THE
SCAPEGOAT

THE
SCAPEGOAT

Mary Lee Settle

 Random House New York

Published in the United States by Random House, Inc., New York, and
simultaneously in Canada by Random House of Canada Limited, Toronto.

Library of Congress Cataloging in Publication Data
Settle, Mary Lee.
    The scapegoat.
    I. Title.
PZ4.S497Sc [PS3569.E84] 813'.54 80–5266
ISBN 0–394–50477–1

Manufactured in the United States of America
98765432
First Edition

And the goat shall bear upon him all their iniquities into a land not inhabited: and he shall let go the goat in the wilderness.

Leviticus, 16:22

And he that let go the goat for the scapegoat shall wash his clothes, and bathe his flesh in water, and afterward come into the camp.

Leviticus, 16:26

I

3:00 P.M. to 5:30 P.M.,
Friday, June 7, 1912

Let them. Just let them investigate until they're blue in the face, and bring it all up again and embarrass my papa. They'll never really know anyway. I know. I didn't miss a thing.

Senator Borah and Senator This and Senator That are sitting in the West Virginia State Capitol having what they call a Senate investigation. Some people call it the Capitol of the bastard son of political rape, but that's neither here nor there. They go on and on about the Bull Moose armored train and the final shooting up of the miners' camp, and the strikebreakers. That all happened *later*. They don't ask how it all began, oh no, not with that bunch of lawyers acting like they've got springs on their bottoms. I know, but of course I'm too young, so I haven't been invited to testify. Every redneck on Lacey Creek and every coal operator is invited, but not me. I went to the Investigation and I was just dying to be invited.

I've even practiced what you do. I would wear the hat Lily left when she went away, the one with the plume Mother made her wear. It would make me look more mature, but not too mature; men love sweet sixteen. I'd wear a white dress with gores and lace not short like I wore last year when I was only fifteen, but right down to my button shoes. I'd be very dignified, of course, when the man says swear to tell the truth so help you God and my voice wouldn't shake like some of them do.

Then I'd have to tell my name, as if everybody who is anybody didn't already know it, but that's what they call procedure. So I would say, slowly, "Mary Rose Lacey, the daughter of Beverley and Ann Eldridge Lacey of Seven Stars, Lacey Creek, West Virginia."

And then I'd let *fly*. I'd say you just chew on it, like a dog with a bone, but you always talk about the big battles so you'll get your names in the papers and spend the taxpayers' money. You've got it all wrong. It didn't start with the big battles and the National Guard. Papa says you're just trying to get votes. *I* ought to know when it really began. It was a day when I would have been broken-hearted but I had too much on my mind.

It was last June. I think it was a Saturday. It started with the Gatling gun and that's the truth of the matter. Papa did want it, no matter what he says now. Of course he did. Why wouldn't he? I heard him call Mr. Baird at Big Diamond mine on the telephone to borrow it. "I know we're not on Imperial property," he told him. Papa only raised his voice on the telephone. "I've got to protect my girls," he said. "Things are bad here. They've been setting people out all week. Dumped them down in my creek bottom. I can't stop it."

It wasn't his creek bottom. He just thought of it that way. The tents were mostly on Jake Catlett's land, and if *he* wasn't a traitor I don't know who was. Essie wasn't, though. She still helped Mother out. I mean at first she did.

Papa wouldn't have let anybody touch a hair of our heads. He made Uncle Obadiah wash off the porch every morning so we wouldn't get red dog on our white dresses. That's red dust from the slag heaps. You wouldn't know about red dog. Of course, the trees that hide the railroad track and the town and the rambler roses on the porches kept most of it away. Papa was doing the best he could. We wouldn't have been there last summer if he'd had the means. Two summers before we went to Europe, and the summer before just to White Sulphur Springs, quite a comedown, don't you know.

It was three o'clock in the afternoon. I can't forget that; Althea and Mr. Anderson Carver and Captain Neill were having their pictures taken around the machine gun on the front porch. That idiot Mooney McKarkle was looking down at his Kodak and backing back. I was standing out of the way waiting for him to fall down.

They didn't ask me to be in the picture. Not that I wanted to be. I didn't care. I wanted to be far enough away so Althea wouldn't notice me and use me to be clever in front of the men.

I was teasing her, inside of myself: Althea wears a rat, Althea wears a rat—but of course I couldn't say it out loud. She could take a terrible revenge, a pink revenge that would last for days. That was the year I was finding colors for everything, like when you say you're blue—or they're blue in the face, or a black look, or a purple passion, or you see red. You know. Well, a pink revenge is slow and light and bedroomy and interminable and almost undetectable and absolutely killing. Althea is the queen of the pink revenge. She inherited thin hair.

She was leaning too close over the gun with her head cocked sideways chocolate-boxing Mr. Anderson Carver—you must know that look. Her bosom was gracefully caressing the gun barrel and I saw she was getting gun grease on her pretty lace peplum she wouldn't let me borrow. I wanted to laugh. She was acting oh I'm so afraid Mr. Anderson Carver and the gun wasn't even loaded. I expected her to start rubbing herself against it like a dog against a man's leg. Pearl of the Mountains, Mr. Anderson Carver called her like she was a hillbilly when we're Laceys and kin to half of Richmond. Once I caught them in the dark behind the trellis and he had one hand on her titty and the other, well! That wouldn't have done any good. I'd helped her dress and her corset went all the way from her knees to her ears. Not only that, there were thirty snaps, hooks, and eyes in her waist alone. Imagine undoing all that in a purple passion! I'm not supposed to know about things like that but I do. Althea warned me. She said, "Don't you run up and down the creek now that you're fifteen. They'll get you—all those foreigners. They're not like us." She said "get" but I knew what she meant—a fate worse than death. I don't know how *she* knows. She's only one year older than I am, but she's more experienced. She knew every single girl on Lacey Creek who was going to have a baby and who the father was and I don't know how she did it. Althea says the word "sex" is tacky, so she doesn't call it that. She intimates. Mother says it's not a word you use in polite society but she won't tell me what you say when you mean that. Isn't it funny how much time people waste over something there isn't any word for?

The gun sat like a big iron spider, right in front of the front door. I heard Mr. Goujot call it a rapid-fire gun. He was older than the others in the Baldwin Feltz detective agency, the best in the country, Mr. Baird said. Mr. Goujot had been in the Army and he got a medal at San Juan Hill. A lot of the guards had medals— Mr. Goujot had the Congressional Medal of Honor, but he didn't come to see us. Some of the guards were our kind of people and some weren't. It was all part of the unwritten law. Dear Lord, if the unwritten laws were ever written down they would fill a million volumes.

Mr. Anderson Carver and Mooney McKarkle and Captain Neill were different. They were the only Baldwin detectives who were invited to dinner. They were like the superintendents and the doctor. It's always been that way here. You just get to know, sometimes the hard way, like Lily, who was taught by Mother with a hairbrush not to play with the foreign children. After she whipped her she combed her hair with a fine-tooth comb so hard Lily hollered louder than the whipping. It didn't do any good. She was headstrong, high-handed and highbrowed, and look where it all got her.

No it wasn't Saturday. It was Friday. It just seemed like Saturday because everything was shut down. Mother came out of the front door just as Mooney took the picture, and ruined it. They waited for her to move, but she didn't. She just stood there, her hands on her hips, not saying a word. I remember wishing she wouldn't stand there in that belly-at-the-washtub way she had when there was nobody around she respected.

My mother is plain people from Pittsburgh. She has very high standards but they aren't like other people's. For instance, she won't let a colored person work in the house, only in the yard, like Uncle Obadiah. Papa says we've always had colored people and she says, "You don't have to tell me," and shuts him up. You see, it's generally known that Papa made a misalliance. You take our names. Lily is really Lily Ellen, and Althea is Ann Althea, and I am Mary Rose, family names for Papa's side and flowers for Mother's. You see the misalliance right there.

I can still see her. I guess that's because on days when something's going to happen, the pictures in your mind are more vivid, like where you were when McKinley was shot. It was a regular tableau vivant; Papa way down beyond the tennis court ignoring us all, Mother without her corset, my sister Althea all lace and simper with a mind and a mouth like a steel trap. She can pinch and bite all she likes, but she'll always have mean lips.

Mr. Anderson Carver lounged against her in white flannels and a striped coat and a straw boater. Mooney was tripping backwards on the grass, heels down, trying to wind the Kodak. He had on yellow boots with little buttons. His white flannels were too short. I could see his galluses. He was wearing a striped shirt with a white collar and a big bright bow tie and a very undignified straw boater with grosgrain ribbon in Joseph colors. You couldn't imagine the miners being afraid of Mooney, even when he pedaled up and down on the railroad bicycle past the tents, all dressed up in a black suit with a revolver on his hip and a rifle across his lap.

Captain Neill was different. He was older and quieter. He'd already been touched by tragedy. He'd lost all his money. He wore a black suit with a gleaming—yes I'd say gleaming—white shirt winter and summer, even on guard. He has one of those bodies that don't crease clothes. If I had been desperately in love with anybody last summer, I would have been desperately in love with Captain Neill, but I wasn't. I was too busy trying to perfect my seat so Papa would let me ride Lady, and besides, there was so much love all around me that it quite disgusted me.

He was a black unsmiling shadow that day on the porch. He had a wide black hat and a gold watch chain and the first thing he did when he came upriver was to find the best nigger laundress to wash his linen. Papa says not to say "nigger," to say "colored." He says he doesn't know where we pick up language like that. Sometimes Captain Neill disappears. Althea says he rides No. 13 up to Thurmond to gamble and visit the tenderloin district. She says he's a rounder and a rogue. I don't believe that. I think he's desperately lonely and misunderstood—I said so and she laughed and said, "Child, that's the way they get the women!" For "child" she means jackass. She makes me furious sometimes.

Captain Neill went to Princeton. So did Mr. Anderson Carver but it didn't take.

Captain Neill is absolutely wild about my sister Lily. No wonder. They both move around like intelligent shadows. He hasn't a chance, though. Lily is a socialist and Captain Neill is dedicated to protecting the miners from union excesses and outside agitators. Papa told Mr. Baird he thought the scandal that hung over that family made him bitter. I don't quite know what the scandal was. It had to do with Senator Neill being what Lily called a crook, but I don't think that's fair. Have you noticed that when people lose money they are called crooks and when they make money they're called good businessmen? Anyway, Captain Neill's granddaddy, Senator Neill, lost his shirt in the Tennessee Coal and Land Company in 1907 and after that his father shot himself in the garden across the river at Beulah, and all that's enough to make a saint bitter.

Mother said, "The mills of God grind slow, but they grind exceeding small." She cried a little bit because they were distant relatives and she remembered seeing Captain Neill's father driving a four-in-hand as if he owned, she said, the mineral rights to the Promised Land. They had to lease out Beulah Collieries for a song. People say that. I've always wondered what the song is.

I heard Althea say, "Everything's too quiet," echoing Papa. Mooney sulked because his picture was ruined and Mr. Anderson Carver teetered on the edge of the steps and stared out toward the trees where the creek valley was—only you can't see any of it from where he stood. Papa saw to that. He had put in trees, shrubs, and in the spring a whole border of lilacs. Granddaddy planted the Blue Cedars the year we leased out the first mineral rights. That was the year I was born. Imagine being as old as a tree.

"Don't you worry about a thing, Miss Althea," Mr. Anderson Carver said and patted the gun like he owned it instead of the Big Diamond Coal Company. It wasn't as if we had the only machine gun in the valley anyway. Up at Glen Pratt there was a Browning—that's supposed to be the best. There was another one at Godley in a concrete blockhouse and the guards rode another one up and down the railroad track on a railroad bicycle, turning it back and forth to show who was boss, and there were two mounted on the armored train that brought in new miners who wanted the freedom to work at the up-creek tipples.

Most of them didn't speak a word of English. Papa said they were grateful to be in America and Lily said something I didn't hear, and had to leave the table. Like when she brought the pamphlet written by Eugene Debs and left it around so we would all find it. Papa came to the table and slammed it down and said, real low, "Who brought this filth into my house?"

"I did, Papa," Lily said. She acted like she was George Washington caught with the axe.

Papa made Lily sit there while he read it in the special golden preacher voice he used for jokes, every word of it. We nearly died laughing. Then he said, "I will not have such men mentioned again in my house." And *that* was *that*. Lily knew it. She didn't say another word. She just sat like she'd swallowed a ramrod and sulked in that kind of lavender way she had.

I'm sure the Baldwin men never meant to use any of the guns. Why, they were nice men, just as nice as they could be. They didn't break any of the unwritten laws. Papa judged people by like wearing your hair parted in the middle, or shooting your cuffs, or smoking cigarettes instead of cigars, or saying who you were kin to before you were asked. They were gentlemen. Do you think for a minute Papa would have let one of them come to see Althea or Lily if they weren't? That's all the proof I need, thank you very much.

Lily was standing apart from the others, acting like she was above it all. Captain Neill didn't take his eyes off her. I have never ceased to be surprised by that. Althea had the men and Lily had the brains, poor soul. Even after a year, there are just whiffs of her left in my mind, faint, very faint, mingled with the scrink-scrank of the swing in the left cupola where everybody was sitting that afternoon.

Mr. Roundtree said Lily was handsome. I guess so—you wouldn't call her a raving beauty, though. He said she was chic, too. But that's the way he talks. Mr. Roundtree is the superintendent of Imperial Collieries No. 8 Mine. He's an Englishman and is very well traveled. He's been all the way around the world and says that means he can put both elbows on the table. Lily has an ironing-board body and a critical soul. She's had a profound effect on our lives but God knows it hasn't been a happy one. To put Lily in a nutshell, she has always refused to let us *not* notice things.

It wasn't that way with Althea. She's beauty's slave. She knows

9

all the tricks, burnt matches and rice powder, toilet water and, well, rouge. You would think butter wouldn't melt in her mouth, except when she bawls out songs to show she isn't bent or broken when Mother makes her stoop to do her own laundry. I'll say that for her. You can't break her to harness, although Mother certainly tried for her own good. One time she stole every petticoat in the house to swish around Luna Park, and Mother made her wash them one at a time, and iron and starch them, and she stood over her and made her do right.

I have a swan neck. Mr. Roundtree says beauty has touched me. Althea laughed and said too bad it didn't stay. Well, she's jealous. Sometimes I go into her room to borrow something, combing my hair down, down below my waist. I can sit on it. She combs hers into a newspaper. She's saving up for a rat of her own hair. She says that wearing the hair of some trash that sold it is like wearing the dead. I heard tell that Maria Pagano sold hers last winter when No. 8 and Seven Stars stayed shut down too long, and her short hair curled up like a nigger I mean a colored person.

I wasn't missing a thing—not a thing. I watched Mother stomp across the lawn. She's a clodhopper. Now that is what I mean when I say Papa made a misalliance. Althea said Mother was overeducated and underbred and that was two strikes against her. Mother tried, though. When we had to give up Miss Hattie the governess ugh in 1907, Mother taught us herself. We weren't allowed to go to school. You'll never know what you'll pick up there she said, and she didn't mean cooties either. She meant men. There just wasn't the ready cash for boarding school that year. She really kept Lily's nose to the grindstone. She said it was a crying shame to waste a brain like that. By 1908 Althea and Lily could go away to school, but only to Stuart Hall. I'm there now and I hate it. Althea got kicked out for smoking, and Lily went to Vassar.

Mother made the world come to us. She made us keep up our French after we went abroad. When Althea yawned because she was bored with lessons, Mother said, "Veux-tu couvrir la bouche?"

Mother treated the coal town beyond the trees like a black abyss we would fall into if we weren't armed with manners and protected with white dresses and taught to cover our bouches. I don't know what she was scared of. She'd taught school herself. She was hired by Mr. Godley.

Everything threatened to go on forever at four o'clock on that afternoon in early June, flowing into all the afternoons of June. There we were, three princesses, ha ha, in durance vile. I could see Althea lounging back on the wicker chaise lounge. She had just learned to be languid. Mr. Anderson Carver was forever raising a glass of lemonade toward his mustache—wishing it was something else, I suppose. Captain Neill was sitting in the porch swing but not swinging, gazing on Lily, and Mooney was sitting on the steps leaning against the porch column with his leg stretched out down the steps and his button shoes showing and the gun, the new plaything, straddle-legged on the porch, forgotten.

Lily had walked away from the others to the other cupola and was leaning against the wall behind the east-trellis roses. She had her hands up in front of her for some reason, like she didn't know what to do with them. She was ignoring us all. She had eyes only for the upriver train to spirit her away to pastures green, east across the mountains. Mother said she came home from Vassar with atheistical ideas.

Well, Mother had some pretty atheistical ideas herself, but she didn't call them that of course.

All that was missing but *not* missing in my mind's eye was the angel Gabriel in white raiment with big gold wings and a gold trumpet perched like a bird over the central peak of the roof, surveying us all and ready to blow the trump that followed Adam and Eve out of the garden. I can see them, holding leaves from Papa's fig tree, going down the old road, full of shame.

I knew why Mother was tracking Papa across the lawn. She was going to start it all again—seams and rights, rights and seams and leasing out. She hadn't talked about anything else for a month.

Papa explained it to me. The first time Grandfather let go of any of the land was when he sold outright to Mr. Pratt, who was buying up useless land on spec. That's speculation. He paid Grandfather $250,000 for the five miles up-creek and said he certainly would keep the tenants' leases. By that time Grandfather had tenants all the way up Lacey Creek. Mr. Pratt said that was the least he could do, in all honor, but of course he bought them out for a hoot and a holler. Papa laughed and said, "So were they all, all honorable men." He made me learn that speech later for elocution.

That was the most money Grandfather had ever seen in his life. He had his own mine, Seven Stars Colliery, and he had opened Godley, and he said he didn't want to be bothered with any more. Well, Mr. Pratt wasn't interested in mining it himself. He leased out his mineral rights to Imperial Collieries and whatever wildcat operators he could find. The hillbillies up the creek went to work for the Godley mine because of the name. They are believers. But it was just the name of one of the new coal operators, Mr. Godley, from guess where? Pittsburgh! Only he wasn't as plain people as Mother was. Grandfather sold to Mr. Godley outright because he was a gentleman. They raised carnations together.

Papa said that even if it was new money, we weren't new people. It didn't go to our heads, not like some of the others who were coining money hand over fist by selling off scrubland so steep you couldn't pasture a goat on it. "God! What some Yankees will buy," Papa would say and glance at Mother. She never did deign to recognize the value of anything but bottomland.

And she would say, "Don't use the name of the Lord in vain." I thought for the longest time she meant vein, like blood, or a vein of coal!

They had the same conversations over and over. "Anyway," Papa would say, "Mr. Godley came down full of a lot of fire and sass. He poured money into building a fine company store and houses with stone foundations. He said he was going to stay on the property until hell froze over."

Well, hell froze over mighty quick. He sold out to the Imperial Land Company in oh seven. He would have been wiped out in the panic if he hadn't. Papa said the people who made a killing in oh seven were bears, and it was better to be a bear than a bull. They had safe cash and always won out in the end. They lease the whole valley, except for us, and Papa says they've bought every vote in it. Lily called this a downright lie, but Papa said that in the last election Mr. Baird voted his mine mules for William Howard Taft. Mr. Baird is the superintendent of Imperial Collieries' Big Diamond Mine but he's not an Englishman. He's just a Virginian. I think Papa said that just to get Lily's goat. He can't resist teasing her, mispronouncing the words she brings back from Vassar, that kind of joke.

By the time I came along in 1897, there were eight mines opened, and a spur of the Chesapeake & Ohio twenty miles up the creek. Of course there weren't enough hillbillies to work all that. They brought in lots of foreigners, but they certainly don't look like the foreigners we saw in Europe, not by a long shot. By the time Imperial took its slice of pie and the C&O took its slice, and the operators took their slice, there wasn't much pie left. Papa said it was a mighty big hog and there were an awful lot of folks on the tit and Mother said, "Don't use that sort of language in front of the children. I don't know where you pick it up."

Which is why the rapid-fire gun was sitting like a spider on the front porch and Mother was tracking Father.

Lily is either totally silent on the subject or she blurts out things at the dinner table in front of anybody who is there. She calls the Imperial Mining Company bloated capitalists. She always says "bloated" and mother says, "Hush, Lily," but her eyes look, well, agreeable, and that I don't understand at all.

Once Mr. Baird teased Lily about votes for women (Lily thinks the sun rises every morning out of Carrie Chapman Catt's head). He said the women he knew weren't smart enough to find the polls, much less know what they were for, and Lily said, "At least, Mr. Baird, they're smarter than mine mules," and Mr. Baird said, "The mule is the most intelligent of domestic animals," and Mother said, "Hush, Lily." Althea says Mr. Baird was flirting and I said that was the dumbest way to flirt, and she said, "Oh, Dodie!" and sighed. That's my child name and I have absolutely refused to answer to it for two years.

I suppose you have to know why everybody was shooing me away like the cat that Friday. I had been in Coventry ever since the day before because I had disobeyed Papa.

I knew from the carryings-on in the kitchen Thursday morning that something important was going to happen. We *never* have company on Thursday. It's usually Essie's day off, but she was there and she looked like a thundercloud. That's the way she looks when she disapproves. Mother says she acts like Moses come down from Mount Sinai. I asked Papa what was going on and he said some associates were coming but he didn't want it trumpeted all up and down the creek. Uncle Obadiah was wringing the necks of some of mother's best Leghorn pullets. They were flapping around the backyard. Now a backyard is a backyard and not a lawn. You can't say "the back lawn" when a passel of headless white chickens are flapping around it spraying blood on the grass, now can you? Papa was in the wine cellar for hours choosing wine, some that Grandfather had laid down. You say "laid down" for wine; you don't say "stored."

Papa said that we were to be dressed and ready by eleven o'clock, that the train was coming in at eleven-thirty. He kept looking at the sky hoping it wouldn't rain. Now, No. 4 comes through from downriver at ten-thirty, and No. 6 from upriver at twelve o'clock. There isn't any eleven-thirty train. When I pointed that out he said, "Don't sass, it is a private train. Now, Dodie, I don't want you to set foot off of this property." When he called me Dodie I knew he meant business.

A private train! You don't know what that connotes in this valley. "Connotes" is a Lily word. She says it's more than what it means. She says it's what it *hints*. I can tell the whole thing in terms of trains. When you're well-off you ride the parlor car in the daytime and a Pullman berth at night. When you're well-to-do, you have a stateroom. When you're just plain rich you have a private car hitched on the back of the regular run. You rent it from the Pullman Company. But when you're real rich you have a private train. We used to be well-to-do, but since oh seven we've just been well-off. I'd seen lots of private cars, but I'd never seen a whole private train before. If you think I was going to miss that you are vastly mistaken.

I had to be careful, going against Papa's orders, so after I'd brushed my hair two hundred times to make it look rich, I put on my white Sunday dress. Of course it wasn't long last year, but it did have a lace bertha. I sneaked out to the barn and hitched up Nelly, that's our old pony, to the trap. It was the only wicker pony trap in the valley. It was shiny white and had striped canvas seats—green and white like the porch awning. I drove down the old back road lickety-split around the eastern spur of the hill, standing up like Ben Hur. I always did that until I got too old.

We only used that road when the creek was high, so I knew there wouldn't be anybody on it. There almost never was. I tethered Nelly up behind the trees and sneaked down to the Depot.

I saw Papa waiting at the wheel of the automobile all in his overcoat and his black hat and gloves and of course a black cravat. Uncle Obadiah had polished the brass lamps and put a rose in the bud vase. He was waiting in the landau to follow the car in case it broke down.

The whistle blew beyond the hill. Then the train came in sight around the upriver curve. I've never been more disappointed in my life. It looked just like any other train—an engine and two Pullman cars. That was all. Then I began to notice as it slowed down. Underneath the coal dust it was painted with dark green carriage paint like our landau. It had small gold numbers on the cars, not names like some of the more ostentatious new-rich ones I've seen. You know, actresses and people like that. Instead of a caboose, the last car had a perfectly beautiful observation platform with striped awnings (green and white of course) and polished brass railings. I thought to myself, Good grief, rich is quiet, isn't it? Lily says they're hiding their ill-gotten gains from the socialists, but I think she's wrong. It's just good taste.

The train stopped. The brakes sighed, and all the striking miners, who were leaning against the Depot because they didn't have anything better to do, started to move up to look it over. Well, naturally, they didn't get very far. The Baldwin detectives, who were on guard on the platform, herded them back with the flat of their guns so the gentlemen wouldn't be bothered with a lot of riffraff.

Mr. Osborn came out of the ticket office. It was the first time in my life I ever saw Mr. Osborn in a coat and a derby hat. Usually he was in his shirt sleeves with garters around his arms and a green eyeshade.

The door of the last car opened and a man got off—not a porter—more like a butler. I've seen lots of butlers—well, not lots but some, and that's the way he was dressed, in a swallowtail coat and striped trousers. No hat, of course. That was the only way you could tell he was a servant. Of course you have to step down to our little old country Depot, and he helped first one gentleman

15

and then another onto the platform. Papa went up to shake hands. I wish the rich didn't always have to be old. There must be some young rich men in the world. If there are I don't know them. All the young men we receive from Canona are either just well-off or struggling back from the pit of adversity like Captain Neill from Beulah.

There were seven of them, giants in the earth, and they *all* had stomachs and skinny legs. There's no use telling you their names, but I will anyway. There was Mr. Pierpont and Mr. Cabot and Mr. Peabody and Mr. Pratt and one without a Prince of Wales beard, slightly younger but his face was plumping up to forty. Later Papa said he was one of the minor Rockefellers, whatever that may be. Then there was, oh, Sir Archibald Inchbold—Sir Archibald Eyeball Althea called him later. He was wearing a monocle.

Maybe you will get the full import of the trainload of gentlemen if I call them Imperial Mining Company, Pratt Land Company, Chesapeake & Ohio, Peabody Sand and Gravel, Standard Oil, and a Philadelphia lawyer! Oh, and of course Sir Archibald Eyeball who represented—shhh! a secret—the Crown of England. Papa says the English interest is a dead secret but I don't know why you call a secret dead. It's only dead when it isn't a secret anymore. Not even Standard Oil can sell the Crown of England short. Good grief, I just realized I've touched the hand that touched the hand of the King of England. It's an awe-inspiring thought.

Well, those were the men who were coming all the way up Lacey Creek to see my papa, and Papa joined the rest, the black coats and black hats and white collars and gold watch chains and discreet gold-headed canes. I was watching from behind the water tower and you couldn't tell one from another. They moved on down the platform and into the automobile.

Uncle Obadiah cranked it and they started off up the road with the dust rising behind them. It wasn't until they were out of earshot that one of the boys around the Depot yelled, "Get a horse!" Uncle Obadiah followed along behind them in the empty landau, keeping General and Lady Gray to a trot. General is Papa's trotter. He can do a two-minute mile, almost.

Papa says the C&O and Standard Oil don't *own* any land—it's all Pratt Land Company—but he says there's Standard Oil behind it, whatever that means. When I ask, he says it's because of Teddy the Trust Buster. "Don't you worry about that," he says. Why would I worry? I guess it's just what Mr. Rockefeller meant when he said, "Pay nobody a profit!" Just think, coming to see Papa like that. Lily says Mr. Rockefeller said, "We only want the big ones, the others—unfortunately they will have to die." Lily has read Ida M. Tarbell and she thinks she knows everything. Papa says she has a lot of intelligence and not a grain of horse sense, and that she uses more big words than an educated nigger. Well, you can't say "educated colored," can you?

I knew it was the only chance I would have, so I marched right up beside the butler or whatever he was. He'd already picked up the step to put it back aboard, and I thought I could kind of peak around him and get a glimpse. He said, "Would you like to see inside, little lady?" I guess he could see I wasn't one of the ordinary people that hung around the Depot. Mr. Osborn had already gone back to his office and the others were still watching up the road after the automobile. There were only the Baldwin guards and a little knot of foreigners left on the platform, those Paganos from up Italian Hollow, waiting for No. 6 to come in. I didn't care if they saw me. What Lily and even Mr. Roundtree can find in those people I can't for the life of me imagine.

I was so scared I just nodded and he handed me up the step like the little princess Papa says I am. I stepped aboard with great dignity.

Holy cow, it was some punkins! Masculine punkins, not feminine punkins. There weren't any frills. There didn't need to be, just a deep turkey carpet all over what he called the observation room, and those real deep punched leather chairs that look like they're stuffed with money. A big table was in the middle covered with green plush, but I couldn't see much of that because there were business papers and maps all over it. Some man—a secretary, I guess—was gathering them up. At the end of the room there was a mahogany bookcase full of those leather engraved office books that look like nobody reads them, and beyond an archway with carving down the sides and over the top I could just see a big mahogany desk with a typing machine like Lily's on it. There was a perfectly beautiful electrolier in the ceiling, and big square windows with dark red velvet draperies. (Mother says "drapes" and she really shouldn't. She knows better.)

I wasn't letting any of it impress me, even when the secretary said, "Good morning, madame," and the butler grinned at him. Just then the train started with a lurch and I thought, My stars, white slavery! But the butler said they were going to the private siding. I acted like I already knew that. So I got to ride for a few minutes anyway.

We walked along a corridor (please note, same turkey carpet) and he let me look into what he called the master suite. He was showing me around like he owned the place. Inside there was a whole brass double bed covered with red satin. That didn't look very masculine. Lily says they keep mistresses on those trains. Wouldn't that be awful—just shunting around forever with no future? No wonder Mother is trying to keep us all on the straight and narrow. There was a dressing table, mahogany of course, with a gold mirror over it. A colored man was cleaning the bathroom —a real bathroom with a marble bathtub and a shower and a washbasin made out of that kind of marble that looks like potted meat (what's it called?—onyx) and silver faucets. I never knew before that firewood, tobacco, polish, whiskey, clean linen and coal dust is about the *richest* smell in the world.

That was only the beginning. After the master suite, there were three or maybe four staterooms, like you find on other trains, only grander. You know, real bedspreads and more turkey carpet and real closets all carved. When we got to the dining saloon, I couldn't believe my eyes. There was a real fireplace with gold candlesticks on the mantelpiece. A golden bowl of red store-bought roses sat in the middle of a big round dining-room table covered with white damask without one speck of coal dust on it. You could smell the coal dust, but you couldn't see it, not a speck anywhere. Another colored man was clearing away the breakfast. I'd never let Lily find out how rich it all was. She'd burst a gasket. Some of the silver was gold! There was a big gold compote piled with the kind of fruit you get at Christmas time.

"The gentlemen start the morning with prayer. Then they have champagne for breakfast," the butler told me when he saw me staring at the bucket with three bottles turned upside down in it.

He really did act like he owned the place. "This is the finest private varnish on the C and O road," he was saying behind me when I peeked into the kitchen, where a cook and a kitchen boy were putting a huge roast of beef in the oven. What they were doing cooking roast beef on a Thursday morning I couldn't think. That's for Sunday. Besides, they certainly couldn't have been cooking dinner for the gentlemen after we'd killed all those chickens.

By that time I was in a panic to get home before I was missed. But I had to wait until No. 6 from upriver pulled out of the Depot before I could get back across the tracks. When it did pull out there were the Paganos all hugging yet another Italian who'd gotten off the train. You could tell he was an immigrant. He had one of those cheap suitcases tied around with rope. Even the men were hugging him in that way they do.

A paper suitcase! I was relieved that the gentlemen didn't see *that*. Maria Pagano was looking all red in the face. She's pretty in her way, I suppose. They develop early and fade early, Mother says. Anyway she was all over the new man, hugging him close, right in front of the Baldwin detectives. It was shameful and you could tell she knew it.

The only other passenger to get off was a little old lady in black bombazine with a frilly black hat and a lace jabot. I only glanced at her. I do remember she didn't have any luggage, just a few things wrapped in a black shawl she had draped over her arm. She looked like somebody's grandmother, not the grandmother of one of the hillbillies or foreigners, but, well, maybe the script clerks or the men who ran the company stores. I mean a hillbilly would have been wearing a poke bonnet, but she had on that old-fashioned black hat. You could tell she had trimmed it herself. You understand the difference, I'm sure. Mooney McKarkle went up to her. I remember thinking how polite he was. I was surprised at that. He escorted her off the platform like you would a lady. Well! If I'd known then what I know now, I would have looked closer.

The last I saw of her was when I was untethering Nelly. She was walking up the dusty road all by herself carrying her black shawl like a sack. She looked kind of lonesome. I would have given her a ride but I didn't have time. Besides, I had to go back by the hill road and if I'd let her off at our stable, she would have walked right across the lawn to get down into the town.

Imagine if that infamous outside agitator Mother Jones herself had walked across our front lawn while Papa was entertaining important people from the East! Lily said she was the most famous union organizer in the United States, but I don't believe that. Famous people don't ride the day coach with their things in a shawl.

I thought I'd gotten back without anybody missing me. Well, that certainly proved to be a fool's paradise. I could see the gentlemen all sitting on the front porch. Mr. Roundtree was there from Godley, and Mr. Baird from Big Diamond, and Captain Neill.

I sneaked into Papa's library but I couldn't get near enough to hear a lot of what they were saying. The library window was shut onto the porch. I didn't dare open it, but I curled up in the window seat and heard what I could.

I was absolutely furious! I counted noses and I knew there wasn't a chance of sitting at the first table. I hated the second table. It was usually just us girls, and leftovers. After all that getting ready and washing our hair. What a ritual that always is! First you heat rain water, then you break a dozen eggs, then after you've washed it, oh Lord, it's heavy when it's wet, you use a vinegar rinse. Always use a vinegar rinse if your hair is chestnut or roan, or lemon if it's blond. Althea uses Golden Glint, and she thinks I don't know. Then you hang your hair out of the upstairs window until it's dry, or of course, when there's nobody to see you, you can sit outside on the lawn. But always keep it moving. Mother lets us use her cupola room up at the top of the tower if we promise not to touch a thing. To tell the honest truth, I still don't like to go there all by myself.

One time Althea dressed Mother's dress form up as the headless woman in white who is supposed to haunt one of the abandoned entries in the Seven Stars mine. The miners say she's looking for her husband who got squashed by a slate fall. Anyway they closed the entry out of respect. Althea put the form outside my door so I'd bump into it when I got up to go to the bathroom. It scared me to death. I still see the headless woman up in Mother's cupola but I wouldn't admit it to Althea. Mother calls the cupola her sanctum sanctorum. It's where she takes her naps.

So after all the getting ready, there I was with my dress smoothed out to keep it clean, and my hair just right after the drive; you know, little loose tendrils. I stared at the etching of the Colosseum of Rome by moonlight over Papa's desk, and then at the busts of Dante and Shakespeare and then at the big plaster Victory of Samothrace. Mother brought them all back from Europe. Those men murmured and muttered outside on the porch.

I caught a few words but I didn't really connect them until later.

Somebody said, "You drive a hard bargain, Mr. Lacey," and somebody else laughed, and said, "We have to buy the mare to get the filly."

That scared me for a minute. I thought they were talking about Lady, and she was the horse I was going to learn to ride sidesaddle. Mother bought me a riding habit in London. But then I realized that Lady didn't have a filly and it was just their way of talking about property.

Oh, one other thing. I heard Captain Neill say that if they brought any more transportation in—he meant foreigners, they call them transportation men—he would have to have more guards. He was talking about the Baldwin detectives. The reason I remember it is because Mr. Peabody said, "Well, now, Captain Uh"—he forgot Captain High-handed and Low Income Neill's name, ha, ha— "that's hardly our responsibility. We're here to protect our stockholders. We'll just foot the bill, with Imperial, of course, and leave the decisions to you." Mother hates that use of the word "foot." She says it's tacky, so I was surprised when a Peabody from Boston said "foot."

The other thing that sticks in my mind was what somebody— I think the Philadelphia lawyer—said, because he touched on something Papa and Mr. Roundtree were unalterably opposed to up to that time. Papa has set his foot down (that's correct use of the word "foot"). He had said no New York firm was going to bring in immigrants to Seven Stars if he had to stay closed forever. Mr. Roundtree had said that about Godley, too.

It's funny that Mr. Roundtree wasn't saying more. I guess he was shy in front of somebody close to the King of England. That was too bad. He certainly knew more than anybody else on Lacey Creek, and he would tell you all about it at the drop of a hat. Mother says he doesn't converse. He instructs. The times I've seen him instructing that trashy Eddie Pagano! Talk, talk, talk like they had big secrets, but I know they were only talking about rocks. Mr. Roundtree knows all about them. He's a geologist, Lily says. Eddie Pagano isn't anything but one of the Italian miners. Like Lily, Mr. Roundtree is no respecter of persons.

I knew he was unalterably opposed to bringing in strikebreakers. He said so often enough. I could hear him and Papa talking it over and over in the library at night.

But that day the cat had his tongue. It was very disappointing.

The lawyer said, "If you bring in more men, the Williams Employment Agency is the most efficient. We use them in Pennsylvania and Colorado."

Mr. Baird said, "I'm glad you think so. We have a contract with Mr. Williams to provide labor. He has a close view of our problems. We're going to keep the up-creek mines open. Don't you worry about that." Neither Papa nor Mr. Roundtree said a word.

Althea and Lily and Mother were waiting in the parlor across the hall. I could just see a flounce hanging down from the mahogany rocker and I knew Mother was in her best dress. They were sitting like the sword of Damocles was hanging over their heads.

Somebody, I forget who, said, "He uses sociological methods based on the scientific facts of supply and demand."

Then somebody else asked, "What services does the contract include?"

I guess they were still talking about Mr. Williams and I knew Papa didn't like that. He showed Mr. Williams the door when he came to see him and told him, "We don't see eye to eye, Mr. Williams. You see labor as a commodity. I have my own men." But he didn't say a word on the porch when they were talking about Mr. Williams. I waited.

"It includes a steady supply of labor. It's an efficiency system. It also includes the cost of transport." That was Mr. Baird.

22

"We subcontract with Williams for extra guards from Thurmond . . ." That was Captain Neill.

I wished they'd quit. It was already two by Papa's clock. It was so still in the library that the tick-tock and the back-and-forth of the brass weight were putting me to sleep. If they didn't go in soon, I knew it would be four o'clock before the second table sat down.

Mr. Pratt suddenly sounded bored and fidgety. Rich people can't sit for too long. Have you noticed that? They'd already been ironing things out for nearly two hours.

He said, "Gentlemen, I only have one thing to say. We bought this property for development. The cost in time and money has been vastly greater than we thought. Now we control the railroad and the leases. We haven't the capacity to enter upon the learning of a new business. That's up to you gentlemen. But let me tell you this." His voice was loud enough for me to hear every word, and whatever I forgot Lily told me later. *She* didn't miss a word. She wouldn't. "Two of you strategically placed gentlemen wish to negotiate with the union. I am unalterably opposed to this. The philosophy in this matter is greater than what is going on in one little valley in West Virginia." I knew he meant Papa and Mr. Roundtree and I was embarrassed to death.

Mr. Pratt was still for a minute, and Mr. Roundtree started to speak at last. I knew it was him because of his English accent. It was different from Sir Archibald Eyeball's. Mr. Pratt interrupted Mr. Roundtree. "All we want are our royalties and our railroad fees and we want them steadily. One cannot cover the whole earth with our responsibility."

Mr. Roundtree finally stood right up to him. "A person who owns as much of the earth as the people you represent, Mr. Pratt, can cover a large part of it."

I heard Papa say, "Gentlemen, gentlemen . . . you must realize that my people are *not* transportation. They've lived here many years." He talked about "my" people like he'd borned them.

Mr. Pratt laughed and said, "Mr. Uh, that's an admirable but dated concept." He was going to eat our chicken and he didn't even bother to remember Papa's name. "This concept has caused

23

a lot of trouble. How many miners on the blacklist have moved down on your property? These two operations are forming a bottle-neck right at the mouth of the creek." For a man who hadn't bothered to learn the business, he seemed to know a lot.

I think he must have, you know, put into words what he didn't mean to, because the lawyer from Philadelphia started that kind of quiet muttering lawyers do. Suddenly Mother had me by the elbow. She whispered so close to my ear I could feel her spit. "I saw you, young lady. How many times have I told you not to leave this house when there is a strike on, unless you are accompanied by an adult? I will deal with you later." She hauled me up off of the window seat and marched me into the parlor. Althea grinned.

So when the gentlemen came in to meet the ladies, there we were, all in our white dresses, Althea, Lily and Rose. Mine was smocked by the nuns. Lily really did look stunning in dotted swiss, with eyelet embroidery, all frail and sagging. Althea was furious. Mother had made her wear a simple white dress trimmed in satin piping and lace. It was apropos, of course, but Althea didn't know that. She never does. Anyway we looked slim and costly and that suited Mother. She was quite splendid in purple georgette and taffeta that made the right noise, with cream-colored Val lace at her throat. She wore the garnet necklace that was wrong for her complexion but it was an heirloom, so she had to. We sat like Papa's pride and riches. Lily and Althea were old enough to shake hands when the gentlemen were introduced, but last year I still curtsyed and Mr. Pratt said "Charming, charming" and touched my hair. He seemed an entirely different man than the one who had gotten so fidgety on the front porch.

We did get to sit at the first table—for decoration I suppose. Imagine having to sit through an interminable dinner knowing you were going to have your hide tanned. They didn't leave until four o'clock and by that time Mother had such a sick headache she forgot to whip me. The Eastern Interests turned their noses up at our lowly chicken and I know why. But they certainly did lay into Papa's wine!

So don't you see why on Friday everybody was treating me like a red-headed stepchild?

I knew as if I were standing right with them down beyond the

24

tennis court, where mother had cornered Papa at long last, that she was trying to get him to make up his mind about some offer that had been made the day before. I still didn't know what it was then. I did know one thing. Some kind of a threat went with it, oh, not a threat like a punch in the nose, it was some businessmen threat that I must have missed when their voices got too low.

Anyway I knew Mr. Roundtree would discuss it with Papa and Papa would obviously discuss it with Mother and Mother always used Lily to talk things over with, and I had ways of getting things out of Lily. All you had to do was make her mad and she'd blurt things out like she was on a soapbox. I told you she had socialist ideas.

When Papa wanted to tease her, and he seemed to want to a lot, you know, take her down a notch for her own good, he'd say, "Miss Lily. Oh dear, Miss Lily, you don't quite grasp the idea," in that real amused patient voice that Southern gentlemen use for intellectual ladies. It's a very attractive quality in men. It makes you feel frail—I mean me, not Lily. It makes her mad as hell, if you'll pardon my French. "Miss Lily, you don't seem to have a problem taking the sweat of the poor to clothe you and educate you and send you to Europe. Your concern for the poor is pure silken googoo!" That's what Papa said. All I had to do was call Lily a silken googoo and she'd tell me anything I wanted to know and never know she'd done it.

So there you are. That's the way it was, if you want the truth of the matter, which in my humble opinion you don't.

Anyway, that's what I have been practicing in front of Lily's chifforobe mirror, just in case I do get invited to the Senate investigation, which I won't. After all, it's as good a place as any to start unless you want to go all the way back to Methuselah and who wants to do that?

What Mary Rose did not remember was that when she stood alone in the grass she was crying and she was afraid to go too near her mother. She caught the familiar scent of her mother's dress. It mingled in the sun with the new-cut grass and patchouli and gun grease and rose water and glycerine and shaggy vines and wood drying in the afternoon. The porch all around the front was like white lace from the white roses and the carving, and the outside woodwork that was painted every spring shiny white to keep the thought of black coal away.

Mary Rose knew what the patchouli was: Anderson Carver's breath. Her mother said he drank and tried to hide it with patchouli or Sen Sen when he came to call. She said it didn't cut any ice with her even if he was a Carver from downriver. She said a downriver fool was just as much fool as a ridge-running fool. She made them leave their guns on the parlor table and she treated them all like stones in her path. She did it then, walked right past them down the front steps, straight as the gate to glory and called to Mary Rose, "Have you seen your father?" and didn't wait for an answer. Mary Rose watched her going hell-bent for election down through the rose garden.

She decided to swing, high and dangerous on the sweetheart swing; it was near enough for her to watch her father and pray for him to rescue her. She felt like a secret princess with a heart of sorrow and didn't know why. She reminded herself that Mr. Roundtree had said she was as graceful as a tender plant. To have to swing alone in a sweetheart swing: nobody should have to. She had to use her petticoat to wipe her eyes. She put her feet apart on the green slat floor, and grasped the uprights and pumped with her knees. She flew—higher and higher until she could feel the swing frame teetering on the ground and she sang as she pumped to keep herself from crying any more. "Flying"—pump—"so high"—pump—"in a flying machine something up"—pump—"you go . . ."

Ann Eldridge hadn't bothered to look at any of them. She didn't care to. Her girls were in no danger in broad daylight. There was that at least to be thankful for, with all she had on her mind. She was worried sick. It had made her feel heavier and heavier for a month, ever since the trouble had torn her safe valley apart. It was not like her pregnancies, not heavy and low in her body, but the same sickness came with it. It made the garden swirl and she had to stop for a minute. She snapped an overblown rose, disgusting thing, and put it in her pocket.

She let the garden settle again, and marched on. She saw him down beyond the tennis court, watching the town.

The only sign that Mr. Lacey was half out of his mind with worry, or at least ought to be, was that he'd dragged out his old white linen suit. It fitted him like a sack. He said it came from New York, and made him feel rich again. A fat lot of good that did. A fat lot he cared that she lay awake beside him, night after night, when there was no more to say, waiting for the first birds and the white dawn and him to *do* something. He took everything for granted, and she believed in taking the bull by the horns. That was the difference between them and always had been.

She didn't know why he hadn't taken the matter into his hands when it started. It had been going on since April, one train or two a day up the Lacey Creek spur instead of six, the air clear for once, nobody who seemed to be going anyplace.

Way off down by the creek there were groups of men fishing, and beyond the creek little white squares where the tent colony was, four or five tents at a time put up on Jake Catlett's farm, and some on their own property. Mr. Lacey didn't say a word when they started putting up the tents. He explained to Captain Neill that he had no jurisdiction over Jake Catlett. Captain Neill said he was creating a trouble spot but he said, "There's nothing I can do. I've got to go on living here," and waited for Ann Eldridge to speak out but she just folded her mouth. It was more effective.

Ann Eldridge wasn't a fast walker. She was too dignified for that. But she prided herself on being sudden. She bore down on Mr. Lacey without a sound. His body shook when she touched his shoulder, and he looked at her as if he'd never seen her before in his life.

"I've been looking all over hell's half-acre for you," she told him, not meaning it. She turned again in the grass without saying any more. She knew he would follow her. She saw Mary Rose making a fool of herself in the swing, as usual, and called, "Mary Rose Lacey, quit that. Do you want everybody to see your sash?" Somebody laughed. It made Ann Eldridge look up at them at last. They were all sitting in the shadow of the porch on the new wicker furniture. Althea was fanning herself with her ostrich-feather fan she got for her birthday when she'd told her and told her to save it for parties. She shooed Mary Rose out of the swing and gave her her walking papers.

"For the love of God go find something to do. You've been mooning around all day. Your father and I have business to talk." She flicked her handkerchief over one of the seats to wipe off the red dog nobody admitted came through the cedars that already shaded the tennis court and the front garden and the croquet lawn and made a green darkness even in the hottest days.

She made herself go over the whole situation once again, step by step, remembering to keep her patience. Beverley sat opposite her, still without saying a word. She hated that closed look that meant if he could get through the next hour everything would be all right. She knew he was just waiting for her mouth to stop moving, not listening to a damned word she said.

She felt then a disgust which she mistook for compassion: poor, shrunken thing, sitting there so forlorn with despair and bad habits, insisting on wearing that old white summer suit from better days. He was only forty-two years old and he looked like an old man. He was going to die. She'd known that for a long time, taking it so for granted that she made it a part of her planned anxiety. The only way to get away from him was to let her eyes retreat around the circle of their property. It had been such a pleasure before the trouble to stand in the rose garden she had planted herself, mistress of all she surveyed, a green bowl around her, lined by a moat of trees. Of course that was a summer vision. In winter she couldn't ignore the coal-black rails from the Seven Stars tipple that ran up the slope and thrust into the drift mouth on the raw hill.

She didn't have time to keep on battering at that deafness he called self-control. Her head was killing her and it was time for her rest and her laudanum.

"Oh, Mr. Lacey, you don't pay attention to a word I say!" She got up and left him there without waiting for an answer.

She walked slowly back up the slight rise of the lawn, hoping and praying for a nice green sleep up in the cupola room, her sanctum sanctorum where the top branches of the sycamore tree brushed the tower windows.

She was relieved to see that Althea and Lily had left the porch; the hammock was still moving. Mr. Anderson Carver and Captain Neill and that young McKarkle boy were just disappearing through the side gate to go on duty.

She looked back once. Mr. Lacey was still sitting in the sweetheart swing. He hadn't moved a muscle.

Ann Eldridge climbed the fifty-five steps to her only peace and quiet, closed the door, and leaned against it, exhausted. The room was octagonal. Four paces took her from wall to wall, but it was hers. She felt like she was swimming in the heat that the room held in June, collected from the day, suspended and palpable. It made the sweat run down under her arms, but heat or not, the tower room was her citadel. She allowed herself to stay exactly one hour by the gold ball watch that was pinned to her shoulder.

She looked at the piles of sewing, remodeling, relining, rehemming, constant redemptions to keep three girls and herself from advertising to all the world that almost every stitch they owned was three years old. Althea's summer evening gown from Paris hung on the dress form, stuffed at the bosom with tissue paper. She was larger there than the others, a thing to be watched.

Ann Eldridge let herself smile. Someone had draped a pink lace flounce around the headless neck, and reeling down one shoulder, a rejected fall of beaded net from her own old Paris dress, the only thing she had left from when they went abroad. The tucked waist had long since gone to Althea, the lace trimmed skirt to Lily, who had forgotten it and left it at Vassar. The underpetticoat, white mousseline, had made a Sunday dress for Mary Rose. The dress form looked like a dignified decapitated drunkard. She knew someone had been seeing herself dressed up like that, probaby Mary Rose when she was drying her hair. She couldn't wait to grow up, poor child. Oh God, if she only knew.

Ann Eldridge folded the beaded lace away in tissue paper. She flung the pink flounce on the pile of scraps in the corner. What she had done to Althea's waist was right. There would be trouble with the guimpe, but she was prepared for that. She looked at

29

the skirt and sighed. It looked tattered, cut from the waist to the floor to take out the gores of lace to make flounces like the dress Althea had marked in the *Ladies' Home Journal*, opened for so long on the sewing machine that it looked wilted. She fingered the leaf-green charmeuse—it felt soft, soft and expensive under her fingers. There was so much to do, tissue paper banked against the wall to pack each dress, each chemise, the exquisite linen, the eyelet embroidery, satin stitches, French knots, tatted buttons, piping, frogs, the exquisite Val lace inserts, all that delicate armor to protect the girls' bodies from the world: a private domain of patched, torn, outgrown, out-of-style clothes to be kept together, up-to-date, a reconstructed bon ton, an ammunition dump in a war against letting people read the change in circumstances, the barometer of money.

The only brand-new thing in the room was the dress box from Miller and Rhoads. It was Lily's birthday present. Ann Eldridge didn't need to open it. She knew the feel of it in her hands, the white crepe de chine, the dear little feather-stitching forming flowers, the ruching, the tucks, the dress that would make Lily look like the girl she knew she could be.

The offering lay in its tissue paper, waiting for Lily to change, change into it, when she got rid of her nonsense. The evening gown was almost sleeveless, too daring she supposed, but then Lily's arms were her best feature, lovely willow arms. Ann Eldridge's eyes filled with tears. They had come too easily lately, over just anything at all. She rubbed her fist across her eyes, annoyed, and remembered to take her laudanum.

She stood at the window waiting for clarity to begin to spread through her, to untangle her worries and make her mind it all a bit less.

Then she saw them, tiny figures in the summer haze, strolling up the back road toward Seven Stars, not caring who saw them; Lily and that upstart Eddie Pagano. She knew it was Lily. She knew the white dress, every stitch of it. She never spied, she could have sworn she didn't. But she couldn't help seeing. Her fingers tapped at the window ledge and she wondered how to get Lily through June and July without more trouble.

She said, "Lily don't go up there honey oh God don't go up there don't throw it all away," as if Lily could hear her. She knew for a chill second that Lily would do that very thing, headstrong as the girl was. Oh God what am I to do, her heart called and her fingernails bit into the windowsill and the room was a trap.

There was, as always, Mr. Lacey to deal with. Sometimes she wondered why she still called him Mr. Lacey, even in her mind, after twenty-two years. I'm just used to it, she told herself. She had had to push him into too many decisions for much to be left of the marriage she had once thought was so grand. What was left was in his proud name. She knew that the girls wanted to know— she'd heard them giggling over it and had broken that up with the flat side of a hairbrush—what she called him when they were alone in their room . . . well, in bed. "Nothing" was the answer; she couldn't do it. Jake Catlett called him Beverley, and Uncle Obadiah Mr. B.B., from his childhood. She turned again. He had not moved from the sweetheart swing.

She could see Captain Neill and the other two appearing, then disappearing, between the trees that lined the creek road on their way to the Imperial Club House. I can't stand men like that, she told their backs, and summed it all up, all the resentment and fear and denial, with the two words "coal men." That covered a multitude of sins and sad times in company towns before Mr. Lacey rescued her. She had to give him that.

It was the smell of tobacco on their clothes, the way they stood, legs apart, in their leather puttees, a strength in their bodies she didn't dare name even this late in life, preferring whores to anything she had to offer. They made you feel safe when you knew you weren't safe, not by a long shot. That was their power, their crime against women. If there had been one, and there had been—there was in every girl's life, she knew that—his name was "they" now, and they had to be kept away from her girls.

They, the three of them, Captain Neill's hat a black circle against the pale dirt of the country road, had gotten beyond the trees. Away in the distance, their shadows stretched across the road—stick men with long stick legs and guns—then fell behind them when they got to the steep rise up to cross the railroad track.

She knew in her hands the awful sweet touch of the bones beneath the flesh of Captain Neill's hips where his gun belt was, arrogant citadel, remembering iliac, Ilium, that great wall.

She didn't know whether it was memory, like that memory blindness of Mr. Lacey, who still saw the huge farm of his childhood when he looked at Seven Stars town, but the valley seemed, that afternoon, somehow shy, if a landscape could be shy. The foliage was so heavy hiding many a grief, so lush it could have been any village dotted with white houses and many trees, and squares of gardens and overcast with sleep. The Boarding House and the Company Store were fine buildings and so was the church, old Mr. Lacey had seen to that. Across the creek and into the hollows, she could see Catlett houses where Catlett women—they always married good workers—kept things neat.

Seven Stars! That pretentious name had been given the valley by old Mr. Lacey because it was surrounded by seven mountains. He called them the Pleiades. Across the valley, she could glimpse the up-creek finger that was Italian Hollow, then across from her, the finger that ran between the mountains beside Jake Catlett's house.

Further down-creek, she glanced at Nigra Hollow, and glanced away again. It was full of Laceys too, but nigra Laceys, and when she said anything Mr. Lacey laughed and said they took the names of the people who had owned them out of loyalty.

Loyalty, my foot, she told herself. The head of the clan, old Aunt Toey, had belonged to the Neills, across the river at Beulah, not the Laceys. She knew they had chosen Lacey just to embarrass the family. She couldn't stand the pesky, slovenly things. She feared way down in her back that arrogant John Lacey who looked you straight in the eye. Mr. Lacey said it was because she was a Yankee and didn't understand. "He goads me," she said to the leaves, and again, "He just goads me."

The long lines of Jenny Lind houses up the creek bottom beyond Mr. Lacey's property line were gray bones in the summer sun, a plague of empty shells. A heavy chain was stretched across the up-creek road on the other side of the track. She could see the chicken-scratched little yards pounded flat by the children. The miners up at Godley just didn't care anymore, not, she had to admit, like the Paganos and all that brood up what she'd heard that awful young man Mooney call Dago Hollow until Mr. Lacey corrected him in no uncertain terms.

The Paganos had not been set out of Italian Hollow yet. It was too far out of the way, or had been forgotten, or too many kin were still working. She didn't know the ins and outs of it, and she didn't want to. She only knew that no matter what the Baldwin men said, teetering on the splendor of their leather legs that the miners called yellow legs, that setting people out of their homes was wrong, absolutely wrong. She was proud of Mr. Lacey because he refused to countenance it no matter what the extenuating circumstances.

She could see children hanging around the snake fence of Jake Catlett's land. Every inch of the Catlett property had a tent set up on it, or if not a tent, a piano crate, or quilt laid over a clothesline and pegged out for shelter. God help them if it rained.

All the men had left the creek. Nobody was fishing. The children weren't playing. Godley and Seven Stars paused for her nap, the exact hour when she allowed the reins to slip from her hands and her soul to be restored.

"What are we to do?" she asked aloud. "It's all we've got in the world." The words drifted into what she called considerations. There are considerations, she thought. She sank onto the old daybed and leaned over to push off her shoes. She loosened her hair and lay down. The considerations drifted into focus. She saw them lost, ignored, anonymous, but the words for them were, "We're somebody here. Downriver we'd be nobody, no matter what the girls say."

By "we" she meant herself, and the nobody within her she had had to fight ever since her marriage, her good marriage, where no matter how hard she tried, she couldn't help feeling demeaned and lonely inside with all her learning. In an old defiance she signed herself Ann Eldridge Lacey, even if the Eldridges were plain people. The daily wish crossed her forehead that Mr. Lacey would finish his dying, and after it shame at the thought. Self-forgiveness winged close on shame. Anger tightened her throat. She remembered to relax her mouth so the etchings of worry would go and she'd be pretty again.

The house, the hill, the round of trees were all the safety she had ever known, and her fingers clenched the iron bed railing as if she were in danger of being torn off it and flung down broken by the tracks like the detectives were doing to the miners' truck, their sticks and bones of furniture, when they set them out of the houses up the creek.

She felt a breeze through the high branches outside the window touch the summer sweat of her forehead and hoped it would bring some relief to her headache.

I'm getting too heavy—one hand loosed from the bedstead and caressed her bulging body. Oh well . . . time was! and she giggled like a girl, up there in the tower room by herself like that. She felt such a fool, but a little pleased at the same time with the memory of a fine flat stomach.

She pulled her mind back to her worries, read them one by one. It was her way of loving her girls. If I can just keep Lily from making a fool of herself, if I can just guide her through the rough places . . . she'll get someplace. She's the one with the brains. Oh Lily I will guide you, hold my hand. How dim it is. Let me guide you. I've never been further than this but I know it's there and you can go there and I will guide you where I've never been. The dim glimpse of the blank unknown had brought unjudged tears and they slid down into her hair. She brushed them away. They felt like flies.

It was Althea's turn to march, defiant, into her mind to be judged. Something in Althea always frightened her when she thought of her and she felt shame, taking for granted that the shame was Christian guilt over not—well—feeling as close to Althea as the others. Althea was the one who made her lose her temper in a way she didn't understand, Althea with grass stains on her skirt refusing to say where she'd been, not bothering with even the kindness of lying to her.

As for Mary Rose—she was still too young for the major worry, the crossroads, the fearful place she didn't name. She promised herself to pay more attention to Mary Rose. She had reached the year when a girl cried too easily. Ann Eldridge had found her in tears in the milk house. She took it for granted that the child was sorry at having disobeyed the day before, but when she told her that the punishment was over, Mary Rose had thrown her arms around her as if she were five years old and sobbed, "Mama Mama I'm scared. Are they going to make us go away?" She patted the thin shoulders and said, "Never mind. Your papa will look after us, you know that." She made herself hug the girl then, even though Mary Rose's high-strung shivering body made her cringe because she hated being touched. She always had.

Near sleep now, duty almost done, she let herself see the fear that held them, that made them all stand still where they were, frozen, forgetting their little chores. The trouble spread out beyond the trees, to the knots of men, who acted like they didn't see her when she went to the Company Store, to the women staring straight at her when she had to pass the tents. She went herself on errands she would have sent the girls for. She had to do that—walk through that quietness, the wrong kind of quietness, silence you could cut with a knife. Her fear was in the language of a thousand small duties that still tumbled through her mind until they began to fade as she moved nearer sleep and she sank beyond fear, safe because she was where she was, the only place she had ever known where she was safe—no, not was, but *felt* safe. I'm no fool winged into thought. I know the difference.

She fell on toward sleep. It was not a green sleep.

Out beyond the protecting trees she heard the hosts of Midian prowling and prowling, even though nothing moved. She began to climb, and went on climbing high gray walls. If sounds like branches breaking came through the window, they only made her pause in her climbing and then go on up the bare walls of forbidden cities, where a song, "Shy Ann Shy Ann hop on your pony," became a plea, always a plea, "Ann, oh God Ann my love take down your hair for me."

There are men to whom nothing happens. Beverley Lacey firmly believed this. He had seen it all his life. His father had opened a coalfield, made money and lost money, made decisions, used all his mental and physical muscles, been to war. His voice stayed in Beverley's head, uninvited. "By God, son, I was on fire for the right. I *knew* what it was. Now I ain't so sure." Beverley answered, "Goddammit, I ain't been on fire for a thing in my life, not even my own death. I'm cold, just cold. Born in the middle. Born between things."

He made the sweetheart swing move as he turned his back for the sun to warm him. Here it was June and he was seeking the sun with his body like an old man. It looked like the men his daughters were going to have to marry would do something—go broke, or even, though it seemed unlikely, find a war to go to. "Me, and men like me, mild men of, well"—he had to use the word— "taste, were somehow exempted by our times." He saw it in his face in the mornings when he shaved around his fine silk auburn mustache. He looked, to himself, at least, like a worn version of the boy who had come back from the University of Virginia with little to show for it but a set of habits that made people trust him, and what his mother had called "a certain style." Sometimes he couldn't believe that he was already forty-two years old and had three grown daughters he ought to worry about more than he did. Things had been done for him, a background prepared, the decisions all made, the worrying all taken care of by somebody else. His father had not let go of the reins until he died, sitting on the porch one afternoon six years ago, and dumped it all in his lap. Even then Ann Eldridge had taken over.

It seemed to him as if he were still a fair-haired child, a Golden Boy. He remembered his mother as so different from the woman the others still talked about as if she were alive; her legend was more gentle in their minds, even the girls'. His mother, his private mother, was implacable. The only things she could forgive were either becoming her or serving her and when things changed and there were fewer servants, and the town grew around her, her soul still wanted slavery, even though she was from Philadelphia. She had always known what he was thinking, and told him so in no uncertain terms. He had never loved her, but he had honored her, as he remembered it, every minute of his life.

When he married, her only comment was, "If you must," as if he had shown some weakness. Ann Eldridge was like her, even though she came from a different background. He'd always heard that you married your mother, but that wasn't it. Maybe you fashioned a woman by what you expected of her, honed her down to it, refused everything in her but what you'd been led to expect.

Therefore (he liked the word, its summing up), unbelieving and unprepared, he sat in the swing, facing with real resentment the decisions that were being forced upon him, and gently, without knowing, put his foot out on the grass and made the swing move faster. He watched the treetops sway back and forth. This time they were all wrong. He was not thinking about the offer, the blasted offer.

Ain't it the damnedest thing, he was really thinking, here I am sitting in the same place in the same swing I helped Uncle Obadiah put up. I couldn't touch the floor with my feet. It had been raining and I got mud on my boots but we couldn't either of us wait. Now I'm like a picked chicken. God Almighty I'm going to die and there's not a soul knows it but me and old Doc Carver, thank God Ann Eldridge don't know. She'd care me to death. I'm so sick of people caring for me. I've been cared for all my life. Seems to me there's always been some damned woman with wet eyes watching me and waiting for me to say it, whatever it is they want to hear. God almighty my hand looks like it's made out of paper. I'll swear to God it does. They're all watching my mind, waiting for it to, to what? Tumble down one side or the other. Ann Eldridge, watch from the tower. Mary Rose, honey you drive me plumb crazy, watch from the lawn. Mother, you watch from the big blank. You can't leave me alone even now. I swear to God one of you comes near me I'll cut your goddamned throat. What none of you know is that *I don't give a damn in hell.*

He tapped his paper finger on his white-linen knee and looked at it as if it was going to die separately from him. He wondered what it was going to look like dead and thought, Goddamn it's three-quarters dead already. Paper. Uncle Obadiah suspicions and so does Jake. I can tell the way they look at me. Now a man looking at you is different. I don't know why. Yes I do. They ain't waiting with bated breath for you to tell them. They're just there. They ain't thinking "What about me?" like a woman. That's a chorus that women sing, "What about me?"

He let the swing slide back and forth and watched the lawn

flow under it, shadow-green, didn't think anything for a minute, didn't let himself, just watched the floorboards brush the grass, and felt the sun through his linen coat.

Doc Carver's advice hadn't been worth a damn. "T.B., Beverley," he told him. "Go on get on the train and go to Cincinnati. Get another opinion. I told your pa not to make you go down the mine. I told him you had weak lungs. He was too goddamned bullheaded to listen. He said you had to learn from the coal-face out like he had. He said if you were going to ask men to work for you you had to do right. I don't know. Bullheaded . . ."

He didn't have enough ready cash to go across the creek, much less Cincinnati.

He remembered his father's voice, too, hearing them both far away as if he were already on the road to where he was going and they were calling after him—senseless excuses, unimportant apologies.

"No boy of mine," was the way his father had said it, "No boy of mine is going to lay like a hog under a chestnut tree eating chestnuts and never looking up to see where they come from. I don't give a damn how much education you get. If you don't know the coal business you ain't worth a nickel." That was the year Beverley graduated from the University. He came back with a yellow linen waistcoat, a red cravat, and kid gloves to work in the mine.

Goddamn, nine-tenths of what makes a man he don't have a word to say about. Beverley had thought that ever since he could remember. When a man's fate has already been decided for fifty million years because his land happens to be over a seam of coal, he's licked before he starts. Coal and ideals. Goddamn both of them.

He wouldn't have been there at all in the sweetheart swing and he wouldn't be about to kick the bucket if his father hadn't been an idealist. An idealist can tear hell out of a family. Look at Lily. His father had gone to Washington College in Lexington before the war when it was a hotbed of abolition and he picked up a lot of wild ideas and went against *his* father. Beverley had never had a chance to go against him like a boy ought to. Beverley had never laid eyes on his grandfather, but that didn't stop him dictating what his life was going to be, not by a long shot. "He never forgave me for going with the Union," his own father said it oftener and oftener as he got older. "But blood's thicker'n water. He sent me a letter and deeded me what he insisted on calling the Western Virginia property that had come down to him all the way from Great-great-grandfather Brandon Crawford. It was useless land in his eyes, God knows, but he'd used it to run for office from a western county, and then they don't see hide nor hair of you after you're elected. So that was partly why he got so mad at West Virginia and cast such slurs upon it."

Beverley had grown up with the letter—more than memorized, it was tattooed in his brain: "Three thousand acres of worthless land among a worthless traitorous crew. I will never understand why the western counties voted to go with the North when the gentlemen from the valley were all away fighting for the South. You are a gentleman, at least I thought so, a Lacey from Richmond." His father fought for the North up to the day he died. He lost his arm at Sharpsburg and he never let Beverley forget it. He would always call it Antietam and embarrass him in front of his friends. He took pleasure in it.

So Beverley's father brought his mother, a Philadelphia bride, to what he called Father's Revenge. He said that after all that, there was nothing else to do. He used to say it over and over again. "Well. The three thousand acres consisted of about eight miles of narrow creek bottom, mostly just wide enough for a road. The rest was little useless mountains. Little mountains," he would say that and laugh and pat the stump of his arm. "You should have seen your mother's face when we saw our inheritance for the first time. Here she was, married to a man with one arm whose only asset was some backwoods creek bottom he'd never laid eyes on. Lord!"

When she was still alive he would look at her and say, "You should have seen your face. Lord!" and she would always smile at him as if he'd never said it before. Beverley dreamed sometimes that he was with them in the carriage when it first went up what they called Signal Creek before it was Lacey Creek. He resented it when he woke, his father's life invading his sleep. Signal Creek was the Shawnee war trail and the red signals were painted on the rocks. His father had made him climb all the way up the mountain shortcut when he was no more than five years old to look at the Indian signs and he remembered seeing the creek far below, as crooked as a dog's hind leg.

The mountains imprisoned it on both sides. His father told him when Uncle Obadiah first drove the carriage with the horses at a walk through a tunnel of trees that they crossed the creek eight times in two miles. They came around the western spur of the mountain and there they were. His father said it was the mountains hiding heaven from profane eyes, a meadowland all deep with grass and clusters of trees, a lost valley a mile across in a round bowl with the mountains to guard it, seven of them, he said, like the Pleiades, and then, "I knew right then I'd come home."

Old Man Lewis Catlett had already built a cabin at the mouth of one of the hollows. His father said Lewis Catlett knew they were squatters, but they'd been there so long he couldn't throw them off the land. "You can't do that, you know," he told Beverley, as if he hadn't been weaned on responsibility for property. Lewis Catlett had fought for the North, too, so his father had sympathy for him even though he said he was mean as a snake. He sold him and his family some of the side hollow land. The day Old Man Catlett got the deed he began to fence off his ten acres with a snake fence. It took him five years.

"Now, son, you have to understand why I did that . . ." his father would say when he was old, trying still to make Beverley see, talking and talking and talking about mineral rights and coal seams on the porch swing in summer, in the library in winter, with the door closed to keep the women from interrupting his train of thought with what he called their chicken voices. "We liked having some people around," he'd say and pat his arm stump. He wore his coat sleeve in his pocket. Even when he was old it made him look more dashing than Beverley ever would. "They'd had an even harder time than we had. The war had left them about half starved."

Then he would laugh and pat the stump of his arm—he always did that when he laughed. "The joke was on Father. How was he to know the whole place was underlaid with a five-foot-thick seam of coal? Lord!" and he'd laugh and pat.

And he would tell how he, with his one arm, had opened up a

coal seam with the Catletts and two or three others from up the creek.

Beverley could still see him coming back from the mine in the evening, so black that his mother wouldn't let him into the house until Uncle Obadiah and Aunt Minnie Mae had washed him down in the washhouse and helped him change. After that they would dress for dinner. His mother insisted. He stood between them, looking up when his father said it was the damnedest silly thing he ever heard tell of, back there miles from nowhere, and his mother said, "Standards."

Would dying be dark, an abandoned entry, would it be like that? He remembered that after the initial fear of the mine, there was peace, just a round light from the lamp, and the chuck chuck chuck of the picks.

He had known for some months that he was going to die, but knowing with his mind wasn't like knowing the way he did, suddenly, in the wine cellar when he was picking out wine for those rich sons of bitches. He had simply given up, could feel it as a physical weight shifted, a blankness. He had sunk down on an empty rack. He was holding a dusty bottle and it had happened, the knowledge in the pit of his stomach. He sat dead-still, the bottle didn't even shake in his hand, and he said to the lines of nearly empty racks, "Goddammit I'm going to kick the bucket," and then, "with all there is to do." He saw his hand, holding the bottle, and he'd been looking at it ever since, watching it do what it had to do, dress him so they wouldn't know he was broke. You couldn't let fellows like that know you were broke, the strike was breaking you. Broke, a broken man.

He'd watched it on the wheel of the automobile, under his kid gloves hiding its white death, watched it shake hands, heard himself saying Mr. Peabody, Mr. Cabot, Mr. Pratt, Sir Archibald, going through the motions as if any of it mattered.

He wished Jake Catlett would come and sit with him in the swing, but he knew he wouldn't. He hadn't done that for nearly a month. Jake said it wasn't fair to his boys, him coming up like that just to set awhile, with everything like it was, even though Aunt Sara had practically raised Beverley, too. She said when he and Jake's big brother, Jethro, were born, she could hear the cries on both sides of the valley. His mother said she exaggerated, and added, "Women like that do." His father said, "Nothing of the kind. She was a Lacey from Crawford's Landing, no matter how far she has fallen," and added ". . . the war." His mother said she certainly had lowered her standards, but she let Beverley be raised by her to get him out of the house.

But he made himself be careful about the wine. He'd always liked entertaining, the way he did it, country manners, seeing to everything himself. There were things, little touches that a woman forgot.

He watched them drink the last of the '97 and couldn't think of a damned thing except his hand that was letting him down. He wanted to care the way the sun touched the wine, and taste its color, that spilled color of red light on the white tablecloth. That always used to pleasure him, the color of hospitality. They sat there drinking his wine, all set to buy him out of house and home. They smelled blood all right. He could tell that.

They knew when to close in. Foreclose. The foresight to foreclose. That's why they were rich and he was broke. Foresight. The only foresight that made any difference was the foresight in the wine cellar, where he wouldn't let anybody else go. He kept the key in his pocket. He didn't want a living soul to know how empty it was.

Spontaneous combustion. The gob-pile set itself on fire and burned and burned like the slow burning in his body, spontaneous combustion of death.

He supposed he'd have to do something. He made himself think. You have to consider the girls, he told himself, and wished he'd brought a cigar out with him and couldn't go and get one. One or the other of them, the waiters waiting for him to move, would trip him on questions, the big question, "What are we going to do?" and he'd never get back to the swing. He watched the sun rock back and forth through the trees.

Wouldn't Ann Eldridge be surprised if she knew I was planning nothing, nothing at all, that I don't really give a tinker's dam. The thought made him smile.

Women as women, as horses, white-eyed, or complaining, or shy, shadows beyond every doorway, sudden screaming as if the fox of anxiety had gotten into a chicken yard. God, he had them, a flock, a legion of them. Althea wouldn't be happy cooking for angels; she had a tacky streak, she showed her fear with too many ruffles, too many curls, too much tremolo when she sang. Lily, aloof, lovely Lily—he'd never known a truly gentle woman, but she came nearer to that than the others. She was teasable and sad, more attractive and more vulnerable. She needed more care and knew it less. That was a dangerous combination. Some men would take advantage of that. He wanted, for a second, to warn her, and then forgot Lily. There was something about Mary Rose that kept her safe—a mixture of curiosity and lack of caring for anyone but herself and whoever was prepared to serve her, please her, listen to her. In that way she was more like his mother than the others. She would be lonely at times, but only for attention, not for love.

He remembered Althea playing the piano. It was night and raining, he knew it had been raining outside and he was depressed and drank too much brandy. It was February, and Althea was playing the piano and singing a song he liked. They laughed at it because it was a train song and not their sort of thing at all—not like the sheet music they sent off for, the latest thing. What was it? He hummed and rocked the swing . . . something, sick child . . . Set a green lamp in the window if she's living, hmmm, set a red lamp if the angels took her . . . something I go to . . . Oh, he couldn't remember—got to get the train in on time . . . Hell, he couldn't remember. He only remembered that when the others had laughed at the song, he'd suddenly burst into tears right in front of them in the parlor, and said, "I don't give a goddamn if I was the engineer running Christ's body through to Jerusalem. If it was my child I'd stop." He wondered why he'd felt that way over a song and not over his girls, his real girls.

He could feel his eyes close. He let himself retreat into the only relief he knew, to remain tranquil, very still, not even letting the swing move. Tranquillity was the only form of panic he allowed himself.

For twenty years Jake Catlett's wife, Essie, had put on her hat at a quarter to five every day except Sunday, and walked down the

Catlett side of the valley, across the town, up through the Laceys' garden and into the big kitchen to help out. She hated being late. Time, to her, was a series of chores, from morning until she, as she said it, fell into bed.

She was running late. It was already four o'clock by her alarm that sat in the daytime on her own kitchen windowsill, and at night on the floor on Jake's side of the bed. She finished wiping off the kitchen counter, looked around to see if there was anything she had forgotten, adjusted Jake's shaving mirror he kept on a nail over the pump, and put on her hat. She gave a chunk to the fire in the range, checked the beans, went back to the mirror to give her hair a last pat, re-drove her big tortoise-shell hairpin in her bun so she could feel it secure against her scalp.

She had worn her hair flat and pulled back in a bun ever since she was thirty. Ann Eldridge had said, "What you want to do that for, you're a pretty woman."

"Pretty is as pretty does," Essie had told her, and that was that.

She glanced into the living room for a last check to see if the couch was straightened. Ann Eldridge had given it to her when she remade the parlor after the Madame died. She said it was Chippendale, and Jake called it Chickendale, teasing her. Over the couch there were the two oval pictures of Jake's ma and pa, Lewis and Sara Catlett, young and stern, not old and mean like she remembered them. She wondered when stern turned to mean, then brushed the thought away. She didn't have time to moon around, not with that bunch she could see out on the porch, still at it. She wanted to do some things over at the Big House before Ann Eldridge came down from her nap. Essie didn't like to be interfered with. It slowed her down.

It wasn't any use. She just stood there rooted to the kitchen floor. Essie had the second sight and it was nothing but a burden to her. She knew it and Ann Eldridge knew it. Premonition. She had labored under it ever since morning.

It was mostly that old woman turning up like that without so much as a by-your-leave. It wasn't that Mother Jones brought trouble. She just appeared where trouble was. That foul-mouthed old woman looked like butter wouldn't melt in her mouth, took over the strike like the whole valley was deeded out to her.

Essie wanted to tell Ann Eldridge about feeling psychic all day. Sometimes she felt like Ann Eldridge was the only friend she had, even though they were in different circumstances. It had started out private, it had to—and it had stayed that way. They used to make excuses when the Madame was alive that they were going up to the tower room to patch. What they did was they worked the Ouija board. The Madame sat on the porch all the time and stared out at the up-creek mountain like she was seeing through it all the way to Philadelphia. If she had known what they were doing she would have cast aspersions on it. After both the mothers-in-law died they quit using the Ouija board. They just got out of the habit, but Essie laughed and said they quit because they were scared that their mothers-in-law would come back and lay down the law like they had in their lifetime.

Essie missed it, though. It wasn't so much the messages from beyond the veil. They didn't make all that much sense anyhow. She missed the talks with Ann Eldridge when they were young and didn't have anybody else to complain to. She didn't know, but now that Ann Eldridge was the Madame she got more like her every day. They still talked in the kitchen, though, but Ann Eldridge quit introducing her when company came. Things like that. Essie told herself not to dwell on it. She didn't except on days when the premonition weighed her down. She didn't care about the Ouija board. She had better things to do with her time.

Took Ann Eldridge fifteen years to rule the roost at last, and her, Essie, well, around twenty. You had to wait until your turn came. That was all. Your own ways just had to wait.

Ann Eldridge hadn't lost a week after the Madame died. She couldn't stand having colored people in the house, all those black Laceys taking the same name after the war, come over from Beulah when the old man was alive. She let them all know it wasn't her way of doing, and Lord's love, she certainly had a clear field then. Beverley didn't say a word. Why, the Madame's death pritnear broke that boy's heart. He was closer to her than she'd ever seen a son, never seemed to take his eyes off her. Devotion.

She considered all this while she stood there. Her body just wasn't ready to go. She reckoned she had done the same—little touches. Taey's Valley touches. Flowers in the house, and doilies, and new curtains.

Essie wasn't from around there. If anybody forgot it, she reminded them, "I ain't from around here," as if that told it all, which, to her, it did. She was a Carver from down around Putnam County, no kin to that Anderson Carver, though, thank God. They were fine people, even if the Madame when she was alive looked down on her. That Yankee woman never did learn who anybody was.

Sometimes Essie went back in her mind to her own people and rested there when she got so tired, so hemmed in in the narrow hollow. She was used to looking out all the way over Taey's Valley. The little black cloud of sinful despair that was on everybody's horizon only most people seemed to be able to keep it little just come over her until she wanted to go behind the privy and blow her brains out, sin or not. She talked to it, the black cloud, told it about the hard births, two breech and one untimely, all three dead, and the other three, all boys. Nobody to lift a finger to help her. Jake's pa, that old s.o.b. (she thought that but wouldn't have let such a thing pass her lips—you couldn't help thinking, though), laid down the law for the first ten years of her marriage.

He was a terrible old man. If ever a man stewed in Christian hate that man did. Prayers full of hate over the beans. She could still hear him, "Lord, thou hast promised to make my enemies my footstool. When? How long, oh Lord, how long?" sitting right in there at the big kitchen table come from Beulah. Jake did it over. The two big chairs come from her side of the family.

But in his life the Lord never did, not even when Old Man Catlett leased out the mineral rights to the hill farm at Beulah for next to nothing. He was too bullheaded to take Senator Neill's advice, his own brother-in-law.

Lord knows, the poor old man died hard, not a thing left in his mind but how he'd been done by. Cursing! Jake said his last word was "Usurped," but Essie said it wasn't anything of the kind, more like, "You were," accusing somebody in his mind's eye or what was left of it. Anyway, after that he asked for a drink of water. With all that good bottomland, he lay there grasping that old whip with the silver handle and cried like a baby. Afterwards they had to pry it loose and Jake took and made a carving knife out of it. The whip part by that time looked like a sick rat's tail.

Only afterwards was the Senator brought low. Old Man Catlett used to say there was only one difference, the difference between hill land and bottomland, he was better blood than that shanty Irishman. There wasn't a thing he could tell Essie about that. She'd seen too much in her lifetime, seen people pritnear starve because their land was hill land, not bottomland. Lord's love, after every rain topsoil come down to the bottom, and the hill farm at Beulah the old man talked about like it was the land of Gideon wasn't worth a red cent. They were better off where they were, over on Lacey Creek with four or five acres of bottomland.

She looked out of the window to where Jake had let all the families set out of their houses when they struck put up tents. It was going to take a year for them to get the land back to where it would yield a thing.

It was all a piece of foolishness anyhow, stirring up things, and she wanted no part of it, except for her feelings for Jake. He was a good man and she loved him, God Almighty, strong as when he was young and pretty. So she did what she had to, cooked for that bunch of deadbeats, made gallon after gallon of coffee, but she was not about to stop helping out at the Big House when Ann Eldridge needed her more than they did, not listening to a word she had to offer. Besides, she had to admit she liked a little egg money of her own.

Jake, in that gentle voice, had pointed out she didn't have to do that, not with what they had. But it wasn't that, not anything of the kind. She didn't point it out, because she didn't want to hurt his feelings, but she had started it partly to get away from the old man and the old woman, and, oh she didn't know, she just never did quit. Later, when the boys made a racket, she went because it was quiet up there, and Ann Eldridge was what she was used to. She come of quiet people, and she'd been through the sixth grade down in Putnam County on a flat farm in Taey's

Valley, not flat, what was? But Lord God, it wasn't nothing like Lacey Creek, the whole valley surrounded by hills like mule blinders.

She wouldn't of been there at all if it hadn't of been for the C&O railroad.

Ann Eldridge wouldn't of been there if it hadn't of been for Mr. Godley. Essie had already been stuck there a year when Ann Eldridge married Beverley and she was never so glad to see anybody in all her born days. The Madame high-hatted the poor little thing and Essie was having her own troubles and it just drew them together, even if Ann Eldridge was older, but lines were drawn. Old Miz Lacey would have set her foot down if it had been any other way.

When Essie put on her hat instead of her poke bonnet, things were different. She wore it to church and she wore it to weddings and funerals and square dances and graduation exercises and she wore it every day to walk across the valley and help out. It showed every one of them that she wasn't no servant. She was a friend and helping out wasn't the same. In the winter she trimmed her hat with grouse feathers Jake shot for her, and on the day before Easter, every year, she put the satin violets on it that Ann Eldridge gave her. She said old Miz Lacey had left them to her, but Essie knew she hadn't done anything of the kind. Ann Eldridge only said that to make her feel good.

Pretty! Not a soul had looked at her, except Jake sometimes and that was after everybody had gone to bed and she was a lot younger than she was now, and had a seventeen-inch waist. He'd whisper "Essie, honey?" a question, and if she could hear the old folks snoring and none of the youngins was sick she'd say yes. But not so much anymore. Jake was their least one, the last shot out of the old man's gun. She hoped she'd have another boy, she still could, one to look after them like Jake did his ma and pa. None of her three boys would do it, she knew that.

Her mother-in-law sat on the front porch for five years after old man Catlett died, with Aunt Toey, that old colored woman from Beulah, and they would laugh and fight like they kicked the end out of the same cradle.

"Now go 'way, honey," she'd say to Essie, treat her like she was ten years old, "can't you see we're talkin'?"

Essie had to wait on her hand and foot while she sat there. Sometimes the old woman talked to her Jake like he was dirt under her feet. She lost her mind and thought he was his pa, called him Lewis three-quarters of the time. Essie had never heard such snakes come out of an old woman's mouth. She proceeded to tell Jake when she thought he was his pa everything she had thought about him and hadn't had gumption enough to say for the fifty years they were married. She called that fifty years a living hell. "You put me through living hell," she'd tell Jake. "I was gently nurtured and you treated me like a pack mule!" Jake just sat there and said, "Yes, Ma," and she said, "Don't you Ma me you old devil." Essie didn't know how he stood it. The other boys were not a bit of help. He just sat there and took it all.

He said, "Ma ain't herself, she can't help it."

But Essie knew she was more herself than she'd been since she was little, maybe more than she had ever been since she come out from eastern Virginia, little Sara Lacey. My Lord she rubbed that in. "Those Laceys"—she'd point across the valley to the Big House —"they're only distant connections," and then she'd tell how gently nurtured she had been and Essie would listen in Christian charity.

"Thus are the mighty struck down," she'd say, and smooth and smooth her skirt, thinking about it. She said after Lewis Catlett died she lost her religion, talked about it like it was something rolled off under the bed. "I'm tard," she'd say, and brush her hair out of her face, and say, "I honestly don't care." Essie like to worked herself to death while she set on the porch and let everybody call her Aunt Sara like she wasn't no better than they were, and she was. She was kin to the Neills, and God knows they were on the hog front titty. "If anybody were giants in the earth in those days before they struck down!" Miss Sara would say, and then she'd answer herself. "That's the God's truth and no lie."

When Miss Sara heard what happened to Senator Neill all she said was, "That little Irish bastard," and she'd never said a bad word in her life before no matter what else she let go. She just sat there laughing. She laughed all one day, little peepee titters. She seemed to be somewhere else watching something in her own head and when Essie tried to get her to eat she just shook her head and pushed at the air and went on watching whatever it was. Essie got her to bed, but the next day she was back in the rocker with the rain coming in on her. Along about one o'clock Essie went out to try again to make her come in and she was dead, sitting right there in the rocker seventy-five years and three months old, never been sick a day, just lost her mind. Something had made her mad. Her jaws were so clenched they couldn't bury her in her teeth.

They were all going fast, Senator Neill, then her mother, then Old Man Lacey, then the Madame. No. That was wrong. She died first. It gave Old Man Lacey a few years to himself. Essie never had liked her, she had Yankee ways; she put too much salt in the butter and a lot of the time didn't speak when spoken to. When Old Man Lacey found out Miss Sara was Brandon Lacey's daughter, he claimed kin. He even knew just how it was, and she would nod her head and say yes that's how it was, but the Madame —well—she never claimed kin, but then she didn't know any better. She never did learn.

Essie was glad Old Man Lacey couldn't see what was happening now. She wouldn't have wanted him to see that, not that he wouldn't of dealt with it like he did in oh two, laid down the law to the whole coalfield. "Now you settle," he told them. "You do right. These fellers ain't got a pot to pee in, no wonder they come out." He never talked that way at home, and he wouldn't of in front of her. He didn't know she could hear. He was only telling Old Man Catlett what he said.

That was before so many strangers come. It was all their fault, nothing but Englishmen and Yankees and Dagoes and field niggers and eastern Virginians and all the white trash both sides of the river come in there with the railroad, Yankee fellows come in on a private train, setting there murmuring and muttering on the Laceys' front porch all decked out fit to kill, while she and Ann Eldridge put on the big pot and the little one.

Now here was that damned old woman come in from way out

West, busting into something wasn't none of her business. Old woman looked like the queen of England, and called herself Mother Jones like she borned them all. Cussed like a section foreman. Essie never heard such language from an old woman. Her and her lace jabot. Essie had heard tell she used to run a whorehouse, but didn't anybody say that in front of the boys. She heard tell that down in Logan County they took and spaded some feller come in there and said that. They thought she hung the moon.

Things had changed since Essie come on the C&O from Putnam County fifteen years old and scared to death. People living in rented houses and going to the public works. It was the first step. It always had been, except for Old Man Catlett and his boys. They had always helped out Mr. Lacey and gotten paid for it but it was different than just laying out to work for wages like the strangers. You couldn't expect any better of them. They were a different class. Jake said they wasn't any difference down the mine one man was as black as another, and she remembered when she first came Jake and Old Man Lacey come out of the drift mouth black as niggers and she said that wasn't what she meant and he knew it. It was a difference you couldn't put into words.

The strike had gone on long enough anyhow—too long—all those people not allowed up-creek to put their gardens in and here it was already June. She made them put in gardens in the down-creek lot, Jake asked her to. She thought it was the silliest thing she ever heard of and said so, and Jake said, "You don't mean that, Essie," and when she started to answer he said, "That's enough. I mean it," and he hardly ever spoke to her like that.

I've got to go, she fussed at herself, but still she didn't move. Lord's love, they were still at it out there. Jake was right and that old woman was wrong and she was glad to hear him lay down the law.

He said, "You ain't going to fool around with them guns nowhere near them girls," and then he was still for so long she thought he'd finished talking, and then he said, "Let me catch anybody."

But what else they had to do she couldn't hear and she wasn't one to eavesdrop. She could see some of the boys in a row against the porch rail, with their hats down low over their eyebrows, looking like more and more weathered versions of the same man.

She knew what ailed them. What none of them liked was having to do it a certain way. The way somebody told them. They weren't used to that. Of course if anybody had to tell them, there wouldn't be anybody they respected more than they did her. Her? She was their angel, The Angel of the Miners. Essie would of had plenty to say about that but nobody would of listened. Why she wasn't no more than a paid rabble-rouser, three dollars a day for going up and down the creek stirring people up.

"What girls?" she heard Mother Jones ask Jake. Sitting there dumpy like a sweet little old lady, about the shape of a keg of dynamite. She could see her through the window in old Miz Catlett's rocker, the boys treating her like she was Miz Aster's billy goat. Essie wanted to spit.

"Them youngins of Mr. Lacey's, he means . . ." she heard Jethro say. He hadn't spoken for so long his voice growled in his throat.

"Now that's just sentimental. That's the way they get you." Mother imitated the way she thought coal operators talked, and they didn't do anything of the kind: "How's that boy of yours, Mr. Miner? Is he still going blind working as a breaker boy while my boy goes to a fine Eastern school?" Essie heard her slap her hand on the chair arm. "You boys make me sick. You don't get the message. Those fellas have been squeezing you dry for years and when time comes to act . . ." Mother's voice had risen. It was part of a speech Essie had heard her make that morning up in the bull pasture beyond the barn.

Softly, way underneath her voice, Jake laid down the law. He said, "Ain't nary a one of my boys firin' nary a gun up around that house scarin' nary a girl. Mr. Lacey wouldn't like that . . ." He usually called him Beverley like he always had since they were boys and Jake used to follow Beverley around like a pup. He said Beverley was good to him and put up with him tagging along and Jethro was mean as a snake. Essie remembered Old Man Lacey saying Jethro was a chip off the old block, meaning Old Man Lewis Catlett. Of course after they were men five years didn't make any difference between Jake and Beverley; they were as close as two sides of a walnut, those two. So when she heard Jake call him Mr. Lacey she knew he meant business.

God Almighty, there she was eighty years old, Mother Jones, nothing but a little woman in her black dress with the prettiest lace jabot Essie had ever seen, even at the Big House. Essie just wanted to feel it with her fingers. She didn't know what got into her. She didn't covet it. She wouldn't do that, just feel with her fingers, that was all. She knew Jake felt proud to have her choose his house, and Essie just couldn't see that, but she had to respect it.

The rest of them never even looked up when Essie walked past them and started down the hill path, but Jake did.

He smiled. "Don't let them beans burn," she told him, and he nodded. He watched her all the way down to the valley. He was worried. It was already five o'clock and Mother wouldn't quit laying down the law and let him go on and do what he had to.

Mother Jones got up and went to the porch rail to look over the valley. She motioned the boys out of her way so she could lean. She'd been arguing with those goddamn hillbillies for two hours. For a minute she felt defeated by the slow voices, the breeze as slow, the flowing creek, the faraway calls of children.

What you wanted to do was you wanted to give them something to do. Shit fire, she ought to know—make it more like a strike and less like a goddamn picnic. Now she knew, and Jake Catlett knew, the boys liked to go on watch, made them feel like soldiers, even if they were in their old everyday citizen's clothes. It was where that they couldn't see eye to eye on. Hell, standing around on some damned mountain where there couldn't anybody see them wasn't a bit of good, but she prided herself that she knew how to give in on little things. But she was waiting a minute; let them wait, let them stew in their own juice.

She squinted her eyes because the western sun behind her had splashed the opposite rise in the distance with light. The Lacey mansion shined like a whited sepulcher stained with gold. That bullheaded hillbilly wouldn't let anybody near it. She was dog-tired and she didn't want her boys to see her that way. She had decided she would die as soon as the strike was won. There had been so many. Somebody else was going to have to look after her boys sooner or later. She felt a little round sentimental tear in her eye and wiped it out with her lace hanky. She said, "You goddamned old woman . . ."

Jake followed her. He didn't want to set down after she got up; it wasn't good manners. He didn't know what to do when she said that. He knew he wasn't supposed to hear. He felt a loss of something. It was language. He knew things but not how to say them. Strung between Beverley and the union, both of them pulling hard, he told them both silently, "Don't you forget it."

Not seeing eye to eye with Beverley made him sad. He wasn't used to it. Why, he thought more of Beverley than he did his own blood. Right could be on your side and God knew it was. He knew it, too, but you didn't have to jump up and click your heels about it. It was easy for the old woman to breathe fire and brimstone. She wasn't kin to anybody and she hadn't been raised with anybody.

She stood, a compacted pool of a woman who knew how to rest in little minutes of silence. He had seen it the day before when she come trudging up the path by the branch. He'd watched her stop at first one tent, then after a while another. He had stood on the porch, and read the gestures, hesitation, alert awareness from the far figures, then recognition, arms pointing toward the Catlett farmhouse.

She was trudging, not with heaviness—she was a graceful little woman—but with the weight of age. She'd walked two miles in the June sun all by herself and she was covered with a veil of summer dust. He just couldn't believe it was really her, paying that much attention to one little strike; his disbelief kept him rooted to the porch until she was almost up to him and she looked up and said, "Well, Jake, it's been a long time. What the hell are you boys up to?" He said then, "How dee do, Mother," and began to move, take her arm, and her parcel wrapped in the black shawl.

She hadn't changed a bit since she'd stood in the middle of the creek in oh two and signed her boys up for the United Mine Workers. My God, he could still see her, that little old thing with the water in winter up to her ankles, and in the spring up to her knees, and her with her black skirt tucked up to her waist, showing the lace on her bloomers and not giving a tinker's dam. She said she was seventy years old and they wasn't no man interested in her sash.

Mr. Godley and Old Man Lacey were the only mine owners let her come out on their dry land. She'd sat on a log right up in front of Mr. Godley's Company Store and sworn his boys in.

He remembered her setting there with her boys around her. She had her shoes off, drying her feet and she looked up and shook her fist at the Company Store when Mr. Godley came to the window of his office. She called out, "You call yourself Godley, you capitalist paternalist son of a bitch," and Mr. Godley opened the window and called back, "Ma'am, I would be honored if you would come into my parlor to discuss the matter," very formally, "if," he added, "you can see your way to taking a mite toddy with a capitalist paternalist son of a bitch."

She laughed, and the men around her started to laugh, too.

"I'm no fool," Mr. Godley hollered over the laughter. "I don't want you coming down with political pneumonia on my property." She went right across the dirt road, barefooted, straightening her hat and flicking a bit of dust from her black dress, and they negotiated right then and there over Old Overholt whiskey. Jake could hear them inside jawing together like men playing cards.

"I come to help you boys—" She climbed up the porch steps and settled herself in the rocker his pa had made one winter while he watched him boil the wood and learned slowness from the old man, how to use slowness. She was just as slow. She settled into the rocker his ma died in as if she'd always been there and told him in the middle of a conversation they'd never started, ". . . So I was out in Montana in the West and I went to the station and I said I'm going into West Virginia. They've brought in Baldwin thugs. I'm needed, and he said 'You be quiet, Mother, we're all with you. That there's Russia. That's the land of slavery. You go in there and give 'em hell.' Now, Jake, you remember in oh two, and that feller whatshisname, used to be governor? Not little old Glasscock, Crystal Peter, who's the governor now—I'll settle with him too. He sent his slaves of capitalism and they put me on the train and said 'We don't want to catch you back in

West Virginia, Mother.' Well, I go where the trouble is. When I got off the train today one of them Baldwin thugs he come up to me and said 'What the hell are you doing here' and put his hand on my arm. I said 'Take your hand off my arm or my boys will blow you all the way across the river.' He dropped my arm and let me alone and I come on up here. I sure would like a cup of coffee . . ." and she went into one of those minutes of closed-in old silence like she was doing now, leaning against the porch rail, just plumb wore-out.

Jake wanted to say, "I know. I know what to do," but it would have come out, "Look here. Now you just lookee here," not what he meant. He felt young, even though he was forty-five years old and head of the local. At the mine they listened to him, by God they did.

So he waited for her to speak up. But he knew that finally it would be him who would do the deciding. He lifted his hands, as if the movement might make her understand.

Her waiting went on until she had rested, leaning there collecting the valley, measuring it. She liked Jake, even his bullheadedness, the kind of man he was, the way he knew when to bother her and when not to. She told herself that he had already learned to time things right, not like some of her younger boys who went off half-cocked. She had liked him from the time she had seen him standing on the porch the day before as she had walked up toward him after that train ride that had almost worn her out. She liked that way he stood there, thick in his chest and arms from mining coal, his eyes like a raccoon's from coal dust. No matter how much a man like that washed it was in his skin. He was a big feller. She came up to between his elbow and his shoulder. She liked that, too. It was a fool thing but she liked to feel little beside a big man. He wasn't a bit bent or broke, not like some of them. She hated to see a man let his chest cave in and his eyes go blank. You couldn't depend on a defeated man or a whining man or a scared man. They would as soon shoot as argue, like that little shave-tail guard, the boy with the rifle, grabbing her arm when she was old enough to be his great-grandma, shame on him.

"Them," she spoke aloud to the white paint on the opposite

rise that gleamed in the late sun. "They don't do no dirty work. No, they just hire them damned guards. They're clean. Mr. Banker and Mr. Operator they're clean. They go to church on Sunday morning and tell you to give your money to learn about Jesus . . . Why, Jesus don't know no more about you than a dog does his daddy." She'd said that, too, in the bull field.

Jake rumbled in his throat. He had to. In half an hour the sun would be right and the men in the right place for what he thought they ought to do. He'd seen three of the Baldwin men, them sons of bitches, come out of Beverley's yard and he knew how long it would be before they went on duty. She went into her own world of grief or anger or her own past and forgot what time it was. That was the only way you could tell she was old.

He might as well have tried to stop No. 13 on its tracks.

"I know them fellers. Oh I know them fellers on sight. Now, son, you don't know them fellers like I do. What you don't know is that feller over there wouldn't do nothing for you. Oh, he'd try, and then he'd give in and feel guilty and tell it all to Jesus. I've seen them fellers shrivel up and die over what they done as if that did any damned good. He'd protest, oh wouldn't he, though, and he'd do it to you in the end. You wouldn't do nothing to him in the first place, that's the big difference. Them fellers over there . . ."—she leaned her head over toward the shining tower where the sun had hit a window and made it glow, a prism of light—"they just squat in these valleys and draw your spunk. They don't have to do nothing. They got Baldwin men."

"Mr. Lacey ain't hard no guards. Just Imperial and Mr. Baird so far . . ."

"Oh shit fire, Jake. It's only a matter of time, you know that." Every time she cursed like that it shocked him, a little electric shock. He couldn't help it. She was suddenly as businesslike as if she had been waiting for Jake, not he for her. Even her face was different. The grandmother was gone. She looked like an old schoolteacher Jake had had once, laying down the law. Her eyes were littler. It surprised Jake how that could happen so quick, large and wet to little and dry, like clouded stones. Animals did that when they died. She was saying something.

"All right. You boys go on up the mountain. In a minute. I got to get the lay of the land. Now that there . . ." She pointed to the side hollow up the creek from the shining house. "Is there a mine up there? I forget . . ." There was no way to see in June whether there was or not. The woods were so lush that they covered the tracks, the tipple, even the gob-pile from where they were. Only the smell of the burning slag heaps kept it from being a land of Canaan; his pa used to say that every time he sat on the porch.

"Now that there's Mr. Lacey's mine," he told her. "Seven Stars. Some fellers are still working. They don't like to let Mr. Lacey down."

"Who's working? We start right there . . ."

"Them's local fellers, a few foreigners, nothing else."

"What's been done to bring those men out? God Almighty, ain't you fellers ever heard of solidarity forever?"

Of course he had. He decided he was tired of her acting like he wasn't dry behind the ears. He meditated on the valley and dammit to hell he made her wait a minute until he decided what to do. He looked way off up the creek from under the thick eaves of his eyebrows; he was squinting from the lower lid, a measuring hunter's squint, up through the heat haze of summer, imperceptible and heavy, that made the faraway dirt road quiver in the light. Slowly he raised his arm when he was good and ready. He pointed up-creek to where the great chain stretched across the road from post to post.

"Up yonder, the first mine is Godley. Now that ain't Godley no more, hit's just called Godley. Hit's Imperial Coal Company."

"Pittsburgh," Mother said, "English money."

"Yes ma'am. Pittsburgh." He wanted to spit but didn't in front of Mother. He wished he hadn't started to chew when he came out on the porch. It was a habit. Essie wouldn't let any of them chew in the house. He respected that.

"Love of God, spit," Mother told him as if she could read his mind. Some people said she could, said worse things than that about her, but not in front of any of her boys if they knew what was good for them.

Jake spat, a long, satisfying stream of tobacco juice, over the rail of the porch, missing Essie's late sweet peas and her early black-eyed Susans. He was ready now to talk. He felt in control of things.

He talked deep in his chest, the mumble of a man who spends the center of his time in silence or darkness.

"Mr. Roundtree is the superintendent. He's a right good man even if he ain't nothing but an Englishman. He's got a foreman he brought with him from Scotland name of Mr. McLeod. He's meaner than a damned rattlesnake. Looks like one too. One of them flatheaded fellers. But he's fair on the weight, I'll say that for him. He don't cheat you on weight."

"Anybody working there?" she interrupted.

Jake went on with what he had to say. "Now, that there's our mine. We done worked for Godley ever since it belonged to Mr. Lacey's pa. Him and Pa dug the first coal in that mine, them two and one mule. Then he leased out to Mr. Godley and Mr. Godley sold out to Imperial. He said he got tired of living halfway between no place and hell." Jake allowed himself to smile.

"Go on up the creek, son." She seemed to know there wasn't any use being impatient. At least he'd gotten that straight with her.

"Well, now, the whole of the rest is leased from Mr. Pratt. He owns all the way up to High Tower—fifteen, twenty miles. He don't mine no coal himself. He leases out to other fellers. That there's where the main trouble is."

"Standard Oil Company," she stated to the valley.

"No'm. Mr. Pratt bought from Mr. Lacey's pa. He didn't want it. Mr. Pratt don't mine no coal." He repeated that, partly for himself. In all the years he'd never understood how Mr. Pratt could be so damned rich when he didn't mine the coal. "They lease out to a bunch of fellers—Imperial, Mr. Baird, Mr. Peabody, Mr. Cabot, oh Mr. Baseheart, all them fellers—six, eight mines up there."

"Standard Oil Company. I told you," she insisted. "Pratt's a vice president of Standard Oil."

"I don't know what else he does for a living," Jake told her slowly. "Now, from the chain on, that's where the guards are. They got an armored car they call the Bull Moose after Roosevelt and they bring in transportation men to work the mines."

"I know," Mother told him. "Some came in with me on Number Six. That fool youngin tried to hustle me off the platform before I saw, but I saw all right. I just stood up there behind a tree and seen them shunt them cars over to the spur and couple them onto the new engine. All the blinds was pulled so I knew what they was. Them guards was all over the cars—some of them riding on top when they passed me. They had guns. Two of them was astraddle of the cowcatcher . . ."

Jake had seen them, too. He didn't see any sense talking about it but he reckoned he had to. "They ain't one single local miner —white, colored or foreign—working up there. They're all out. Hit's all transportation and most of them fellers never been inside of a mine before. A lot gets killed but they don't care. One time on the telephone Mr. Cordell bragged. He said 'We use Dagoes for mine props' . . ."

Mother couldn't trust herself to answer for once. Talk like that made her sick. Then she thought, That'll come in handy in a speech—get more foreigners to sign on with the union. She believed in putting everything to use.

Jake thought he ought to explain about the telephone. "They ain't but one line up the creek—nine, ten parties on it. We got . . . uh . . . access to a telephone. We knowed a transport was coming up yesterday when it left Thurmond. Now they was a few local fellers working Godley—you know—some Italians, Finns, but when Imperial hard the guards, they come out, too. Hell," he finished, forgetting she was a woman, and then remembering, added, "Pardon, ma'am. I don't know why they brung them guards and them armored cars and machine guns up here. We wasn't fixing to shoot nobody. Other side of the river they settled peaceful with the union. They wasn't but three, four guards over there and they pulled them off first week in March. They wasn't on strike more'n a month. Here hit's been four months and folks is getting hungry, Mother . . . We done shared out and shared out. We can't go into winter on account of them kids."

It was as if she had climbed onto a wagon bed as she had that morning in the bull field. The same voice, those blue eyes all alive again, damnedest eyes he ever saw.

"You may have to. That's what they're trying to do, starve you. That's why they bring the guards in. That's why they set you out. Starve and freeze you. Are you going to stand by until they throw

60

your wife and children and your precious belongings into the creek? Are you going to cave in before—"

"We own this land," Jake interrupted, but quietly so as not to be rude. "Can't nary a one kick us off. Them tents down there is on our property. I don't know, Mother. They're setting so many out." Then he got to the gist of the matter. "What I reckoned was we just scare some of them shave-tail boys they got up there out of the holler . . . not hurt 'em or nothing . . . Folks are mighty upset about how they're setting 'em out. You know, hiring niggers to throw their truck in the creek and standing around with rifles laughing. Hit's mighty sad to see how mean and trashy things look when they're setting in a creek all broke down."

"Oh no, Jake, don't hurt 'em or nothing. Don't do that." Jake ignored the irony. He wasn't having real shooting and she knew it. She knew he'd do what he wanted to anyway. He was that kind of man.

Mother hadn't forgotten about the pickets. She was a real one-track-minded woman, Jake told himself.

"How are we going to get pickets up-creek beyond the chain? Is that the only road?"

"Yes, ma'am. They ain't no other way to get up there save over the mountains. Me and the boys will watch from the hills. Now that the leaves are thick they can't see us. We don't miss nothing. We got somebody to listen on the phone . . ."

"Who's that?"

"Well, I'd like to tell you but I can't do that . . . Now if we laid out to picket anywheres else it would get some of our boys shot, Mother, and besides, it couldn't do no good. Mr. Williams called up Captain Neill on the telephone last night from the King Coal Hotel in Canona and he told Captain Neill that pursuant to orders that new shipment didn't speak no English . . ."

"What else did he tell him?"

"Nothing important." Jake was tired of talking. It was time to go on watch.

"I'll decide what's important." Mother didn't mean to be impatient. She smiled, a little flirtatious twitch. "Anything my boys know . . ."

"He said 'I'll be a son of a bitch if I'll spend another night in this shit-hole' he said that ma'am I'm sorry but you asked. He said 'Some fellers tried to break down my door last night.' He said 'These here are the meanest sons of bitches I ever had to deal with' . . ." Jake allowed himself one snort of a laugh, and then turned back toward the porch. His brother Jethro and Elsworth Tremble and a couple of boys from the tents were just standing there, waiting for him.

"Well, they won't shoot women," Mother said to his back. "I got to see the path you fellers use, and I got to find me a woman speaks Italian—a woman with some spit and vinegar. I don't want no whiner."

"That would be Annunziata Pagano, her and her daughter Maria," Jake said without turning around. "Boys, let's go." They started down the steps carrying their rifles sloped.

"Mother, it's a mighty steep path," Jake said as they filed past.

"Holy Saints, this ain't the first mountain I've had to climb." She heaved herself off the porch and started around the house toward the narrow path that disappeared ahead of them up into the trees. She reminded herself not to talk that way again. One thing her boys didn't like, that was Catholic talk.

Jake was worried. The strike had gone on too damned long. It wasn't a crisis anymore, but a deep anger they were used to, a way of living. His boys were as restive as hounds in a wind. She was right. He had to give them something to do. He couldn't hold them back much longer. Every time a family on yellow-dog contract got thrown out of their house they got madder. He reckoned it was better to draw off some of that. Anyway, it might do some good, what he'd decided. It probably wouldn't but it might.

They went single file past the pigsty, past Essie's chicken coop, past the corncrib, past the side path to the privy. As he got into the rhythm of his walk, Jake felt tall again, but he still wished he could talk to Beverley. He always had.

Samuel Tremble saw them coming up the mountain. He'd been sitting on a rock by the trail all afternoon waiting for a sign. He'd been waiting a long time and he was getting pretty tired of it. Everything—God's leaves, Jesus' sky, and the signs of the Holy Ghost in the raccoon, and, once, a squirrel that came close to him without fear—became less hallowed as the afternoon stretched on. He'd come up there damned bound and determined that he was going to see a sign if he had to stay there all night. Besides, he was tired of Samantha acting like she hog-tied him and delivered him to Jesus when he come to Jesus all on his own. Lord, after all that drinking and fighting, he could lick anybody on the creek, Jesus touched him and it was over, except once in a very great while.

He wished they weren't on strike. Ever since he come to Jesus he'd liked working in the mine. He thought of all the years he'd wasted hating it and cussing it, ever since he was fifteen, ten years ago, when he first went to the coal-face after being a breaker boy and sorting coal since he was twelve. He counted off the years on his fingers slowly. Now he saw the entry he worked as a kind of dark church where he could get away from women's voices and talk to Jesus whenever he wanted to, lonely no more as the hymn said I come to Jesus, lonely no more.

He watched Jake Catlett and his brother Jethro and his own brother Elsworth and a couple others coming nearer. Sweet glory of God, they were being followed by that little old woman, now wasn't she something, puffing and blowing up that hill like a little old mule?

When they got near enough he knew Jake would look up and see him without either one of them saying a word. Jake never did say anything. He respected him. It was his own brother Elsworth who couldn't leave him alone.

"You heard yet, Samuel?" his brother called as they passed.

He made himself turn the other cheek. "No, Elsworth, I ain't."

"He's waitin'," Jake told Elsworth. "You got to respect that. Leave him be."

"He's my brother," Elsworth muttered, but he didn't say any more, just plodded on by.

Mother watched the boy, who had turned his head away from all of them. She caught up with Jake even though she was heaving so hard she could hardly talk when she took him by the arm.

"What's the matter with him?" she panted.

"Well, ma'am, he got saved and he won't do nuthin' without

a sign. He says the Bible don't say nuthin' about no union. You got to respect that. When he gets a sign—"

"Hell's fire. I'll give him a sign. We need all the fellers we can get. You wait right here."

She was gone and Jake couldn't leave her behind, so he turned to watch her. He leaned his shotgun against a tree and then leaned himself beside it. It was time to rest anyhow. They'd gone nearly to the top of the mountain and Elsworth was sweating like a pig. Elsworth was too fat. He had a beer belly. Jake didn't trust a man like that.

Mother stood over Samuel, her hands on her hips. She didn't say anything for a while, just looked at the top of his head. He knew she was there. He felt humble, Mother Jones herself standing over him. Her watching him like that made him freeze. He couldn't move his head. Something was happening, though. He knew that. He could feel it, an excitement, a little trembling down inside his chest.

She said, "Son, you're wrong."

He didn't dare even take a breath after he'd waited so long.

She said, "Don't you know your Bible no better than that?" Her voice rose. "You want to know who started the union, son? God Almighty started the union. The children of Israel looked up and said 'Oh Lord, how are we gonna make bricks without straw?' and God said 'Organize!' "

Samuel didn't say a word.

She said, "Didn't you know that?"

"No, ma'am," he mumbled. "I didn't know that."

"Come on, now," she told the top of his head.

Jake watched Samuel pick up his rifle and unfold up off his rock. He had to smile. Samuel was six feet five and he made Mother look about as big as a peanut. "Elsworth," Jake said, "swear to God you say one word and you're gonna git this here gun butt right upside your head."

They walked single file for a mile over the mountain. Jake had stopped from time to time to let Mother rest, only he didn't say that was the reason. She didn't seem to like being looked after that way. They stood where Signal Rock jutted out over a line of trees, level with the top of the tipple of Godley Mine on the opposite hill. They kept their guns down by habit so the sun wouldn't glint on the stocks, even though they stood in the deep shadow made by the summit behind them. They could smell the dews and damps of evening in the deep woods. Quiet was heavy on them. Three hundred feet below them empty tracks cat's-cradled the narrow treeless bottomland. A tiny old towel still hung on a clothesline. Doors sagged open onto the porches of the long line of empty houses along the creek. A piece of brown paper tumbled up the road, caught in the evening breeze, until it lodged against a gatepost. The gate was ajar. Behind it the big wooden Boarding House seemed shut down. All the windows were closed, the blinds drawn against the sun. The Company Store and the Club House were as still as tombs. Both the store and the Club House were big solid wood buildings with stone foundations. Some of the houses were streaked with old whitewash, but the rest had never seen a paintbrush; dirt-colored Jenny Lind board-and-batten shacks, sprung-doored privies, bone-hard yards.

It looked like a town people had escaped.

Jake whispered, honoring the silence, "We come a mile over the mountain, old Shawnee warpath. It's like this here." He put down his gun. He splayed the fingers of his left hand between her eyes and the opposite hills. He looked like he was blessing the valley. His palm covered the bottomland. His fingers thrust up the hollows. "Now"—he pointed to his little down-creek finger—"we come from there up this here hogback. You see, up here on top." He pointed toward his wrist: "You can get mighty lost, going down the wrong hollow. They all look alike . . . fingers. Now take if you come down here"—he moved his left finger down between his right forefinger and his thumb, passing the finger where he wore his Royal Order of Odd Fellows ring he bought himself. Essie didn't have a word to say about it but he bought it anyway. It had a diamond in the middle of a triangle, a secret sign. Every time Jake got to looking at that ring it took his mind off what he was saying. Essie said it ought to have been a watch fob and he said why when he didn't have a watch and he didn't have a watch chain. He was proud of his lodge. They'd all joined the union together, but you didn't get a ring for the UMW, only for the lodge.

"If you come down here . . ." Mother touched his finger.

"Why, you'd come out of the side hollow seven, eight miles up the main hollow. Now we're here, right over Godley." He pointed to the tip of his middle finger. " 'Tain't but half a mile up from where we was. This here's a real narrow hogback. Italian Hollow is the next one up-creek, and then, he wagged his little finger, Nigger Hollow." He didn't like to call it that, but that's what everybody called it.

He folded his hand like a map and put it in his pocket. He picked up his gun again and went rock-still. His hand had covered the road and hidden them.

They stood in the road below, leaning against the Club House fence, five men in black coats. Mother could see their leather puttees and their black slouch hats, pulled down toward their eyes. A little puff of smoke rose from one of them and was carried away by the afternoon breeze that was beginning to make her eyes water and the men below swim together. She dabbed at her eyes, turned aside so Jake wouldn't see.

When she turned back she had a flick of a vision, like a glimpse of her death or the intrusion of a dream. Down below on the road, and there with her on the cliff, were the same men; the black coats, the slouch hats, the guns, the still, straight backs. They seemed to be one mirror image, waiting, not ready yet. She knew it was a weakness of age. She had to make herself see the difference.

"That there tall one is Captain Neill, he's the boss." Jake mumbled, as if they weren't three hundred feet below them, tiny men. "He's a right good man—from across the river." He didn't tell her the boy was his own first cousin once removed. She wouldn't understand about that. "Them others—Goujot—he's a butcher. Then Carver, he ain't worth the powder and lead to shoot him. Then there's little Mooney." He let himself grin: "And that there lanky fellow they call Pat Hand. He used to be a miner and a union man too. But he got mad and quit."

66

The names had helped. She could see them now as the thugs they were, and she let fury clear her mind.

A tiny figure came out of the Company Store and bent down to lock a door. It seemed to be in a different sphere from the men against the Boarding House fence.

"That there's Mr. Roundtree coming out of the office. Lookee there. He acts like them guards ain't right there watching him. He don't want them. He made that clear on the telephone. But it didn't do no good. Pratt went against him . . . and that Englishman come in here yesterday."

"Well, what are you goin' to do?" she demanded.

"We ain't aiming to hurt nobody. We don't want to give them no excuse to start a shooting war up here. We're just aiming to shoot around them a little bit. Them three won't scare out, but Mooney and the rest of that riffraff they hard will scare right out of the hollow when they smell smoke. We're aiming to fix it so they can't get no more men to come up here."

He blew a little like a horse, then went quiet again, gun sloped, faded into waiting with the others, watching the narrow valley.

"This here's a waste of time," Mother fussed. "I'm going back. Where do I find this Pagano woman?"

"They're up Italian Hollow. This side." Jake pointed down to where the right-hand hollow that wound below them disappeared into the mountain. "They ain't set them out yet. Mr. Roundtree won't let them. The old man is still working for Mr. Lacey. You got to go down a path about a hundred yards back. Now be careful. Don't get lost."

She turned, halfway along the path. There they were, waiting, black silhouettes against the opposite sunny hill. She wondered why everything was so silent, why nobody made a move. How much of what had to be done consisted of men standing around casting their shadows. It made her shiver.

The guards stood together in front of the Club House gate, squinting into the sun, afraid to speak. They knew better. They knew what was the matter with Captain Dan Neill. He'd seen Miss Lily and that Dago go up the mountain. They knew that. Mooney had told them. His window was right below Captain Dan's. He'd seen them himself and then looked up when he heard Captain Neill's window slam shut and knew there was trouble.

Captain Dan was a killer. His boys said so; Anderson Carver said, "Hell, you fellows don't know the difference between a killer and a Princeton man." They didn't pay much attention to that. Pat Hand said Anderson Carver was a flop-mouth. He couldn't hold his licker and he couldn't hold his words. The way you tell a real man is when he goes quiet, like Captain Dan. It was what they talked about, what made a real man, how you could show you were one, how you could tell. Captain Dan was being that way now, quiet, just quietly standing there. Goujot said he never saw a man whose skin fit his body so well in his black clothes that the road dust didn't dare to get on.

Mooney was imitating him, leaning against the fence too, his slouch hat a little too far over his eyes, his belt a little too low on his hips, his revolver a little too ready for a hand that couldn't hit a barn door, staring too as if he had a mind to make up; his eyes looked sleepy, not sad and cool like Captain Dan's. Oh, Captain Dan was a killer all right. Anderson Carver didn't understand that was not a description. It was a high compliment, as near to an endorsement as they could bring themselves. They didn't bother to tell him that. If Anderson didn't already know that there was no use telling him.

All that Dan Neill hoped for was that nobody would speak. What they judged as coolness in him—and he knew they did, hero worshipping, on the whole a vulgar mistake—was simply a wary mistrust of all of them, all the second-rate material he had to work with, and whose presence, whose eyes watching him and seeing only a parody of what he really was, brought an inner shame. If the others slouched at the side of the dirt road, their boots, he noticed, crushing the Queen Anne's lace, he, Dan Neill, stood in hell, and resolved, having no choice, to make the best of it.

Oh, the men said they would have followed him through hell and high water but he knew better. The only one who had earned his confidence was Goujot. Goujot was an Army man until an ungrateful government discharged him over some damn fool thing when he had earned the Congressional Medal of Honor in Cuba. He didn't tell why and Dan Neill didn't ask. It seemed disrespectful somehow. He was so much older and had actually been in a war. That set a man apart. Goujot had been there, done that unnamed thing, been tuned and hardened, had survived in a place beyond imagination, a place you come back from without speech. Dan Neill knew he could not hope to emulate him. He had no crucible of battle to give him purity of form, to answer the question beyond love in a man—"Which way would I jump?" He sought his own proof, not an image. Sometimes, he told himself, this valley was his proving ground, the strike his assay, the danger his distillation, his answer. That made him feel better. It seemed, then, purer. He sensed, in himself, a strong, proud justice.

The other reason he didn't pry too far into Goujot's business was that he needed him. Together they tried to train the men they led, thugs and candy-ankles picked up from around the soda fountains, parodies of gentlemen. Dan Neill set patrols along the ridges and he knew the men skimped them. They didn't dare meet the mountain boys. This made him smile. It was a slight smile but it eased the men around him; they shifted their positions against the fence, slouched a little more. Mooney took another drag of his disgusting Fatima that made the air around them smell like a brothel.

It was damned hard to keep men. When one of the trains had got to Montgomery, a whole contingent, ex-militia from Virginia, had turned around and caught the next train back east. Some union man who got on at Thurmond with the new guards had told them the mountain boys would cut their balls off if they caught them working for Baldwin and Feltz. Dan had tried to find out who it was. Every time he thought his blacklist of organizers was complete, another agitator sprang up. It was a disease in the whole New River and Kanawha field. Sometimes he thought he alone had been sent to stamp it out.

At that moment, standing against the fence, he was trying, and not succeeding, just to keep his mind on his job. He hadn't said a word for five minutes. He hoped to God the riffraff around him thought he was planning the patrol. He lifted his eyes with some effort from staring at the dirt around his right boot. He made himself scan the opposite hill, from the upriver curve across the mountain face slowly, his hand over his eyes to keep out the sun. He seemed to be saluting, like a real soldier.

He knew the valley and he had studied the contours of the hills. He knew there was little chance of ambush from the hillsides, no matter what the men said. The leaves were too thick by June. May was the worst time, when there were enough leaves to hide a marksman, but not enough to obscure his aim. Besides, he knew the miners weren't aiming to shoot anybody, any more than he was. It was a game, a game with guns, played to a standoff. He did not know Signal Rock existed.

It was no use. Lily came back, the damned bitch. She came and flowered in his brain, her face forever turned away from him. Her wrist turned as it had, separate and alive, on the porch where she stood in the shadows, as if at last she'd made up her mind about something, and she grasped the rope of the hammock, pulled it away, rejecting it, and turned and walked off the porch around the house without even thinking to say goodbye.

Memories of her every movement were as incisive as a knife in his brain, dry, dry, a dry knife—he saw being in love as a dry knife—or he knew he was in love and he kept seeing, in his mind's eye, a dry knife. He knew that the state he was in made everything too important, too urgent, too green, too bright, too etched. He hated it, this fatal consciousness where everything, hallowed by her, was intensified and therefore unbearable.

He had seen Lily and the Dago from his window at the Club House, seen them going up the hollow road toward the Seven Stars, known of course who she was with, could follow them on beyond the tipple to where the road turned to a path that wound up through the trees beside the branch, where in tiny meadows, unbearably green and soft, they could lie, and he could gently, evil as darkness, take off her belt, unbutton the thousand little tatted buttons of her waist, lift her camisole, all so slowly his filthy hands among the lace and expose her breasts to June. He followed the black hand that left its trail of dirt across her white skirt, among her petticoats, buried itself in lace and dotted swiss, pulled it down and lay crushing the lace, the dotted swiss, and her, her frail body, worming, entering her, his other hand across her mouth, his hard look reflected in her eyes, gone blank, Dan was sure, with horror. Oh Christ, he had taken down her hair. He had his hands in her hair, the goddamned black Dago Wop, while Dan was forced to honor her as a sister. It made her more to be desired than ever, damn her for her aloofness and her strident opinions.

He lowered his hand from shading his eyes. Of course, the whole thing was one problem, one battle, one Grail you might say. She was a victim, just as he was, victim of invasion and circumstances. Any other time she wouldn't have had the strike to feed her fool ideas. What the devil she'd picked up at Vassar he didn't know. There certainly wasn't any of that sort of thing among his friends at Princeton—oh, maybe in the outer darkness among a few swats, but not among gentlemen. He was a little ashamed of himself at that thought. He'd outgrown all that undergraduate snobbery when the facts of life had demanded that he, quite frankly, grow up in one week when the Neill mansion at Beulah, the pride of the valley, went after all those years into some maw of failure called the Tennessee Coal and Land Company. Senator Neill, his grandfather, overextended, gone senile without taking one word of advice, sold up lock, stock and barrel, leased out Beulah Collieries. After they were ruined, their ruin part of a vaster plan, then Morgan stepped in and bargained the rescue of the United States from panic for the Tennessee Coal and Land Company he'd had his eye on all the time.

Dan could no more have left the valley for long than he could have left his skin, or Hercules his coat. He'd tried. He'd worked in New York for two years after college as a common clerk. Times were hard and he took what he could get. He'd walked all the way from the Bowery to dinner in Gramercy Park, his coat buttoned up to his neck to keep his evening shirt clean and not a cent in his pocket, but striding along, what the riffraff called a swell.

The letters, brutal with their self-centered sorrow and fear, followed him, whispered, whined, "Dan, honey, come back, please come back. We need you." His sisters, his mother, his aunt, all called, "Dan, honey," until they fused in his dream to one call, incessant, made up of voices and the sound of women's clothes. "Dan, honey, you come on home, we need you," as if his father didn't exist anymore instead of sitting, a courtly husk of a man, on the front porch of the Neill mansion on Canona Street he couldn't even pay the taxes on, but waited until the delinquency was advertised and made his mother cry. Then he made the gesture that he had meant to be tragic and which had turned out to be a damned nuisance and an embarrassment. Dan could have told him that tragedy is never planned—the planning itself changes it to bathos. On the day the tax delinquency was advertised, such a small thing after the events that had towered and crushed them, he had taken the labor train upriver to Beulah, and had shot himself in the corner of the lawn of what was now the Club House of the Mark Hanna Coal Company.

Inside the Canona Street house, the forms of failure were cool plants and poverty and freshly laundered patched tablecloths and what was left of the Duncan Phyfe, and the portraits in the parlor, Grandmother Melinda, and the Senator looking like he owned the Union Pacific Railroad instead of crushed like all the rest by the Eastern interests. Dan hated it, hated not so much the poverty: it was, he had to admit, the lack of taste. They advertised it with their bravery, their excessive neatness. Five years had stretched into a detested way of living, the blackmail of that awful hopeless polite courage of noble poorhouse Tories.

He, God's gift, Captain Dan from Beulah, their pride and joy, thoughtless, fast-moving, a fine horseman, crawled home from ambition. Now stranded, he stood beside the dirt road in the only job a Neill could get after the Senator had brought so many to their knees along with him, against an Imperial fence on Imperial property guarding an Imperial tipple that had been built by his distant cousin Lacey from Richmond, guarding it from mountain men he at least respected even though they were little children, led by outside agitators, and Dagoes, and, he had to admit, people with the same half-baked ideas as Lily. Lily was as far from him as he was far from his own portrait of his future. It contained her at times, but he rejected her when it did. He had had too much disappointment.

He straightened up slowly from the fence, heavy with the weight of his sorrows. He moved the butt of his rifle like a crutch, nearer his boot, fine leather, cared-for, English, seven years old and timeless, standing for something, a comfort. He stood then, watching across the dirt road. Mr. Roundtree the Englishman, not many years older than he was and already a superintendent, walked out on the porch of the Company Store and turned his back to lock his office door as if he didn't see him when he knew he damned well had.

Oh, the Dagoes in Dago Hollow were good enough for Round-tree, and at night he could hear him laughing and whooping it up with Mr. McLeod, that sour-faced Scotch bastard. But he, Captain Dan Neill, whose family had settled the damned valley, was something the Englishman ignored in the road dust.

If the outside agitators and the red-necks and the googoos and the Eastern interests were bad in the valley, Dan thought, men like Roundtree were worse. They were compromisers. He and Lily's father, who just wanted to stay out of trouble no matter who paid for it, set a dangerous precedent like the Hanna interests had set at Beulah and all up and down the north side of the river by negotiating with the socialists. He was glad when Mr. Pratt had laid down the law on Mr. Lacey's porch, that it was principle, a principle that a man like Roundtree couldn't grasp.

"The philosophy in this matter is a greater question than what's going on in West Virginia," Mr. Pratt had said, and then looked at Dan as if he understood. Dan knew right then that he was on his way, that all he had to do was have a little talk with Delaney Baird as soon as he'd proved himself in the present trouble.

"Princeton? A Princeton man," Mr. Pratt had said when Delaney introduced him. He said it like he was filing it away in his mind. When Dan thought of that, Lily came nearer, near enough to touch.

Neville St. Michael Roundtree had not seen Captain Dan. His mind, for the moment, as he locked the office door and went toward the steps slowly, slowly, looking at the porch floor, was someplace else. It was facing defeat, and that defeat was too hard, literally hard on his spirit. He and Mr. Lacey had been so outnumbered, so outpowered, that he couldn't, still, bear the weight of it. He had turned and tossed while the nearly full moon came up, flooded his room, then set, and the light darkened to false dawn, then it was true dawn, bringing color back, at first faintly. Then it was seven o'clock and he could hear Maria Pagano down in the kitchen and smell fresh coffee.

He was, he had to admit, rather proud of that sleepless night. It was a kind of triumph over weakness. If he had one fault beyond all others, it was an unfortunate faculty of mirth. He simply could not stay unhappy or anxious for long. He hadn't the sustaining capacity some people had, but he had to admit that while he envied them, since he knew his fault had cost him sympathy, and once it had cost him love, most people's capacity for suffering bored and offended him.

It got in the way, clogged friendship, dimmed the clarity of the eye. When he had finally got away, with a shameful lack of guilt, from his parents, who were Plymouth Brethren and who he could not remember having even seen smiling, he was the victim of an explosion of what he could only consider was un-English and un-seemly joy. It bubbled up, as if it had lain under pressure.

Most of this Mr. Roundtree managed to hide from everybody on Lacey Creek but Mr. McLeod, who was from the Outer Hebrides and therefore sentimental. They did, from time to time, indulge in laughter, whiskey, maudlin homesickness, and dominoes in Mr. McLeod's rooms over the Company Store.

Mr. Roundtree had sentiment, too, as an added secret burden, though that seemed, somehow, more forgivable. He cried as easily as he laughed, not at events but at—he could only define them as sudden clarities that brought tears to his eyes. No one ever saw either of these weaknesses. They were bad for business.

He affected a carefully trimmed spade of rich black beard, which, because he had a habit of tilting his head back and sighting down his too small nose, stuck straight out in front of him most of the time. He smoked a collection of pipes from Dunhills in St. James's Street. He wore, day in and day out, in series, three oatmeal-colored suits, Norfolk jackets and plus fours, exactly alike, made in Savile Row. He had heard that Bernard Shaw did this and it seemed a good and economical idea. He hid, with a habitual squint against the sun, the wide brown eyes of a curious child. He considered himself lovable, though no one loved him at the moment, a circumstance he had fully resolved to do something about as soon as the strike was settled and he could put his full mind to it.

After all, Miss Lily was at home all summer and it was only June. Her primitive charm, her spirit, delighted him. He saw potential there, to be very carefully broken to harness so as not to destroy but to tame. Sometimes he had glimpses of such piercing domesticity that he labored for an hour or so afterwards from the recognized and enjoyed illusion that they had been married for years.

He had forgotten to put on his hat. He put it on now, a deerstalker, oatmeal like the Norfolk jacket, suitable, he thought when choosing it at Lockes, for whatever back of beyond he had consented to go to.

Up on Signal Rock, Elsworth Tremble drew a bead on Mr. Roundtree's hat brim. He followed him through his gunsight down the steps and out into the road.

"Put that gun down," Jake told him.

"I wasn't doing nuthin'," Elsworth said. "I'se just taking the range." It embarrassed him to be called down in front of his brother.

The sight shook on the tiny brim of Mr. Roundtree's hat three hundred feet below as if it didn't want to leave. Slowly Elsworth lowered the gun.

Mr. Roundtree knew that his sleepless night had come more from dammed-up ambition than frustrated justice. He did not allow himself to be deceived about this. He saw no reason to be tied to the other operators on the question of negotiations. A strike was, to him, a failure, a business failure, and he had pointed it out, quite rightly.

"Oh you're quite right, quite right," Sir Archibald Inchbold had told him, "but don't you see . . ." the bloody old fool, the old pink-faced rich fool. Not all the Locke hats and Savile Row suits in the world could get through the barrier of that rich stupidity. He could see Sir Archibald peering through his disguises with that damned eyeglass, through the Locke hat and the Norfolk jacket to the Plymouth Brethren underneath, not judging—not intelligently—not even very interested. Men like him saw stupidly. They missed nothing, stupidly, and that was unforgivable.

Mr. Roundtree understood with a quiet, furious clarity that the decision was being made someplace else, by minds in committees remote from the reality and dirt of the coalfields, ledger minds, old and brutal with stubbornness. It was to them a principle. There was a "they," abstract, and for a few hours the "they" had been concrete, and had sat on Mr. Lacey's porch in well-cut trousers and fine white linen, wielding their blind and awful power.

When he pointed out that the Seven Stars and Imperial No. 8 at Godley held a bottleneck to the whole of the Lacey Creek field and that if they negotiated the others would have to go along, Baird had said, "I'll be goddamned if I deal with a bunch of rednecks and outside agitators." Sir Archibald had only muttered, "No doubt, no doubt." He had been wined and dined and softened up all the way from New York, the damned old fool.

After the long polite lunch when Lily had sat like a slim, solemn young Daniel in a den of bearded old lions, he had finally managed to get Sir Archibald aside to try again to explain the local situation. Sir Archibald had interrupted with: "Fine job, young man, frightful place. You've been very brave. I'll see what I can do for you. Oh, yes, see what I can do," taking for granted that he was asking a favor. He had patted his arm. Sir Archibald had finely kept pale fur on the back of his pink hand. There was a faint scent of Floris lime.

Mr. Roundtree had visions from time to time, which he hated and denied. He was having one right now. He saw a vast and senseless power that fed itself on its own body. He saw intelligence, this time a tiny bitter David, again with Lily's face. He saw himself and Jake Catlett and McLeod and the others, even Mr. Lacey who didn't do much, between the two forces, just trying to get the coal out and wanting to be left alone. That amorphous and pulsing power source was even interfering with his falling in love.

Finally, after a day of damnable indecision that drained his soul, he knew that he had only two choices: throw up his job, and with it what he saw without shame was "a fine future," or go along with the others. He did not like to admit to himself that a large part of his choice rested on the fact that he did not want to leave the Lacey Creek field, not while there was—well—hope. But he did admit it manfully to the cow parsley he was studying. It seemed inefficient not to, and he disliked inefficiency, even in his hopes.

The only thankless job left to do was to tell Mr. Lacey that he had decided, finally, to give every help and assistance to the Baldwin agency in the—what was it that gray solicitor had said?—pursuance, that was it, of their duty. He was going to reopen No. 8, using the transportation brought in the day before.

The real decision had, he was bound to admit, been made and implemented over his head. This had been told casually among the crystal and the damask and sleepy big dinner shadows over mounds of fried chicken, gravy, and biscuits that the men toyed with while they drank Mr. Lacey's wine and exclaimed, politely. Neill, that bastard, had stared at him, not bothering to smile. Lily had looked thunderous. Her mother was keeping her quiet by sheer will and once in a while a whisper, "Now, Lily," and a worried shake of her head, a no, that nobody but he noticed.

It had taken him all night to face the fact he was *not* going to throw away the best future an ambitious thirty-year-old man could have for a set of principles he couldn't define. It bothered him that he could define theirs, both the right and the left in their entrenchments, but he couldn't define his own. It was, he thought, a balance rather than a principle, but there was no metaphor for balance, no definition for, well, a poised style. He knew it was urgently important, but he couldn't define it.

He hardly noticed stepping over the chain that separated Godley from Seven Stars, but the rattle of wood as he walked made him stop and stare down past the widely spaced boards of the bridge over Lacey Creek. He told himself he had first to tell Mr. Lacey and then go with McLeod to have a look at the transportation that had been lodged in the Boarding House all day, locked in, while McLeod waited for him to move, getting more impatient by the hour.

Mr. Roundtree clamped his pipe in his mouth and stared at the maidenhair fern along the bank. The movement of the water weeds and the water flow washed the whole problem out of his mind. He watched like a patient child until the sand and stones of the creek had defined themselves in his eyes, watched for the movement that betrayed the protective coloring of the crustaceans among the flora. He saw, at last, transparent and graceful, a crayfish feeding, slowly moving upstream, intercepting the microscopic algae flowing down toward its mandibles.

That sense of touching the timeless center of an event that never ended made him feel cold with awe. Water flow, the feeding fauna, current that grew in force, all the elements were there before his eyes.

He moved beyond the quiet creek into the dark depths of swamplands where the ferns, the maidenhair, were eighty feet high and the wild rain-laden leaves were platters of damp and if there was sun it never touched the swamp through the hot blindness of the mist. Deep, deep fallow falling slowly burning through an eon, it was gone and Mr. Roundtree was in an ocean as perpetual, an inland-sea sand floor taking a million years to cover the swamp under it. He saw a rhythm so slow of sea and sand, sea creatures, slow pulse of change to swamp and ferns and mist and then the systolic sea, and then the diastolic swamp, continuously overlaying. He saw the inexorable pressure of pulse and change, the mountains forced upward and, for the time being, saw himself within an eon, taking the future as much for granted as did the sea creatures, the swamp worms. The patient water, the greatest of all forces, moved again in Lacey Creek below his feet, gently, gently caressing the water weeds that flowed like streaming hair.

He, Neville St. Michael Roundtree, stood thinking he was using his intelligence to dig out the coal formed by the hot swamps. Once in a while there was a clue, the bole of a great tree that made a dangerous petrified plug that could fall out of a mine roof and kill a man. From time to time a perfect form of a fern frond kept its grace forever pressed by the coal as girls pressed flowers in books. Mr. Roundtree paid a quarter to any man who would bring him the fossils of worms, of leaves, of clamshells from the sandstone of the sea ceiling they worked under. *Productus cora, Spirifer bonensis, lingula*—Mr. Roundtree had been to grammar school and was proud of his Latin.

He saw the *lingula*, the Venus's-shell, in Lily's dear white hand. He felt her concern about the fossil as warmth in his soul. She

78

seemed to understand, just for a pause while she held it, an old, old bond between them. She spoke, then, some abstraction of hers, and it was gone.

The only other bond they had was Eddie Pagano. At least he hoped and prayed it was a bond, and not, well, no, that was unthinkable. He told himself sternly, as he did when envy crept into his mind, that she, too, was interested in Eddie's development, as he was. He tried to see it as another bond and almost succeeded. The boy cared so much to learn from him, and he was grateful for that. It assuaged—he liked the word—the loneliness of his mind when Lily was gone. Only Eddie, of all the men he worked with, knew that the trapped gas a pick could release had waited there for fifty million years to kill a man.

He had tried to explain it once to the others and had afterwards had an embarrassed visit from Samuel Tremble's Baptist preacher. He said they didn't hold with nothing it didn't say so in the Bible. "Six days and on the seventh day he rested," the old man said, looking at the office floor and turning his hat brim, his Stetson, around and around in hands as gnarled as roots. He said God made the land in layers like it was: sandstone, slate, shale, coal, fire clay, sandstone, shale, coal, bedrock, all the way down. He said God done that for a reason it wasn't for us to judge.

Mr. Roundtree apologized and said he agreed about that part anyway, that it wasn't for us to judge.

Mr. Roundtree straightened up from leaning on the log railing watching the creek flow and made himself go on across the bridge to talk to Mr. Lacey. Around the road turn he could just see in the distance the commanding white tower, Mrs. Lacey's sanctum, over the trees, but part of him still walked through rain forests with ferns as tall as oaks. He couldn't shake the vision. He thought if a man could be still enough, patient enough, he might catch a glimpse of that slow rhythm, that change, and saw the trouble of the afternoon, saw the decisions as so minuscule compared with it, that it was hard to take them seriously, although he knew he had to. His life-span might be as short in the face of all that as a moth's, but he had things to do and duties to perform.

He never knew, walking under the trees beside the railroad track, when he crossed the line between constructive thought and uncontrolled dreams. He only knew that when he heard the shots he was the governor of Rhodesia and Lily was Lady Roundtree. Sex, with Mr. Roundtree, tended to take ambitious forms.

Jake's first thought was slow, as the moment of an accident, its irretrievable time, slows, stops forever on the other side of the act: I shouldn't have brung Elsworth up here.

But it wasn't Elsworth who said anything, it was Samuel Tremble. He made one funny choked sound as they all watched the doll-sized Mooney McKarkle subside slowly onto one knee. "I never hit him. I never. I seen where I hit. I hit the gatepost beside him. I seen it hit. I fanned him, like you said, swear to God."

Jake could see young Dan kneel down beside Mooney and his white hand on Mooney's black pants leg, then he seemed to cut the cloth with his knife and Mooney's knee was white and red, or maybe the red was imagined, they were so far away. He saw Captain Dan look up at the gatepost. Carver, Hand, Goujot and four or five new fellows closed in around them. Then Goujot started scanning the hill. He seemed to be looking straight up at Signal Rock.

"Don't move a muscle," Jake said.

"Swear to God I never . . . why, I wouldn't do that," Samuel was still moaning more words than he usually spoke in a whole day. "I fanned him like you told me." Jake was watching Mr. Roundtree run up the road.

"I know you did, Samuel," Jake said, watching Dan get up and go over to the gatepost and bend down, out of sight. "What you done is you hit the gatepost and a sliver must of got shot off and hit McKarkle in the leg. Nothing more than a big splinter. Think about it that way."

Samuel had been praying to shoot straight and not hurt anybody and he had shot straight, he knew that. Hell, he always followed his shot. The bullet, it wasn't no more than a twenty-two, had to go and tear a sliver of wood off of the gatepost and drive it into Mooney McKarkle's knee. Samuel had heard him yell and was still hearing him.

"Goddamn, Samuel, now you've went and done hit," Elsworth

whispered, as if they could hear him all the way down there in the road.

"Shit fire, Elsworth. I never shot nowhere near that little candy-ankle," Samuel said, forgetting that he had been saved. Then suddenly he burst into tears and stood there crying, his red face creased like a baby's, but not making a sound.

"Hit ain't nothing to do with you, Samuel. You wasn't nothing but God's chosen vessel, hitting that there gatepost. I reckon hit was more like God's will that the blood of one of them bastards should be shed," Jake whispered to comfort him.

They went on watching until the knot of men spread out. Mr. Roundtree ran down the road again toward the doctor's house. He called something over his shoulder—"Wait"? or "Hate"?—Jake couldn't tell. It was a wisp of sound. As they moved back from the cliff edge, he saw Goujot and some of the new men dogtrotting toward Dago Hollow. Captain Dan and Pat Hand were helping Mooney toward the Club House. He looked like he'd been hurt in a football game, one leg bent, his arms over their shoulders.

Mooney lay very straight on the cot. He wasn't comfortable but he didn't want to complain. They'd been so good to him, tucking him in like that, treating him like a real soldier in a real war.

It wasn't until they had lifted him to his feet that he had really known he'd been hit. At first he just sat there, surprised, and watched blood seep through his pants leg. All he could think was Captain Dan's being awful good to me and wondered how he could make it up to him. What he had to make up he didn't question, just something. Captain Dan was a man you wanted to repay all the time.

When they did get him to his feet, Mooney could have stood on that leg, but Captain Dan told him not to. He said, "Don't put weight on that leg. You have to be careful with a wound like that."

A wound! His knee didn't hurt much, but it had scared him, blood running down his leg from being shot at. Shot at! Even if the bullet had just made a wood sliver ricochet and hit him, he had been under fire. That's what they said, "under fire." They all talked that way. He had been proved as a man, good God and him only nineteen years old.

Sometimes, as now, lying in the bed while Pat Hand still leaned in the doorway, watching him like he was worrying over a sick dog, Mooney didn't want to go at all, just stay and be one of them —a man. Pat told him when he said that, "You go on back up to the University, you little shave-tail. You want to end up an ignorant old fart like me?"

When they got him up to the porch they had talked back and forth over his head, like you do somebody who's wounded. Pat said, "We got to get him to bed here or to a hospital one," and then, "It ain't nuthin' but a flesh wound but you can't tell about them things."

Captain Dan said, "We'll see what the doctor says," and then, remembering he could hear, "Are you in much pain?"

Mooney said, "Not much." It was true, but it sounded more brave than true.

There he'd been on the ground giving instructions—well, almost —like he was somebody to reckon with. He said it to repay Captain Dan more than to accuse anybody, he wouldn't do that. But the shots had come from the direction of Dago Hollow, and he knew Captain Dan hated them and he knew why. Telling about how he had seen the new Dago socialist coming in yesterday on the train and the Paganos meeting him kind of redeemed him for not making that old bat Mother Jones get back on the train. He couldn't. She wouldn't let him. So if he did act like he didn't know she was even on Lacey Creek, it wasn't a lie. It was just that he was embarrassed. When Goujot went up to the bull pasture in the morning to take names at the UMW meeting for the operators' blacklist he didn't let on at all.

He didn't need to be embarrassed anymore. They'd all paid attention, almost like they'd been waiting for that sliver to hit his knee.

Captain Dan had said, "That's enough. Goujot, set them out. I don't give a goddamn if two of them are still working at Seven Stars, one of them struck against Imperial and they're on Imperial land. I want every goddamned foreign agitator closed out of

82

my territory." Nobody had said, "What about Roundtree?" Nobody bothered, now that there was blood.

Somebody had said, "Hey, let's us get us a Dago," and Goujot said, "Shut up, men. On the double."

There was blood. When they got Mooney on the bed, it had seeped right through Captain Dan's fine white linen handkerchief. They hadn't any more than got him onto the bed and taken his pants off when Aunt Trudy Daingerfield, the club housekeeper, came flouncing in and pushed them aside. When Mooney grabbed the sheet to cover himself she said, "Hell's bells, son, that ain't the first dickey I seen. Now get me some hot water and iodine. Pat you know where it's at. Let me take a look."

She talked to Pat that way because he was her paramour. At least that's what Miss Mary Rose called her. She used fancy words for things. Mooney couldn't believe that. Pat Hand chewed tobacco and only shaved once a week, and Aunt Trudy gave them breakfast in her old pink satin wrapper that had seen better days, with her gray and red hair hanging down her back, not even braided. They sat at the kitchen table long after everybody had gone to bed and played setback. Old Pat took off his glasses and clamped them in his teeth and held the cards right up against his face. That wasn't the way paramours looked. Maybe he couldn't see her; all those veins and those big jiggly tits under that satin, and that rat's nest of hair. Sometimes at night you could hear them in the kitchen all by themselves, just laughing fit to kill. Sometimes he'd hear "Kiss Me Again" running down on the Victrola and he'd go in to wind her up and find them both passed out in the parlor. That wasn't the way paramours behaved. He could have told Miss Mary Rose that but she wouldn't pay any attention. She was as high-hat as Captain Dan's sister Sally Brandon, who looked like she'd swallowed a ramrod. Well, by God, Mooney wished they could see him now, a wounded man, the first wounded man on Lacey Creek.

Pat went on leaning against the doorjamb, watching the boy and not seeing him. He knew that when he straightened up, turned around, walked down the stairs, he was going to walk straight into the kind of trouble where everybody talked and nobody listened, real trouble where somebody could end up dead. He felt almost as if he could keep it from generating if he just went on leaning against the door, frozen there, not moving a finger. That damned fired little candy-ankle, wouldn't he get in the way of a fanned shot? Wouldn't he? He and Captain Dan and Goujot knew what it was; they all knew that if any mountain man wanted to hit them from the hillside, they would have hit them right in the head, no two ways about it. They knew they were just trying to scare that bunch of cake-eaters like Mooney out of the hollow.

Dammit, he knew and Goujot knew and Captain Dan knew and he had watched them let it turn into something else, something more than a damned-fool accident. He saw them fit it into something he didn't like at all. Not that he liked Dagoes any better than they did, but the way they were using it, as an excuse, no more than that, well, that wasn't right.

No, it was more like he was watching a lie begin, one of those lies where nothing was said but you acted like something happened you really knew didn't. That damned kid, scared shitless of a little bit of blood. He was still so pale green that his freckles stood out like goat turds. Trudy, that dear old girl, had combed his hair and parted it in the middle and slicked it down. He had never seen Mooney so shined up. She should have had fourteen youngins, who never had airy a one.

Pat did love her, carrying on like that, getting all dressed up when the doctor come, Lord God she was a thing to love, the old bitch. He wondered if he could get her to go on down-creek before some damned fool shot up the Club House. He could hear her down in the kitchen, humming, happy now that she had somebody to nurse. Hell, if he told her to leave she would laugh in his face. He wanted to go down there and slap her bottom, but he still didn't dare move.

The shots were fired at dead on five-thirty. The breeze carried most of the echo up-creek where it skipped through the trees, became faint, left silence.

Down-creek at the tents, they heard it as a crack in the sky. The women stopped. The men froze. The children went on playing down by the water. The women moved first, ran down to the creek and jerked their own children by the arms. Some of the men were beginning to grin. After all the waiting something had happened. There was not a man who didn't know where the message came from.

In the sweetheart swing Beverley woke up from his nap, but he didn't know what had waked him. He had a crick in his neck.

In Mrs. Pagano's kitchen Mother Jones smelled gunpowder. She looked around the table. Nobody said a word.

In Nigger Hollow on land that still belonged to Beverley, John Lacey picked up Aunt Toey, chair and all, and took her in the house. His wife, Loada, herded the children in. All up and down Nigger Hollow, they burrowed away from white men's wars. There was the sound of doors and windows closing, then no more sound.

At six o'clock only one man moved across the deserted valley. It was Jake Catlett. He was going up to tell Beverley what had happened. He thought he ought to explain it was an accident. Besides, he wanted to borrow Beverley's wire cutters to cut the telephone wire before they got through to the sheriff to deputize every damned-fool guard on Lacey Creek. He decided not to burden Beverley with that knowledge, though, when he had so much on his mind. After all Beverley wouldn't want a bunch of white trash deputized either. He knew that.

II

5:30 P.M. to 7:00 P.M.,
Friday, June 7, 1912

Except for Mr. Roundtree, for whom she had a tenderness, Lily didn't care what anybody thought. She knew that everybody at Seven Stars took for granted, when they saw them disappear up the tipple road, that she and Eduardo Pagano were making love in the grass. Lily most assuredly was not. She was doing her duty.

Sometimes, when the duty had to do with her political opinions, the importance of doing it made her feel almost ecstatic. It was surprisingly like the way she felt when she ran into Mr. Roundtree.

She was in disguise for the moment, as a pretty blond girl in a white dotted swiss dress with a voile sash and a lace collar, and at her throat a red, red rose, and white kid shoes on her pretty little feet. She wanted to giggle outright at the deception, but patted the cinquefoil beside her hip instead, and thought of the socialist state.

She watched Eduardo's hand on the flowers. Of course she was not conscious of the hand, like Althea would have been, not that way at all, but more interested aesthetically. She made a mental note.

She was sitting on a mountain plot high and clean up beyond the Seven Stars drift mouth, on a blanket of tiny blue scented flowers called Quaker-ladies and sometimes innocents. Lily thought, wouldn't it be wonderful if the air were scented with asphodel instead of plain old innocents, and wondered what asphodel looked like. She saw it in her mind's eye as lavender.

She was sitting as straight as she could against a tree. Eduardo was lying on the ground. She could see the faun line of his ear and chin as he lay with his head turned away from her. She could have stared at the living pulse of his throat but would not have done anything like that, of course. Even glancing at his throat made her lose her place in Montaigne.

His eyes were closed, his hand lay palm up, peaceful, as if he had forgotten it. She saw that the coal dust ground into his torn fingernails made his hand whiter, more genteel. He was a natural Jeffersonian aristocrat. She'd always known that. She was sure that if she touched the palm, so trustingly exposed there, she would feel what Bernard Shaw called the Life Force surging, no, not surging, something more delicate. Flowering? Well, something like that.

She went on reading Montaigne, skipping a bit. She didn't want to bore him. Softly, softly. She tried to make her voice that way. She had long had the habit of luring him, not like a woman lures a man, not like Althea, she would have scorned that, but as a Muse, for instance, would lure a poet, out of his feral shyness. She had written the word "feral" in her diary and resolved to use it, not aloud, not on Lacey Creek, where no one understood, but in her thoughts.

Where she was sitting made her hair shine in the leaf-filtered sun and she did feel guilty knowing that she was pleased about that. She stopped reading. She had a feeling that he wasn't listening.

She looked over the book and tried to ignore the way Eduardo's hair curled on his neck. She found the place again, still searching for exactly the right lines to read. She smoothed her skirt, feeling patient, and made a little hum in her throat to draw his wild attention to her voice. His eyes were closed.

She told herself about how exhausting manual labor was and resolved to experience it sometime. She went on waiting, now frankly watching him as he lay on the flowers. That he was her pride, the symbol of her defiance, was something she took for granted. She had recognized that for all the years since she had found him, as you find a wild animal, out in the woods. She had seen his eyes, staring at her through the rhododendron leaves.

Of course, the language of Eduardo had changed. Then he was her playmate, secret and possessed. Afterwards he became her battle shield.

She brought back to him as her duty all that she was being taught at Vassar. She told herself that if mathematics had gotten Stendhal out of Grenoble, so Vassar College, once removed, would get Eduardo Pagano—oh, pagan was so right for him—off the Seven Stars coal-face.

She had never, since she first saw him through the leaves, questioned the fact that that was what he wanted. Now that she was home for the summer, and he was on night shift, she made him take advantage of the time to meet her every afternoon for lessons. She was determined to take him—she made him see that —out of the mine forever, a fine intelligence like that. She knew she wasn't wrong. Mr. Roundtree saw it, too. She suspected and hoped that Mr. Roundtree noticed her dedication.

She was proud, too, that the union trusted her enough to find a use for her. She felt like a soldier, a Vera or a Vanya of the 1905 revolution that the youngest Pagano sisters were named for. She loved the listening awareness of the telephone: one ring Seven Stars office, two rings Father's library, three rings Godley, four rings Bairdsville, five rings Mucklow, six rings Wacomah, seven rings Peabody, eight rings Glen Pratt, nine rings Glen Cabot, ten rings High Tower, and then the ghostly whirr of the bell when somebody was ringing Central to call downriver on the telephone. She listened and made careful notes.

She experienced, knowing it every time, the quick awareness of danger, the thrill of slipping into the library, the closing of the door, mostly to keep Mary Rose from hearing her. Mary Rose was nebby; nobody else cared. Once her father had thrown open the door while she was taking notes on a conversation between Williams, the transportation man, at the King Coal Hotel, and the superintendent, at Glen Pratt. She told him she was making an order, what she didn't say and he didn't question.

She heard herself reading the passage she had marked. She read it slowly so he would know how she felt about the whole thing:

"He that will free himself from this violent prejudice of custom, shall find divers things received with an undoubted resolution, that have no other anchor but the hoary head and frowning wrimples of custom, which ever attends them: which mask being pulled off, and referring all matters to truth and reason, he shall perceive his judgement, as it were over turned, and placed in a much surer state . . ." She looked at his hand and explained to it, "What Montaigne means is, you see, it doesn't matter . . ."

Her voice slowed, then stopped, and she sighed. Eduardo was asleep. There was total silence at first. Then she could hear the water of the mountain creek, the leaves turning, the hum of air. She wanted to cry, Take me in, let me be in on it, please take me in, and couldn't understand her own words. She tried to be stern with herself and question, In where? In on what?

"I'm not asleep," Eduardo answered from the grass, his eyes still closed. "Go on. And don't tell me what things mean."

It was a reprieve. She began again, trying to untangle her joy from the words and keep them strict, objective.

"All right, I won't. I understand . . ."

"Won't what?" He'd already forgotten, but she willed him not to look away again, not yet.

"Explain things."

He was smiling at her, and then he closed his eyes and turned his back on her and withdrew his hand from the grass.

Eduardo said when Steve kidded him, "Sure, I go up there with her. I go up there a lot. Jesus. Why do you want to know?"

Steve told him why. He said it was because of the telephone, but what it came down to was putting Lily's innocence to work. Eduardo didn't like it, but Lily acted like she was the queen of the strike, all that carrying on with handkerchiefs tied to trees like it was a game.

It was embarrassing for Eduardo to admit, but to tell the truth, he always did run when Lily called him. He defended himself on that. He said she was the first person in that shit-hole that treated him like anything with a name, much less anything but a Dago. On Lacey Creek, Dago was a race. They had houses for white, black, and Dago. That's what they called it. Dago Hollow.

When he thought of that, lying there among the innocents, he saw Steve being fooled, too. Steve thought he went up the mountain on strike business. Steve saw everything in terms of the strike or Dago. You say "Dago" to him one time, only one time, you got his foot in your mouth, he didn't care who the hell you were. It was his strike and he was its hero.

Poor Steve, that big condottiere in his overalls. Poor big brother. He had a crush on the United States and Eugene Debs. Steve didn't like Mother Jones. He didn't know why, but Eduardo did. He was a Dago and she was a woman, and he didn't like her laying down the law. He said she was blasphemous. Steve wasn't religious. He just thought Christ was Italian. When she was there in oh two some fellow come up Lacey Creek, said he was bringing Jesus to the miners. She got him run out of the hollow. She said Jesus Christ ain't needed up here. This here belongs to the United Mine Workers. She said the fellow was a Baldwin spy and Jesus didn't have nothing to do with it. If Steve told that story once he told it a hundred times.

Steve thought he cut himself off from the past. He would call his own father and mother Dagoes or Wops when they did anything old-country, but he was already too old himself when they came over. He never lost his accent. Mr. Roundtree said Eduardo sounded like a ridge-running hillbilly. Mr. Roundtree said to get rid of it. He said, "Buff them all off, all your habits. Travel light."

Eduardo didn't move for fear Lily would interrupt his thinking. Why did everybody think he was ambitious? He didn't give a continental damn. Now Steve, talk about ambitions! Whoa Nelly! He had taken in more of Mamma's dreams than any of them. Osmosis. What he expected of himself. All that bravissimo. Oh boy. Steve was a goddamn walking shame. What he could have been he didn't come to America too late!

Lily did bring messages from the telephone. She made up that hanky signal out of one of her books. Talk about La Eroina, oh Miss Lily, every day a story she made up. She would tie her handkerchief to the wellhead where the Trembles' old shack used to be before they built the tipple. Nothing left but the well and some Rose-of-Sharon still struggling in the coal dust from the train tracks. Lily washed the coal off the blossoms.

"Hey Eddie," the driver would yell when they came out on the man-trip, "she wants ye!" Riding out of that blackness into day, first thing they would see was that fresh-washed lace hankey, snow-white. So Eduardo would go and meet her. So much of it was games—games with real people and real blood. Jesus.

Who wouldn't have gone up there with her? Why he did, not a one of them could have understood except maybe, just maybe, Mr.

Roundtree. He wasn't in love with Lily and Eduardo wasn't; not like that Neill fellow followed her with his eyes like a sick pup, the son of a bitch.

It was because . . . it was something Eduardo was always looking for, a place beyond the voices. What was it? Maybe what you hear when all of them stop, the sound of the machines and the picks' thunk and the train hum and the shunting and pulling and hauling and the buzz of the telephone wires and the tall tales and the women stop, and you can just stand there. Nobody knows that quiet but saints and coal miners. No sound. All blotted out. Not even an echo. He lay with his eye an inch from one of those little blue flowers and watched and waited and made plans.

Not dreams. He didn't like dreams. Jesus, he had to live in enough of them to last him one long lifetime. Lily's dream had him by the throat, and Mamma's. Mamma. She lived on hers. Almost from the time she touched this side of the water, the family had to live on them too, just to keep the peace. He didn't remember her that way before. Oh, he knew what it was. There in Italy her hopes had been in the future, but here in America her hope was to find something that was past. She lived in a past that hadn't even happened. That was how it was with her.

A plan beat any dream going. A plan was like a map of hopes, not like the clouds that day through the tree branches, that rode the high wind, making him feel like he was moving and they were still—not an illusion like that. Illusions were not for Eduardo. He'd seen enough of them.

He glanced at the tilt of Lily's chin and the blond drift of hair, the pale hands. He watched her fingers moving on the back of the book, some dumb thing she was reading. She was wearing a white dress, clean and smelling of ironing and sun and a faintness of Florida water she wouldn't admit she wore. The lace at her cuffs stopped halfway up her arms. He could see her skin through the lace, and the hint of her skin through the sleeves she called dotted swiss that he wanted to touch but didn't dare. That would have been asking for it. She looked like Mamma's blond plaster Virgin with her doll feet on the sins of the world.

When he was little, in Perugia, they used to watch the Virgin in the light of the near streetlight in the Via Canerino and when somebody passed outside the statue seemed to move, waver, and they teased Maria about it, "Look, she's breathing. Mother of Mercy, Maria, a vision, look." Lily looked like that; she was graceful and frail, breakable. A woman ought to be anchored solid.

He never could understand what it was that Lily expected him to be ashamed of. Sure, mad. Goddamned mad, sore as hell, and tired, Jesus. Something in him had been rubbed dry, worn-out, for a long time. Some—he tried to think what it was—ability to be surprised, that was it. It came back, once in a while, from before he was ten, a kind of newness suddenly in him. It wasn't hope, it was something else. Jesus. He had enough plans for twenty men, and he knew what he had to do. He had been following his plans as careful as if he put his finger on her wrist and followed the vein right to her dear, dumb surprised white dotted swiss banner of a heart. When he went into the darkness of the mine, it was with the same care, his fingers telling him where he was, and the clues of wind direction and water flow, five miles into the coal vein right to his own room, his coal-face, his parlor he lay in then, la sua chiesa, sanctum sanctorum, black heart of hell.

Another thing. That day was different. He almost didn't get away because of Carlo Michele. Everybody was performing for Carlo Michele. Oh boy. Mamma was one new lady. She made Maria throw her arms around him at the Depot even though Maria cried. She was only sixteen. She said, "You got to, Maria. I'm your mother," like she said when they were all laid off and there wasn't enough to eat and she cut Maria's hair herself and sold it for ten dollars to a man come to the door and Papa cried with Maria and Mamma just looked at him disgusted.

Papa didn't say a word of course, he didn't much anymore, and Steve said Maria had to do what Mamma told her. So when they got to the Depot, they all stood around Maria while she kissed him. Carlo Michele was so surprised he didn't say a word. That boy, you could tell he'd once been one bellimbusto, all new tailored clothes to look rich to his American family. After twenty-six days in steerage, and through Ellis Island, and then all night in the day coach, he looked like the same dirty Dago as anybody else.

Maria took a deep breath and ran up and threw her arms around him while they all made a big noise of hugging and kissing, a real

Dago dance around their cousin. When Maria kissed him, she took out of his pocket the gun Steve told Carlo Michele to bring and put it down between her breasts. She was bright red. They didn't speak or look at each other all day. Mamma made him lend Carlo Michele his Sunday pants while she cleaned his clothes, and ran her fingers over his coat and trousers, over the seams. She made little mooing noises.

"Bring a gun, but don't put it in your suitcase," Steve wrote to him. "It's the first thing they steal." Carlo Michele took that to heart. The suitcase looked like he'd sat on it all the way across the Atlantic Ocean. Late that night Carlo Michele told Eduardo it took him two whole years to pay for the ticket and the clothes. The gun was sent by their grandfather. It was his most prized possession. He had used it to fight for Garibaldi when he was fourteen years old. Steve said he needed the gun to fight the capitalists, but he really wanted it so he could swagger around like the mountain boys.

Carlo Michele thought Steve told him to bring it to America to shoot Indians. That's how dumb Carlo Michele was. No. He wasn't dumb. He just hadn't been out of Umbria before. He was still walking in a dream and finding it different from his hopes, shock after shock after shock. You could see it in his face.

Mamma killed the fatted calf. Jesus, you should have seen the tomatoes, the peppers, they got them earlier than anybody else, and the conserves from the cellar his father had dug under the hill, and the chickens, her chasing pullets down by the creek, and the smell of bread in the outdoor oven. She sold the bread when people had money. The foreigners all bought from her. There wasn't one inch of that strip of level land by the creek his father hadn't planted in vegetables. They called it wasteland, but it was his for the asking, a miracle. Jesus. He had it terraced all the way up the south hillside.

When Mr. Godley saw the stone walls, and the stone heads he carved, he said they could have the house in perpetuo. He said, "In perpetuo. You made the desert bloom." His father was not like those zaccheroni, his mamma called them, the Americans, who never lifted a finger to grow things, and ate bread from the Company Store made out of air and putty.

What Mr. Godley did not know was that to them, the twenty-foot-wide creek bottom was a kingdom, an Eden, miracoloso, paradiso. What none of them foresaw was that in perpetuo was only until the next padrone.

None, that is, but his father. He never did trust the new owners, but he went on building walls and planting on land that was his on promise and carving monster heads out of stone. He said they were to scare the animals out of the garden, but really it was because that's what he had always done, carved the teste di mostri they used for cornerstones and house eaves in Italy.

That was what he did. He was a stonemason, but he wanted to be Michelangelo. He thought in America he would be. "You can be what you want there," he told them before they came, as if you want to be Michelangelo, then you can be Michelangelo. But he still carved the same heads he always had, mostri e mostri. That's what a dumb Dago his father was for a smart man. He thought in America he could be Michelangelo.

But even if he only made the same heads he always had, he looked so alone at such times that not even Eduardo's mamma went near him. He looked like he was getting his life back, feeling it enter his body again. He looked like he was listening to something close to his ear, not happy—better than that. He looked intent. Rapt intention, like rapt attention. Papa. Jesus, Eduardo couldn't forget what a handsome man he had been. You could still see traces, like something beautiful left out in the weather. There he was, smart, a smart man, but unused, neglected.

He never went beyond the Scuola Umberto Primo. He was apprenticed when he was twelve. The priests wanted to educate him, the Jesuits, but his grandfather wouldn't hear of it. He was educated by the priests himself and could read Latin and he still hated them. He blamed the Jesuits because he had only two sons, four daughters. He had fought with Garibaldi and he was an idealist soured by broken promises. He made rules and his sons suffered them.

"A long history"—he banged the table—"of the castration of the intelligent poor to keep power for the capomostri. That is the Church," he would yell to the street, "they weed you out and educate you and teach you not to use your cazzo, your tool, the way God intended, or they kill you in wars and break their promises, or when all else fails they martyr you with your feet pointed down and make you a saint. My sons," he would say like his father wasn't there, "are men of the people, laboring men. Pane e lavoro. Don't forget that," he would say to Eduardo.

His father was in the middle between the grandfather's ideals and the grandson's chances. Jesus, Eduardo knew how trapped he was. He couldn't free himself, might as well stop the water flow down-creek.

Every spring it brought topsoil down over the little strip of bottomland. It was like a blessing to a woman like mamma who had had to keep her chickens in a cage on the roof in the Porta St. Angelo. The chickens had names and the children made a show of crying when they were killed. But they were glad for the feast the old birds made when they finished laying, Saint Bonaventura, Saint Claudia, or whoever it was. His grandfather always named them for saints. Like a lot of atheists he never had the Church far from his mind.

So in Dago Hollow, his mamma would smooth her apron down and count her chickens, all white, every day to be sure some of the canaglia came to work in the mines didn't steal one. Sometimes they did. You had to be careful. None of the stranieri like Lily's family would even try to understand what kind of people his people were. They tried to make something out of themselves. Plenty of guts, like his mamma and the chickens. One time she followed the white feathers to the back door of the Godley Boarding House, bunch of Hungarians come. She marched right in the kitchen, took the boiling chicken off the stove, brought it home, cleaned the pot, took it back, and ask this Hungarian fellow spoke some English how they made the dumplings. Eduardo went with her to speak the English. He always did.

Yes. His body was up there with Lily that day, but he couldn't find any peace, not for long. His mind stayed down in the valley. He kept listening for something down the mountain. He didn't know what it was. Something worried his peace he didn't want to recognize. Part of it was because nothing had happened for too long and he knew it had to bust, a false peace, but not at their table—no peace there. Steve worked at Godley and they were out but Eduardo worked at Seven Stars and his father drove a mule and they were still working. His father wouldn't let him go out on strike. For once he was stubborn like the old days. Nothing could change his mind. He said, "Mr. Lacey is a good man. He was good to me." That was because Mr. Godley left them to Mr. Lacey like a litter of pups.

Eduardo hated it and Steve hated it but his father was old-country, he needed a padrone to love and to hate. Funny thing, a lot of the mountain people were that way too. Jake Catlett was a strike leader but he spent half his time setting in that swing with Mr. Lacey. You could hear them talking hour on hour. You could see them through the trees.

Eduardo heard something. It could have been anything, a rail snapping, a branch falling, but he was worried. It had sounded too damn much like shots.

He said so. Lily said no, it was a backfire. She would think of that. They had the only automobile in the valley. But the sound wouldn't leave his mind. He wanted to go back down the mountain, but Lily wouldn't be hurried. She knew as soon as she gave him the telephone calls he'd go, so she kept putting it off. He had long since learned she had a mule streak in her would go cold, cold and polite, when you pushed her too far. He was jealous of that, that stonewall you couldn't get through. She never would fly off the handle. She would just stop and look at you like you were a stranger. She would look rich and tall. She wouldn't honor you with anger. She just went where nobody could climb unless they were born knowing the way.

He was careful with her, lots of reasons. She was so damned young, not only in years—she was only eighteen. Even if she knew this place, this circle of hills, like she did her own body, she was more of a stranger than he was and always had been. His mamma did not understand this about her. She called her a witch. She said, "There is no place the strega walks her soul does not own." That was assurance, that ownership with the back straight. Eduardo knew he had to find it. He had had it once, God knows, that freedom, that ownership of the ground. The difference between them— with him it was there, inside, trying to get out. With her, Lily, it was only skin-deep dog training.

She trusted him like she did few other people. That was a burden, that kind of trust you haven't asked for—a worse burden than tears. He glanced up at her. She was looking out across the creek, watching and not watching something on the mountainside beyond, just being there, as still, for once, as a plant.

Her wrists were frail and loose in her lap, not like when she folded her hands together, sure she was right and spoke about money as if he agreed. That was the privilege she enjoyed so blindly that it made his muscles clench. Most of what she tried to teach him he did not need. He could earn it on his own. But he never could learn her easy and high-flown hatred of money, as if it didn't matter or was at best a convenience, at worst, shit too low for her concern. Even so, she talked about it more than he did, thought about it more, took it less for granted. She kept chewing at the subject, worried it, pointed things out about it. She had even connected the dull book she was reading to money.

"At least here's some use for it all, don't you see?" she suddenly said with a little worried frown as if his thinking about it had waked her from her stillness.

He was used to her reading his mind. So was she, but she did it less than she wished she did. Oh Jesus, Lily and money. Once she said she understood about Saint Francis. "He felt guilty because his family was rich. I understand him completely." Lily could be a damned fool sometimes. That innocence that festered in her repulsed him.

Her preoccupation with money was just a game, not the disease that he had seen twist his papa and make his mamma's arms too thin. He looked up then at the veil of Lily's lovely hair but it made him think of Maria with her short crop, and how they had eaten her hair. "La mia putta," Mamma had said, caressing the short curls when Maria and Papa cried. Steve said, "Speak English," like he always did.

"So, Mr. America, what is the English for la putta?" his mamma said, going on caressing Maria's head. She knew he didn't know. Thinking about Mamma and Maria, Eduardo felt a thousand years older and a thousand miles away from Lily, even with her skirt within touching distance. He wanted to smile but he didn't dare. He knew she would catch it and make too much of it.

Sometimes he hated the weight of her reactions, the interference with his plans, and even her curiosity about the trouble he was born with. He hated her easy unearned answers out of books and the demands that he feel with her, share her eyes, her senses, her opinions. Sometimes he felt raped by the strength of her wishes but he stuck around. If anyone had asked him he would have been too proud to tell, and a little bit too ashamed. The truth was she and Mr. Roundtree had what he wanted, and when he felt ashamed of it he told himself he gave as good as he got.

Mr. Roundtree wanted to educate and he was there to lap it all up. Once he looked at him and he said, "Eddie, you don't know a damned thing but you will find out things that I will never learn." He doubted it sometimes; other times he didn't. He wouldn't let himself. Doubt was a luxury he wouldn't let himself have. Lily. Well, if Lily was his door, he knew he was her cause, and things balanced out.

He did have to be careful. She wanted, she didn't know it then but she did, she wanted to slam the very door she was offering him. Her dreams meant trouble she didn't know about. He protected her since she was after all a lady, a signora, as dumb as hell about being a woman.

Like that day. It was typical. There he was nearly asleep, floating in relief for a minute, the weight of his troubles lighter at least, but he still felt her eyes move over him as if she had touched him, a blond feather touch. God knows it wasn't love. Love was not blond. It didn't float. Love was dark red, a solid sacred heart.

Under Steve's old pants he lay there afraid to breathe, with the private body of a prince. No Dago coal miner. That was what they all saw. In secret he sensed his muscles, his height, his slimness. He felt handsome.

He doubted if Lily had ever felt that way in her life. Poor little girl. She had come unasked into the house of his mind, and moved in there to stay. It worried his mamma so much that when she knew he'd been up there with her, she looked at him and shook her fingers in the air and said, "You think I don't know what is going on?"

"Boredom and handsome boys," she said. "How can they resist, the vossignoria with nothing to do but twiddle their thumbs and their hair and no religion? You choose the woman. Let me warn you, it is not that Lily who will suffer, it is you. She is only a fool and God looks after them, sciocchi ubriachi e bambini Dio li proteghe. I don't know why. I don't ask."

She would tuck her hair behind her ear, self-concerned, to show that the conversation was over and she didn't care anyway. It was that one gesture of his mamma's, making him see her neck where her fingers touched, that made him tender toward her the same way he was with Lily, her wrists and her feet, those vulnerable places in a woman that he distrusted. It was not breasts. He knew there was strength there. No, the danger was the back of a woman's neck, her wrists, her feet.

Lily's foot in white kid was as near as his hand's stretch. He wanted to touch the little pearl buttons, trace the outline of the bone, but he didn't move a finger. He traced the skeleton under the white kid in his mind's eye.

What he loved to understand was the structure, the shape of things, not Lily's justice and Lily's beautiful thoughts. He only trusted things he could touch with his hands. Mr. Roundtree called the human foot a miracle of engineering. He was right. Eduardo thought of the use, thought of the balance, but he wouldn't have touched the foot for the world. It wasn't that she would have misunderstood, it was not that. She was taboo. She was forbidden, because she had chosen him.

The choice of him was in the set of her delicate jaw, raised in judgment on what she referred to always, as if she were reading it aloud, as her unearned privilege of birth. He was what she believed was right. She never knew that it made her choice of him an insult.

At first, he had felt more than chosen. He felt rescued. He had stood in the creek, his feet distorted and pebble-colored under the running water. He was eleven and she was nine when she found him there. Even then she sought him out to play with. She said nobody at her house understood her. They didn't like her. She was blond, blonder than he had ever seen. She shook her hair. He couldn't even then believe the sun in the strands of her hair and the green blond of her skin through the leaves. After the black-haired women with their dark pools of eyes made huge by shadows under them like tearstains, she seemed the color of disappearance.

She said, "Let's wade together, let's play like . . ." His own sister Maria was only seven, and had more dignity than to ask like that. Maria had the bella figura of a lady. His papa said so, out of his mamma's hearing. She had waded into the pool that first day, a little frail girl. If he turned his head he could have watched the same pool through the innocents. It was now just a small basin of water caught by the rocks, but then, at eleven, it was big enough to be a swimming hole. It had been embarrassing to watch her, her white skirts and the white lace of her petticoat held wide and her water-distorted bare branches of legs and her blond hair almost to the water. She stopped in the creek quite still and said, "Who am I? You guess." He wanted to say Our Lady, for she was just then like Our Lady standing on that serpent and holding aside her blue plaster robes. He dared not say it because that was blasphemy, so he said instead, "I don't know," and it made her mad.

She said, "You don't know anything," and he knew he had to walk away, teach her right then how she could talk to him. She put her hand, palm out, on her forehead, and one side of her skirt fell into the water. She acted like somebody in the moving pictures and said, "Come back, Eduardo." She called him by his name.

He heard that call all the time he was growing up. She was the first person outside of Dago Hollow to know his name.

Then the lady, her mother, was there and had grabbed her shoulder and pulled her out of the water. She kept shaking her by the shoulders to hurry her while Lily struggled with her stockings over her wet feet. She hauled her, draggletailed in her wet skirt, down the path and away crying, "I was a nymph, I was a nymph, please Mama please, I was a nymph." "I'll nymph you," is all her mother said. There he stood barefooted, and the lady never even looked at him, not through the whole thing.

It was evening and his papa had not come off his shift yet when there was a knock on the door. His mamma went to open it, wiping her hands, and she was half smiling. She loved company. Lily's mother stood there under a big hat that sat like a ship on her head, the same hat as when he had first seen her. He was ten.

She had marched from the landau across the Depot platform, followed by her three daughters, looking like three expensive dolls. They were all in white dresses with white lace and big white lace hats and button shoes. The biggest of them had red hair hanging down to her waist. That was Althea, he knew later. There was one with a blond fall of hair, that was Lily. The one with dark thick curls was Mary Rose, only five years old but as poised as the others.

His mamma clicked her fingers at him to come to speak English to the lady.

The mothers stood there watching each other over the barrier of the doorsill. He'd seen Lily's mother lots of times since the first time, between the Big House and the Depot being driven to the train, but he never had seen her come all the way up to Godley before. He looked out to the road for the landau. It wasn't there. She had walked almost a mile, a long way for a lady with a ship on her head. There was plenty of time to think and notice all that because they just stood, nobody saying anything. The lady's eyes were veiled in the shadow of her hat brim. He could see the hair in her nostrils and the shape of her big front teeth under her tight upper lip. There was a little film of sweat from her walk.

"Mrs. Pagano," the mouth moved. His mamma said, "You tell him. I don't understand too good." She pushed him by the shoulder toward Lily's mother, but she didn't tell him. She just went on moving her mouth at his mamma. He didn't dare look up at her eyes. Her mouth was mean and thin and she didn't move it very much. Just enough for the words to come out.

"I hate to speak about this." He translated this: "Questa non mi piace, this does not please me." In Italian "hate" is a big word: odio, avversione, detestare, and the worst, nemico. Nemico senza compassione, detest without compassion. It was a curse. He couldn't tell his mamma the lady had said something like that.

"My daughters are not . . ." Whatever that was, the mouth didn't finish and he waited while his mamma looked at him. Then Lily's mother looked down. Her eyes didn't even dislike him. Nothing. He was only in her way.

"You are not to come around our place. I have spoken to Lily.

104

If you don't know why, I can't tell you." She turned away from him to his mamma. "Oh why don't you understand?"

She had been looking at him without seeing him, but he saw her and all like her, and he detested them without compassion. He had learned that in one minute and it was a double burden. He hated and he didn't want to be bothered.

He wouldn't tell his mamma but she read the message in his eyes. It called through the silence between them. There was no way to go back before the words. Even after nine years his mamma still carried those words, lodged deep.

Didn't people know words were things released or thrown, sensed with your skin, not to be taken back? He knew his mamma understood by the way her face hardened under the skin of her jaw, and the way she turned and played Dago for the lady, the worst insult she knew. "Signora, what you want? You want buy something?" and stared at her without saying another word until she stared her backwards off the stoop and down the steps. Then she turned and caught him by the shoulder and with her other hand hit him and hit him again until his ear ached and felt hot. He wanted her to keep on to stop the other hurt, but she was more hurt than he was and he knew it.

No. Hate was not the word for the vossignoria to use. Hate was a stone that waited to be thrown. Whenever he forgot that, like now a little too comfortable on the grass, he made himself remember his mamma's face that day, and the hate came back hard and useful like a stone that fitted his palm.

His mamma had slammed his hand on the table, that hand with the coal dust already ground into the fingernails, no matter how much she made him wash. She banged on his palm with her finger.

"What you know is this. Here. Piazza Grimaldi. Here"—up the thumb—"the Corso Garibaldi. Your grandfather fought with him. Here. Via Canerino. Here"—at the palm—"Porta Etrusco. What do these barbari capiscono?"—up the little finger—"the Porta Sole. Dante wrote about it."

"Dante, Dante, Dante. You can't eat Dante," his grandfather would have said.

She looked out of the window over his head but her eyes were sightless. "This place, this little desert, this sporca fossa di morti speranti, is her kingdom, capisce? That pittonessa, strega. There is no place her foot falls she does not own and this"—she slapped his palm again—"is yours." She was right. She put it in his hand, a place you could not go to but was always there, the flowers always in the whitewashed olive-oil cans, the embroidery always on the bed pillows, the stove always black, the stairs always narrow so that they said when both shoulders touched the walls you knew you were grown up. Your father and your grandfather tested themselves the same way. There were the gates of stone and the high walls and the huge brutal past of things, not the rawness of Lily's kingdom that his mother called this ditch of dead hopes.

Later that night, when his father came home from his shift, there was a silence that kept the children out of what his mamma called the salotto even though they ate there, and then sat there in the evening around the table sharing the lamp. There were rules she made and one was cleanliness. Their father was in the salotto and he hadn't even washed yet. He was still black with coal dust. He never came into the house before like that. Eduardo could see him through the open door, his face handsome and shadowed with coal dust, his head against the wall close to the photograph of his parents, wild bearded Grandfather and that old woman with the straight back who could not read or write. His father was as still as a picture himself, his head laid back beside the carved wood frame of the painting of the Holy Family they had brought from his parents' house.

She sat at the table with the supper plates all ready and the wine casting a red glow from the lamplight. Her head was down in the safe protective circle of her arms, her beautiful rounded arms. He could see from the doorway the parting where her hair had tumbled loose, and from under the hair her voice repeating, "Mi prometti, prometti."

His father never looked at her. Eduardo saw him unmanned right there, saw the impotence in his eyes because he could not push the weight of the world off her shoulders, saw him for the first time, his beautiful feared father, made small by circumstance.

106

Eduardo vowed right then never to promise anything under the blackmail of love if it did that to a man.

His father finally spoke, "We will only stay long enough . . ." but she interrupted, "Un bel domani, one fine day!" and shouldn't have laughed, not right then when his father was so alone. When she raised her head she looked at him like she didn't know his name. Eduardo saw her take the reins of power in her hands right then, long before the accident, even if she didn't remember it that way.

Afterwards, it was as if she had given up the pain of caring. He could sense it in her voice, something missing even in her prayers. She lost the tension of her anger. If she hated, it was abstractly. More and more she seemed to replace it with another energy, a protection of the past, and she dared them to take her memories away from her. She had built a wall of safety in her mind, and behind it a house in Perugia, and she dared them all with her eyes and her silence to challenge her and say it was illusion when all of them, even she, knew what she saw in the past was untrue.

Reality shrank the fine villa in her mind to his grandfather's house, where they had all lived, three rooms up a narrow stone stairway worn down four inches in the middle. Eduardo had measured it with his first ruler when he went to school. It curved upward toward the dark. Century after century of feet had worn it, first the monks, and after the Risorgimento, his family. He seemed to hear their chanting like the moaning of doves, to feel the Umbrian wind caught in the folds of their habits.

He learned to be afraid from the smell and shadow of the Little Black Monk Steve told him about. All the boys said he appeared on the stairs when there was going to be a birth or a death. Eduardo practiced the fear, the little chill, enjoying it.

The Via Canerino was their home, his grandparents, mamma, father, sisters, brothers, uncles, aunts, cousins, a street connected by blood from house to house. The landlords took the buildings after the Risorgimento, and his father's family had filled the rooms ever since, paying the padroni for forty years after the centuries of the monks.

To protect them in the New World, his mamma had brought the Virgin and Saint Ercolano, his wooden face and body as starved and stern and driven as the Umbrian winter. She wrapped him and the bust of Dante in quilts in their one trunk, with the painting of the Holy Family. The Christ Child looked like a potato wrapped in pink icing. There were the fiaschi and a plate from Gubbio that she had bought when they went there for the festa. She showed them as her treasures, and hinted at so many more they had to leave behind, and sighed.

When she lit the kerosene lamp, if anyone was there besides the family, she sighed then, too, and said, "We had the electricity in Perugia." It was the streetlight she remembered outside the kitchen, where the children slept in the smell of oil and garlic and boiled pasta and light piss. He remembered the first night after the streetlight was put in. It kept them awake in awe of it, shining in the window like daylight and throwing the shadow of vines on the ceiling and making the Holy Mother breathe.

The Holy Mother was in the kitchen then because Grandfather wouldn't allow her in the living room. Grandfather thundered so, you could hear him in the street below when you were coming home in winter hoping for supper, yelling at his father so the whole street could hear, loud, Dago, Porta St. Angelo father booming. If Lily could have heard that, it would have driven her notions of impoverished nobility out of her head, she who'd seen only the palazzi, and those glimpsed from the street on the way back to their hotel.

His grandfather was the idealist of the family, a risorgimento all on his own, left to grow old in a street five houses long off the Corso Garibaldi, a Garibaldino.

So his father, his own father, a man of more beauty than any of the paintings in the Museo, could only read his name and little more. The old man, not knowing he was old, when he drank wine and it ran all bloody down his gray beard, yelled at Eduardo's father at the table, as if he were still a child. "Better a good mason than an idiot trained by the priests! They wanted you, they wanted your cazzo, that's what they wanted," and his grandmother would mutter "Basta," and he would say "What?" "Nothing," she would say.

"That is how the priests get you," he would tell them all, again and again, all the faces just at table level, and he up there near the ceiling like God, all wine-stained. "A history"—his voice would go down—"of elimination of the brains of the proletariat. Take them into church and keep them from breeding. It's a plot of the nobility." He had been to the Seminary and he knew, he told them.

"I tell you. You would not have been born," he would announce, at the table, as if he had never said it before. Sometimes when Eduardo came up the street off the Corso in the dark, in winter, with wood for the fire—precious windfalls the boys went out at deep twilight to steal from the landowners—he would hear him.

That's what Lily insulted when she talked about money like it was shit.

You start thinking back to what the causes were—how it all had to do with what happened. You go back and back, all the way through your blood, to a cold street and that voice booming, "Mostri sono mostri ma i padroni sono capomostri!"

Lily moved and stretched out her arms. She wanted attention. She could sense it whenever he withdrew his mind from her, and she punished him with her patient educating words which he thought of as fool talk said in a fool voice, unreal and unimportant. There were no facts, maps, blueprints, nothing to hold and turn over or feel or think about like the fossil shells he brought to Mr. Roundtree or like kisses or money or the color of the shadows, the grass, the innocents, the trees, or even her thin wrists. Those were facts beyond Montaigne. He didn't mind Montaigne if it made her feel useful. It gave him a chance to rest from the perpetual knot of trouble and decision and danger downhill.

Steve said he took too much time to get her report, but he had to explain that there was no other way. She demanded attention.

He knew Lily was going to say something. She couldn't stand the silence. He knew that not many women could. It scared them. She said, "Eduardo?"

He tried not to answer. He wasn't ready to come all the way back yet.

"Are you asleep?"

"Hununh." It was time to go anyway.

"Papa said there wasn't a night shift," she told him.

He knew what was coming.

"Take me in," she said. "Please take me in."

It sounded like a deeper thing with her than just going into the mine. They'd been arguing about it for a long time. Lily was damned, bound, and determined that she was going to do it. "I want to go right in and touch the coal-face where it all comes from," she said, every time.

Eduardo sat up on the grass. He told her once again that it was bad luck a woman went in the mine. He told her the miners thought the right entry was haunted ever since some woman went in looking for her husband after black damp got some miners, and black damp got her, too. Lots of miners had seen her, all in white, without a head.

Lily said, "But don't you see? They'll never know I've been in. Even if they see me, they'll think I'm the ghost." She laughed. "I've got it all figured out."

Eduardo unrolled from the grass. "Once and for all," he told her, "no. It's too dangerous for you."

She got up and that little kid shoe stomped the grass and innocents. "Don't treat me like a woman," she hollered. She never looked more like the woman she was than when she stood there with that red rose at her throat, furious.

All the way down the creek path he knew he shouldn't have laughed, and shouldn't have left her up there, mad as a wet hen, without letting her have the last word. She was calling after him, "The phone calls. You forgot," but she had that tremolo in her voice that would make any man run for his life.

From where they were hiding there were only whispers on the wind that Carlo Michele couldn't understand. From so far above, a bird's view, the movements were slow as disasters are slow, run down and deliberate. He watched from behind an outcrop of rock above Annunziata's house, where the old woman had brought him, not letting him lift her even when she fell. He was afraid to take his eyes off the toy house below. It was his last link with anything he knew, a part of a great circle he could almost see sometimes.

He had planned all along to travel in a circle. It was his safe and abiding dream. But here it was as thin as a spider's thread, tenuous and transparent. Carlo Michele was cold for a second under the sweat of his climb. The old woman cringed down without shame, muttering noises to herself like his grandmother did.

He hated the indignity of his hiding. He thought, This is happening because they stole wood. He had caught Annunziata in another lie. The wood was not there for the taking. That was obviously not true anyplace. Those men below were the contadini hired by the padrone, the landowner, and the world is the same wherever you go.

The raw house below was part of his sacred circle, his mapped route, a stop on the way. To get to it at last had been a relief from the fear that was so secret no one could spot it except for a straightening of his back. It was the fear of being at the end, of not knowing where to turn. Against it his only protection was dignity, and, he hoped, grace, not the religious kind, that was no help, but in the bella puzienza, the fall of his clothes. There had been more than one recognition of that fear, which surprised him and made him sweat.

He had slipped into it, as a cold place inside himself, on the road, in the port of Genoa, in the days on the boat deck, at Ellis Island, waiting anonymous on the long bench, goaded and numbered, a sheep in the shambles. It made him afraid of being sick with no one to look after him.

He straightened himself, lifted his chest inside his clothes, trying to lean casually against a huge tree that clung to the mountainside with roots like snakes. He drew on aloofness, all he had to depend on, ignoring the fact that the old woman, when she remembered him at all, jerked at his pants leg to make him squat beside her. There was no one to see him but her, no one in mile after mile of trees, a fortune of trees.

He was not used to country violence where there was no sound, no shouts slapping the stone walls of old buildings, no running feet on city streets, no risonanza, only silence, not broken, but brushed by wailing words as faint as the turning of leaves in the twilight wind.

Below him in the distance the wooden rawboned toy house vomited from its toy windows and its broken front door, blankets, quilts, clothes, furniture turning in the air and falling, tearing, breaking into trash slowly, deliberately. A tiny stove was hauled out of the back door, dragged across the porch and let go at the top of the back steps. It parted without sound into several small black pieces by the border of the flower garden. One black square fell across the chicken yard, and dots of chickens scattered, bright white in the twilight, some toward the creek garden, some where the corn and tomatoes had been stamped flat, some toward the woods.

The wind carried a ghostly yell, but the words were English and not ones he knew. He could see Annunziata, with Maria and Vera and Vanya, standing close together in the front yard where Francesco's statue lay like a dead man at their feet. They seemed to be totally calm in the middle of the running men, the stranieri he had seen at the train in their black suits and their clean linen and their fine boots. There was no use asking the old woman what was happening. There were no words in common, only gestures and those misunderstood.

So Carlo Michele Pagano, named by his grandmother for Carlo Marx, and by his grandmother for Saint Michele, the Archangel, twenty-one years old, uomo elegante, dignitoso, aware of being slim, of his clothes fitting, straightened his trousers and leaned as casually as he could against the tree, an instinct as deep as blood not to let his fear break through the pride of his body, or show like a wound. What he did feel as waves of cold was shock, new-world shock. He was aware of a new harshness, not of something pent up and bursting—he was used to that—but a new thing, slow and strident. He could see it below, methodically destroying Annunziata's house. He could smell it in the air, sulfur mixed with green leaves and running water and mast.

It was the smell of America beyond the cities, raw in the wood of the house below him, wild in the trees, disheveled in the trash thrown now in the yard, now in the creek, frightening as the ghosts of laughter from someone below. It was as ugly as the railroad tracks that led from the high mine mouth to the tipple, a black gash parting the green woods. Its voice had clipped him, his name even, to Mike hey Mike, like the yap of a dog.

He had been caught in a long line of dirty human beings at Ellis

Island, some awed, some crying, some mute, all shuffling, body to body, through a bottleneck in a building as high as a cathedral. It smelled of sweat and vomit and disinfectant. He had been given his new name by a man whose hands trembled and who needed a shave. There was a huge echo, a raw echo, of people and feet and heavy faces and heavy sorrow as they were pushed toward the doctor who used a buttonhook to fold back their eyelids and stare into their panicked eyes. But Carlo Michele had made himself step lightly, dirty as he was from three weeks without washing, so he would not confuse himself with the others.

Nothing in these endless mountains had been covered yet. In shape they were like those he was used to, but where there could have been a city, gray and white, there was still this fine savagery of trees, as if he had stepped back a thousand years. The old woman was wiping her eyes with a white linen handkerchief edged with lace. It surprised him into thinking of women covered with a polite and beautiful language of clothes, language of wool and silk and linen. He tried to bring back the circle to his mind of which all this was a part. I am not a fool, he told himself, and I am not patient—uomo pazienza, to whom everything comes.

He reminded himself, to keep his spirit, where he was really going. He let himself walk the same Corso he had always walked, as handsome, nearly as young, but this time he wore a sky-blue cape to his ankles like the blue capes of the nobili, the officers. The dream would not stay. Between himself as he had been in the Corso, in the clothes that took him two years to pay for, good as they were, and himself as he could be someday, in the blue cape, there was America, rough as a chapped hand, and a new name, Mike hey Mike, and the breaking of a house into trash, and the old woman crying beside him, making no sound, just letting the tears run out of her old filmed eyes into a white linen handkerchief trimmed with lace.

What had begun the dream, the circle? He tried to find it. That at least was strong, directional, not impotent, as his fury, hidden by his studied casualness against the tree at what he saw below, could not understand, felt shut away from and mute. He had seen the men in black before the women did. It was his instinct to go to the salotto door, but the old woman had grabbed his arm, and

113

pulled him toward the kitchen, surprisingly strong, surprisingly fast. Maria had run after them, urgent, calling, "Avanti, presto, avanti con la Madre Jones!" No one told him what was happening. There was only Annunziata's sobbing, "It will be worse for us if they find you here." He who had done nothing, had no choice but to run away with an old woman, and watch like a deaf man who can only see and cannot understand.

La Madre Jones! That old woman? Her handkerchief? He thought then of one of the visions that had fired him with hope beyond the others, the vitelloni, the easily satisfied, the day-by-day ragazzi. It was, he had to admit, nothing very fine, no idealismo like his grandfather, anarchismo, socialismo, whatever it was. No. It was a white, chaste, unattainable mountain of white lace and white linen, fine, frail, and taunting—as certain as the sky-blue cape; a froth of American women's underwear piled to the ceiling as light as feathers, even the stains an excitement he could still feel, unseemly as it was, as he stood against the wild tree. But he did feel it whenever he thought of it.

He had lost his virginity in that soft mountain of lace and linen, overpowered by it and by the peasant laundress on duty, who laughed and bounced as on a feather bed and called him il suo signorino because he had been educated by the priests and had more delicate ways, even though he could only find work carrying the laundry and he knew he was lucky to get that in a bad time. Because of the manners the priests and his mother had taught him, he was put into the uniform of a porter.

The threshold of the rooms at the Hotel Palazzo was a great gulf six inches wide. White arms stretched across it to take the laundry. The rooms behind their heads were a frame for women, red walls, great gilt mirrors, the heavy tables, high-backed brass letto matrimoniale. Their heads were in clouds of lace, their faces egg-smooth. He liked to see their eyes, ravaged under the cloud veiling. Their skirts swept the rug and made no sound but a sigh. Once in a while, one would motion to the bed and let him enter and for a second, in the perfumed air, he saw himself as singular and immortal, opening all doors, crossing all thresholds, even that one, that great gulf six inches wide. He glimpsed and smelled choice, for the first time in his life, headier than their perfume, more intoxicating than their fine linen.

Sometimes one, too old, too easy, would touch his hand too long, tipping him. It made him feel as if she didn't see him, but an animal in his place, an animal to pet. "Per bellezza," one said once, and he ran. That was not in his plan, not the way he saw the circle. Solicitudo mater divitiarum. Care is the mother of riches; pazienza, the key.

He forced himself, demanding, so as not to feel so lost in the alien woods, the safe retracing of his movement around the circle. He saw it as a changing corridor that one day would meet itself again. How far he had come already! If he could follow the past that had brought him to the trees, then surely the future led beyond them. It only took courage, and he had that, he knew, from the cut of his trousers to the set of his head.

So he made himself repace the corridor as he marched down between the houses in the Corso Garibaldi on his way to work at the hotel, past the University for those with money, down the hundred steps narrow between the gray walls, passing the nuns, the priests on their perpetual errands. The Porta where he lived was, his grandfather said, as priest-ridden as a brothel, and beyond it, down, down among the carpenters, he passed his cousins, who called out "Bellimbusto," or meowed like cats.

He was not like them. He was lucky, he told himself. He had gone to school to the priests. He strolled across the piazza, past the first glimpse of the changed, impossible world, under the arch, sky-high and heavy, that had once been through a prison. He could still smell bodies, excreta, and stone. He kept trying to see it, in retreat from the old woman who pulled his trousers so hard she forced him to kneel, forced him down, so that his knees touched the damp of the ground behind the rock.

The corridor led up through the oldest street in Perugia, old as the Etruscans, a handhold wide. On either side bone-gray buildings turned away from the exposure to the street and his eyes. There were still the iron rings where the citizens had fastened the great chains across the streets, horse-withers-high to keep the nobles out, and the beccherini, the thin ones, who had erupted for centuries from the Porta he was born in to tear at the city walls. That was not his way into the citadel. His way was better. He knew it. Down below, across the dirt road, he saw the kind of chain they must have used in the old times, the only one he had ever seen.

He had walked every day, strolled rather, out of the ancient street into the wide Corso, where he had closer ties than any in his house and everyone knew his name.

That was where he had watched it, a world away caught in the lift of his eyes, dignity, beauty within an open window high above the street. The ceiling was gilt, carved and painted with clouds and gods. There was a heavy gold mirror that plunged up into the carvings of the ceiling. The walls were red damask. A hand flung back a sky-blue cape and reached up to draw the curtain.

That was the glimpse, the first one, even before the underwear of women. He was ashamed that it was such a thing that set him afire, made him move, save, listen to the priests. He had, he told himself, to go through patience, and pain in his shoulders, and the dark night of a twenty-year-old body and soul without a woman, in order that someday he could wear a sky-blue cape, draw a red damask curtain, unwrap a woman from clouds of lace and fine linen, drive an automobile and belong to the English tennis club where the ladies went in their phaetons and their electric brumi.

A yard from his foot a branch released itself from the root-covered ground and began to slide past the old woman within a foot of her black rump. He dared not breathe. It slid toward a crack in the rock, poured down it slowly, six feet of black snake he had thought was a fallen branch. He dared not take his eyes off the ground near his feet. No one had told him to take care, every second, where he stepped. He had been so busy watching the house below, the valley, the tipple, the creek by the house meeting the big creek winding on out of sight toward the river, getting his bearings in his eyes, and in his mind. No one had told him simply to look down.

Because he refused to be afraid, he could feel that same energy turn to fury. For a second it hit on Annunziata, but only for a second. He knew he was being unfair to her. He would have lied too, or been as she was, barocco with the truth. It was not, after all, really a lie. It was pride, the same pride that made them pull the shutters and sit around the table at dinnertime and talk loud dinner talk when his father had been laid off at the post office and they had been out of food so that his grandfather would not find out his son could not feed his family and yell, "See—I told you—ben educato! The priests have taken your cazzo! You have one pair of cuffs and no trade."

He could see the old man, see even him petrified by the snake, and it made him laugh, so that the old woman looked up for a second, surprised. She turned away from him, disgusted, and he knew she thought he was laughing at what they watched.

Annunziata had told them there was a garden. That was not a lie. She had not mentioned the boarders in the upstairs room, who had come in without a nod and gone slowly up the stairs without washing the coal dust away. They were Finns, Annunziata had explained, and until they learned some English she could not scrub them as she did her own men when they came home. He had watched her as Francesco knelt in the backyard over a washtub. She used a hard brush. As he passed the room where the Finns were, he heard a few words of a soft sad murmur of a language nobody knew, and then nothing but the creak of the cots.

When he read Annunziata's letters to his grandmother, the women—his mother, his aunts—stood quietly as if they were in church, even whispering single words so as not to interrupt. But his grandmother, who had been honed by age and by living with the old man, chewed and chomped her gums, unbelieving all the time, and said, after almost every letter, "No. There is no land. It is not like that. You go to bed a donkey. You wake up a donkey."

At least Annunziata thought she was telling the truth. Appearance was comforting, as it was when she stripped him of the clothes he had worn for two weeks and three days, day and night. She cleaned his fine trousers and jacket, exclaiming over them, the cut, the cloth, while he sat in Eduardo's undershirt and clean overalls waiting. She would not let him go out until that was done, even to that little village he could see through the open door.

Yesterday in Eduardo's work clothes, with the grandparents in their oval frames watching him, and the carefully patched table-

117

cloth reminding him of the worn hands of his mother that never stopped until they were folded in death, wax on her yellow veiling that had wed her to Christ and to his mild father, he had felt trapped, as if he had gone nowhere, or had gone all that way full circle, not across a threshold at the Hotel Palazzo, not to the damask room with the gold mirrors, but home to his own salotto. All the saving and the planning had been in vain. Now, looking at the same tablecloth caught on a corner of the porch, and the tabletop leaning on the chicken fence, he knew a loneliness like the slamming of a door. Hopeless. Down below the bulli in their black suits had slowed down. He saw one of them go toward Annunziata. They seemed to be talking quietly. He saw him hand her something—a patch of blue. He knew it was the plaster Virgin with the missing hand.

He had dressed and was himself again when she took him into her garden, the little girls watching every move he made, saying nothing. "Capisce," she told him. "But they don't answer. They have forgotten how. That Stephano! He won't let them speak Italian." And she shook her fingers. "Chi ha prato ha tutto," she said in the garden, and laughed. "You tell them. You write to them and tell them."

But how could he do what she wanted? What she saw as meadowland, a great prato, was only a narrow valletta; all of it except for the dirt road between the hills was planted in vegetables and flowers, narrow rows of them. The land was good, but even so, she could not see the real miracle that rose, tier on tier of trees in the distance, up above him on both sides, the flat green leaves, the smell of sulfur and of green, the smell and sound of water. Acqua e boschi, boschi e acqua, miracoloso, everywhere—an endless paradiso of water and trees.

She told him all the wood was for the taking. She said that as if it were of no importance. Had she forgotten the brown domes of hills, the bare cities? Couldn't she remember the donkey carts, their hollow sound on the old road as they carted the laundry down from the city to the Tiber because in that city, mist-high, a man-carved stone mountain, water was as precious as wine?

She put out her hand and touched the maize already waist-high on her; she was a deceptively small woman. She bent down to squeeze a bug in her fingers and flicked it away, forgetting him. The tomatoes were already forming fruit in early June. She set the seed early, she told him, near the cooking stove in the shed behind the salotto. She was first in the valley. The stranieri were lazy. They didn't care. She clung to what was the same, the outdoor oven Francesco had made for her. She told him about that twice, forgetting she had done it.

Inside as evening came, the Virgin, the saints, the plate from Gubbio, the painting of the Holy Family, the grandparents, the smell of pasta, cheese, and wine, a feast day of food, made his throat tighten with homesickness. That surprised him, and he was ashamed and told himself how tired he was.

After the weeks at sea, where he slept against a stanchion on the crowded deck because the smell and swish of vomit in the steerage made him sick, there were only the same dull faces, the dull sorrows at leaving home. Only sixty hours ago, that? Yes, the dawn sight of the Statue of Liberty in the mist, excitement and fear together as they stood and stared, all quiet, even the children. Already the cathedral space of the hall at Ellis Island was full when they landed, shunted through, and then the clutch of fear until he found a padrone who spoke Italian and exchanged his money. He got much less than he had expected, but the man told him it was a different exchange in America. Carlo Michele knew he was being cheated but he was too confused and the man had his money in his hand when he said it. At least he told him how to get to the train through the city of New York. No one spoke to him. The streets were numbered, so he walked north with the sun over his head and then to his left, not saying a word—strolled, rather, so that no one would know he had just landed. He carried his suitcase all that way, not letting it out of his hand. He had gotten on the train with a sandwich in a bag, one quarter of American money left after the sandwich and his ticket, and on paper from the Hotel Palazzo—a good touch when he had to show it for directions, he thought—an address fourteen hours away, somewhere inside the continent. It was evening when the train left and there were lights as of a city stretching mile after mile.

Then, as suddenly, there was dark, dead pitch darkness outside the train window. The stars did not move. The train seemed still.

There was only the clack clack and the seldom lonely light of a single house, approaching and retreating in black space. Once he had waked and saw long lines of ovens with open red-hot mouths that glowed skyward into the blackness and he was, for a minute on waking with the taste of coal in his mouth, as afraid as when he was a boy and the priest had told them what it was like in hell.

Now, down below, the men were stepping through the flattened flower garden. Annunziata had turned to watch them leave. The old woman had gotten up without his seeing her. She waved her hands in the air, telling him to stay by the tree as if he were a dog. "Do what la Madre Jones says," Annunziata had whispered.

The old woman went down the path and left him alone in the endless world of trees.

Not even his grandfather's laughter at the priests had made him lose that image of inferno when the train passed, ovens spouting a red hell and a red haze in the black sky. If that was hell, then this was limbo, not, as he had thought before, a paradiso. No, if men made hell they also made heavens, the humanness of the Corso, the sound of voices. In the silence he knew that in limbo there were miles of green trees and the smell of wood rot and damp and the awareness of snakes.

He longed for the comfort of the night before, the admiration of Eduardo, even the contempt of Stephano that hid his envy, the shy stare of Maria. Annunziata would not let him sleep until she had taken him through street after street of the Porta, questioned and questioned, keeping him pinned to the table and to home while she kept turning up the lamp.

He tried not to stare when Francesco patted his one foot on the floor while they played morra, waiting for Annunziata to make the supper. He could not keep his eyes from the stump. Francesco had unstrapped his leg at the knee and left it like a cane at the door. The worn shoe on its wooden stump, the straps hanging, accused him of surprise. That that was one of the things Annunziata had not written, a thing like that.

Francesco, Francesco, the name and voice of pride, oh Jesus, his grandmother had kept him at home in her mind, the handsome son. She said, "Go if you must go. Go to Francesco."

That was when he broke the news to them after he had saved

for all that time, that secret saving he felt so guilty about when they needed it at home, saving for the suit of clothes, slow, slow, lira on lira, one hand turn after another of tips from the thresholds of the Palazzo Eterno, as he began to call it to himself. He sat in the piazza in the sun, making lists of lire, the clothes, the fare to Genoa, the fare to America, and then to Francesco, as if he were a city, a goal, and not a man; not that man with his stump and the coal dust creased into his stonemason's hands that were going to make statues when he got to America. "Scultura come Michelangelo," his grandmother said.

Well, he had carved the brute figure standing in the garden. Annunziata said it scared away the birds. He had carved the heads at the corners of the stone walls he made and he had carved himself a wooden foot and leg from the knee down. Now he thrust out his coal-dust fingers playing morra, and when he spoke at all it was to argue with Stephano because he was still driving a mule in the padrone's mine when Stephano had already come out on strike.

"It is not the same mine," he told Stephano. "I owe him."

"Niente," Stephano raised his voice before his father. "Una gamba destra," he said in Italian in honor of Carlo Michele.

When Carlo Michele admitted that he had kept back money he expected his grandfather's fury, but instead the old man laughed and slapped his back and left his arm across his shoulders and called him un bel pezzo d'uomo, a fine fellow, and said he had cool blood.

He had never complimented him before. "You see," he told him, "you go to the priests until you are too old to learn. You have to work like a contadino—not that it is bad," he said, remembering his politics. "You see how well Francesco has done, eh? I would not let the priests take him. Your father—eh, senza muscoli, senza macchia. They could have him. So you know mathematics and Latin, and you deliver the laundry. Do the professors take you into the University without money? Do the priests make an avvocato, a dottore, out of your brain unless you give up your cazzo? That is the way they do it. When they find a poor smart man they give him Latin and mathematics and a good living and take his cazzo so he cannot breed more poor smart men—eh? Sing in the Vatican choir. Not me. Not you. You go to Francesco." It was his own gun he sent, his treasure, when the letter came. "Of course Stephano wants a gun," he said. "For Indians."

His grandmother said that it was right for him to go to them. Even if she didn't believe the letters she said they were his family, and that a mother hen didn't step on her own chicks.

When he remembered Francesco, it made the goal, the long voyage, less awesome. He remembered how rich his voice was, how easy his words. He had been too dignified a man to laugh much, but he smiled and his hand was gentle when he touched Carlo Michele's hair.

Francesco had slammed the table and talked back to his grandfather. "The boy has brains. Let him go to the priests. You want him to be an ignorant bum like me because his grandfather is an idealista? Anarchismo, who does it feed?" Carlo Michele remembered his muscles moving under his shirt, and how handsome he was.

His grandmother had kept the picture alive for him. She would stroke his face with her horny palm and say, "You look like him. Che bella, Che pezzo di galantuomo."

He had seen him first through the train window. He saw the terrible thinness of his face, like the old, old pictures of the saints on the church walls, all bones and brown suffering. He saw that Francesco limped, but he had not known about the leg until he unstrapped it. He had been as shocked as when the pretty girl, Maria, had thrown her arms around his neck and taken the gun from his pocket and put it down her dress between her breasts. When he realized, they both blushed scarlet.

In the night by the lamp, Stephano still grumbled. "You work. Nella mia casa." He was ambitious, Carlo Michele could see that, and proud of his place in the strike.

"La *mia* casa," Francesco had said like a man who didn't use his voice much.

Carlo Michele searched for the Francesco he remembered beneath the dried parchment skin and the new stillness in him that was like the stillness of the woods he stood in feeling foolish in his city suit, sick at the sight of all that pride and lying and work turned to garbage in the yard below. He watched the women and children climb toward him up the mountain path. Annunziata cradled the plaster Virgin in her arms like a baby.

He reached down and brushed the leaves and dirt from the knees of his trousers.

Francesco had changed in all their eyes, but not in his own. He had simply retreated. He had long since passed through bitterness and left it behind. He found the feeling hard to conjure up again. Like rock, it had eroded away in uselessness. Francesco didn't like useless things or noises or even desires. Annunziata told the children in front of him, as if he sat like one of his own carvings, not hearing her, that his silence was despair. She talked about his old ambitions like a lost country.

He could have told her there was no longer such a place, but he didn't bother. He had long since given up trying to break through the demands of her beliefs. It was easier to go into silence as into a room that he had always known was there. When he was young, and his oil ran smooth and heavy in his muscles, he had only visited it in seconds that surprised and scared him. Now, as he sat on the bumper of the tram car, sensing the slow rhythm of the mule's movement through the black tunnel, he welcomed it.

It was nearly six o'clock. He had only a few cars to pick up at the rooms and take out to the main entry for the tram to pick up. The shift was almost over. He drifted through Third Face South toward West Six entry where the sound of his own breathing and the mule's steps died without echo as if, after the machine's clatter and pulse in the main entry four miles away, the silence, like the blackness, comforted him.

Unlike the main entry, which had a ten-foot ceiling and was as noisy as a city street, West Six was only four feet high. Even with the dark ahead he and the mule sensed the ceiling. It bowed its head slowly, sloped it down until Francesco's light shone straight along its back into the wall of black ahead. Delicately, the animal turned without any order into the entry. There were things underground that Francesco had learned to take for granted, that the mule took direction in the dark from his wishes, that the men sensed ahead of time when there was going to be an accident.

Sometimes they made that sense into images, usually images

from their own countries. The Carpathians in No. 2 room saw dwarfs with long beards, and the Sicilians in No. 3 and No. 4 rooms saw the Virgin Mary. The two Russians in No. 5 saw the seductive rusalka, and when they learned enough English to tell what she looked like, the other men said they wished they had seen her and said the Russians needed women. They were both sixty, grandfathers. Francesco wished that his hands could make them a rusalka. He saw her in his mind but not with his hands. She was too delicate. As for the mountain men, they saw only the miner's wife in white, and the little dog.

Francesco liked West Six. It was five miles deep into the mountain. He had helped to open it. If he thought at all, it was in wisps that floated through his mind, intrusions of questioning, and answers he no longer gave to anybody but himself. Drift. He like the English word, the way people used it, drift mine. He knew it meant a mine that intruded into the hill's outcrop horizontally, not vertically, as in a shaft mine. Shaft pierced down. Drift was an act, gentler and less alien to the way the world was made, leaving the overburden alone for three hundred feet, undisturbed above them all the way to the trees on the mountaintop.

The overburden lay in tier on tier of time that Mr. Roundtree told Eduardo about, and Eduardo told him, the sandstone of ancient seas, the layers of shale, the black flint from old swamps with the marine fossils, sandstone, shale, limestone, coal, fire clay, strata of all the surfaces there had been as the earth died and buried itself over and over. Privately in the dark Francesco thought that Mr. Roundtree was as superstitious as the others. The layers of time like the rusalka or the Virgin Mary were his way of explaining things that were enough of a mystery in themselves.

At least, Francesco let the thought drift through him, he knew his images came from his inner eye to be made, instead of waiting out there with the dwarfs and the layers of time and the cry of his father long ago with his pleading atheism and his gnarled hand slamming the table, "The priests lie," nearly sobbing. "I know this."

Moving slowly through the entry, letting all this be in his mind, Francesco was satisfied that he did not know. Stephano was another knower—that they called a know-it-all—and the old woman, la

Madre Jones, was another. If the miners hadn't hated Catholics they would have called her a saint. Her picture in the Odd Fellows Hall had a halo around her head. Of course it was just a light the photographer put there, but they looked at it like Annunziata did the plaster Virgin, soft-eyed, but they wouldn't use the word "saint, sancta, santa." No. The rusalka, the strata, Madre Jones, the passionate nogod, Annunziata's golden city, all past, all future; most of them seemed to see something way out there, way back there, way up there. He clicked his tongue at the mule gently.

The mule stopped. Francesco heard a scurry down by the tracks at the door. A head lamp turned toward him so that it and his own head lamp lit the tunnel to the walls and shone on the ventilator door ahead where someone had written, "Debs for Prez." The door boy, Nipopollis's son Vangeli, his face black, his eyes sleepy, stared up at Francesco as if he hardly knew him. He opened the door, slammed it too hard behind Francesco, and he knew the boy was back asleep again almost at once, not like Eduardo. When he was made door boy when he was fourteen, he read all the time by the light of his head lamp. Francesco, if he considered anything in the past, was proud of that but he let it drift away too, knowing it, enjoying the drift. Drift was a way of testing a direction, an understanding. The stranieri even said it; they caught the drift of things.

He promised himself a little rest before the shift ended. Lately, when he was tired, and sought the silence uninterrupted, he had taken to turning into the abandoned entry, West Four, that had long since been mined out. He stopped the mule and sat on a slag heap, taking off his leg to ease the stump when the memory pain demanded it, and waited for ease and the sound of silence. It had a sound of its own, his own loud heartbeat, the creak and crack of the breathing mountain, the faint sighing of the running gas from the old ceiling.

He let himself have visions without wishes. Sometimes he compared them to Annunziata's visions of the past, or Stephano's and Eduardo's of the future. Sometimes he saw stone waiting to be carved, released. Mr. Roundtree had told him that the Indians, when they wanted to carve, would pray to a tree, and when the spirit of the tree came out to look at them, they would cut it out from the tree's bole, and it would be a mask. He liked that. It was the way he saw stone. There was no ambition in this. Even Eduardo who knew him best was wrong. It was the act of doing, not the results, that calmed him. He knew that when the vision came out through his hands it would not be quite the same as that in his mind's eye. It would be something else, surprising always. The judgment of "good" or "bad" never occurred to him.

That was what he saw when the darkness and silence within him found its room to expand to the shining black walls of the abandoned room, to the dull black of the roof when he turned his head and his head lamp's glow touched the slate. Sometimes, more often lately, he could see his father, as if he were standing in front of him, blessedly quiet at last, as little as the Carpathian dwarfs. Even though he didn't believe in them, he had at the corner of his pool of light glimpsed the ghost of the small feist dog the stranieri said haunted the entry. When he turned his head to see it more clearly, the dog was gone. Once he had seen the woman in white, caught by the black damp that crept without warning, when she came looking for her husband. At least it could have been the miner's wife or the rusalka, or the Virgin, whatever it was. Black damp was like the death it brought. It had no smell, no image. There was, he told himself, no sense in it. English was a strange language of puns.

When he reached day, where the others were, he learned to take the silence with him. He didn't say much, but he told himself that when he did, it meant something, not like the others out in day, whose steady useless chatter sounded to him like empty cars on a track. It nearly drove him crazy.

He liked to be at home in the dawn, when the new sun shone through mist and the trees were scented like a garden, and the house was asleep. He hoed his vegetables then and when the vision was strong, he carved, in summer by pure new light, in winter with his mine lamp, like another hand, moving over the stone. At seven o'clock Annunziata would wake to the rhythm of his hammer on the stone and call out "Mamma mia, basta!" leaning out of the upstairs window with her hair wild on her head. Some good times she would catch the quiet of the morning, and stay there, staring out over their place, not aware that she was smiling. Then she looked like his memory of her when she was a girl and her eyes shone.

He had almost reached the room where the two Finns worked. He could see the two spots of their head lamps. They trusted him to come. He knew that all of them did, the ones who only had a few words in common with him, the two from the Carpathian Mountains farther along the entry, Nipopollis, who worked No. 5 room, the niggers from Alabama in No. 3, though God knows everybody was a nigger after a half-hour at the coal-face. They had that in common. The Spinetti brothers from the Abruzzi in No. 7, the old man from Russia who looked like God, with his head lamp making a halo around his head, and his white beard; they depended on his precision and his fairness, even the foreigners in the new entries where the coal seam was only two feet thick and they knelt all day under the low ceiling to shovel the shining black loads for him to pick up.

Steve was contemptuous of them, the new ones. He said the only words they learned were reach day, coal-face, yes, no, straw boss, whiskey and fuck you. He said he didn't know what he was going to do about them.

Out in day Francesco had the job because he was a cripple, and could only do unskilled work, but in the black entries, in the rooms of coal, crouched under the sandstone, or slate ceilings, slowly moving, all the shift long, he was a power in his kingdom. Sometimes he could feel with the men at the coal-face, hearing him coming, steady as a clock.

He had been one of them ten years before, a Dago under a bad ceiling, depending on a straniero to pick up his full car and take it to day, where the straw boss chalked the load up. His family depended on fairness for his pay. So he worked in strict rotation and they knew it, all of them. They listened to him, not to his words —most of them couldn't understand those—but to his steadiness, and stayed on the job in Seven Stars Colliery. Stephano said he could bring them out in a minute if he only would and Francesco said that was true and went back to his silence.

The Finns' last car was loaded and scragged, waiting at the room entry. Deep in the room, Francesco could see only two tiny smudges of light from their head lamps and hear the faint tapping of their hammers as they set mine props to hold the new ceiling they had exposed on their shift. The lights moved slowly, the tapping was methodical. Francesco liked the way they worked. Out in day the hammer would have been louder, but the cave-room, the coal dust, muffled both sound and light. They were only a hundred feet away.

Francesco hitched up the mule to the full car and scragged the empty one in its place. The mule started back down No. 6 toward the entry without even a signal from Francesco and the rhythm of moving and thinking that had been interrupted by the stop began to flow again.

He stayed on the job, even though Stephano was ashamed, for more reasons than he would tell. It wasn't that he liked Mr. Lacey, but Mr. Lacey had inherited the Paganos from Mr. Godley when he sold out, and Mr. Lacey had stuck to his bargain. He had seen to it that Mr. Roundtree understood about their keeping the company house at Godley after his accident in Godley mine, and he knew that if Mr. Lacey had to shut down, he would be the last man fired. No. He didn't like Mr. Lacey. He felt a twinge of shame about that. He didn't like his shoulders. He didn't think a man ought to advertise his sorrows with his body like that. He felt sorry for him, though, trying to keep his head above water. That was another English phrase that Francesco liked, and used a lot in his mind. It was hard for the padrone to keep his head above water with those horseleech's daughters of his who cried Give, give. Sometimes out in day when he saw them, Francesco would translate their white dresses into coal, how many shovelsful, how many tons.

He headed for No. 4 entry and a few minutes of rest with his leg off. It was only a few minutes. He had cleared the last full loads of the day, and he told himself he needed a little peace before he began the five-mile trip back to day. The mule stopped and sighed. He eased off his leg and rested his head against the shining black wall. He had taken refuge in forgetfulness about the accident itself, except when the memory pain brought it back and it intruded, uncalled for.

He could hear again the high whine of the chain cutter. He sat again, his legs straddling the machine, on the board held level by the wooden trestle, holding on to the undercutter, guiding it into the coal wall. His scraper crouched, ready with his shovel to clear the cut. At the moment that the trestle broke, his scraper had time to fall back clear of the cutter. It came to rest, still running, still cutting, but his right leg instead of the coal-face. He didn't remember any more. When he came to, he was in the fore-man's shed on the worktable and the company doctor was lowering an ether cone over his mouth and nose. He remembered the big clock on the wall. It said twelve o'clock—midnight.

He had been proud of his job.

Now, in the deserted entry he thought only of how quiet it was on the day shift when there was no scream of the cutting machines, no clatter of the electric trams, except along the main entry. He felt disloyal, after Mr. Lacey had kept his promise to Mr. Godley to keep him in work, and Mr. Roundtree had kept him in his house even if Stephano was out on strike, but he was glad Mr. Lacey couldn't afford any more noise.

He was nearly asleep when he heard the sound of a man running through First Face South. His heart lurched. A man running could mean gas, black damp, fire. He hobbled out to watch the bobbing light appear in the distance. It was the third Sicilian brother, the one from Godley who had gone on strike, not like his brothers who had families to send for. He had been in the mine only three months, but his voice was already low and muffled.

"I have seen it," he told Francesco holding him by the arms. He spoke the strange Sicilian slowly so that Francesco would understand—"The house, the garden, everything."

Francesco hopped slowly back to his leg. He sat down and strapped it on. He unhitched the mule and walked out of the entry, leading it. He had not said a word. Even when the Sicilian boy went on talking, he seemed not to hear him. He turned into No. 6 and shook the door boy awake again. At the first room he touched the Carpathians on the shoulders. They were setting mine props. He motioned to their water bucket, leaned down and turned it over. The water that was left made the slate glisten. They

129

followed him to the next room. He turned over the second water bucket, then the third, then the fourth.

The only thing he was heard to say was. "Mostro è mostro; il padrone è capomostro," and then in English, "A monster is a monster, but a padrone is one king monster," even though the men following him couldn't understand that either. Only the Sicilians understood him, but the turning over of the buckets was a language they all knew. Seven Stars Colliery had come out on strike.

They began the five-mile walk, a glowing circle of their head lamps lighting more and more of the walls as they gathered the shift from the rooms, a long line of men bent under the four-foot ceilings of the entries as if they had the weight of the world on their shoulders.

Lily, standing on the road above the drift mouth, saw them come out. She thought the shift was over, and decided then what she was going to do. She looked at the sky, and at the little gold watch pin her father had given her for her eighteenth birthday. Away down the hill she could see Eduardo running up the road. He stopped for a minute at the chain on the Godley road with a man she didn't recognize so far away. Lily smiled. There was plenty of time and she was safe from Eduardo. She watched him vault the chain and thought, Animal spirits. They have that, and then sadly, more than we do.

Mr. Roundtree saw Eduardo away in the distance, running toward the chain where Anderson Carver lounged against a tree, bored and half asleep. He glanced up and saw who it was. He shifted his rifle and the gesture made Mr. Roundtree start, ready to run. What he thought, the thing that stopped him, was said by Mr. McLeod when it didn't need to be: "Wee Eddie will no want to see you."

If Mr. McLeod had any opinion about the last setting-out at Godley, he gave no sign. His opinion of the way it had been done was another matter. He said, "Tis the maythod I abhor, Mr. Roundtree." He read a lot, mostly speeches by Keir Hardie. "Ach, the wee sons of bitches, they brought trouble." Since Mr. McLeod never left the obvious unsaid, slowly and carefully, Mr. Roundtree had learned not to listen.

He couldn't get out of his mind that Lily would blame him. He knew how unfair her passions made her. He had been scanning the road for Eduardo ever since he'd seen the Baldwin men coming down out of Italian Hollow. Goujot was carrying papers. The others seemed, in the distance, to be joking. Mr. Roundtree had known then, before he was told, what had happened. He wanted to catch Eduardo and explain that it wouldn't have happened if— if what? He had been there? He'd been on his way to Mr. Lacey's when he heard the shots. He had almost convinced himself that he had gone on then, but he hadn't. He'd known. He must have known, he told himself. When he got back to the Club House with the doctor, there were only Neill and Pat Hand still there. He hadn't seen the others go up Italian Hollow. He wanted to tell Eduardo that when he got to the chain. The boy seemed to be running in place in the distance, prolonging the moment.

The road in front of Mr. Roundtree's window was as empty as only a road at six o'clock in the evening in a deserted town could be. Usually at six o'clock there was the sound of children at the creek, and a crowd of men on the porch of the Company Store in summer, or on the big log across the road near the company Boarding House. Now there was only dust in the last sun, and there had not been a movement since Neill had sent Anderson Carver to report formally that the last of the strikers were out of the houses. Anderson Carver couldn't stop that slack-jawed grin of a lush all the time he was making his report. He didn't say who had been set out, and Mr. Roundtree didn't satisfy his grin by mentioning their names, but he knew. Mr. McLeod had run all the way up Italian Hollow and back and for once he didn't say anything when he got back but "they've set the Paganos out and thrown out their wee bits and pieces."

He saw Anderson straighten up in loose sections, saw him hold the rifle across Eduardo's body, heard his voice far away, a thin yell, "You can't come in here you Dago redneck sonabitch." "You cannot be both," Mr. McLeod said. "Either you are a redneck from the hills or you are a Dago from Italy. Although I've heard it said that the phrase 'redneck' originally came from the followers of Garibaldi."

Mr. Roundtree saw Eduardo stop. The boy seemed to cave in

for a second. He knew what it was on his face, the fear of power from another man for the first time in his life, blind power like a wall in front of him, the dangerous stupidity of it. Mr. Roundtree had sensed it, that caving in called growing up, the first time he had obeyed a stupid order from a man more powerful and less intelligent than himself; knelt, in his mind, to that force. It crossed his mind that you never got over that choice, and it was, after all, a choice. After the first time it had been easier, and he had even seen, with his intelligence at least, the reason for that split-second decision to survive without trouble. He knew the boy wouldn't be the same after that, whether he ever knew it or not.

The boy said something, he couldn't hear what. He saw him vault the chain. Anderson Carver called after him, "I let your mother keep her little statue," and then he was back leaning against the tree and staring down the road even before Eduardo came abreast of the Company Store, running.

Mr. Roundtree must have made a second move to go out and stop him, or call out the window. He had a need to tell him something. But Mr. McLeod held his arm.

"What have you to say to him?" Then, in his Keir Hardie voice, "You would do it only to ease your own capitalist conscience." Mr. McLeod was a socialist, but he kept it all for evenings when they drank together. He did not let it interfere with his work.

Mr. Roundtree knew Mr. McLeod wouldn't let him find any more excuses not to go to the Boarding House. They waited until the road was clear to go across to talk to the transportation men, who had been locked in there for thirty hours waiting for him to make up his mind. From the middle of the road, Mr. Roundtree could see them at the windows, watching him. He felt vulnerable, exposed to their eyes and their silence.

Then somebody yelled from the window. "Hey, Jock, what are ye doing there? We ain't dogs, you know."

McLeod said, "As ye no doubt remember, there are some Yanks in there, a wild and dissolute lot."

"I thought they told Williams not to send anyone who spoke English." Mr. Roundtree stopped, annoyed, as if he'd heard this for the first time. Mr. McLeod, for once, did not play conscience. He knew how a man's mind could pivot toward something else when his real fury lay deep and impotent.

Up the road at the Club House, Dan Neill watched Eduardo run into Dago Hollow. He still held the incriminating documents, as Mr. Goujot called them, forgetting to put them down. When Goujot made a move to go after the boy, Dan Neill said, "Let him go," and looked back at the paper in his hands.

"He's on company property," Goujot told him. He hated that manicured hand holding good evidence like it was something dirty.

Dan Neill said nothing, but he thought, The dumb bastards. Out of the whole turnover of the house they had found only a dated copy of the *Labor Argus*, and old UMW journals. Who the dumb bastards were he didn't bother to think.

The birds were back, as after rain. It was so quiet in the hollow that Eduardo could hear the evening breeze high in the trees. Everything that had been familiar stood out in the stark detail of a new, strange place. He saw something shining in the creek, where the last filter of sunlight touched the water. It was Annunziata's painting. Even that was false. The Virgin and the potato Baby undulated in the water. It had only been paper pasted on board. The water had loosened it. A final tug of the current released the paper print. It floated downstream past the bust of Dante and curled around a rock.

It seemed important to set Francesco's statue upright again, even though there was nothing for it to guard. The yard where the flowers had been was tramped flat. Down at the creek the vegetable garden was flat, too. Annunziata's chickens picked and scratched at the broken plants.

Eduardo found an orange crate that was still whole. Maria had lined it with red silk to hold her comb and brush and her jar of Pond's cold cream. Eduardo tore out the lining and set it aside to use as a cover. He paid more attention to his separate movements than he ever had before in his life. He was conscious of how slowly he moved. It took him until seven o'clock to round up eight of the chickens and get them into the crate. All the time he tried to

133

take an inventory in his mind of what was worth coming back for. Thrown out like that, it looked dead, nothing but broken junk, all that pride of hers, a pile of junk. He kicked a frying pan as hard as he could, watched it tumble across the back porch and then ran to retrieve it. Then he combed the empty house for clothes. The only thing that struck him as obscene, that made a sense of wanting to kill rise so fast in him that his teeth clenched and he couldn't swallow, were all the clothes, tipped out on the floor from the old trunk they'd brought from Italy, torn out of the closet Francesco had made, with its carved door and its finished shelves. It was the finest piece of furniture in the house, but it couldn't be moved. He had built it into the wall like American closets, New World.

The mattress, stained with old love, old childbirth and children's night-wetting in whitened patches where Annunziata had scrubbed and bleached them, lay half on, half off the brass bed, the letto matrimoniale, the center. It was polished nearly white. It shimmered in the mess, reflecting a last streak of sun. It had been too big to get down the stairs. Francesco had taken the stair rail down to get it into the bedroom. Eduardo remembered that from when he was little. He put the mattress back on the bed and folded the clothes, the private clothes that no one ought to see, very carefully on the bed, more carefully than he had ever done when Annunziata nagged him.

He found an old sanitary towel that Maria had hidden away until she had a chance to wash it. They shouldn't have touched it, the men, flung it out on the floor like that. His tears dropped on the stained rag in his hand. He hid it as carefully as Maria had.

When he had finished he walked down the stairs, seeing from above them glimpses of the deserted rooms. Annunziata's wallpaper, the big red roses from the Company Store, Francesco's yellow paint, all the attempts to make theirs what was not theirs seemed pathetic against the bare boards, the essential emptiness of the house, its echo, its raw-wood smell now that the cooking was gone.

He was glad to get out again into the evening and hear the chickens clucking under the red silk cover of the crate.

He knew better than to go back down the hollow. Up the path on the mountain, he saw Maria's comb. He heaved the chickens upon his shoulder, took the frying pan in his other hand and started up the mountain. He climbed through twilight and into darkness. If he thought anything at all he never remembered it, although he tried later. The next thing he remembered was coming down the path toward Jake Catlett's house. In the window he saw Annunziata and the children at Essie's table. Steve and Jake and his father were talking by the stove. He watched them go out to the front porch. The old woman, Mother Jones, and Essie went on washing dishes. It was all calm. It looked like a family, any evening. He noticed, for the first time, how gray his mother's hair had become. He hadn't known that before. He wished she'd straighten it. After all, she was the Catletts' company, for the first time in ten years.

He could just see Carlo Michele, not part of anything. He was leaning against the wall, in his self-conscious Italian hat. Everybody seemed to have forgotten him. Eduardo suddenly didn't have any idea what to do with the eight chickens in the crate.

Even though he knew there were thirty men in the Boarding House, spread somewhere through its eight rooms, the house seemed barren and empty to Mr. Roundtree as he unlocked the door and stepped into the bare hall. For a second he had a wild hope, or despair, that they had all gone, that he wouldn't have to deal with them. As he let himself think this, he heard one of the cots creak upstairs, the sound of a body turning and turning again. He knew then that the absence of voices was the silence of waiting.

He knew that McLeod had told them all, conveyed as best he could, what was expected of them, but there were so many he couldn't get to over the barrier of language.

There was no smell of cooking, only dust, bare boards, and the smell of men who had been locked in for thirty hours, sweat and full chamber pots, from the opened windows a scent of breeze and green leaves.

He found something to say. "How long since these men have eaten?"

Mr. McLeod was a little offended. "One cheese sandwich for Jews, one ham sandwich for gentiles only an hour ago. They've no complaints. I brought food to be cooked this morning and the men threw it out of the upstairs window."

Mr. Roundtree opened the first door. Already the men had formed themselves into pools of isolation. Two Orthodox Jews sat on one of the cots, side by side, in black overcoats, with their hats on. Even after being locked in a train for sixteen hours, and then in the Boarding House for thirty, they managed to look neat and calm. They simply waited without any emotion at all, sitting together.

On a cot by the window a young boy lay with his face to the wall. He was crying, or had been; the deep breaths sounded like after-sobs. A young giant with a heavy face and yellow hair cut with a pudding bowl sat on the fourth bed. He seemed relaxed except that his hands gave him away. They were clenched so that the knuckles showed white against dirt and hair.

Mr. Roundtree said, "Do you speak English?" very slowly, to the room.

The giant answered, his voice gentle and small for such a man. It had not been fury but nervousness that made his hands clench.

"My name is Joseph Brodowski. I am Polish."

"How do you do?" Mr. Roundtree held out his hand, and it was grasped in a great paw. Joseph Brodowski smiled, and Mr. Round-tree realized that he couldn't be more than eighteen.

"You understand why you are here? You signed on willingly for a job with Mr. Williams." He consulted the manifest that Mr. McLeod held out.

"My name is Joseph Brodowski. I am Polish," the giant boy said again, grabbing for Mr. Roundtree's hand.

"Christ, does anyone here speak Polish and English?" Mr. Roundtree asked Mr. McLeod.

One of the Jews got up from the cot. "How do you do?" he said, "I am Joseph Rabinowitz and this is my brother Chaim. I am speaking Polish, English, German, and Yiddish. My French? Enh!" He came forward, his carefully kept, now very dirty hand held out politely, drawing Mr. Roundtree into an embarrassed handshake. "There was no use in speaking until we were very sure of someone in authority to whom we could explain that there has been a grave error." He said this calmly, a man who seemed quite sure that with patience and wisdom, in the face of any circumstances, there would somewhere be logic, reason, and justice.

"No mistake." Mr. McLeod pointed to their names on the manifest. "They won't eat."

"May I explain?" the speaking brother went on politely. "We were told in New York that there was a need for our trade in this place. We have relatives in Canona. So we consulted together with each other and thought to come here under this contract would not present so great a burden on our relatives."

Mr. McLeod was getting restive. "You signed on." He hit the manifest. "Here. You signed . . ."

"Yes, but as tailors, you understand. We were told that there was a need for tailors."

Mr. Roundtree erupted. "Why the hell didn't you tell me these men spoke English?"

Mr. McLeod yelled back, "Look at them. How would I know? Some nature of Wog! Do they look like they speak English? I bleedin' ask you."

The talkative brother cleared his throat. "I see that you have been put into a very unfortunate position to which you are reacting with anger. Now there are several points my brother and I have discussed in order to place them before the proper authorities." The boy on the bed sobbed aloud once, and the young Pole smiled at anyone who said anything, as if the recognition that they were speaking would somehow help him to understand.

"First, we would like to wash."

There was dead silence in the room.

"We would also like to be escorted safely out of this place, since not only were we misinformed about employment, we were also not informed that there was a strike."

"You were told there was a strike." Mr. McLeod told this to Mr. Roundtree. "Williams said every man was told there was a strike."

"I am most exceedingly sorry. We were not informed that there was a strike."

"Don't you call me a liar," Mr. McLeod's face and neck had begun to swell. "I'll break your goddamned haid."

"Goyim nachus," the brother on the bed pointed out.

"He doesn't speak English as well as I," Mr. Rabinowitz explained. "As for food. We most certainly did not mean to cause offense, but we follow strict laws. Kosher."

The young Pole had caught the word. Kosher. His face went dark and he stood up. He spoke very loudly in Polish and then he sat down again.

"He says he is insulted to have been put into a room with Jews," Mr. Rabinowitz explained, still in the same calm, polite voice. "Poles are very proud of their anti-Semitism. This is our main reason for coming to this country. Now, in parts of . . ." He seemed prepared to explain all this, but Mr. Roundtree had had enough.

"Go out into the hall, and take your bags," he told the brothers. "If you will interpret for me I will see that you get to Canona . . . I speak only English and some French," he added apologizing.

They picked up their carpetbags, some books, and moved out into the hall, where several men had gathered at the sound of voices.

The Pole grinned and tried to grab Mr. Roundtree's hand to shake it again, but he missed. Mr. Roundtree had gone over to the boy on the bed.

"Sixteen years old. French." Mr. McLeod read the manifest with some contempt.

Mr. Roundtree felt more secure about dealing with the crying boy, who lay quite still, his legs drawn up against his chest as if he knew they were standing over him but was afraid to turn and face them. Mr. Roundtree had been to France several times and had, he told himself, gotten along rather well.

"Comment allez-vous?" he said to the boy's back.

"J'ai du mal," came from the buried face.

"Très mal!" Mr. Roundtree tried to sound stern. "He says he is behaving badly," he explained to Mr. McLeod. He wished he knew how to say "Pull yourself together," but he knew it wouldn't have done any good unless the boy was English. So he said instead, "Votre nom?" He lilted this at the end carefully to show it was a question.

At the sound of French words the boy had begun to unfold. He sat up and rubbed his fists into his eyes. His face was streaked with dirt and tears.

"Now that is a distasteful sight," Mr. McLeod grumbled. "I told you Williams had sent an inferior transportation. I also told you

138

that it was getting harder to find foreigners who don't know about the union troubles. I also—"

"I know you did. Eh, uh, maintenant . . ."

The boy began to explain something in rapid-fire French, none of which Mr. Roundtree could follow.

"Parlez trop vite! Parlez lentement!" he ordered.

The boy looked confused.

"Votre nom?"

"Jean-Paul Sonier." The rapid French began again.

"Shut up," Mr. McLeod told him.

"Pardon me, I beg of you," Mr. Rabinowitz pushed past them and sat down beside the boy. He put an arm around him.

"This boy has also been misled. He is an apprentice chef de cuisine, a cook. A French-speaking employee of this Mr. Williams told him cooks were needed here."

"Very well. We will send over some food and he can cook for these men. Now—" Mr. Roundtree turned around to the men at the door and said loudly, "How many miners here?"

One of the men at the back shoved the others aside. "There's ten of us here worked for Mr. Williams before. You ain't got nuthin' to worry about. You git 'em a pick and shovel and we'll git 'em to the coal-face."

"Where did you work before?" Mr. Roundtree started to take the manifest from Mr. McLeod to check it.

"Pennsylvania, Colorado. We're strikebreakers. Couple days these men will mine you some coal. There's two rooms full of Dagoes upstairs; they been raisin' hell."

Mr. Roundtree was suddenly very tired. He had taken a step in the wrong direction and it had led him deeper and deeper in slime. He called Mr. Rabinowitz, "Will you come with me, please?" and pushed on through the corridor of men in the hall. He trudged up the stairs slowly. Mr. McLeod, behind him, read his bowed back.

"If you lie down with a beggar you get up with fleas," he told him.

The upstairs hall was full of men. By the time Mr. Roundtree got to them he knew what he was going to say. He motioned to Rabinowitz to stand beside him.

"Tell these men that they have been misinformed. There is a

strike on here. They should have been told. Now, they have signed contracts to mine coal and they are in debt to the company for their transportation, for their board, and for picks, shovels, helmets, and shot that will be issued to them in the morning. They will have a hot meal served to them as soon as it can be cooked. The company cook was the wife of a miner and has left town. The shift will go into the mine at five o'clock tomorrow morning. The men will be guarded. The miners here are not violent. However, there may be some verbal abuse. And you men wash at the pump in the kitchen and clean this place up. It's a pigpen. There's no use trying to run away. The guards will see that you fulfill your contracts."

He pushed his way through the knots of men and walked away from Mr. Rabinowitz, who had begun speaking softly. He felt sick as he crossed the road, unlocked the Company Store and kicked open the door. "McLeod, goddammit come here!" he yelled across the road.

Mr. McLeod crossed the road slowly. "I had to check the rest of the manifest to see that none of them had run away."

"Where the hell could the poor buggers run to? Most of them don't even know what state they're in."

Mr. Roundtree had found a Kellogg's Corn Flakes box. He threw it to Mr. McLeod. "Put all the fresh vegetables and bread you can find in that."

"But it's our own supply," Mr. McLeod said. When he saw Mr. Roundtree's face he, for once, did as he was told without any more comment. Mr. Roundtree was throwing corned beef, sardines, baked beans into an orange crate. The Company Store had been closed for a month, and the dust was thick. Red dog covered his clothes and his face. "Goddammit to hell," he yelled when a can missed the crate.

Mr. McLeod lugged it all over to the Boarding House in the dusk. He motioned to the French boy to follow him into the kitchen. He grabbed him by the arm, pointed to the stove, pointed to his own mouth, pointed to the tin plates, the huge pots, made chewing noises, stabbed the air with his free hand six times to show thirty, herded the boy over to the box and the crate, and shook an ear of corn in his face. By the time he had finished the boy was in tears again and the crowd of men who had followed them were in an uproar of laughter, pushing at each other so they could see better.

"Mr. Rabinowitz!" Mr. McLeod yelled.

"I am truly sorry but it is against my religion to touch that food," came Mr. Rabinowitz's soft voice, "except, of course, for the vegetables, which we will prepare for ourselves."

III

7:00 P.M. to Midnight,
Friday, June 7, 1912

Jesus Christ! If you want the truth of anything that happened, don't listen to Mary Rose. She'll tell everything exactly as she wishes it was and believe every word of it. Poor little old thing, she's so careless with the truth by now that if I didn't love her I'd call her a damned liar. She's thirty years old and I swear to God I hear her voice on the telephone and she still sounds fifteen like she did that awful summer in 1912 she keeps dwelling on. She was a pretty little thing then, too. Looked like Bessie Love? Mary Pickford? No. One of the Gishes. A Gish with some bitch in her. Now she works in the library and has two shirtwaists and looks like a picked chicken. You know that neat look the genteel poor have? Come to think of it, there's a lot of chicken running in our family.

Not me, though, not Althea, thank you very much! I got married and I was the first one to bob my hair.

Mary Rose has rearranged her whole puny little past to suit herself. She always swore all those wise men from the East came the day before the first real trouble happened. They did not. She only wants it to be that way. My God, you'd think old John D. himself came down to consult Papa to hear her tell it. She just can't stand it that nobody gave a damn.

I don't know when they did come but it was earlier. Little bit earlier. How do I know? Must have been at least May, though. We were in white and Papa insisted, by the calendar, that his girls greet the May, as he called it, in white dresses. He made a little ceremony out of it. Poor Papa, he liked things like that. Mother made fun of him, but he had a sentimental streak. Talk about victims. Why, he was as handsome, upright a man as you could hope for until that day. It was after that he began to go downhill. Bunch of outside agitators and foreigners came in there and interfered when everything was going so well. They lied, too. They all lie. Papa's men just worshipped the ground he walked on. They never would have let him down unless they got all stirred up by outside agitators.

I know it sure God changed my life. Althea Lacey, the Pearl of the Mountains! Look at me now, if you care to. God knows I don't give a damn.

Strike, strike, strike! I'm sick and tired of hearing about it. Who cares? It's old water over a forgotten dam. Nobody got killed or I would remember. Besides, they said he was a socialist anyway stirring up trouble. They! The biggest liar on earth. *I* could tell them the facts of the matter. People always want to know what *happened* to everybody. I could tell them, but who asks me? Althea's got a wet brain. Althea tells everything from her own pointaview. Well who the hell doesn't? They never did treat me like I had sense enough to come in out of the rain.

If you want to know why I was not consulted about any of the decisions at the time, whether they affected my life or not, I'll tell anybody who'll listen. They're afraid of my truthful tongue and they always have been. I can tell what happened better drunk than the rest of them can sober. Remember fifteen years ago like it was yesterday. Hell yes. Dreams and gin are no respecters of time.

Why in God's name do I wake up in this crumpled bed morning after morning, just fell asleep, if anybody wants to know the truth, but who does? I know I never did. I went to bed with a bunch of magazines, Sister French doll with the long, long legs I had to buy myself. Nobody thought to give me one when they are all the rage. Brother Gin from the bathtub, and the radio playing "I can't give you anything but love." I woke up to some fellow with the news and I turned it off. Who invited him into my bedroom? To tell the truth, since that's what I'm trying to do, I passed out.

Most of this room is designed to get my goddamn sister-in-law's goat, the *True Confessions* and the *Photoplay*, the French dolls and the Spanish galleon, and the fringe and the balls. I hate them. They're all to remind Sally Brandon Neill McKarkle of Country Club fame that it's no use taking me to raise. She thinks I just don't know any better. I've heard her say it out of that mean little mouth. "Poor thing, she just doesn't know." Oh yes I do, Miss High and Mighty, better than you ever will. The trouble is you come to, wake up, and there you are for a minute naked as a jaybird to anytime, anyplace, anybody your dreams have brought you, and to me, this morning it isn't morning and I've been with that son of a bitch Broker Carver. Look at him now, took that wartime coal money and parlayed it into a fortune. Anderson Carver!

Lord's love, I can't think what we were then. It was something like that Lily used to spout. Then was, was then, who cares? She was always holding forth, carrying on, and if she thought the boys cared for that kind of behavior she was vastly mistaken. She never fooled them, not for a minute. She only fooled herself. You don't go up the mountain to "read" to the boys with a rose on your skinny little throat. Lord's love, I could have told her that.

In my dream—I'm lying in the hammock, right after supper. It's deep twilight, almost dark, and I'm thinking, if you want to call it that, about Anderson. All that golden summer I missed Anderson and when I dream I miss Anderson, just like I did that night, not like he is now God knows but like he was then. I'd slipped up and loosed my stays. It was too late for Mother to notice and send me upstairs. She watched me like a hawk, how we ever got born I'll never know. She'd gone to bed with one of her splitting headaches, so I felt safe.

Oh God I missed Anderson. In my dream I'm lying there with one foot on the porch, swinging and missing. The longing was a heavier weight on me than Anderson's body. In those days, he was light, all the kinds of light, including being half-lit, but I didn't care. I can still smell his skin and his white linen shirt and the patchouli and the feel of his smooth stomach against mine and the night and the damp grass and the release of the honeysuckle still warm. Anderson was the great love of my life. I was crazy about Anderson, wild about Anderson. I hid a towel in the potting shed so she wouldn't find grass stains on my skirt. Can you imagine your mother inspecting you for grass stains these days, girls high-tailing it around in skirts up to their heinies, sassing their parents?

Ah well, last year's crop of kisses! Lily said I was making a fool of myself. All I have to say is they all had one thing in common. None of them have ever been in fool heaven like I was that summer, when you're more than you can be and yet you are, and everything seems to glow and every least little thing is remembered, a note in the bushes, a shirt button dropped. I treasured one note, one shirt button, a handkerchief and a powder box with an old-fashioned lady in a lavender skirt for a lid he gave me for my birthday. It was just trash but it was pure gold to me. He got it at the Company Store. It's right there on the chifforobe that used to be in Lily's room but I got it. I love to use that word "chifforobe" and watch Sally Brandon Neill McKarkle cringe. She's very careful to say "chest." She also says "chest" about breasts. Well she's right about herself there!

I didn't give a shit about the strike. I thought it's brought me Anderson. Later it was a different story, I'll tell the world. It ruined Papa and it was the ruination of me, but then that evening I just lay in the hammock and waited. My beautiful titian hair was loose around me. I had the most beautiful hair in the family. When I got it bobbed I cried all day. I'll never forget it as long as I live, lying there shining on the black-and-white tile floor of the barbershop. The barber turned the chair around to the mirror and I had this little tiny pinhead. When I cried all day, Dan Neill left the house. He didn't deign to understand. He said, "I'll be back when this one is over," and he walked out. As if I lost my crowning glory every day of the week.

I lay there in the hammock feeling that Anderson would come. I've always felt things. I'm psychic. One thing was—I was a favorite of somebody. Lily was Mother's favorite and Rosie was Papa's. I never had been anybody's favorite around there, not until Anderson. He had a soft voice then and cool hands and he called me his Pearl of the Mountains.

I could just hear a buzz of voices in the library. They'd slammed the window down so I couldn't hear anything they said. I didn't give a damn anyway. If it had been Rosie the Eavesdropper she'd of been glued to the window, but I, oh Lord's love, didn't I my love, didn't I, though, have better things to occupy my mind? Of course, even if I hadn't seen them troop in I would have known from the tones who was there. I remember they were in the hall first. Papa's lovely quiet voice, "Now gentlemen, I'm sure . . ." Jake Catlett's mumble. Papa said when Jake was mad, he talked so slow you could hear his voice creak—"Bev, gawd dammit," were his last words before the door shut and just those words had carried him all the way through the hall. They had that Dago Pagano with them, right in the library like a white man. Mother would never have allowed that if she'd been well. Then of course there was Dan Neill's voice, beyond all mortals, his poorhouse Tory drawl from way up at Princeton above the lowly world. "Surely you must know, Cousin Jake." He always called Jake Catlett cousin, but he made it sound like he was condescending. Condescending. I think my in-laws condescend to shit. "Surely you must know, mere mortal!" He still says it all the time.

So does Sally Brandon, the stuck-up skinny-necked bitch. Surely you must know, oh whatever it is, whatever pin, whatever needle she wants to stick in me. You don't wear this with that and you don't eat that with this and you don't use them with those and these with they, to which my answer to my beloved sister-in-law is Fuck you Miss Sally, if you'll pardon my French. They make me downright sick. All of their Senator Daniel Neill this and Senator Daniel Neill that. Senator Neill was a war-profiteering son of a bitch and they all know it. My granddaddy said he bought his Senate appointment and everything else that wasn't nailed down after the war until the bubble burst. If I have to hear one more time how "Pa and Ma" got married in Washington and the President himself came—Chester A. Arthur, for the love of Pete! Standing on such a rock I look down my nose! Well, we know what happened to "Pa"! A shot in the head. She says he took the gentleman's way out. I think he just got damned sick and tired of listening to them. What in the name of God she's got to be putting on airs for I don't know. Well I remember when Mr. and Mrs. High-toned McKarkle lived up Catlett Creek and he ran the mine and voted Republican and they went to the Methodist Church and she called Crawford McKarkle Mooney like everybody else. Don't think I don't remind her when she's up on her Democratic Episcopal Country Club high horse either, the persnickety thing. Even her collars are little and mean.

All that and she hasn't even been abroad. I have. I was a girl, just lovely. Oh I was the loveliest thing when I was a girl. Mother had bought me a hat in the Via Condotti in Rome. It was the loveliest thing you ever saw and it cost the earth, pale gray clouds of georgette with pink rosebuds faint behind them. I can still smell that smell of a costly hat before the Great War, smell of tissue paper, silk, and straw and hear the sound of the weightless lifting of it, a rustle and a falling breeze of tissue paper, and it had no weight at all and I moored it to my head with my best hatpin, filigreed gold, oh absolutely lovely, and I sallied out to meet my dear one who had followed us all the way from Lausanne. We were madly in love.

Shit. I don't even remember his name. But I do remember the black trees, and the old, old shade, and I remember the hat, perched on the grass like a gray dove and I lost my cherry in the Borghese Gardens, which is more than they can say. Mary Rose's still got hers. You can tell by her face. She's only got Bubba Leftwich for a beau and God knows he won't take it without benefit of clergy not with Mother on the prowl. He drives a Stutz Bearcat but it doesn't help. Mother can't abide him. Mary Rose got a permanent wave but that didn't help either, just frizzled her hair. She's no vamp, God knows. Mother hit the roof.

Anyway there I was flat on my back in the Borghese Gardens at three o'clock in the afternoon. I didn't care what anybody thought. They were only foreigners.

God we were lovely. Our love made us clever and we never got caught, not by Mother and not by you know. I never could see anything wrong with it—it's a need like any other, an act of generosity almost, nothing to be ashamed of. Just life.

We were madly in love but he's not in my dreams—not like Anderson. Why, I sang all that summer in my secret heart of course, the song of Anderson. Let him come. Oh God let him come. Oh now, if I hold my breath he'll turn the corner of the porch and come up the steps oh so light and he will close over me like a great bird in fine linen and sometimes, oh my God, we'd only had to touch our bodies together, only that, we'd waited so long through the long, long day and we were so madly in love. I just lay there in the purple twilight that evening, letting the night come softly, praying and yearning, and I could hear down by the tents one of the Italians singing a love song I thought, just for me, that pure voice drifting up through the trees, some operatic song, the kind they like, and I thought, Bishop Dunne was right when he investigated their living conditions. They are so artistic, and have those lovely voices, and they keep pigs right under the houses. He said they were being led by selfish interests like lambs to the slaughter.

Well, it was Lily who interrupted that little bit of peace and quiet. Going around like that! Not that I want to speak ill of poor Lily but I think intellectual women are more immoral than I ever was. I was always passionately in love and couldn't help myself —but women like Lily, all that don't wear stays and let your body breathe and sashaying around the lawn in your shimmy shirt. Eurythmics. Hunh! Lily was advertising something she didn't know the name of. At least I delivered the goods. Papa was wrong though. He said it was provocative to flaunt yourself like that and Lily said it most certainly wasn't meant to be. Well, meant or not, I could have taught her more than books. Men like all those clothes, all those buttons, layers of sweet surprises, the weightless falling of silk and lace and petticoats. Just like uncovering that lovely hat from its box. These girls running around in skirts above their heinies and nothing else don't know what they're missing, I'll tell the world.

Lily needn't to try to fool me. I had her number. She was after Dan Neill all the time, you could tell that. With her airy fairy Lillian and her airs and graces—all aloof in corners at him. But it was me that got him. I wouldn't have looked twice at him if it hadn't been for her. Her making out to be so high and mighty, her with the rose at her skinny neck. Oh sure, she hightailed out of there and left him to me thanks for everything. I was the Pearl, the Pearl of the Mountains, not you.

Poor Lily! Went out to make the world safe for democracy on what was left of Papa's money. I know you oughtn't to speak ill and all that but Lily was a damned fool and we paid. God deliver me from a reformer.

I always have thought it was something happened that night made her hightail off like she did. She never lived with us after that. Oh, she'd come home to visit but you could feel the duty in her walk and in her look when she did. You know that patience that says how long before the next train leaves? I always wondered if she was raped that night. She certainly came in looking like something the cat dragged in. *I've* always thought whatever it was happened that night upset her equilibrium. Why else would somebody traipse off to a war wasn't any of her damned business? Don't try to fool a drunk. Lily *wanted* to die. I'm absolutely sure of that. She made a will and left me her chifforobe. She knew I liked it.

I'm sure Mother thought it was rape, too, or worse, that Lily had *liked* it because I could hear their voices after everybody had gone to sleep, and Mother had that where-have-you-been-at-this-hour-of-the-night tone she usually saved for me and it can still freeze me so bad that only Brother Gin can melt me, deafen me, relax me, and like the Prayer Book says, grant me peace.

I can still see Lily pussyfooting out on the porch that evening. She was sidling around the Gatling gun like it was a snake. It's funny the way I see her, teetering on the porch steps, still in her white dress, and that damn rose at her throat. She was hiding something and I couldn't let that pass. I just rocked the hammock and let the chains squeak and she turned around like the gun had gone off and saw me. I didn't say a word. I just waited.

She came over and leaned down and whispered, "Allie, please don't tell on me."

My God, as if I hadn't sneaked off in the bushes myself. I had to laugh.

"You won't, will you?"

I played at whispering, too. "I'm just glad," I told her. I lay back and smiled and had a good cat stretch. I was, too. I wasn't the only one. That's why I was glad. I knew exactly what Miss High-Browed was up to. I just nodded no. I thought I'd store up a little complicity for later use.

She ran off the porch and down the side lawn toward the tennis court. It was still light enough to see what she was hiding. It was Papa's miner's helmet with his head lamp. My God why go there —all that dirt!

She hadn't been gone a minute when Mary Rose sneaked out; she was a natural spy.

Of course she asked me if Lily had told me where she was going. I told her it wasn't any of her damned business.

"I know already Miss Priss and I'm going to tell Mother."

"Come over here," I said real sweet, and when she leaned over I twisted her arm. "You'll do nothing of the kind," I told her, "or you'll have me to answer to." I'm glad I did that. Not that it did much good, but in the light of what happened it made me feel better. Anyway I wanted to get her off the porch because at any minute Anderson might come around through the dusk and take me in his arms.

She wouldn't leave. She just pressed her head up against the library window.

"Papa's men have come out on strike," she told me. "They've set the Paganos out." Then, "Mooney's condition has improved."

"If you don't go back in the house I'll never lend you anything as long as I live," I told her. That made her skedaddle. Poor little Mary Rose. I remember how pretty she was then. Now look at her. She slaves in the library all day long and then goes straight home to look after Mother. I'd do more but, after all, I am married, if you want to call it that.

I knew then that Anderson wouldn't come, but he did—just long enough to hold me. All of the night flowers had released their scent and it was that purple last light I just love. He came over me in the swing and it was a moment of joy, especially when they could have come out on the porch any minute. I touched him there and there and he said "No, honey, I've got to work" but it was too late. I still have the handkerchief. It was the least I could do with him so worried.

How was I to know it was never, never again and God knows I'm high and dry now, waking up like this morning after morning. Where's the money I was brought up to expect? Where's the man I was given every reason to suppose I would love?

Don't mention troubles to me—mine troubles or men troubles or money troubles. They're all the same when you come to think of it. Dan Neill seemed so capable and aloof. Why didn't anybody *tell* me? After my papa died and he took over and things were booming he was our white hope. Even Mother said so. It was a rescue. All he lacked was a white horse. He got me, the most popular of the three girls, and a controlling interest, and none of it's worth a hill of beans.

The sun hurts my eyes. This room needs dusting. I'll have to speak to her. They're not worth a nickel these days. Not like it was. Powder on the vanity, dust on the chifforobe. I could write my name on it. Mrs. Daniel Chester Neill after Chester A. Arthur. Tragedy hell. It's all very well to bleat over what's happened to them but what about me? Sitting here day after day with Sister French doll and old Brother Gin. Where's Dan when he's needed? Sitting in the Riverview Hotel playing poker, or getting hauled home dead drunk with two black eyes. My best friend is the Crosley Radio Corporation in Cincinnati. Just tell me that. What about me?

On Friday, May 7, 1915, a month before Lily graduated from Vassar, the *Lusitania* was sunk with a thousand Americans lost, including Charles Frohman and Cornelius Vanderbilt. Her mother wrote that war was certainly no respecter of wealth. Lily decided what she was going to do without saying a word to a soul. Her mother, still in mourning, and Mary Rose and Althea in white came to see her graduate, and she told them nothing. All through the ceremonies she had the familiar sense of being in the wrong place, on the wrong side of a gulf, that the heart of things was somewhere else. This time the heart of things was war.

When she read the advertisement in *The New York Times* by the Imperial German Embassy warning Americans not to travel on ships flying the flag of Great Britain, she booked her passage on the Cunard Line. It seemed the right thing to do. When she didn't go home with her mother, she lied to her for the first time directly instead of by evasion. She said she had a job in New York. She timed the letter home so that it would arrive too late for anyone to stop her. Her mother cried over the long-distance telephone and said it was a selfish thing to do, but to go to Altman's and buy what she needed and not to forget that anything stronger than senna pods upset her stomach.

So Lily went to war with a 1910 Baedeker guide to France, a case of Hines Honey and Almond Cream, senna pods, heavy underwear from Altman's, and on the advice of the British Army recruiting office on Broadway, a large supply of gramophone needles, popular records, and chocolate for the troops. It was not until she went to Paignton in England as probationer nurse in a Voluntary Aid Detachment that she found out that she spoke a different language.

In May 1916, she was posted to France, to Voisincourt on the river Ancre, in the first detachment to open a hospital in the château. She looked it up in her Baedeker, which she kept hidden because it was published by a German company.

"The Château at Voisincourt is famous for its formal gardens. Part of the Château is fifteenth-century. It was enlarged in 1856." When they walked into the empty great hall it still smelled faintly of potpourri and polish.

The Matron, Armistead, pointed out, because she took for granted that Lily wouldn't know such things, being American, that Ward One, forty beds, was a smaller imitation of the Orangerie at Versailles. She had looked up at the gilded cherubs, and the painted ceiling. "God, it's dreadful," she had said. "Whiten it."

That was an order. Lily, terrified on her ladder, thought of trees, girdled with whitewash in front of Jake Catlett's house, and then of whited sepulchers and heard in herself the language still, no matter how hard she tried. When she thought about it in the dead of night she heard the old hymn, and the hosts of Midian prowl and prowl around, which had been her image of terror of the dark outside her window when she was a child. She couldn't make her memory white, a tabula rasa. Sometimes, in piercing moments of homesickness, she didn't want to.

But aloud, she had learned to speak and understand a new language—a language of England, and soldiers and ladies. She found that her alien drawl frightened men who were too wounded, and any deviation from Matron's iron norm drew forth something in her eyes that was frigid and amused. I am blotting out Europe, Lily thought as she blobbed whitewash on a cherub's face, and remembered Italian hotel rooms—one, she couldn't remember

which, all red velvet and gilded mirrors with cherubs, fat ones—
and wanted to giggle, but didn't with Armistead standing, for once,
below her instead of looking down.

Lily heard Armistead call, "Now the ceiling, that dreadful false
Tiepolo. It was bad enough when it was real. My men won't want
to lie staring at obscene lovers."

Armistead had laughed, directing the orderlies and the proba-
tioners on the sixteen-foot ladders, clinging there more afraid of
her than of the height. She knew that, and it amused her. "This
is not the time," she had said below them.

There was nothing she could do about the wall of mirrors. In
the daytime they made a double room, the forty cots made eighty.
She had put the men with face wounds with their backs to the
mirrors.

In two weeks, the Orangerie was white. The black curtains between the French windows were clean columns in the daytime.
That pleased Armistead as if she had changed the prewar setting
of a play to one more fitting for a theater of war. Now it smelled
of lye, iodine, and Jeyes Fluid. Beyond the light of one small hooded
lamp, it was, at three o'clock in the morning on July 1, 1916, a
cavernous black space behind the regulation black curtains that
made the château a dark heap, huddled under the perpetual dawn
of bombardment.

When Lily made her rounds she took with her a flashlight that
pitched shadows over the sleeping men. She had been grateful on
the two o'clock round, guiltily grateful, that they were all, at last,
exhausted enough to sleep.

She looked at her little gold watch pin and did not sigh, kept
herself from it, too relaxed a gesture. She could not understand
the drowsiness that kept trying to close in on her. Then she heard
silence, shocking silence, after a week of bombardment, after night
duty on night duty, of men lying in silent stupor, kept awake by
the noise. Some of them stared at the white ceiling as if they
dared not shut their eyes. Their skin twitched and flowed even
though their bodies were dead-still. The nurses knew it as "from
the front" shock and waited for their voices, at first terrible, and
then slowly some of them found their names again, and their pasts.

They lay, the conscious ones, in a luxury of cleanliness and silence. They asked for small things—biscuits, chocolate, a cigarette, an apple. When the screens were put up around men about to die, the others heard them cry Mère, Mum, Mother, Mutter, ami, Kamerad, old pal, and once, one clear voice, "Get down, George, you bloody fool."

The nurses called each other by their last names, imitating the military, but the soldiers called Lily Sister Yank, and held her hand when Armistead was not around. They seemed to understand that it would get her into trouble. One time, at midmorning, in all that rush, Armistead had stopped, and watching her, said, in front of all of them, "We"—she used the imperial "we" easily—"know why you're here. Volunteered for personal reasons, I'm quite sure." What she thought they were she didn't say, but she made the unnamed reasons sound beneath contempt. "Oh God, American atonement!"

Armistead was a lady "in her own right," the men whispered, in some awe of her that Lily could not yet fathom. It was in her stride, and in her high piercing voice. Even so, she did strange things, like opening the nearest French door, no matter what the weather, if a man had died. "His soul has to be free," she explained.

In the stretched silence of the night Lily let herself retreat, for rest from all of them, back into the valley of her mind, almost homesick. She let herself hear the bird voices of her blood sisters. Althea called, "Lily, I know what you're up to! You can't fool me," and Mary Rose sang, "I'm going to tell my mama on you." The voices made her smile. The soldiers said that at the front, ten miles away, when the guns stopped, the birds sang.

Her attention diminished to the tiny, cozy circle of the lamp. When she looked up to her left, she could see herself in the little pool of light, reflected in a long mirror. She couldn't help looking up from time to time, finding company in her own image, the halo of hair she could not for the life of her keep under the white starched cap for more than half an hour, the rest an anonymity, a belonging in the white starched apron, the stiff collar and cuffs, the blue sleeves, the Red Cross on her left arm. She had earned in that anonymity a kind of freedom that chilled her when she thought of it. She didn't know why, but thought, One day I will understand this, but not yet.

Partly to keep herself alert, partly out of duty, she made herself write in her diary, avoiding, she told herself, abstractions. The abstract words "war, peace, justice" came so easily with fatigue and the dark. She wrote them down: "war, peace, justice, force," and thought, They will make me remember this time but I know they have no meaning. I've learned that at least. She wrote "state, state of war," and marked it out.

It was no protection from what she knew waited for her in the dark, a darkness she hadn't told about, that only she knew. She let it come, let it take its place in her mind, a space there, too, like the night, the demanded space they had always taken in her brain simply by being alive, not by earning it, as friends did, or books, or brave men, or lovers. A valley of them, sisters, parents, playmates; that part of her brain was a house they were born in and would not leave, for all her exorcising. She had tried to forget them and there had been spaces where she had. It was like the relief of realizing that someone she was in love with had disappeared for a while, leaving peace.

Then the letters came, the pathos of their innocence. The letters hurt her more even than what she saw every day and she could not understand that and resented it. She told herself that she let it happen to hide from herself the daily facts. "I can't get help," her mother wrote, meaning that she couldn't find a maid for the new house. She tried to sympathize and she found that her mother's words could make her cry, when she had long since stopped crying from fatigue, or even at death. Too much death, she told herself, becomes mundane.

At three o'clock her mother and her sisters were there in the false darkness, calling to her, more than the soldiers did. She heard a whimper, and in a reflex started up, and her shadow leaped among the cherubs, now white ghosts clinging to the white ceiling. It was a man asleep, fighting his dream. She sat down again and let herself give in to the demand that she remember, as she would have a demand for attention from a patient, as if giving in to it all the way would exorcise it and she could think of more important things. Recall was like a dream, too, the same fragments, some etched, pure vision, then spaces, then other vivid scenes.

She was in the tool shed and it was twilight and she still reached up to get her father's head lamp and his mine hat. She remembered being worried about how to control the oil wick. It must have been after supper, but when she tried to be there in the dining room, it was not that supper, but all the suppers. If there was a time in memory beyond the taken-for-granted dread of the black night she sat in, it was "used to"—a timeless safety of used to. Unlike the others she could not say, "Do you remember? We used to—oh, take the number eleven bus down Victoria Street, go to Epping Forest of a Sunday, hear Marie Lloyd." The comfort of her "used to" was a secret comfort she could neither share nor trust.

"Memory, not the present, which is shared, defines a stranger," she wrote. There was a vivid picture of Eduardo's mother, and of Eduardo's cousin whom she had seen only one time. She was surprised at that. She tried to bring back Eduardo's face, but couldn't. "You can't will recall," she added.

She had not known before she joined up, although she told herself she should have, how much injustice and joy people took for granted. It had taken war to make her recognize within her own memories something she had not known. People can live with terror. There was an inertia of acceptance that at times she found almost holy, at other times obscene. She wrote that down, and wrote:

"Yes," and looked at the word, and then, "yes" again. "We used to eat supper at the same time, all of us at the same places, growing up I suppose, but I don't remember any change. I remember us as always the same. We said 'always' and 'never' easily, especially when we were mad at each other. 'You always borrow my pretty things.' 'You never listen!' Mary Rose's voice. We don't grow. It is a child's memory.

"Althea sits on the other side of Mother. I can't see her face. She is against the light from the French doors. She has her head down. She eats desperately, as if the food might be taken away from her. Obsessive. She'll be fat, or a drunkard. I never saw her this way before, only now, with the light from the window like a halo around her red hair. Mary Rose sits beside her. I hear Mary Rose. She is a vague figure. I see black hair. She is always in movement. Now she is turning toward Papa whom I can't see. I never can. Mother sits between Althea and me, waiting. To speak? To interrupt? Her face is still. She is self-conscious in her stillness as if she were being watched. There is perpetual light there. I think it is natural undisturbed light I miss most, not this whited sepulcher of a hall by day, this cave by night, this monotony. How petty the days of war are, yet kind at the same time. People are tender with each other.

"That room is so far away. There's falseness about it, seeing it gilded with light like that, and smaller than it was, as if this present had diminished everything that came before it."

She stopped and was surprised at not hearing her pen move. No. She knew with her mind to distrust the light, but not with her heart. She made herself go on writing words to speak back to on paper. "Nostalgia consists of remembering things that never were that way," she wrote sensibly. Her pen stopped; after the scratching, silence, and she thought, Why tonight? Why are they here tonight? She knew what it was, the demanding echo. The last letter lay in her pocket. It cracked with the crackle of her apron. She was answering it in a way she would never answer it to them, exorcising with words what it brought to her surface in the darkness.

"You don't understand. You never will. Maybe you do, better than I, although it's quite"—she smiled at slipping into Armistead's English—"a horrid thought. You beg me not to break up the estate as if I were bombarding it instead of just taking my fair share. Letter after letter, that parade of letters please letters please"—her writing was heavier on the page. "DON'T YOU KNOW WHERE I AM?"

Money. Everywhere you turned it made the difference. Armistead said it took money to do your duty. Money had put her through Vassar, gotten her to England, made it possible for her to pay her own way as a V.A.D. probationer. She faced these hard facts. Using it right cleaned it, she told herself. It wasn't—well —the word "tainted" came and she almost wrote it down, and then stopped. She saw her father and Jake Catlett, and Eduardo and his father, and dear Mr. Roundtree, their sweat and their worry and heard the sound of her father's steps, back and forth in the library after they had all gone to bed, and couldn't make herself see it that way, even if the socialists did. She had only taken half her share out anyway.

But that share was an umbilical cord; she couldn't free herself from it. It reached from the coal-face at Seven Stars to the dark where she sat. In the dull boredom of too much horror and too much fatigue, a fatigue that never seemed to leave her, the endless tramp of men going toward the front in the night brought from that center of her memory, another road, another darkness, a corridor of night and marching men.

She was ten again, her face against the predawn winter window. Down along the road the lamps of the miners were strung out in tiny beads of light. Then she remembered putting lamb's wool in her shoes to keep her feet warm. All through lessons that day, she told herself, she had thought of the marching men. She saw them straggling back at evening, already dark by five o'clock. At the edge of her vision, waiting for her, the men marched from night to the black mine to night again. Her first real political thought, she told herself, was a child's phrase, "It's unfair."

She did not know that from too much recall and overuse the vision had become professional, as dishonest as a slogan.

As if the whole drift of thought in the night had been no drift at all but a way out of protective abstractions, she was back at the dinner table, at first recall of winter, comforting, the electrolier casting light down on the white tablecloth, and the sound of Essie in the kitchen, and let it come, what she knew she had been waiting for all the time.

In the winter when it snowed, even at night, she had seen, beyond the French doors and the conservatory, reflecting white across the lawn and down through the skeletons of trees the little moving head lamps of the men shining on the snow. In summer when they ate supper it was still light, a golden western light that made the room float. She remembered staring beyond them into that light. How were they to know that she put on the rose that day, ashamed of herself for the weakness, because she wanted Neville Roundtree to notice her some other way than in the realm of ideas? How could they know what she didn't admit to herself?

She wanted to share his language and his knowledge—that se-

161

curity of body that he had. She wanted him to take her away, as deep a want as any shopgirl dreaming in the cinema. She shared everything they could share—Eduardo's education, all that concern—not knowing what to do about it. She had made it harder for Neville, she knew that now, trying only to make him pay attention. He was such a civilized preoccupied man, and she didn't want to flaunt herself like Althea.

She turned and smiled at her image. Where you find your happiness! My God! Her own smile entranced her, it was so new.

It had taken these months of fighting shyness to get the nerve to write to him at all. He came as soon as he got her letter saying where she was. He rode a motorcycle for ten miles through the rain and mud from where the Devonshires were stationed on the Somme, and they met on the château steps. It was the first time she had ever seen him without a beard. He looked like a boy. He hugged her, mud and all, as if he had always done it. It was the war. Her shyness had been a luxury left over from peacetime. She smiled at that. There was no longer world enough and time.

They walked the road beside the Ancre in the rain, under the perpetual roar of the bombardment in the distance.

When Lily tried to figure it out, all the "time and circumstances," as she called it, he put his hand over her face and said, "Shhh. Be quiet."

He didn't say, "I love you." People don't. He just said, "Lily, dear Lily," then suddenly was practical, trying to light his pipe in the rain and saying at the same time, "We will marry as soon as I have leave." Then, "I think I shall send you to London. I would prefer that. This is no place for you."

She couldn't remember having said a word. The hospital siren wailed in the distance, and he clutched her arm so tightly it left a deep bruise.

"It's only a practice," she said.

He let her arm go, and muttered, "Sorry," down in his throat as he always had when he apologized for things.

Afterwards he lectured her on the geology of the Somme Basin, the chalk downs, and how the terrain would affect the Big Push. He said, "Not to worry," added "darling," a swallowed word, embarrassed at using it for the first time, then a big sigh.

162

She had watched him go slowly down the ragged drive, wheeling the motorcycle to the road, past the waiting ambulances, past the overgrown greenhouses with their broken windows, the last shards of glass glistening with rain. She had stood on the terrace then until the sound of the motorcycle was lost in the sound of the bombardment, and Armistead's arm was across her shoulders, and she said more gently than she ever had to her, "Old girl, you're on duty."

Lily made herself write again, letting whatever came into her mind flow into her notebook. She wrote, "I am in love," looked at it and smiled again, and went on writing, "At least I shared his experiences, even then, although I couldn't tell him. After Eduardo went down the hill and I knew I couldn't make him do what I wanted him to, I stood there and watched him out of sight. I went the long way home, around by the back hollow and across the knoll where the miners' graves were. I really saw them for the first time that evening, little pathetic things with wooden crosses overgrown with weeds already in a week after the women had been up to clean off the graves for Decoration Day. There were still dead rambler roses in jelly jars and a few of those wicker baskets they liked so much. I looked at the names, some too faded to read, some spelled wrong. I was going to do it myself. I had to. I couldn't tell Eduardo I was afraid of the dark. You don't tell things like that, even to one of your best friends.

"The pitch and rhythm of family voices, the sameness, while we ate supper that evening—that's all I can hear now, not what they were saying. Supper went on and on. I had made up my mind after all of that wanting and being afraid at the same time, that I was going to do it, and the fear had turned into something else, an excitement. I knew I was going into the dark. Why do some of us do a thing like this? Why do we go out from the safety most people seek?"

She looked at her watch and read three-forty-five, got up and tiptoed through the corridor of beds into what had been the great hall of the château. Now the bare floor and the bare walls echoed emptiness. The probationer at the receiving desk looked up and smiled, but neither of them spoke. The echoes were too heavy to disturb. It was McKay from Aberdeen. She lowered her head again to the circle of light from her lamp and went on writing. Lily heard only the scratch of her pen. McKay wrote to her fiancé in the First Highland Regiment every night, even though she saw him oftener than the others. He was stationed four miles away.

Lily lifted the blackout curtain and let herself out of the French door to get air and wake herself up before her next tour. After the darkness of the wards the night was light, as if there were a city to the east, and far away, the grunt of big guns; the shelling had started again.

She leaned against the cool balustrade and watched across the great space that had been the formal garden and now was rank with weeds and ragged shrubs. The distant line of willows by the little Ancre River floated in mist, defined by the first faint lifting of true dawn. The rain that had been going on for five days had stopped at last. She could smell it in the weeds below the balustrade. There were still pools of water on the terrace. The statues were stained with black tears and the stone urns were full.

She was there and not there, and again she reached up for her father's head lamp. She hid it behind her skirt, could almost feel again the little bumps of the dotted swiss, went to the shed door and looked out. There was Essie in the kitchen, putting on her hat to walk across the valley. She could hear her singing, washed in the blood of the lamb. She knew, at that time of twilight, where everyone was. She had seen her father, with Jake Catlett, and Eduardo's father, go across the side porch and hoped they had gone on into the library. Dan Neill was with them, and a little apart from them, as he always was. The thought intruded: I have seen so many like him since, bitter volunteers who use the war. He didn't need to. He made his own war that night, and wondered if Armistead was right, if she, too, used the war.

She saw Mary Rose in the girls' room. Her mother, she knew, had gone back to the tower with one of her headaches. Althea would be in the hammock on the front porch, waiting for Anderson Carver. Lily couldn't for the life of her see what she saw in him outside of availability.

It was safest to go through the house so that Mary Rose wouldn't spot her white dress from the window.

She didn't remember Althea. She only remembered walking around the gun to get to the front-porch steps.

The walk up to the mine entry was blank, as if her memory were too anxious to get there and face again what she had done. She did remember, though, that there hadn't been a soul on the path, and that the first lights of evening were shaping the white tents and making them a faint yellow in the town below her.

She had to let her hair down to get the mine hat on. She walked at long last into the vision of the night men marching.

Ahead of her the tunnel disappeared into the mountain. After her first steps into the pitch dark, she only looked back once to see the safe twilight at the entry, already a small opening, so distant that she had a moment of surprise at how far she had made herself walk without daring to think. When she let thought come, she was shocked to find that she was not afraid. The fear had been a barrier, and when she had stepped through it she found that she had left it behind.

She had known the map of the mine, piled question on question, to her father, to Eduardo, and to Jake. She knew the main entry, the only one with tram tracks. She knew that the first turning was into First Face South, and that it was three hundred feet inside. She knew that the mine was being worked off South Six. All that had been with her mind, and, too often, she realized, with her heart. Now she was knowing it with her body, and she stopped, elated. Her head lamp showed along the tram tracks, found the long line of mine props, still with their bark, an avenue of tree trunks that seemed to reach through the ceiling. It was so man-made, so domestic, that she felt tears running down her face. She reached up to brush them away and pushed the mine hat back so that the lamp shone on the ceiling, guttered, and went out.

The blackness pressed her eyes. Her back felt it, like a body forced against her. Slowly, slowly she made herself take off the hat. She held it in both hands, tight, and as slowly moved to her right until she felt the warmth of wood and let herself slide down against a prop. She heard scuttering and knew that the mine rats were there, moving in the heavy black. The mountain groaned and creaked. Something, a small thing, dropped far away. She heard water. She found the matches in her pocket, and managed to light one. She saw tiny bright eyes, not moving, charmed by the light. She made her hands stop trembling and lit the lamp again.

She was in a comforting globe of soft light. The darkness beyond the circle was only there in her mind's eye. She did not move. Across from her the coal glittered, man-cut clean across the five-foot seam. Mine props held the dull sandstone roof. The glow from the lamp caught little stars. She had not known about the stars. She knew it was niter but she was seeing little stars.

A rat sat up and watched her. Her left hand scrabbled on its own and threw a lump of shale. The rat disappeared. She got up, balancing the hat carefully, letting one hand guide her up the wall, and went on following the tram tracks past the old abandoned rooms her grandfather had dug with Lewis Catlett and Jake, nine years old then.

She stopped at the entry to First Face South. No one had told her the ceiling was only four feet high. No one had told her it was on an incline. She bent almost double to keep her lamp from hitting the ceiling. Already a few yards inside the new tunnel her back began to hurt. She was glad it did. This, she told herself, is knowing with my muscles. This is the way you know things, get to the heart of things.

Someone was following her. She crouched, still as an animal. The following footsteps stopped, too. She knew who it was, the woman in white. She had known she was not alone all the time but she had thought it was the atmosphere of work she felt, the careful man-made walls diminished into security by the language of it as of a house. The men said the ceilings were well behaved when they were solid sandstone and there was no danger of three hundred feet of overburden crushing them. The word "overburden" had, for her, the domestic sound of sad women on Mondays. She made herself take a few more steps and the following began again. She had to analyze the sound, place it. It was her own heels, dropping the fine shale from the floor off her slippers. There was no woman in white. She was alone. If anyone sees me come out,

I am the ghost. I am the woman in white, she told herself. There's nobody here but me, myself, and I, and that made her giggle, remembering fairy tales. She had not realized that she was speaking until she heard the voice. From then on up the incline she knew she was accompanying herself. "There is one who walks beside me," she said again aloud. "This is the experience of the one who walks beside me."

The entry reached its apex and sloped downward. She stopped. Her back was killing her already and she knew she had gone only a few hundred yards. She knelt against a mine prop and stretched her muscles. The cold, the damp, the incessant crouching, had made her stiff, that and a kind of muscular fear that would not let her go on. She had to turn and crawl on her hands and knees along the wet floor. She could feel the shale grinding against her palms. She tried to concentrate on the experience but she was stupid with pain.

"Troglodyte," came to her mind, another fairy tale, and she knew it was not real experience. It was flirtation. No matter how much her back hurt, she knew, crouched in wet shale and dirt, that she was trying to get a thrill by sticking her nose in where she had no business. She felt silly and ashamed and she wanted somebody to come and get her. All the danger seemed to fall on her at once, the overburden of it. She had never felt so lonesome in her whole life until now as she stood on the balustrade, watching the trees along the Ancre gradually defined in halos of mist. She was disgusted with her own self-pity. The lifting dawn had brought the birds to their chorus, the noisy clatter and song among the trees against the incessant thunder to the east.

Even when she tried, she couldn't remember the crawl, then the walk back to the mine entrance. The present dawn made the memory of that recede to a tiny vision, as in the wrong end of a telescope, or a dream she couldn't quite call to day. She saw herself again, standing in front of the Main Entry. It was dark. There were the first stars and the lightning bugs. Across the valley the tents glowed in the new night, and she could hear a lovely tenor voice. Down below, her home was etched in light. She could see someone, she thought it was her mother, walking

167

back and forth on the lawn in front of the French windows. She saw again both safeties: the safety of belonging to the tents, the safety of her child house that was not a safety, not with what she knew now with the aching she still felt in her back.

Shall I go down across the valley, or shall I go home? She heard that question as if she had spoken it aloud to the Ancre valley in front of her. She had known then, in a piercing moment when choice was alive in her whole body, that if she turned toward home, the choice would not come again, not until she was too old, and had sick headaches like her mother. I was like Antigone, standing there, she told herself.

She looked at her watch. It was just four o'clock, pure dawn now beginning to dim the false dawn at the east, and to color the fields beyond the river where, so close to disaster, a farmer was already working, plowing and planting. She could see him, faint beyond the trees, following his team of oxen. The soldiers told her they had watched the farmers within yards of the front lines, under the sound of the guns, plowing around the shell holes, clinging to stubborn habit to push away the despair of war.

Had it been that kind of surviving blindness with her own family? She wondered. They asked, usually at the end of their small areas of trouble in their letters, what it was like. How could she tell them, when they already knew or could have known? It had been, literally, on their doorstep. They had seen the night men marching all their lives. They had stepped around the first machine gun she had ever seen, keeping the grease off their white dresses. They had heard the Godley gun tattering the air. They knew the smell of canvas tents. They had lived that night in the impatience and quick flares of temper that meant waiting, waiting for the unknown until they hoped it, whatever it was, would happen, and the tension would break and let the day come. They had heard Dan Neill and the others laughing.

I am in war, she told the white dawn, and the ones who would not leave her mind, tired as it was. It is catching as a disease, as that night was catching. It comes down to this, she tried to explain, a man dead, or a thousand dead, the question to be answered is always one man dead no matter how many times—statistic, or mine prop, or slate fall—a man used and discarded who would be alive but for this. They call it a hate at the front, an exchange of fire, a warm-up to keep the men alert. Someone is always in the way. Its obscenity is that a man does not die because he is a certain person with a name. The act is as nameless and uncontrolled as it was that night.

That night was a hate and they wanted it, men like Dan Neill, war-lovers. How could she, how could Althea marry him? The little-girl competition made her smile, "he was in love with me," and then feel shame at being so childish.

"Lacey." McKay's voice was soft behind her. "It's time for rounds." She came up beside her, feeling the new air and light. "Ach, it's a lovely morning after all that rain."

Above them Armistead watched, and thought of them, and of the men. For a week they had marched along the road beyond the river. There was so much rumor. Everybody knew there was going to be a show—a big one. The signs were there, the quick fights, the impatience, and the singing as they swung along toward the Somme under the pall of rain, the constant drumming of bombardment. They said it would be a walkover, that there wasn't a Hun left in the trenches. They told each other that, over and over, and the tears ran down her cheeks because she knew in the dawn that it wasn't true. How she knew she didn't question. As in a prism she saw the men marching east, a vast naïveté of men.

Down below she could see Lacey and McKay turn back toward the door and she checked her watch to see they were on time for their rounds. Poor little bitches, she told them, you don't know. Why don't you go home? she wanted to call out to Lacey, not because she didn't want her there, but because she was so god-damned gentle.

When Lily went off-duty to her room she was too wide awake for sleep. She made herself begin a letter to clear it from her mind. She planned to make it as entertaining as she could to keep from worrying her mother.

"Dear Mother, it is a lovely morning." She marked out "lovely" because they caught the English use and teased her for it. When she had ruined the page, she tore it up and made herself undress,

169

and was asleep as soon as she lay down. Her last thought was of Mr. Roundtree; even in her near sleep she had trouble with calling him Neville.

She began the letter again on July 5, huddled on her cot in her warm dressing gown from Altman's.

"Dear Mother, there has not been a minute to write. I have never seen so many wounded. We have been on duty day and night, just taking a few hours for sleep. The slaughter has been huge. They say fifty thousand casualties the first day. There isn't enough of anything. Men are on the beds and there are stretchers under them with more men. All the way across the old garden to the river there are so many men waiting to be treated that you can't see the ground. They lie out in the rain. There are always too many of them. I found some wounded from the 8th Devons who could tell me about Mr. Roundtree. He was killed at Mansel Copse by machine gun fire. They say over a hundred and fifty men were killed by one machine gun. They were all buried together in one trench. They put a wooden notice over it. 'The Devonshires held this trench. The Devonshires hold it still.' " She wanted to write, "That's what a machine gun does, Mother," and then, "I want to come home," but she didn't let herself do that, or cry anymore. She went on with the letter. "Please send some Victrola needles and any popular records. The tommys like American music. I am enclosing the bill of sale for the bull field you sent me to sign. I thought all the Lacey Creek property but Seven Stars had been sold after Papa died." She found both the language and the family decisions comforting and important after what she had seen. She went on writing, "I am volunteering for the Ambulance Corps if they will let me in. They need drivers so badly. I will be nearer . . ." She hadn't meant to say that. She tore up the letter.

The bruise was still black on her arm.

Now it is evening on Lacey Creek. The first stars are out. Down among the tents, the children are chasing lightning bugs. They put them in bottles to make lanterns, and run to find a dark place to test how much they shine.

Faint light from the open tent flaps falls on waves of cloth from the acres of clotheslines as the wind catches and tosses them. The canvas tents are faintly shaped by the glow from the kerosene lamps inside them.

The clotheslines bear treasures among the overalls, the shirts, the white aprons and the skirts made from the bolts of sprigged cotton from the Company Store. There are embroidered linen sheets from Italy, heavy enough for a lifetime of wear, that have come with the bride chests; lace tablecloths from Ireland like delicate flags to show the gentility of their owners; embroidered waists from Poland; sunflower, sun-burst crazy quilts made by the women who have come down from the hill farms, that show a whole history in fragments, hour on winter hour, mile on country mile of care, thread, color that tells who they are, their industry; that they, the women, are used to nice things. The women don't want to leave their washing up to dampen in the night dew. They are afraid the children will stumble on the clothesline poles and they will have it all to do over, but Mother Jones has told them to leave it up, and they do. She says that it hides any meetings in the tents, and the mine guards will be on the lookout. She says to beware of informers and tells terrible stories of Butcher Goujot and the Baldwin Feltz detectives.

So the tablecloths and sheets and skirts sway like warning ghosts in the breeze, and the children hide and seek in and out of the lines, catching lightning bugs. They love the tents. It is like a holiday, like the camping their fathers tell them Mr. Godley took them on when they were boys, miles up Lacey Creek beyond the mines where the creek was clean over the rocks, and there was the same smell of canvas, the same soft tent shadows, green reflections washing across the canvas top, and you could reach out of your cot and touch the grass, the smell of dews and damps from the song they sang, the exposure to the huge outside, and still the protection of grown-up voices fading in the night as you went to sleep, and later, part of a dream. They sing the kind of songs they sang with Mr. Godley, songs that float upward and are lost in the night.

In the good old days, they told the children, they could hear Mr. Godley slowly blowing taps. Day is done, gone the sun. The face of a boy would appear over the kerosene lamp, and his cupped hand as he blew it out, and the tent was pitch-dark before the pale night came in, and Mr. Godley played the end of taps in the dark. But all that had ended when Imperial came, and nobody knew the owners anymore. They were just the company, they didn't have names. They said of Mr. Roundtree that he done the best he could, but he was under orders from the company, too.

Earlier, there had been the last sounds of baseball practice, Come on, come on, and the hollow crack when the bat hit right and the calls, Here, here, play ball. Mr. Godley had started the baseball team, too, but Imperial gave orders to put more houses up where the diamond was because they needed the space, so Mr. Lacey let them make a diamond out beyond the cemetery. That was the old man, before he died. He even built them a bandstand. They remembered when Beverley was young and they let him play ball with them.

They have played later than usual, now that Seven Stars has come out, because they are afraid Mr. Lacey won't let them use the field while the strike is on.

Mr. Lacey has let a lot of Godley people put up tents on his own bull field, but all evening the sound of hammers on tent pegs has sounded a broken rhythm and by night Mr. Lacey's land is clear. Where Catlett land stops, the tents stop, too. The older tents have board floors and wooden sides, but the new ones have to be on the bare ground. Some are made from piano boxes, and some from old quilts. But it is June and evening, and now that Seven Stars is out, too, there is a sense of celebration. It is, after all, the beginning of summer, and they have planted vegetables on what was Catlett pastureland while Essie pulled her rocking chair out into the weeds by the clearing and sat and bossed like a section foreman to see they did right.

The Italian women have brought the Paganos down and the men have set up a tent for them. If they have resented them during the month because Francesco has gone on working and Annunziata has let them know that nobody can move them like they are a sack of potatoes, none of this is mentioned. They treat her gently because she has been fooled, and they respect the humiliation of her finding out. As if she has been stripped of clothes they want to cover her with kindness, lend her things, and touch her hair. The younger Paganos have disappeared among the washing, chasing lightning bugs with the others.

Annunziata, Steve, Eduardo, Maria, and Francesco and their cousin Carlo Michele sit together, part of a circle of the Italian families. The Italian girls look at Carlo Michele sideways and smile. Mother Jones has told them to have a party. They pass fiaschi of wine across bodies. Even if it is a false party they are enjoying it after all the trouble. Young Giovanni di Pietro has been chosen to sing. He has the best tenor voice in the camp. The men listen, pleased with the sound. It is too early to meet for a strategy meeting, but there are little knots of men outside the lighted circle, consulting in whispers while Giovanni sings.

Eduardo still has trouble paying attention to the singer. He is watching his mother. She looks happy and bright-eyed with fury, which she seems to be enjoying. He wonders how many of the illusions she has lost were a burden to her. She seems years younger. The dignity that kept her so carefully apart from the others has been lost and she even sings, lugubriously, best opera style, "Sca-aappa!" and "Addio!" when the singer waves his arm and says "Tutti." She sits with her legs easy on the ground like a Calabrian contadina and not like an Umbrian from a great city. She feels him watching her and smiles. He worries that the wine has made her a little drunk after the shock. She seems to sense this and puts her hand on his leg and whispers in English, "You wait. It's all right," and goes on singing.

Giovanni's voice is so pure that it quiets even the children. It floats upward. It reaches Mr. Roundtree and he stops reading *Daniel Deronda*—he reads ten pages a night—and blows out his lamp to lean out of his living-room window. He has been to Covent Garden and heard Tetrazzini and he misses the opera. He tries to place the aria and decides it is Verdi but can't remember which one. Down below him he sees the Italian transportation men leaning out and listening, too. He can almost feel their homesickness like an ache in his body.

"E um sciopero, voi siete crumiri," Giovanni sings, improvising his own melody, "Le guardie sono armate," his voice soars up to the stars and holds on "ah" until no one could hold it longer and the aria subsides into "guardate, attenzione!" and finishes with a lingering "Addio, amici miei."

Mr. Roundtree knows he recognizes that line. He is absolutely sure it is Verdi. After the pure sound, pure silence in the dark, and he can hear applause and some laughter. He can see the distant steady glow above the trees of the electric lights in the Laceys' house. Nearer, down at the Club House, he sees the Baldwin men through the open window playing cards. He hears the faint cry, "High, low, jick, jack and game."

The lights go out in the rooms of the Italian transportation men. They have been told by the improvised song that the mines are on strike, that they are scabs, and that the guards are armed. Many of them have families in New York waiting to be sent for. They have to decide what to do.

Jake Catlett stands in the shadow of his porch, waiting for the meeting that will happen under cover of a square dance in his barn. He has cut the telephone wires with the wire cutters he borrowed from Beverley. He looks up toward the dark mountain opposite. The moon has not risen, and yet, he sees, he really sees, a light moving in front of the mine entry and a woman in white caught in the glow. He knows it is the ghost and he is not surprised, not even scared, really. It's a warning. It seems inevitable. He decides not to say a word about it. He doesn't want to listen to the fear of the women and children.

He has seen Lily, holding up her father's mine hat, with its lamp lit. She has paused there, caught by the song. Her long hair blows around her. She knows the words. What can happen and the night and what they have done to the Paganos, the mixture of beauty and fear and anger have made her cry again so that the warm lights of the tent colony shimmer in the distance. It seems to her to be a thousand miles across the valley but she knows she belongs there with the oppressed of the earth.

The litany of Mooney's apology never varied. To him, the definition and Dan Neill's name would be inseparable. Whenever he was mentioned, he would say, "Captain Neill was a gentleman to his fingertips. You didn't know him like I did. I will reiterate, he was always a perfect gentleman." Then he would add, "Whatever else." People took for granted that it was Christian charity but it wasn't. It was the central core left over from when knighthood was in flower.

His memories of what happened changed focus, grew protective covering, were censored by self-comforting, faded like everybody else's. Not the repetitions. They remained the same, same words, same certainties. "Now you've got to understand. They weren't the way people say. Why, some of them were Elks and Shriners, those kind of fellows."

He would find old laughter. "First fellow I have saw could use two hairbrushes, same speed. I'd of given a year's pay then for a pair of silver hairbrushes."

But on that night at ten o'clock, Mooney McKarkle was nineteen years old, and could account for every cent he had in the bank, where and how he had earned it for another year of college. He had gone over it in his mind, lying up there in bed, useless and forgotten after all that fine, brief attention he had had. He couldn't even feel his wound anymore, except for an itchy sting. He had to face the fact that it wasn't any damned wound anyhow, just a scratch, about like falling on the gravel and skinning your knee. He gave up trying to figure out how much he had and how much he still needed. He got up to a hundred and seventy dollars including a winter coat, stopped and sighed. He worried about whether he was going to make it to Morgantown in time for football practice, and yawned. Then he just let himself lie there and listen to the sounds of men, the setback game, and the rise of white mule in some of their voices, especially Anderson Carver's. He listened to the game turn into a gathering, a real meeting. There was a new kind of laughter, men's laughter he thought, the kind that women never hear except through closed doors. That was the way he was hearing it and it made him feel neglected and unmanned. He could hear the horses coming from up-creek, and voices out in the dark.

Aunt Trudy Daingerfield had been sent to bed. He'd heard Pat Hand call to her up the stairwell. "Now don't you worry none, honey, you just gwan up there and git your beauty sleep." She was still grumbling when she passed his door, but he couldn't hear any separate words, just the grumbling. He just had to get up and find his pants and go on downstairs, remembering to hobble a little bit out of pride.

He was surprised at how many of them there were, guards from the up-creek mines, and even some from the Cain Creek mines over the ridge. There must have been thirty or forty of them. Out in the road along the fence he could see their horses tethered in a row, and away down-creek he could hear a faint pulse of music.

Even in the middle of all the noise, Captain Neill sat there looking like the Arrow Collar man. When he saw Mooney in the hall too shy to come in, he seemed to understand. He said, "Come on in, son. Are you sure you feel all right?"

Mooney limped into the room and tried to say, I thought you might be needing me, but it came out, "Un-hunh, sir." He wouldn't have admitted to a soul that he wouldn't have missed anything that was going to happen, that wild horses wouldn't have kept him up in that room.

Of course there weren't any wild horses anyhow, just company nags and hacks. "Nobody would bring a good mount up here," Captain Neill said. He talked like that all the time. He didn't even have to think about it.

They let him go with them out into the dark road. Captain Neill said he could. That was all part of the new wonder of the night and the wound and the white flash of his bandage and the horses in the dark of the moon. Lord God, that wasn't swearing, that was recognizing—why, they were steeds, their hooves splashing through the creek, with the fine veils of water spumed up around the night riders for justice like at the Biograph. He just wished Captain Neill's sister, Sally Brandon, could see him now, the stuck-up thing. There wasn't any doubt about it. Captain Neill was making a special friend of him, almost a page when he motioned him to ride beside him.

He knew he was doing right on the side of law and order and protection of property. Mooney feared his pa more than God and his ma more than his pa, and his pa said that it was niggers and anarchists and foreigners and, worst of all, outside agitators, that were the trouble. "Look at Pullman," he said. He swore that Eugene V. Debs was a dipsomaniac with an unhinged mind due to overindulgence, who smoked cigarettes, coffin nails.

Riding along like that, Mooney felt like it was Chancellorsville and Waterloo and the Rough Riders and when knights were bold: everything he'd ever missed in his life. He was glad they rode horseback instead of taking the railroad bicycles. Captain Neill just naturally did things right. It was all the Calvery he'd ever heard about, and there he was a member of the Calvery, even if they were in citizen's clothes instead of uniforms.

They passed by the faint circle from the single naked bulb on the railroad water tower. The breeze made the circle sway, and oh my stars that diamond stickpin on Captain Neill's black tie flashed even after they went again into the dark, or seemed to. He couldn't tell where the light was coming from but it was on the diamond and he followed it like the knights of old.

His feet knew they were getting near when they started patting the sturps to the sound of the fiddle and the stomp of feet on the wood floor of Jake Catlett's barn, a huge drum for all those feet. Stomp bum bum bum Stomp bum bum bum. He felt that his feet were being disloyal, carrying on like that when he was supposed to ride tall and quiet like Captain Neill said, a night rider.

"Pass the word back to the troop," Captain Neill whispered. "Ride close and quiet." Troop! Now, wasn't that something? It was getting harder to keep them quiet with all that white mule wanting to holler, but Captain Neill had the voice of command even passing along a whisper, "and no gunfire"; he passed that along too. He said they only had their rifles for self-defense in case the enemy opened fire. He didn't quite say it that way, but Mooney liked to think he did. What he said instead was, "We don't want the sons of bitches to have an excuse to start another shooting."

When they rounded the last slight curve he gave the order to halt on the edge of the light from the tent colony. Except for the music from the open barn door the whole place seemed asleep. Only a few of the tents still had their lamps lit. Through the open tent flaps they could see the shape of the colony and an acre of washing moving like flags in the night. Up on the side of Jake Catlett's hollow his cow barn was a big dark shape around the light from the open door. Inside, he could see the dancers, whirling, and hear the stomp of their feet. The light cut a wide path down to the colony. Another beam from the hay door stretched right over onto Jake Catlett's porch, where Mooney could see the dark shapes of people sitting in the rocking chairs. The hanging lanterns in the barn made the paths wiggle and sway to the rhythm of the music.

Captain Neill kept his hand up until there wasn't a sound, except somewhere behind them a horse blew, and another one whickered and Mooney could hear bits champing and the faint clank of a harness, and saddles creaking.

They were near enough to hear the caller, "Ladies and gentlemen, promenade," but that sounded far away under the stomping.

Of course everybody knew it wasn't a regular square dance. In the first place you don't have a square dance on Friday, you have it on Saturday. In the second place, when some of the young fellows started passing around the white mule like they always did outside the barn door, not in front of the ladies, Jake Catlett went out and they heard him say, "Now, they ain't going to be no more of that there." He took the bottle and told them to git on inside and goddammit dance for the UMW. After about an hour, though, it was just like any other square dance, only there were more young fellows and the ladies didn't have to dance with each other. There were the older ladies sitting around the sides like dignified statues. The pat of their feet was their only movement. They were a lot more solemn than they were in church, looking straight ahead, their dresses and their aprons smelling of ironing and sun as if they trapped the breeze and light in their clothes. The kids were underfoot as usual, some trying to dance, littler ones chasing each other, babies in arms setting up a wail until their mothers whipped out a breast to feed them, still staring straight ahead at the dancers, still tapping one foot.

There was some breeze from the open barn door and some from the big hay door that opened with a ten-foot drop to the creek bank. Once in a while, when the kids ran too close, a woman would say, "Git away from thar." Jake Catlett drove the cows in morning and evening, all four of them, to milk, but in summer he kept them in a cow field further up his hollow. He sluiced out the floor every evening, strike or not. At ten o'clock it was still damp and cool, and the big room was sweet with the scent of hay.

The fans waved back and forth in rhythm in the ladies' hands, some palm leaf, some paper fans with pictures, Jesus Saves and Suffer Little Children to Come Unto Me and Bull Durham.

But the stern upright stillness of mountain women at a party was more urgent than their habitual silence. Their voices usually were low in their throats and slow anyway, except when they let out a banshee yell for a cow or a hog or a child, quiet from being alone a lot with too much work to do to stand around talking, and from catching silence from their men. Their ears were cocked listening for something to happen, they didn't know what. They knew it with their skin.

Essie, watching too, said to Old Ant Annie next to her without turning her head, that the Angel of Death was louring over the valley and Ant Annie said yes it surely was.

The main difference, though, was that the other side of the barn was filled with Italians for the first time ever at a square dance. Steve Pagano told them they had to. They sat as solemnly, as ironed and starched, their printed cotton skirts from the same bolts of cloth from the Company Store, except for the women in their strict Catholic mourning black. Both of the rows facing each other wore their clean dresses boiled in the washtubs set up on stones outside the tents, and dried in the sun, but each side was convinced that the other was dirty.

Once in a while a mother fed a baby, or grabbed a running kid and pulled it close and whispered, "Basta!" under the stomping and the fiddling and the fast calling they couldn't understand. They were beginning to enjoy it though, even Mrs. Pagano in her borrowed clothes.

Eduardo and Carlo Michele stood with the other young Italians in a tight group. They didn't dance because they didn't know how to do it, but the music entered them and they pushed each other from time to time, just friendly pushing, high spirits, and once in a while the only laughing out loud in the barn made both rows of women glance around, hesitating their fans.

"They ain't got no business here," Ant Annie said.

"Jake told them to." Essie turned her head then and just looked and that ended the matter right there.

Up on Jake Catlett's porch the meeting of what Mother Jones called the executive committee had ended but they all still sat there rocking, not saying anything, just enjoying the stars and listening to the music.

They had gone over their demands again so that everybody had them straight. A couple of miners from No. 10 over at Cain Creek said they agreed in principle but they thought they ought to picket anyway when the transportation went into Godley at five o'clock in the morning. Jake Catlett argued. He said he didn't want any bloodshed and Mother Jones said, "Sometimes you got to," and he argued even with her, he said, "Not in my hollow."

Mother Jones laughed and said, "It ain't your goddamned hollow. It belongs to company thugs and sons of bitches."

He said not his land and she said, "Hell's fire, you don't own nothing but the overburden." That shut Jake up. His biggest shame was that Lewis Catlett had sold the mineral rights under everything to Mr. Godley for a dollar an acre when he didn't know what it was worth and was too proud to ask his own brother-in-law Senator Neill, who had made a killing on the north side of the river. They hadn't spoken in some years. Jake wondered who had told Mother about that, but she surely knew. She even knew the Latin for it. "Ad coelum ad infernum," she said and laughed again. "You used to own from heaven to hell, but your pappy sold hell to Imperial."

He wanted to say it wasn't Imperial, it was Mr. Godley, but he didn't. There didn't seem to be any use.

One of the Italians from the transportation had jumped out the window of Godley Boarding House and was sitting down at the end of the porch. He brought a New York *World* with the ad that the padrone at Ellis Island had translated for him. Steve Pagano read it out. It said, "Steady employment at good wages in the mines of West Virginia. No strikes. Free transportation."

He said that the Italians had believed the man. After all, he was a padrone and he looked after them. He got their families a room in Little Italy, and said he would take the responsibility of sending them down when the men sent him the money for their keep and the train fare. It was only when they got there they found out that their own train fare and their tools were going to be taken out of their pay, and that they were crumiri, scabs. Steve translated all this and Mother Jones went on rocking and listening and looking at the stars.

"How many of them got the guts to stay out?" she asked Steve when he finished.

"Some of them got families," he said after he'd asked the man, and she didn't say a word. They could tell she was thinking, so they all kept quiet.

"How many professional scabs?" she finally asked.

"Ten or fifteen as near as he can tell."

"Now," she finally said, "I've decided. These here are our demands. Recognition of the union, permission to buy someplace else outside the pluck-one company stores without being blacklisted, you men pick the cracker boss, and you have a union checkweighman see you don't get cheated on your tonnage, no yellow-dog contracts that say you get set out of your houses when you strike, company rents lowered, and them goddamned Baldwin detective thugs out of this hollow before we deal with them."

All this had already been discussed and discussed again. Under the protection of the square dance the men nodded at each demand she repeated, checking them off on her fingers, hardly listening though.

"I've decided about the pickets. Couple of you men get up there before dawn and set mine props, one on each side outside the drift mouth. Make them eight, ten feet high so everybody can see them. On top you put big bunches of daisies. Every one of the scabs know what that means. This side you look at the daisies. Go beyond the poles we lay 'em on your chest when they berry ye. Now, you all know that a strike is won over the cookstove and it's been my long experience you give the women something to do they will go through hell and high water better than the men. All right, Jake, you win. We won't have no pickets. We'll have a prayer meeting."

"Where?" Jake was suspicious.

"In the barn," she said.

"I don't hold with no women being put to risk," he muttered. She ignored him.

"The telephone wires are cut, ain't they?" she asked Jake for the tenth time, and he said yes and didn't remind her because she was old. "That way they can't call the sheriff and get deputized and they can't get no men from over to Cain Hollow."

After that it was time to be quiet and watch the stars and listen to the music.

They heard a yell and heard the horses before they saw them. The men poured off the porch and ran down toward the branch and up into the barn.

Mother Jones went on rocking. There wasn't a damned thing she hadn't seen before and there wasn't a damned thing she could do about it. She didn't even turn her head when the music and the stomping died. They didn't just stop. They ran down.

"Everybody keep calm," she heard Jake Catlett yell. "Stay right where you are."

She did hitch the rocking chair around just enough so she could see both the camp and the barn without having to turn her head too much. She saw the horsemen crowd the barn door and two of them dismount. There was only the sound of their boots across the bare wood floor.

"You goddamned rednecks are having a meeting and that ain't legal!" That was Butcher Goujot's big loud mouth. She knew him from oh two.

"Who says so?" somebody yelled.

"We are deputies. We got the right," Butcher yelled.

"Oh no you ain't."

Butcher laughed. "We deputized each other, you goddamned redneck."

"Now, gentlemen, let's discuss this rationally." That was another voice. She didn't know that one, some piss-ant gentleman's voice. Then he said, "Jake, you know better than this."

She could just barely hear Jake say, "They ain't nuthin' illegal in no square dance."

The valley was so quiet she could hear night birds and the men's voices and a faint breeze in the trees, high up. She thought it sounded like the Angel of Death and then swore to herself because Catholic thoughts from Ireland had begun to bloom up lately in her memory and she hated that.

The horsemen at the back were getting restive. They were beginning to holler back and forth to each other as if they were far apart instead of in a huddle of horses. White mule. That was the sound of white mule. Somebody whooped and hollered and it stirred up some yelling from inside the barn. Mother went on rocking. Some of the men at the back turned their horses away from the light of the barn and into the dark. She saw them appear again in the glow of the tents. She watched them ride full tilt into the clotheslines. The white sheets and shirts and quilts and lines tangled among the horses and she heard men swearing and yelling. A tent went down and caught fire. She never saw such a tangle of horses and men.

"Goddammit, Dan, control your men," she heard Jake Catlett yell. The flames lit the sky so she could see better. They rose up and turned the trees green. A jumble of men—some dismounted, some running down from the barn—stamped and tore at the tent. It was a God's blessing she thought that the wind was blowing up-creek and the flames were not catching the other tents, but they would catch at her boys' hearts. She knew that.

In the light of the fire she could see the horses tangled in the laundry and was pleased. Her plan had protected most of the tent colony and her other plan had worked, too. She knew the women would be so riled up about it that she could lead them into anything.

"You women stay in there," she heard somebody yell, but that was pissing into the wind. Some of them had crowded in the barn door and had seen what was happening. They flowed down into the mess like a bunch of Harpies. Mother Jones smiled and went on rocking.

"You get you some damned fools and some white mule and you got yourself a union," she said, even though there wasn't anybody on the porch to say it to.

She heaved herself up from the rocker, patted her lace jabot and straightened her hat. She got out her powder puff and dabbed her nose. She lit Jake's porch lantern and adjusted the wick. It was time to go down and put a stop to all that foolishness before somebody got shot.

She had long since learned to control her always present anger until she had use for it. Now that she had timed the raid's rising, watched it engulf the tents, and recede into a lot of milling around with nobody going any sensible direction, she let the anger rise. She could feel it, hot in her face, tight in her dentures clamped together, in her jaw, and ready in her throat.

She was mad about another thing and that's why she had ridden on the day coach all the way from Montana. Goddammit, she had handed John Mitchell the Kanawha field on a platter back in oh two. She'd stood in the middle of the creeks in February over seventy years old then, signing her boys for the union, because both banks were company property and the water was a rightaway according to the law, and she didn't like to see all her work go to hell in a handcart on account of John Damned Rockefeller and Jesus Pierpoint Morgan.

Step on a piece of ground and you step on an injunction. Jake Catlett might be hard to handle, God knows his pappy had been, wouldn't let her on his place in oh two, but at least now they had some land, UMW land, Jake's property, the surface anyhow, and she wasn't going to see a bunch of Baldwin dogs run her boys off it.

Mother Jones marched down the path, a one-woman army, holding the lantern up so it would light her face.

Lily had been wandering for two hours, not knowing where to go or what to join. People looked different as they passed the faint light paths from the tents. She had to be so careful of the high, blinding corridors of clotheslines. Once she stumbled on a pole and tore her skirt and skinned her leg. She stood there bracing herself against the swaying pole to keep the heavy quilts from falling.

She had never been a stranger in her own valley before. People she had known since she was born passed within a foot of her in the half-dark, walking so busily that she told herself she didn't dare cross the gulf of their intentions. It wasn't that they didn't recognize her. They seemed to be choosing not to see her at all.

She had started down from the mine mouth toward the sound

of the lovely tenor. The song was calling right to her. "Vieni fuori! Vieni fuori!" She knew that meant come out. It was like a sign. "It's a sign!" Essie always said, but a sign of what she never explained, just a sign. She said that about Halley's Comet and when a bird flew in the house. It was all the same.

Lily walked toward the end of the song through her favorite blue-purple time of the evening, seeing Venus and not forgetting to say "Star light star bright grant the wish I wish tonight color of his hair color of the clothes he's going to wear," and she giggled because Mr. Roundtree's clothes were always the same. He had explained about Bernard Shaw and how sensible he had been. She felt the familiar shame of thinking about unimportant things like that when she ought to be aware of crossing into a new world, well, the same valley, but at least a new life. Essie called it born again. Her father said Essie was born again every Wednesday night, and her mother said it was the only social life Essie had. Lily almost skipped along the familiar path, down to the foot of the mountain and to the trees that lined Lacey Creek, close to the blue cedars at the bottom of her lawn. She sneaked close to the fence and dropped the mine lamp inside under the lilac bushes.

By the time she got to the main dirt road away from the light that fingered down the hill from the Big House and crossed the bridge over Lacey Creek that took the wagons up to the mine, it was pitch-dark and the stars were so bright that she seemed to see through a depth of them, not flat as they usually were but deep into the dark. She wondered if that was a sign, too. She couldn't remember seeing them that way before.

The singing had stopped and she walked in night noises, the frogs in the creek, the up-creek wind in the trees. Under the trees little dots of lightning bugs floated in black space. She didn't hesitate, even in the dark, not down her own road, through the heavy scent of honeysuckle on the fences in front of the company houses. The honeysuckle held the sun in its blossoms to breathe out for her in the night.

Ahead of her, the tent colony seemed to shine. She was so intent on the bowl of light that she came slap up against Jake Catlett's snake fence that surrounded his property before she remembered that it was there, as many times as she'd climbed it to go see Essie. Essie's voice came as it always had. "Hold that skirt down when you climb the fence. Somebody's gonna see your sash." Obedient still without realizing it she climbed carefully, only lifting her skirt a little when she had to.

The people around the singer were getting up and walking in pairs and threes and fours toward their tents. They were all Italians and she didn't know any of them except the Paganos. She was relieved when she saw Eduardo walking along with his mother, and the new cousin and Maria. She walked faster remembering to say "scusi," to get through the crowd.

When she touched his arm he dropped back and said, "Don't let my mother see you."

She caught his whisper. "Why?"

"We got set out. You go home. You got one to go to."

He left her there alone by the last down-creek tent, just left before she could say, "I know. I want to help."

Nobody spoke to her again until she found Essie, who looked right at her. She was grateful for that at least. Essie didn't stop. She said, "This ain't no place for you, honey, you gwan home where you belong," and the words trailed after her as she disappeared out of sight.

There was nothing to do finally except lean against the snake fence and watch.

She saw one light after another being lit in Jake Catlett's barn. It poured out of the barn door, where she'd gone so many times with Essie to watch her milk the cows. It lit the water of Jake Catlett's branch, out of the hay door where Essie had told her, "I told you stay away from that door you'll break your neck. That there's a ten-foot drop to Kingdom Come." When she was little she thought if she fell out that big door she would be snatched up in midair and taken to Kingdom Come before she hit the water.

When the music tuned up and the fiddle began to fill the night, she thought at least they wouldn't keep her away from that. After all, it was a square dance and anybody could come to that. She walked up the steep path, but when she saw the boys crowded in front of the door, she didn't dare go nearer or even move for fear of one of them seeing her.

She was near enough to hear them brag. Somebody was telling a story, "So this drummer come up Cain Creek he sold shoes to the pluck-me Company Store. He's ridin' the platform behind the caboose. The train was only goin' about four, five miles an hour. He seen some fellers setting outside the scrip office. He hollered out you rednecks you rednecks and one them fellers tuk and shot him right between the eyes blowed him off that caboose and he lit ten, twelve feet beyond the track deadern four o'clock. They don't like that kind of talk over aroun' Cain Creek."

Somebody said, "Goddamn!"

Somebody else laughed.

She could hear them passing the bottle and jostling around until Jake came out and herded them inside. She heard the bottle splash in the creek and one of the boys say, "Hail's far."

She just thought that if she stood in the doorway, halfway outside, nobody would mind that and she stayed there with the music making her foot pat, wishing she could go in and dance, too, like she used to when her mother got softhearted and let the girls come to the dance, which wasn't often. She managed to get by with it for a long time until Essie glanced up and saw her, and came right out through the dancers and grabbed her arm and turned her around toward the path.

"Now I told you to go on home. This ain't no place for you. These people catch you they'll skin you alive." She stopped talking and looked at her. "Look at yourself! Where in the name of God have you been? You're dirty as a pig. Hair hangin' down to your tail. It ain't decent. You oughtn't to come up here lookin' like that. Now git."

Essie turned around and left her there, half in, half out of the light. When Lily looked down she noticed for the first time that her white dotted swiss was torn and covered with coal dust and her hands were like her father's when he came down from Seven Stars, and even if Essie hadn't even said "honey" to soften her anger, she was proud of that. It was the dirt of the people after all. She hadn't noticed that the women inside were all as clean as new pins.

She couldn't go home anyway until the lights were out that still glowed from the windows on the hill opposite and she couldn't put up her hair because she had lost her hairpins in the mine. She had to wait to sneak in after the bedroom lights were out or she'd catch holy hell and she was too tired for that, tired and almost, well, heartbroken but not all the way through. Something might happen yet to show them where she stood. She felt about ten years old instead of a grown woman. She found a stump to sit on and wait. What she was doing was right and she had tried to be of use, but Eduardo had told her to go home and Essie had told her to go home. She began to cry. No. She wept and would not be comforted because there was none, out there in the dark, despised and rejected.

She was sitting near the up-creek gate and she heard it open. Somebody was trying to be quiet about it. She didn't hear any voices at all, but she looked up, so used to the dark that she could see a few of the horses against a fragment of sky between the trees and hear their champing and the clank of a bit. She knew what it was. Her body didn't know what to do. It wanted to throw itself in front of them. It wanted to run up the path and stop the dancers. For a second she saw herself there, noble in her white dress, standing in a ring of silent grateful people.

At the pause before she could get to her feet, she heard Dan Neill yell "Forward." Even then she felt a giggle at his foolish pretentious voice rise in her throat. They swept up past her, up past the light of the last tent, up the rise of the path to the barn door and she could see their shapes bunched there, blotting out most of the light. She couldn't move, couldn't get past them.

Somebody yelled inside the barn, but she couldn't hear what he was saying for the talking of men almost over her head and the turning of their horses. It was like one of those long nightmares that last a minute or two, where she was frozen and couldn't move among the alien and the heartless men who didn't smile or listen, just kept on coming, a mob of the heartless.

A man yelled, "Hell, this ain't nothing. Come on, far the tents. Git the rednecks!"

Six or seven horses were turned at the back and the ones in front of them seemed to catch direction and follow.

They rode out among the tents. She saw one of them ride too close to the nearest tent peg. The tent folded down over its kero-

188

sene lamp. The flames shot up, lighting the sky, a bonfire. She had to get behind a tree away from the horses. They were beginning to panic at the sight of the flames. Some of the men had dismounted to try by instinct to put out the fire, forgetting they were going to fire the tents. She could hear others in the distance, their horses mired in the clotheslines, hear them yelling but it was a melee of voices, no separate words.

The women ran down the path past her, pushing at the horses, whipping their flanks, trying to pull the men off. Voices died down as the fire finally died down into the ground.

Then she saw her, the little old handsome woman. She stood above them on the rise up to Jake Catlett's house, holding a lantern so they could see her face. She had a voice like a foghorn, coming out of that little old body.

She yelled, "Goujot, are you down there?"

Lily saw the whole mass of running jostling people stopped in their tracks by the voice.

If Goujot was there he didn't answer. Nobody did.

"Goujot, this is private property. If you don't get these men out of here I got eight hundred armed men up in these hills won't leave a goddamn one of you alive."

Nobody answered. Lily saw Florence Nightingale and Joan of Arc and herself in her visions standing there with the whole crowd of them reined in by her voice. Mother Jones the Miner's Angel. Lily knew what it was to be in love.

Mooney had been swept along with four or five horsemen. He couldn't see who they were. They followed somebody down along the snake fence out of the way of the clotheslines. Whoever it was called out, "The goddamn fools got themselves caught. Come on, men. Let's git back on company property." It was that Anderson Carver, that braggadocio full of white mule. "Git down here and tear down this fence." He hollered orders like he thought he was Captain Neill.

This wasn't like any battle he'd ever heard tell of, this was just a bunch of loudmouth drunks, now throwing down part of the old fence, but he followed them through. He just wanted to get out of Jake Catlett's land where he had no business. He started to turn his horse toward the creek road but Anderson Carver heard him. "Here, you git back here. We gonna let a bunch of Dagoes and rednecks run us off?"

The horses were head to head in the dark beyond the fence on Mr. Lacey's property. Mooney stayed away from their rumps, but he didn't dare move again for fear Anderson Carver would hear him. He couldn't see a damned thing. In the distance he could hear a woman's voice yelling like a preacher. He knew who it was, that old devil Mother Jones they said used to run a whorehouse, but that was far away behind the talk of the men. They hadn't paid a damn bit of attention to Goujot or Captain Neill. They was just ready to take the bit in their teeth. They wasn't any knights of old anyhow. They was just a bunch of pool-playing white trash full of white mule like hung around the courthouse and bragged. His ma would have taken a strap to him if he hung around like that.

They were arguing, "Let's git us a Dago."

Somebody laughed. "Git a Dago woman. I heard tell them Dago women got wells instead of slits, you disappear inside and go to glory."

Mooney didn't feel like a knight or a Calvery man or nothing anymore. He wanted to say, Please, oh please don't do that. Please don't do that, but he couldn't speak. He was about to cry or vomit. He just sniveled up snot. Already their drunken minds had veered past getting a Dago woman.

"Let's us git ourselves a Dago! Git him on company property. Bushwhack him."

"Do Dan Neill a favor." Somebody laughed.

A voice in the dark: "I wouldn't feel right we didn't git us a Dago. That one come in here spreading socialist propaganda, that new one."

"Hell, I can't tell one Dago from another. Let's git one somebody knows anyhow."

The horses champed and stomped. The men whirled them around, maniacing them like they were thoroughbreds.

"Gittin' run off like that don't make me feel good."

Turning and turning of men and plans and horses.

"No." Anderson Carver's voice in the dark. "Worst one is that Eddie Pagano. Everybody knows him, sniffing around the ladies."

"Captain Neill sure don't like that," one of the men said. They were all drunk with their planning.

They tried to concentrate on which Dago they were after until one of them got tired of it. He turned his horse and whooped and hollered, they all followed, whooping and hollering around the snake fence, safe on company property, to show they were still full of piss and vinegar.

The center of the camp was in darkness except for the lantern Mother Jones carried. She had parted a Baldwin man and one of her boys in a fight. They stood there while she made them listen. "You boys ought to be ashamed. Now, they ain't going to be no more of that." Their bloody faces showed in the lantern light.

Mother Jones found Goujot. He and Dan Neill were helping the men free their horses from the clotheslines and hold off the rest of the women. Dan Neill was trying to lead his own horse and slap the women away. The horse plunged, crazy with terror. "Get out of the way, it's dangerous," he kept saying.

Mother Jones took Goujot's arm and looked up into his face.

"You heard me," she said.

"Howdy, Mother." Goujot grinned.

"Don't you Mother me, you son of a bitch." She sounded almost casual.

They stood like two people who meet on the street who haven't seen each other for a long time.

"Now, we don't want no trouble," she told him. "Your boys was just high-spirited but you and I know it could turn worse."

He still didn't say anything. He just looked over her head then like he saw somebody in the distance.

"Who's this here candy-ankle?" she turned to Dan Neill.

That made Goujot laugh. "Why, this here's Captain Neill."

"Why Captain? Captain Jinks of the Horse Marines?" Some of the people in a circle laughed.

That made Goujot laugh again. Whether it was the little old woman or Goujot's laughing at him in front of all those people, Dan Neill's back looked like he'd swallowed a ramrod.

"Captain of the troop," Goujot said.

"Well, Captain, you better git your pretty little butt out of here before these women take your jewelry." Another relieved gust of laughter swept around the circle of men nearest them.

"Git back on that horse and walk it out of here. Can't you even control a horse?"

It was as if she had stung and stung Dan Neill until he remounted. His face, high over them, was white with fury, lit from below by Mother Jones's lantern, a death's-head in that light.

"Now you folks stand back, let these men through. Keep away from them horses. They'll kick ye." Mother slapped a horse's rump as it passed her. "Now, git!" The horse skittered.

Some of the guards waited for Dan Neill to start. After all, he had said he was their platoon leader. Some of them still hesitated, watching Goujot. After all, if you didn't obey a Congressional Medal of Honor, who did you obey? Not Dan Neill. "Hell's fire, he just done what the old bitch said like she was his mother," one of the men complained.

"Besides, now that some of these horses had been lamed by the goddamned redneck clotheslines we got to see to them. Goujot told us and told us 'You lame a company horse you got to reimburse the company.'"

"I wisht we had of come down here on railroad bicycles, that damned fool," Pat Hand said. He was leading his horse slowly. It was limping. "I didn't want to come down here nohow."

One of the men from Cain Creek said Neill was too goddamn high-hat anyhow.

They made a slow parade through a path made by miners, wives, children, who had been as silenced by the old woman as the Baldwin men had. Nobody even dared laugh or yell sonabitch anymore for fear they'd turn around and use the rifles they carried. Jake and Mother Jones reviewed them as they passed. Jake said, "By God the white mule's done gone out of them now."

Mother Jones said, "It's too soon to say. They can always get more," and her voice rose up to her orator pitch. "Now you women git this place cleaned up. You got to rescue what them thugs ruined. When you finish come on back up to the barn. We got business to attend to."

She didn't seem to care if the last of the men disappearing through the up-creek gate heard her or not.

Mooney heard her. He was walking slow along the outside of the fence. He'd tethered his horse to a tree on company land where somebody would find it. He knew one thing. He quit. He didn't want anything to do with that kind of going-on and he wasn't even going to ride their horses anymore. He was too sad to worry about any of the miners catching him, although it was enough on his mind to keep him away from any light. The camp was all lit up again and he could see the women untangling lines and poles and torn laundry.

They shook and folded and straightened like the whole camp was a house they had to red up; overturned washtubs, broken chairs that they'd been sitting on outside the tents, a torn mess of clothes. One woman, a foreigner, just stood there making a mewing noise and smoothing some rag that had been a shirt down and down across her breasts and her tears fell on it. Most of them looked too furious to cry or to say a word. Mooney could see their hands clenched over the clothes in the shafts of light.

He saw a woman grab a sheet from another one with a small spurt of fury, but she was only starting to help the other woman fold. They folded once, folded twice, walked together, their hands touched. One leaned down to take the bottom fold. It was some kind of bedspread, embroidered with peacocks. One hunkered over a bushel of corn that had been trampled trying to pick out kernels that were still whole. The only sound was a woman out toward the downriver tents, "Now git," to a child in the same imperious voice Mother had used on the men.

Then, good God, Miss Agnes! If there wasn't Miss Lily Lacey, dirty as a miner, helping one of those Dago women fold a sheet.

He had to tell somebody. It had been a big decision. He still needed a hundred and seventy dollars. He leaned over the fence and called, as soft as he could, "Miss Lily? Oh, Miss Lily."

When she came over to see who it was, he said, "I quit."

All she said was, "You oughtn't to have started in the first place. You better run. If these women catch you they'll tear you apart."

"I ain't got nowhere to go. You think I could stay all night at your house?"

"No." She was just like a schoolteacher, that same no. Her face looked final. "We aren't going to harbor a Baldwin detective, not after this."

They both knew that wouldn't be true, not if he went up and knocked on the door. Besides, he said he wasn't no Baldwin man no more. He'd told her that. They didn't see anything wrong with the Baldwin men anyhow, especially Miss Althea. She said that Anderson Carver was a courtly man. Courtly hell. Courtly my foot.

Lily started to turn away. He couldn't let her do that, not yet. He was too lonesome. He had too much to tell.

"I'm gonna be a lawyer and defend the rights of property, but I'm never goin' to do nuthin' this way anymore."

That made her turn back, just enough to say, "You'll just use men like that to do it for you. Keep your shirt clean and your hands clean like Pontius Pilate."

That was a mean way to talk after all he'd been through, and it was too much of a thought for Mooney to consider right then. She didn't give him time to say it wouldn't be that way. The way he saw it there was going to be law and order through the courts. She was gone. He could see her walking behind that bunch of redneck and foreign women who had started to gather toward the barn again. Now, that was illegal, meetings were illegal, but he guessed it wasn't illegal when it was just women, only when it was men.

He said "Women!" as if that settled the whole awful thing in his mind for the time being.

Lily thought she had earned the right to follow them and at least listen outside the barn door. Her back was sore again from an hour's fast work. She was experiencing the kind of tiredness they felt every day. The only other time she ached like that was when they rolled out the tennis court every summer. The new tiredness was cleansing the shame of that life away like when Essie said she'd been "warshed in the blood of the lamb."

Jake Catlett sat in the same rocking chair Mother Jones had quit,

rocking in the same rhythm, waiting too. For once he was by himself. He could see the women trailing up toward his barn, not chit-
tering like critters the way they usually did, their brains flowing out
of their mouths. There was something he knew he had to do, and
he had to do it alone, not ask anybody, not have no damned meeting about it. He thought of his two pastures. They were going to
need a lot of work after the strike was over. They were trampled as
flat as ground after a circus had left town.

Mostly, though, he was watching the Big House. Lord God, he
must have sat out there and watched it a thousand times from his
front porch. He knew every move in it at night from watching the
downstairs windows darken, watching the girls' light go on, then
later, watching the Madame's light go on. He wished he liked her
better for Beverley's sake. But you couldn't turn who you liked
off and on like they did the electrolier in the dining room. It still
lit the lawn through the French windows. It made a skeleton of
black lines in the light that etched the conservatory. He watched
in the summer when he could just faintly see those real flimsy curtains breathe and sigh when the breeze billowed them out over the
lawn, and sometimes he watched in the winter when the lights
met the snow that seemed to shine white even at night, and then
he watched the girls with their store-bought sleds run belly-flop
down the hill, their yells from all the way across the valley sound-
ing as pretty as birdcalls. He would stay out there until Essie
would come to the door and say, "Git in here. You'll freeze to
death." Essie never did quite understand that there was where he
did his thinking, as he was doing now, just like his ma had before
him in the same rocker, the seat worn thin.

He was waiting for all the lights to go out but the light in the
library. It had been on later and later since the trouble began. He
was worried about Beverley. He looked like death warmed over,
but he didn't ask him about it. He figured that Beverley would tell
him when he got good and ready. Beverley was as near to him as
his own brother, nearer. Jethro was bone-idle, a bully and a jackass,
and Ephraim had passed on. No. Him and Beverley had something, a stillness together. They had shared their hours ever since
he'd followed Beverley around like a pup, and Beverley never did
chase him off, not like Jethro. He hoped the lights would go off,

all but the library before the women got through with their meeting, but if they didn't he was going to go up there anyhow. He wasn't going to explain to nobody. He was on his own damned property.

Mother had inspected the barn before the women got there. It gave her something to do to clear her mind. By the time the first ones straggled in and stood against the back wall, trying to hide in the shadows under the loft until it was time, she had found a feed-box that suited her, and turned it over to stand on so she would be high enough above them for everybody to see her. She had blown out the lamps at the back so more light shone on her, and they would be in the half-dark. She had reminded herself not to sound too educated and scare them.

She stood on the box waiting for the women. She didn't move, or smooth her dress or finger her jabot. She'd already done that.

She knew better than to use the language in front of the women that she used in front of the men, or to herself. She knew what they had all heard about her and she knew they had to see something different from that if she was going to get them to do what she had in mind. She looked at her little watch pin to pace herself in the time she had. It said eleven o'clock.

In another five minutes the barn was nearly full. The women clutched together, Italians on one side, hillbillies on the other. They looked toward the feedbox, waiting for her to begin, and she let them look and shuffle long enough to see a pretty little old lady, more like a schoolteacher or somebody's aunt than the hell-cat they expected. Some people said she looked like Queen Victoria, and she used that when she negotiated with the bosses, but she knew none of the women knew Queen Victoria from a hole in the outhouse. Even the voice was different. She started out low and easy just like they were having a talk over the fence.

"Now all us women," she said so low the ones in the back had to crane their necks as if that helped them hear her. She could see them in the half-dark, necks stretched like chickens about to be fed. Well, by God, she felt ready to scatter her words like grain. "We know what a strike is better than the men. We are the ones got to keep a bunch of tents clean and our youngins fed and do our washin' and arnin' best we can. We're the ones watch our babies' bellies swell from not enough to eat and see our men brought in beat up by thugs or worse. Worse?" It was time for her voice to rise. "Is that there worse than seein' 'em brought back mashed in the mine and no compensation?" Several of the women at the back began to nod, not the ones in front. They were too self-conscious still, too near the lights.

"Is it worse than bein' borned by a company doctor when he's sober or if he's got time? Is it worse than seeing your youngins schooled in a company school four months a year, and your boys dragged out to slave in the breaker shed as soon as you quit changin' their didies? No! Nuthin's worse! I seen the rising generation, yes the little ones, yes the babes, look to the little ones, look to the assaulted women!"

One woman said, "Amen," like she was in church.

Somebody said, "Hush up there."

"I feel inspiration in me! I feel inspiration like I never felt before from you women tonight." It was time to ring the chimes. Mother let go. Her voice pounded the barn walls. "The womanhood of this valley shall not be beaten, robbed and violated like you was tonight by a bunch of company bloodhounds. NEVERMORE." She paused for the Amens, the yes, yes, she knew would come, always did come from the Baptists and the Holy Rollers.

They caught the Amens from each other. Nobody said hush.

"Nevermore will you be married by a company preacher, owned by a company store, put in a company house that ain't fit for nuthin' but a hawg, ready to fall in on your head, berried on company land your loved ones can't even put flowers on your grave if there's a strike and your men are on a yellow-dog contract says they git set out if they stand up for their rights. Nevermore would the operators steal your men's labor by docking their loads of thousands of tons of coal a year."

She heard one of the Italian women translating for some others that were clustered around her, so she slowed down as much as she could without losing pitch or rhythm. It was that Mrs. Pagano she'd helped get up to Jake Catlett's house. She could still see in her mind's eye that woman's poor belongings thrown down the steps like sacks of potatoes. She sensed that it was time to step right out onto dangerous ground.

"And the church!" She let them have their little stir at that. "Now I don't say nuthin' about your church as such. But it ain't your church. It's company church, you can't even use it to git berried from when there's a strike. It don't belong to God. It belongs to the company with a company Jesus. Why, I set in one of them churches and I seen sixteen hundred dollars of your money sent out to teach Chinese heathens about Jesus. Why, that company Jesus don't know no more about you than a dawg does its father! Jesus never saw a penny of it and never will. You don't need no company Jesus up this holler. You got the UNITED MINE WORKERS DISTRICT SEVENTEEN! QUIT YOUR BELLY-ACHIN'! ORGANIZE!"

There was almost a cheer, not quite, mostly from the young women. Mother let her voice drop again.

"It was the United Mine Workers from all over this fair land brought these tents up the holler to shelter you when the blood-hounds throwed your treasures out of your houses into the creek, and it will be the United Mine Workers that sends you food so your little ones won't starve as I've seen the youngins do many a time before. I been in fourteen states of our beloved land took away from us by the Big Corporations. I seen strikes in fourteen states. I been in the mine loading coal with the men. I set with them in the darkness of hell on the gob-pile while they shared their lunch with me and we organized. Who brought the Gatling gun up to Godley? Who built the concrete pillboxes? Who set the Gatling gun up to the Mansion looks down in arrogant contempt on your poor little town? Who hard the Baldwin thugs to murder ye? No. It wasn't no UMW and it wasn't them poor fools locked in the Godley Boarding House. It wasn't even the poor old mine owners we used to deal with in oh two. They was gentlemen when we organized up here before. They was not the Eastern interests and the wildcat operators we got these days. They're the aggressors. They're the ones hard men like Butcher Goujot come up here to violate and murder ye. I wish I was governor of this state instead of Governor Glasscock who for modesty sake we will call Crystal Peter . . ." She paused for the laughter she expected, forgetting they were women and wouldn't dare laugh out loud at that in public. She recovered quickly.

"Why if I was governor for one day I would clear the guns, and the bloodhounds and the blind-deaf operators and their crew out out of this state. I would send them to their God in the repair shop! I'd get rid of the whole blood-suckin' bunch."

She noticed that the women had drawn together in groups, the hillbillies together, and the foreigners together. She waited to use that at the right time. Back at the door in the half-dark she saw the flick of a white dress, somebody too shy to come all the way inside. She made herself sound gentle, motherly.

"Honey, sister? You out there in the darkness. You come on in here and join your sisters. There's nuthin' to be afraid of in here."

She waited until the girl came around the door. The women turned to watch where she looked. Then the girl, it was no more than a girl, dirty as a breaker boy, my God in a fancy white dress with a rose at her throat, and her hair down her back like a twelve-year-old.

Her voice was just as soft when she said, "Yes, you. You come on up here. Come up here with me."

Lily thought she was in heaven. She had listened to every word of her own feelings spoken by Mother Jones. She had not dared to hope to be noticed and used. Now it was happening. The sweet-faced old lady was willing her down the aisle between the women, down toward her. She could feel the welcoming eyes. The crossing of the valley, the wandering in the night had been worth it. She felt her heart. It was really swelling. She hoped she wouldn't cry for joy. She knew then what it was like at the night meetings, knew Essie's heart like her own when she walked down the aisle toward the preacher to be saved.

She was trembling, so that Mother had to help her up onto the box. She was a head taller than Mother, but she didn't feel that way. She felt like a little girl. The barn was dead-still.

Mother Jones clutched her arm hard and held it high.

"Now what have we here?" she asked the crowd. "What have we here out of curiosity and boredom come over to be entertained? Yes, this is a lady! Look at the lady. Look at this little hand never done a lick of work, not worth fifty cents. Why, it's got dirt on it. Coal dust I bet for the first time."

Lily tried to get her hand away but she clutched it like it belonged to her and waved it. "Has she been chasin' her little lost poodle dog into the mine, her dog that eats better than your kids? Has she been callin' out 'Come here, little doggie'?" Her voice simpered, " 'I love you, little dog. Have those mean dirty people hurt you, little Fido?' Or maybe that's dirt from the golf course while your youngins play on the gob-pile. Look at her. Look at her little waist and her pretty dress cost a year's pay. That's not a woman. That's a lady. Let me tell you! Modern parasites made ladies. God Almighty made women!"

Lily didn't cry. She wouldn't let herself do that.

"Now git on out of here. We don't need you. Let me help you down like some nigger done for you all your life."

Essie knew she ought to go with Lily, that old woman treating her that way, poor little youngin not dry behind the ears. She'd told her to go on home where she belonged. She wanted to move, but she was hemmed in by the women. She never had liked Lily much anyhow. She was a know-it-all. Always something hurt her feelings if anybody said boo turkey to her like nobody else on earth had any feelings when she instructed them like she knew it all. Instruct you how to pee!

Lily jumped down as soon as Mother let her arm go. She ran up the aisle. When she got to the door she knew she had to have the last word, and not let herself be treated like that or she'd be ashamed for the rest of her life. She made herself turn around and face all the eyes. They looked dead. She had to let them know who she was.

"VOTES FOR WOMEN," she called out, and ran into the dark.

"Oh shit!" Mother Jones forgot and said it out loud, but nobody heard her. They were still staring at the blank doorway. They had heard the girl, though, and she wanted to put that last remark in its place.

"WOMAN SUFFRAGE!" The yell turned them around again. "That's for ladies. That's a class movement. That don't have no more to do with us than the YMCA! Both of them are capitalist-formed and capitalist-paid-for out of the pockets of people that's bleedin' you to death. What about child suffrage? What about CHILD CRUCIFIXION? Child crucifixion is what I care for and fight for and go to jail for and am gonna die for!"

She finally got the cheer she'd been waiting for all through the speech, the cheer that meant she could get down to business.

Annunziata had stopped trying to translate. When somebody touched her arm and whispered "Quale?" she snapped, "Basta." She was listening too hard. She didn't know a lot of the words, but she knew one thing. The old woman up there had talked to Miss Lily Lacey like she should have been talked to all her spoiled life.

In Annunziata's shoulders, in the muscles of her body, something that had frozen a long time ago was being released. It was hope surging back to the dead places in her. She could feel it thawing her blood. She found that she was sighing over and over. She glanced around. She sounded like a dog panting and she didn't want anybody to notice. Speranza e furore were good for a woman's body, hope and anger. It was an old saying, or she had just made it up. She didn't care. She felt like an animal released from its winter pen. She had a direction, an open field. She could feel her mind quicken and gambol at the old woman's words.

"Now I'm just one old woman, one old woman eighty years old"—Mother Jones lowered her voice again—"What about you young women? What are you goin' to do? I'm goin' to tell you. You're goin' to pray. Yes, pray. You're goin' to do just that. The men are afraid to picket when the scab shift goes in tomorrow morning at five o'clock. They're sneakin' them in early so we won't know. Why, we know everythin' that goes on in this holler. Some of your men make excuses. They can't go. They got an ache in their back. Why, some of them ain't got enough grease in their backbone to grease two black cats. They can't picket because it's illegal. Well, I'll tell you something. I agree with them this time. We don't want no shootin'. We're law-abidin' citizens. But we women ain't goin' to back water. No sir. I never backed water in my life and I'm eighty-two years old eighty-three this summer.

"No. We ain't goin' to picket. We're goin' to have us a prayer meeting and it ain't goin' to be like no prayer meeting you ever saw before. Even Butcher Goujot won't shoot a woman that's prayin' if he values his life in these hills. Now I want you to come up here and meet me at four o'clock this morning. All of you!" It was time to use the path cut between the women. "Look at that! Standing apart as if you wasn't all in this together. Let me tell you. In the United Mine Workers there ain't no Hunkies nor Dagoes nor rednecks. We don't use that kind of language. We're all one. Close up that aisle!"

The women moved obediently together. "Close! Get closer. Now we're all one!"

"Teddy Roosevelt, old Teddy the Monkey Chaser, told an audience in Chicago that we were committing racial suicide. He ought to come up this holler and see you women with two babes on the titty and six more on the floor. Now I want those of you got a babe in arms to bring it up here. Those of you don't, borry one. Don't bring none that can walk. They'll slow us down. The rest of you bring tin pans and tin washbasins and cooking spoons. I don't want no washtubs. They're too heavy. One, two of you stay on watch and wake the others. The rest of you git what sleep you can. You're goin' to need it." She consulted her watch. "It's after midnight. Dawn comes at four o'clock. Any of you got a clock?"

Everybody looked at Essie. They knew she had a clock, so she had to raise her hand but she didn't agree with any of it. She thought it was all a piece of foolishness, and she was not going to have any part of using Jesus Christ as an organizer even for Jake's UMW and she was going to tell him so in no uncertain terms.

"Mrs. Catlett will come and wake you then or I will. Go on git some sleep."

The women began to file out and their voices chirped, beginning to discuss what they had heard.

"Hush up, you women," the voice behind them called. "I don't want the men to know what we're up to. They told me not to do this. A man's a fool to tell a woman not to do nuthin'. Miz Pagano, you stay here. I need you."

IV

Midnight to 8:00 A.M., Saturday, June 8, 1912

Mooney was scared. He could feel it on his back as he trudged up to Godley through the black tunnel made by the trees. In case anybody met him he held his bandanna up to his face and blew his nose once in a while like he had a cold. He could hear the creek down beside him, and the upriver breeze high above him, and the frogs berkekking and those sounds were a comfort. Once in a while a branch fell and it put chills up his spine. He stopped frozen as a deer. Every branch, every sound he couldn't name was a bunch of rednecks waiting to meet up with him, ready to jump out and bushwhack him in the pitch dark before he could explain he wasn't a Baldwin man anymore, that he was going back to Greenbriar County to be a lawyer.

It was the longest, darkest mile he'd ever walked in his life, not only because of the fear, but because of the burden he carried. He knew what he had to do and he didn't want to do it, but that square rock of conscience the preacher said hurt your heart when it turned over was hurting his heart, or his stomach. It was giving him the bellyache. The preacher said if you didn't pay attention to it it would wear right down and get smooth and not hurt you any- more and then you couldn't feel it atall and you would be lost to sin and that the road to hell was paved with good intentions.

He came out of the tunnel of trees to where he could see the light on the water tower. He was never so glad to see anything in his life. He walked across the bridge on his tiptoes but he still made a noise like a troop of horses in that quiet. He was trying so hard not to make a noise that he damned near broke his neck on the Godley chain. He could hear men up in the pillbox. He knew they had the Gatling gun trained right on him. He stopped. He could hear voices, but not what they said. He didn't move until they quieted down so he could make out somebody saying, "They ain't nobody comin'. You're just shit scared."

He did have the sense to creep right close to the concrete so if they did get to shooting they'd shoot over him.

There was still a light up at Mr. Roundtree's on the hill, and one, two windows at the Boarding House showed him the way past. The Club House ahead of him was lit up like a nickelodeon. He could see the shadows of men jump along the road and the houses, and hear the sound of white mule, the sound of men getting mad as hell.

He pushed past them to get into the Club House. He was sneaking upstairs to get his things and sneak out again without saying anything to anybody, but Dan Neill looked up and caught him. He didn't see how he did it, with that crowd of men making the racket in the parlor.

"Come on in, son." There wasn't anything to do but come on back downstairs and stand inside the door until Dan Neill quit bothering him. "Son, you look pale. You got up too soon."

They both knew there wasn't nothing wrong with him, that it wasn't nothing but a scratch. He didn't know why Dan Neill tried to make so much out of it.

Some of the men were arguing that the new Dago started it all, and some others were saying they didn't need no new Dago, them Paganos was troublemakers enough. "You git the snake in the head," Anderson Carver hollered over all of them, the loudmouth drunk, "the way he hangs around." Nobody said who he hung around, but Mooney knew who he meant, and that high-hat Dan Neill knew who he was talking about and he didn't say a word.

"Git one, you don't need but one." Anderson Carver was making up their minds for them and Dan Neill wasn't saying a word. You couldn't even tell from his face whether he was listening or not. He was looking at his fancy boots and when he leaned down to brush some dirt off, Mooney managed to creep out the door and go on upstairs again.

He changed his clothes carefully. He didn't want to be caught dead in those black pants and that black coat and slouch hat he'd paid a month at the University for so he could look like that bunch

206

of trash. He was disgusted with himself. He put on his white ducks and his good shirt and his Sunday coat, not his Sunday coat to go to church in but the one to impress the women, his ukelele coat he called it. He was proud of that coat and his straw hat with the grosgrain ribbon like the fellows wore up at Morgantown, the richer ones anyhow, not the hillbillies come out of some hollow.

He put his straw hat on and packed his other two shirts, his underwear and his pajamas and the books he brought to study but hadn't got around to yet.

Not a one of them even noticed when he walked back out of the Club House and out of the periphery of its light and noise, past the pillbox, and turned up the path toward Mr. Roundtree's lit window. He wasn't taking the road of good intentions, he was taking the road of acting on his conscience. He wished that stuck-up Miss Lily could see him.

He felt terrible about telling Dan Neill earlier about the Dagoes at the Depot, and guilty about letting them make so much out of a skinned knee and setting the Paganos out. He felt like he had started the whole damn thing. There was only one thing to do, tell Mr. Roundtree, and get the hell out of the hollow while his conscience still had hard corners.

He looked in the window. Mr. Roundtree was asleep in his chair; his book had fallen and splayed out on the floor.

Mooney tapped on the windowsill and Mr. Roundtree woke up, not knowing what woke him, and picked up the book again. He just glanced around the room like somebody had caught him sleeping when he was supposed to be reading.

Mooney whispered, "Mr. Roundtree, I'm out here."

He came over to the window and saw who it was. "Why, Mooney, what's the matter? You look ill." He sat down on the windowsill like he was getting ready to have a discussion and Mooney didn't want no discussion of the matter. He just wanted to tell him and ease his conscience and go on home where he belonged.

Mr. Roundtree yawned and said, "Pardon."

"Mr. Roundtree they's gonna be trouble. A bunch of the boys went down to the tents just to have a little fun, and they got thowed out." He couldn't help grinning. "They got thowed out by a little old woman." Mr. Roundtree started to speak but he didn't let him. "Now they're down to the Club House. They's drunk as skunks. They're fixin' to bushwhack a Dago. They about decided to git Eddie Pagano because he's too big for his britches. You better git down there and stop them."

He'd said what he had to and he turned and jumped off the porch with Mr. Roundtree calling after him, "Come back here, Mooney. You must tell me more."

He stopped on the path and called back, "No sir, I quit. I'm going back to Greenbriar County."

He didn't even look around, not at Godley, not at the light on the water tower, not at the tents as he passed them except to notice that they had set them back up and there were only a few faint lights. Everybody was asleep.

He just walked on the two miles to the station carrying the carpetbag his ma had loaned to him, first in one hand and then in the other. He didn't stop until he got to the Depot platform and sat down on the bench to wait for the first upriver train. He didn't care for once what the hell his ma would do to him for quitting. He already decided what he would do. He would get him a job helping with the harvest or he would get him a job soda jerking at Mr. Carver's drugstore. Mr. Carver was his mother's first cousin once removed. He was sure he wasn't any kin to that Anderson Carver from Canona though. They weren't that kind of people. He knew one thing. Anybody would give a job to a fellow working his way through college. The preacher said, not saith, like the Bible, but said. He said, "Set your gauge for Glory. Yawl know what a gauge is for, well, set it higher and higher."

Mooney wondered why you spelled it "gauge" and said gage instead of gawge. Well, he didn't know about Glory, but he felt like his gauge was already rising enough for his boiler to blow. He set his gauge for Greenbriar, not Glory, not right then.

He wasn't going up there on some labor train either. He was going on the Tuxedo Special come in from St. Louis at one-twenty-five. It seemed more fitting to get off of the Tuxedo Special at Alderson. It was almost like a triumph after all he'd been through.

The only other souls around were two foreigners in long black

208

coats and hard black hats. They were sitting on the bench too. He remembered to say "Howdee" to them and then he just forgot they were there. He was too busy doing figures in his head about how much hay he was going to have to pitch to get a hundred and seventy dollars. It was a lot of money. He decided he could do two jobs, one in the day and one in the evening, and then not even his ma could say he was good-for-nothing, quitting a ten-dollar-a-day job you didn't have to pay board and room.

The two other souls were Mr. Rabinowitz and his brother, waiting for the downriver train.

Mr. Roundtree had come back to the Boarding House and got them. He said there was absolutely no excuse for their being there under false pretenses and he lent them three dollars.

Of course the telephone had gone dead just when Beverley needed it. The damned thing cost an arm and a leg and it wasn't worth a plug nickel. The girls had been fooling with it again. He had things to say to Roundtree and he didn't feel like dragging himself a mile up the hollow after him. He wished the breeze would cool things off a little bit. The big ceiling fan creaked and groaned around and around over his head. It didn't do a damned bit of good. Summer lightning made the window livid and then passed, leaving deeper darkness. He tried to tell himself it was the first hot night of summer that made him clammy with sweat under his shirt but he knew better. Night sweats and hot flashes, just like a damned woman, that was what it was. It got worse every night. It kept him awake. He didn't want to go to bed anyhow, not until the women went to sleep. My God, the floorboards still complained of women pacing back and forth, one heavy tread, then light pats of bare feet, like restive dogs up there. He went on waiting for the house to quiet down so he could think, get ready to do what he had to before he left them. It was about as mundane as cleaning out a top drawer. He hadn't expected that. He wanted it to be more awesome, less like his life had been.

He had hoped against hope that she wouldn't come downstairs again but it was too much to ask. He'd told her he had work to do but it didn't do any good. When had it ever when she had something on her mind that had to wait until the girls were asleep? He heard the pacing stop, the upstairs door open, heard her slow heavy tread down the stairs. By the time she knocked at the door he had wiped his face clear of sweat and done what his mother always told him to do—composed himself, as if he were making himself up for a song he had to sing, a song that went yes honey I know honey don't you worry honey, honey, not meaning a damned word of the chorus that would send her upstairs to sleep like a baby, leaving her worries on his shoulders.

She knocked on the door, the same shy knock, the only time of the day or night she had a bit of shyness in her whole makeup. She stood there in her old kimono. She wouldn't wear the new one. She said she was saving it, but he didn't know what for. She did it because she'd been poor, and she wouldn't let him forget it, not when she complained about every idea he had, the tennis court for the girls, anything. She would speak her piece that always ended with, "I have to point these things out. You don't know what it is to have one waist you have to wash every night." Well, she was poor again, the sad bitch, only she didn't know it and he was too tired and too scared and goddammit too hopeful that something would happen to change it all so he could go to his grave in peace. He could see them following him now, hollering down through six feet of overburden, "I've got to talk to you."

Her hair hung down over her shoulder in a lot thinner braid than it used to, a little skinny pigtail when it had once been as thick as a six-foot snake. He noticed that for the first time. Goddammit. You'd think getting ready to kick the bucket would keep your mind occupied so you didn't notice unimportant details, you'd think about God and Eternity, but it was just the opposite. Details he had taken for granted were all new, taunting him. He had no protection of habits or blindness anymore; everything was vivid and terrible.

She said it. She said, "I've got to talk to you." She didn't wait for him to say "I know, honey." She just walked behind him over to the open window that looked down over the town and said, "They had a bonfire down there, all that whooping and hollering, drunk. I couldn't get to sleep." She turned around. The breeze caught her kimono and made it billow out in front of her.

"Beverley, we've got to come to an understanding."

210

He waited.

"We've got to come to some kind of understanding," she said.

He looked at the paperweight that had belonged to his father. It had a little church in it. When you turned it over and then turned it back, snow fell around the church, slow quiet snow.

"We've just got to come to grips with this thing," she said to his back.

He knew what they had to come to grips with and it wasn't what she thought, not by a long shot, but he let her talk since there wasn't any way to stop her.

"We've got to get our girls out of here. I've been thinking. We could rent a house in Canona until we find something suitable."

He knew what she thought was suitable. River Street. A Coal Baron mansion. That was suitable. He turned over the paperweight, and turned it back. The snow drifted down.

"Please, Beverley, consider the offer."

He knew that was coming. The snow floated around the tiny church. It made him feel cooler just watching it.

"Put that thing down and look at me. We've got to take the offer."

Over my dead body, he told himself, enjoying his private joke. For once she was going to have to make the decision and he knew she would do it while the tears still dribbled down on her black bombazine.

"Yes, honey," he said, "we'll talk about it in the morning."

"You always say that." She started to cry. She didn't do that often. It was going to take longer to get her to go upstairs. He sighed. He pushed himself up out of his chair, his father's chair, and took her in his arms. She was thick, she felt soft as pudding without her stays. She mumbled against his shoulder. "Lily didn't come home. You've got to go and find her, please, Beverley, I'm just worried sick. It's way after midnight."

"All right, honey. I'll go down and see if she's over at Essie and Jake's. That's where she goes when she's out like this."

"At Essie and Jake's my foot," she corrected him by habit. "She oughtn't to be out like this. She's with those Paganos I know she is, oh Beverley, please . . ."

"All right, honey, you go on to bed. Take something for your headache. I'll go get her." He led her out of the room as soon as he had pacified her body, not like you do a woman. He hadn't done that in years, but like he would have one of the girls, stroked her back and remembered to murmur, "Don't you worry, honey, honey." Then "Honey?" as he led her out. "Will you promise me? Go on to bed? Go on sleep in your tower, princess." He made himself remember to say that, as he had a long time ago when she took over the tower room. She said she had to have a place she could call her own.

She said yes she would now that he knew. He stood in the door and watched her climb the stairs, lighter, almost like one of the girls. He didn't know why she trusted him like that. She only trusted him at night when she was about to go to sleep and leave him with more than he bargained for.

Beverley picked up the paperweight again. He felt the night breeze on his shoulders. He felt almost chilly after the waves of heat. If he was finding the quietness to sit there by himself and commune with his death, he had forgotten. He tried to sigh. It made his chest grab pain. He was waiting for nothing, to rest in nothing for a little while.

Somebody was tapping on the windowsill. He wasn't going to be let alone.

Jake saw Beverley get up from his daddy's office chair like an old, old man. When he finally got to the window to look out, Jake said, "I brung your wire cutters back."

Beverley said, "Come on in, Jake, I'm glad to see you," like he had a thousand times.

Jake climbed in the window. Beverley didn't ask him why he didn't go on around to the front door.

He sat back down in his daddy's chair and circled it around so he could see Jake. Jake sat down in the bishop's chair like he always did.

They didn't say a word until they got used to each other. Beverley looked past Jake's head. For once he didn't want to look at him. It wasn't time to tell even Jake and he knew he would read trouble way beyond the night in his eyes. He always had. He said, "What's eatin' you?" whenever he read his eyes.

"That damned youngin Lily," Beverley finally said.

"Oh she's all right. Don't you worry about her none. She's down to the tents. Essie tole her come on home."

"She's bullheaded as her mother. I'll go down get her." Beverley started to get up again.

"Naw. Don't go down thar. Ain't nobody goin' to bother her. Ain't nobody been drinkin' but them gun thugs and they're back up to Godley."

Beverley did feel the need to talk, not about the real trouble but about all the troubles that lay over it. "Jake. They're cleanin' me out. Don't you folks know Imperial don't give a goddamn how long you stay out? They ain't losin' a cent at Number Eight. If there's too much trouble with the transportation men they'll just close Number Eight. They got other mines ain't out. They got plenty of stockpile."

"We don't figure it thataway."

"I know you don't. You're damned fools." They were so at ease with each other that they could have been talking about anything, weather, crops, baseball.

Baseball reminded Beverley. He sounded hurt. "Why did you all move your tents off of my bull field? You knew I wouldn't make you."

"Oh it ain't that, Beverley. It's solidarity."

"Don't talk that UMW language with me, Jake. Save it for your meeting." They both grinned.

Jake didn't answer. He just sat back in the bishop's chair and looked at the plaster Winged Victory. "I always thought that was the prettiest thing."

"I'll leave it to you in my will. Dammit I don't understand anything anymore. We never had a walkout at Seven Stars. Father negotiated with the union in oh two. I'm ready to negotiate a contract with you, you know that."

"It ain't that simple no more, Beverley. You only got one mine. Them gun thugs ain't goin' to let you work. Them and the UMW ain't goin' to let you run no coal out of here, don't care who you are."

"I don't understand a damned thing. It just don't make a damn bit of sense."

Jake had to get to the matter at hand even if neither of them liked to hurry the other.

"Beverley, I come up here on my own. They don't nobody know I done it. Them thugs come down and tore up the colony. They's full of white mule. Didn't nobody git hurt yet but my boys are mad."

Beverley started to interrupt. Jake wouldn't let him. "I know. I know we started it. They're up thar saying we bushwhacked 'em. Now you know damned well we wanted to shoot somebody we'd of shot somebody. All we was doin' was shootin' around them white trash they got up thar figured we'd scare em out of the holler."

"It was a damned fool thing to do."

"Yes. I'm agreein' with you. A damned fool thing to do."

They had finished that conversation. They let silence fill the room. They rested in it, both alone, neither one lonesome.

"Company policy." Beverley broke the rest. "Company policy against solidarity and us in between. That's how I see it."

That was how Jake saw it too, sitting up in the library with Beverley, but he knew he wouldn't see it that way down the hill or on his own porch.

"Them Imperial fellows think more of a mule than they do a man," Jake said, mostly to himself.

"You all knew better than move off my bull field," Beverley said, not to anybody. Then he finally looked right at Jake. "I'm goin' to sell out. I've hit bedrock. I ain't got no place in this. Jake, Imperial is taking advantage of the strike to squeeze me out."

There wasn't a damned thing Jake would say when Beverley talked like that. He'd said it before, and Jake knew he'd say it again, every time the bottom fell out of the coal business. He felt disloyal, but he never had liked it when that pity for himself crept into Beverley's voice. His pappy never would have talked like that. The trouble was, Beverley thought he was broke when he couldn't afford to go to Europe. Broke, hell. He didn't have the least notion what broke was. Jake didn't say that, though. He said, "Only way you can make a cent out of this business is when folks is fixin' to fight. War, strike . . . You piled up stocks. I seen it."

214

"I can't move them without guards."

"You ain't never goin' to have no guards." Jake was certain of that, as certain as he was that Beverley wasn't broke. His pappy, alive or dead, wouldn't stand for it.

"But my boys don't know that," he went on aloud. "They seen them guards right up here on your porch."

"They come to see the girls, Jake. I can't stop that."

"My boys don't know that."

"Well, dammit they ought to figure it out. They've known me all my life."

"They've knowed a lot of things all your life. That was a damned fool thing to do, too, puttin' that Gatling gun out on your porch. Hell's far, Beverley, that there's an insult."

"You talk to Mrs. Lacey about that. You know when she gets a bee in her bonnet. She stood over me until I did it."

"Well it was a damned fool thing to do. We both ain't used our brains."

"Things come along too fast," Beverley comforted Jake and himself. They rested in the comfort; Beverley turned his chair back and forth. He wanted to pick up the paperweight again but he didn't.

Jake, behind him, said, "Now what I come up here for is I think you and me ought to go up and talk to Roundtree. If they take them scabs into Godley tomorry they's goin' to be trouble." Jake had refused ever since the sale to call it No. 8. "That ain't no name for nuthin'," he had told everybody. "The boys won't stand for it. That old woman is fixin' to take the women up thar. She's stickin' to the letter of the law. We ain't goin' to picket. But she ain't stickin' to the spirit of the law. She ain't got no idea what that is."

"Hell's fire, Jake, don't come talkin' to me you can't handle your women. I can't handle mine."

"They ain't goin' to picket, but lay a hand on one of them women them boys take to the hills and anybody moves down in the holler is a sitting duck. We got to do something." That was as near to urgency as Jake could go, but his voice never rose. It stayed there slow, low in his throat like it always had.

215

"I've already talked to Roundtree. He says it's as much as his job is worth not to take the transportation in. He's got no more control over that bunch of trash than you have over your boys."

"They want a fight." Jake's voice was slower than ever. He thought for a long time. "I'm goin' up thar and talk to Dan Neill. Dammit, he's my own cousin. Blood's thickern water."

They both agreed that blood was thicker than water. It was at least a new idea, and Jake clung to it. "Yep, I'm goin' up thar and talk to him. Why, Middle Dan Neill was alive I used to go over thar and set with him. That was after Pa died. Eighty years old he wouldn't of let me go." That reminded him. My God, Cousin Dan had looked just like Beverley in oh seven. Same drawed-up face, same sick-animal eyes. Jake was scared.

"Beverley, what's eatin' you? It ain't the strike. You could handle that." He'd finally said it, interfered, didn't wait for Beverley to tell him.

Beverley never wanted to tell so much in his life, but he couldn't. He couldn't bring it out of his mouth.

"I'm worried about my girls," he lied, and Jake knew he was lying.

"I'm goin' to find Dan Neill." Jake had one leg over the window-sill. "If my boys find out what I done they'll accuse me of goin' over. Well, I don't give a damn. I'm goin' to talk to him."

He was gone, out into the dark. Beverley couldn't hear a sound.

Jake had left trouble behind him. Beverley thought if he just rested a minute, got his breath, he'd go too, and find Roundtree, get him out of bed.

Midnight settled in the library, dead of night, dead-still. He took stock. He watched the pile of bills held down by the paper-weight, bills he had no idea how he was going to pay. He took stock of the company books piled on his daddy's big rolltop desk. He took stock of the Winged Victory and the bust of Plato and the picture of the Colosseum in Rome. He took stock of the dead books nobody but Lily touched, the green Thackeray, the brown Dickens, the blue Sir Walter Scott, all dead, all of it.

Beverley's conscience wasn't dead, though. Dammit, he thought he'd settled with it, but in the library in the middle of the night, it came alive. It was a man. It had the face of his father. He had to wrestle with it or it struck him. It was a woman, my God, his mother, his wife, his girls, all the same face. It pricked, that's what woman conscience did, pricked at you until it nearly drove you crazy. His conscience was the strike. It struck at you, bowled you over, made you whimper. "I know, hell I know, but what can I do?" That was no way to ease the prick, the wrestling, the strike.

"You're going to learn every last thing," his father's voice came back as if he had spoken aloud.

He was ten years old. He wasn't standing there before his father in the library reciting his catechism or the multiplication table or the books of the Bible like other boys. "You're going to know this land from heaven to hell, young man. That's how we own it. That's what the law says. Now start."

He started at the trees, and went down, seeing it in his mind's eye, down into the terrifying dark, deeper and deeper, down through the overburden. "Home wood, sandstone, shale, black flint, gassy coal, Stockton seam, gray sandstone, shale, limestone, fire clay, coal," all the way down toward hell. His father wouldn't let him stop until he was down six hundred feet from the home wood of the topsoil and the mountain trees to bedrock. Well, now he was going down six feet. That was all. He was going to be buried in home wood over sandstone.

Goddammit, somebody was knocking at his door again. It was Mary Rose. She came in looking all sleep-pretty in her nightgown. Her fists dug at her eyes. "I had a bad dream."

"Come here to me, honey." He held out his arms and she snuggled up.

"There was this monster . . ."

"Now honey, you're fifteen years old. You're too old to carry on like this." Once she had fitted his strong lap. Now her feet dragged the floor. He could feel her warmth against the bones of his legs.

"I'm not fifteen years old when I have a bad dream." They smiled together. It was their private joke. "Nobody's over five years old when they wake up scared in the night," he had told her lots of times. She let him rock her back and forth in the office chair. They listened to the comforting groan of the big spring.

"I heard somebody talking." She tried to sound as sleepy as she could.

"It was me, talking to myself, honey. Your daddy's gone plumb crazy."

She giggled.

She hadn't been asleep at all. She'd taken Althea's dare.

"Carry me up and tuck me in," she said, little-girl talk. She knew he liked to hear that.

For the first time in his life Beverley knew he couldn't lift his youngest girl. He was so damned weak he couldn't lift a cat, a slim little girl, much less the weight of the world that was on his shoulders.

He teased her instead. "Now you go on. You're big and ugly enough to climb those stairs."

"It's dark," she whined. She had to persuade him in case she met her mother coming down from the tower all scary with the night around her.

"All right. I'll come up with you. But I won't carry you. You're too old for that kind of foolishness."

"I'm sleeping in Althea's room. I don't want to be by myself." She clung to his neck. God, she was heavy.

He patted her bottom to start her up the stairs, and tucked her in as quietly as he could to keep Althea from waking up. She was sleeping like a stone, her body turned to the wall.

He closed the door as carefully as he used to when he came in late on the last upriver train, the Tuxedo Special, after a party in Canona, to keep his mother from hearing him and asking who all was there.

The girls had waited and giggled into their bunched-up night-gowns and whispered together ever since Mary Rose had sneaked into Althea's room and whispered, "Are you asleep? Lily's still out."

"I know," came from the darkness. "I've been listening." Althea wasn't even in bed. Mary Rose could see her at the window, against the lighter darkness of the sky. She was kneeling, with

218

her arms on the windowsill. "Budge over." Mary Rose pushed her to make room. They knelt together in their white nightgowns, playing with their braided hair, and swaying together to the sound of the fiddle winging up out of the valley, lonesome and left out while the dance went on in Jake Catlett's barn.

"I bet Lily's over there," Althea whispered.

"Could we sneak out?" It was only an idea that had to be said. They both knew there wasn't a chance with her mother pacing back and forth in the next room.

Hardly breathing, they listened to her open her door. They counted the steps as she went down the stairs. She didn't leave the library door opened, so they only heard the familiar rhythm of parent talk, not what they were saying. They waited and watched the night. They could hear the music stop, and the sound of shouting. Somebody lit a bonfire but it went out.

"I bet they're all drunk as monkeys," Mary Rose whispered.

"Shhh!" Althea said. "There's somebody else down there with Papa."

"Maybe it's Lily."

"No. It's Jake Catlett. I can tell."

"You can't."

"Yes I can. He rumbles."

Mary Rose had to bite her braid to keep her giggle down.

Finally, there was only the pacing of their mother, this time in the tower room. They took turns going to the bathroom, but they couldn't hear anything.

Althea couldn't stand it any longer.

"Go on, I dare you. Mother's gone to the tower. You know what that means." Althea tickled and prodded Mary Rose until she was dying of silent giggles.

After Papa had tucked Mary Rose in, they held their breath until they heard the library door close again, playing at dying to giggle. Althea released hers first, into her pillow. Mary Rose grabbed her pillow and wiggled and said "Oh Lord oh Lord don't make me laugh anymore. It hurts."

"Did you find out?"

"No."

They lay on their backs watching the darkness outside the window. It was too warm for covers, even for a sheet. The breeze touched them and played over their faces.

"I think she's out in the bushes with that Eddie Pagano." Mary Rose started the game.

"I think she's being seduced by Captain Neill," Althea played.

It was Mary Rose's turn. "I think she's lying stark naked in a patch of poison ivy!"

They both had to retreat to their pillows to giggle.

"Reading a book over his shoulder!"

"Oh that's *killing!*"

There was a silence, but Mary Rose wanted to keep on playing. "I think . . ."

"Hush up."

They waited for the sound of footsteps and their mother's voice saying, "Young lady, where have you been at this time of night?" They waited all the way into sleep.

Fury was an iron girdle around Dan Neill's ribs. It kept him from breathing, as if any deep breath would bring a shout up from the pit of his gut, bring up gall, all the gall he'd ever had to swallow. Nobody. Nobody could make a fool out of him in front of his men and get away with it. The goddamned old woman had treated him like a boy, slipped the reins of his command away from him with that goddamned bunch of rednecks standing in a circle laughing at him. He had not been laughed at like that, alone in a circle that taunted him, since he was in kindergarten and wet his pants. He'd seen him too, Eddie Pagano, heehawing with the rest of them. He killed the old woman. He killed Pagano. He killed Roundtree. His jaw felt so tight he couldn't swallow. His whole body said kill kill kill in time with his horse's slow walk.

Roundtree, that goddamned foreigner with the job he ought to have, had stood there in the Club House parlor, stood there and talked to him like they were alone in the room, arrogant son of a bitch.

"I don't want any more trouble." That goddamned prissy voice. "You're not to take your men on Seven Stars property. No patrols down-creek beyond the chain." He acted like *he* was a goddamned captain, like he was on a parade ground.

"You men." He hadn't waited for Dan Neill to say a word. "You are paid by Imperial and you are working for Imperial." He walked up to one of the men from Cain Creek mines. "What the devil are you doing here? You work for Baird. All of you get back where you belong. I'm reporting this to headquarters in the morning."

He had walked out of the room, and into the night without saying another word.

"Fuck you," one of the men had said, and the talk went on, the brag, the big talk, the white mule talk that made Dan Neill feel defiled when he had to sit and listen to it.

"I don't want. I don't want . . ." he could still hear that god-damned English accent.

He had to say something and say it quick, had to find an excuse to get out of that smell of white trash and white mule.

"I'm going on patrol," he told the men. Pat Hand grinned. "Goujot, set your watch."

"Yes, *sir*." Goujot was grinning, too.

He rode beyond the chain and down the dark road. He wished somebody would shoot from ambush. He could feel himself, too quick for anybody, slip down on his horse's flank, shoot from behind the galloping horse, shoot to kill. He rode in the dark of the moon under the black trees. He passed the naked bulb on the water tower. He came within sight of the camp. It was dark. He could see a light up at Jake Catlett's. Suddenly he knew he ought to find Jake, talk to him. He wanted to talk to somebody, somebody who knew who he was. He didn't pay much attention to where he was going. At least the night was still his. He didn't know who to kill. There were so many. He understood at last why his father had done what he did, to release the unbearable pressure of his fury. One shot instead of many to settle the whole goddamn thing. He understood what the women meant when they said, "I don't know where to turn."

If he didn't know, his horse did. It had carried him too many times on his late-night ride. It even knew when to slow down so he could watch Lily's window, moonstruck, embarrassed to do what he couldn't help doing. He could smell the honeysuckle and hear the frogs as he clattered across the bridge. Then he saw it, something white moving under the trees that bordered Mr. Lacey's property. He brought his rifle to the ready. "Who goes there?" he called. "Come out with your hands up."

Lily never thought that she would be glad to hear Dan Neill's voice. At least it was familiar, one of her own, no matter how much she disliked him.

"Dan." She called him Dan instead of Mr. Neill. "It's me, Lily."

She came out from under the tree. "I had to wait for the lights to go out so I could sneak in. I didn't want Mother to see me like this." It started the crying again. She stood there in the middle of the road below him, and she sobbed, but when he dismounted and tried to touch her, she stepped back.

He turned on his flashlight and saw her standing there so bedraggled and forlorn, her dress torn, her hair loose and tangled, her face streaked with dirty tears. One arm was stained with what looked like blood from being thrown down in brambles—or worse —stroked with a knife. She looked like she was about to faint. He grabbed her shoulders and wouldn't let her go. She needed him.

"Oh my Christ Miss Lily what have they done to you?"

"Nothing." She jerked away from him. "Turn that off. Nothing . . ."

She would say that. He knew her. He knew how loyal she was. He played the flashlight over her body.

"Who did this? You tell me."

"Don't . . ." She started to sob again. He could feel her sobs in his body, releasing all that pent-up fury. He had a direction at last. "Nobody," she sobbed, and couldn't say any more. She ran to the fence away from the shaft of light.

"Let me take you home." He tried to follow her.

"No." She ran back into the trees. "Let me alone."

He shone the flashlight beam into the thick trees and the lilac. He couldn't see where she had gone. Of course she wouldn't let anybody touch her. He realized that. Not after what she'd been through.

He remounted and turned his horse.

*   *   *

Lily heard the hollow sound of the wooden bridge as he cantered across it. She let him disappear from her mind. She sat upright in the sweetheart swing, keeping herself awake in the battle of wills between herself and the high light from the tower room. It was the only light left in the house. It caught the path as it came up through the trees. It seemed to wait there to pin her. The light was her mother watching. She was nearly asleep; she could hardly remember what had happened. She was too tired. She only knew that she had found out something, made a decision at last.

She knew that she was going away. She had to. She was never going to let her own people look at her again that way, dead eyes, not even interested.

A child's phrase "I'm never going to speak to any of you again as long as I live!" made her smile at her fool self, sitting there with no place to go. She held on to a few facts; she had saved almost two hundred dollars. She had saved it over five years. It was her female emancipation money.

It was not cajoled out of her father. She scorned that. "You don't know *when* to *ask.*" She heard Goneril's voice, and Regan giggled, but she, Cordelia, scorned playing her father for what she wanted. She found the sweetheart swing was moving; it was the habit of her relaxed body to pump it back and forth. She was afraid. She put her foot out on the grass, stopped the swing and listened. No one. She *had* cajoled a Corona portable typewriter; well, not cajoled—asked it as part of her plan.

Deep stars and sweet breeze; dirty and sore, she let them cleanse her, let her body stretch, let her tears course in dirty runnels of the past down her face and dreamed into her future, nearly asleep. Her body, her feeling, had had enough, had reacted enough, and cried enough and hurt enough and now she, numb of past, didn't listen to the night sounds, didn't swing, didn't do anything but drift in the future and watch for the tower light to go out.

She had forgotten her fright at Dan Neill's flashlight. He never stayed in her mind long.

Mr. Roundtree knew he had failed. He had heard the fuck you said after him. He had watched from his own path on his hill to see if any of the men from Cain Creek were leaving. No one came out. He stood there staring down at the Club House, making haste slowly as his father had taught him because there were too many variables in the problem, too many mind depths, too many prejudices and hates all stirring in the night and he knew he had to walk between them and get to Eddie and get him out of the hollow. He was a little surprised when he finally let himself voice the conclusion after all the premises. He had thought of it in larger, more abstract terms—stopping violence, seeing justice done, protecting the innocent. No. It all came down to getting that one smart-aleck young boy out of the valley and onto a train because he, Mr. Roundtree, had aided and abetted his getting above himself, getting himself noticed among all the foreigners, and he was responsible. He had let McLeod stop him, let the boy go up Italian Hollow alone. No matter what the expediencies, no matter what the excuses, he had been failing ever since he had given in to the transportation, ever since he had stood on the Laceys' porch in front of the damned Eastern interests with their damned gold watch chains, and let Dan Neill win. Not even the thought of Lily could move him from his recognition of his responsibility. The threads of decision, he told himself, some too amorphous to name, were drawing toward the boy, that boy or another boy, drawing toward . . . an incident . . . and he had to stop it and he simply did not know how.

Finally one man did come out of the Club House. He saw him mount. It was only Dan Neill going for his night ride as he did every night. He looked like a man with insomnia. Mr. Roundtree wasn't surprised. He watched the horse amble across the Godley bridge, and turn down-creek, until it was out of sight in the dark.

Mr. Roundtree watched the stars and named them. He simply waited, standing still in the path where he had first turned to check the Club House, to make the first unerring step toward a solution. After all the complications, the direction was extremely single. He decided to seek out the Paganos.

He stepped down the path, called out "Roundtree here" to the men in the pillbox, and heard "Pass," the word that Dan Neill had told them to use.

Down the road beyond the water tower he came into the night.

It was not dead to him. It seemed naked and sleeping, rumors of night animals, hints of breeze in the leaves, fragments of sighs and whispers and then spaces of silence. It was the time of night a man might turn, half asleep, toward a woman from his dream, and overlay his wife. It was the dangerous time when a man who was alone could spin his mind over bills or insults or sex; ripe time for an acted nightmare for those awake, like Dan Neill, who had looked at him in the Club House as if he wanted to kill him, but didn't dare.

Mr. Roundtree could hear real whispers of men and see, ahead, the bright tip of a cigarette.

"Who is it?" Low voice, mountain boy.

"Boys, it's me. Mr. Roundtree. I've come down here to see what I can . . ." he explained to the cigarette tip.

"They ain't nuthin' you can do."

How many of them were there?

"Do any of you men know where the Pagano family is?"

Nobody answered.

"What you want with them?" finally, a low, slow voice.

"I have an important message." Mr. Roundtree realized that he was matching their voices, low and slow under the black trees.

"Ain't none of us know whar they're at . . ." Somebody at the back of the group spoke for them all.

Their talk began again when they thought he was out of hearing. They were spreading rumor, sex rumor, that came from deep in the night and their fear and excitement. "I heard tell a feller said knew a feller feller's brother them Baldwin thugs cut off a woman's breast at Number Ten. Raped a little girl no it was a Dago woman that was a nigger done that no hit was Goujot Goujot caught that girl, white girl, I heared tore her all inside . . ."

He walked out of range of their private detonators, private excitement, obscene, ready to climax, but not in a woman.

He had to step aside. In the distance he heard Neill cantering back up the road.

Roundtree flashed his torch and called out softly. "Stop, Neill. There's a group of miners on the road ahead. They could be armed."

Neill made his horse careen, by habit.

"Roundtree, those goddamn Dago sons of bitches have hurt Miss Lily. No bunch of rednecks are stopping me. I'm getting help."

"Wait. Who told you?"

"She did." Dan Neill called over his shoulder. Mr. Roundtree thought he heard the word "Dago"; then there was only the cantering horse on the stony road, disappearing, then silence.

Roundtree set off at a run down the road, over the bridge, up through the path among the blue cedars before he gave a thought to anything but the direction toward her.

The boys weren't waiting to fight anybody. They were not aware of spreading rumor. They were just laying out, waiting for the moon to rise so the white of the daisies would show, stark in Jake Catlett's up-creek pasture. When they heard the horse they knew it was that fool Neill. They didn't want any trouble. They stepped back into the trees. He wasn't worth fooling with.

He wasn't the snake's head, not like Goujot. Now him they just plain wanted to see dead.

Lily saw him there, in the shaft of light from the tower window, answer to hope, a dream. She wanted to run to him, let him comfort her, talk and talk, talk it all out, talk until dawn came, but instead she remembered to walk sedately, knowing he liked that, to the edge of the light path, and say, "Mr. Roundtree." She wanted to say "How did you know to find me?" but wouldn't have said such a thing for a farm in Georgia.

She seemed so calm that he tried to stop his panting after the run so she wouldn't think he had panicked. She wouldn't respect that.

"Are you all right?" he managed to say, but his spirit wanted to cry, "Lovely girl, all bedraggled, tender and dirty, dear and dangerous girl, what have you helped unleash?" but he wouldn't have said such nonsense aloud for the world.

"Of course I'm all right." She was a little scornful, he thought; he had to know what had happened, even in the face of that light lithe scorn of hers.

226

"I must talk to you." That was all right to say, business voice, urgent in the right way.

"Of course," she said, going ahead of him. "We can sit in the swing. We have to be quiet so we won't wake Father and Mother. They'd never understand."

What they would never understand didn't seem, by her voice, to mean sitting at one o'clock in the morning with a man in the sweetheart swing. It was something else. The moon was rising over the trees, and it touched her as she should be touched, ephemeral, a ghost of light on her face.

"I just met Dan Neill." He wanted so to take her hands. Under the beginning light of the late moon she was a wraith of white across from him in the sweetheart swing. "He told me you'd been hurt."

"Dan Neill's a fool. I did not tell him that. I told him to let me alone."

Rumor is a seed, planted and nurtured. Dan Neill hated the word "Dago." He would plant it, grow it, nurture it.

Mr. Roundtree knew what he had to do.

"Miss Lily," he said carefully, "I must wake your father. We've got to get Eddie Pagano out of this hollow."

"No." She seemed to consider for a long time, controlling herself against surprise. "Let me think," she said—then, "Wait a minute." She held up her hand, her dear dirty hand. She didn't bother with questions.

Lily was facing up to the hardest fact of the night. It was small and terrible after the great indignity she had gone through. When she should have explained something of what had happened, she had remained silent, run away from Dan Neill. How could she have told him that she had lain on the ground and cried and cried over what one old woman had done? He would have said "Is that all?" and been relieved. Instead she had left his mind to conjure up what he wanted. She saw as clearly as if he'd told her what he wanted to believe. She saw her running away from him as a delicacy of taste, but that was no excuse. Mr. Roundtree waited, as she knew he would, for her to tell him where she had added to the evil. She yearned to discuss the matter in all its ramifications, sit in the swing with him until the sun came up and touched her hair.

Instead she said, "My father wouldn't be a bit of use, you know that. Now nobody would bother Eduardo if he were with me."

"I can't let you do that." Roundtree made the mistake of leaning forward, and said the wrong word ". . . a woman . . ."

"Nonsense." She felt brave. She planned aloud. "I will go with him on the first upriver train. They're all used to seeing me at the Depot. I've thought it all out. I'll go with him as far as Covington. He'll be across the border into Virginia then." She was beginning to see herself again, not in flight, but useful, really useful at last. "You find him. Bring him down the back road at five-thirty."

He wanted to tell her he had to be at the mine at dawn, but how could he tell her?

"Could you?" She was constructing the morning as she wanted it to be. "Oh maybe not . . ."

"Could I what?" He knew why she was suddenly all aglow with excitement, and he faced his hardest fact of the night. She was talking like a woman in love. "Unsuitable," he wanted to say, "oh my old dear, how unsuitable."

"Lend him one of your suits? And a hat. It will disguise him as"—she made a little cough, not liking the word—". . . a gentleman. We must look . . ."—she didn't like that word either but there wasn't another—"rich. It's a great protection."

She was a girl, playing at crisis, and he had no way to stop her except to say, "I am deeply in love with you," and that would have been—not unthinkable—he'd thought of little else for a long time.

Neither of them spoke. The night breeze paused, there was not a sound in the valley.

"Twenty past one," Mr. Roundtree whispered.

"Or twenty to two. Essie says it's the Angel of Death . . ."

"My mother in Devonshire says that. My father says it's pagan. But then he says even Christmas is pagan. I never celebrated Christmas as a child. They are . . ." He paused, then plunged ahead into confession in the night, "Plymouth Brethren." There, he'd said it. He had to tell her, no matter what she thought.

She didn't say a word. She didn't seem to mind at all. She just put her lovely foot out on the grass and made the swing move a little.

"I wish . . ." she said, and nothing more.

They didn't move or speak until the light went out in the tower room.

"I was planning to leave anyway," she said, leaving him a pause to persuade her not to.

He didn't say a word.

"I'll take him to my place." He got up from the swing, knowing that he was not the hero of the drama, and disliking it intensely.

She came with him to the edge of the trees. She was so close to him, he thought, it's now or never. He told himself she was waiting, but of course he knew she wasn't.

"I'll meet you on the back road, just beyond the garden at five-thirty," she finally said, and then she sighed, or yawned. He couldn't tell which it was. He couldn't stand it anymore, her saying it like that, not meaning him at all.

After he had gone Lily stood for a long time under the trees. She was wide awake. She wondered what Althea would have done under the circumstances.

The moon appeared over the east ridge and touched the daisies. The boys spread out in the pasture, picking the stems nice and young so they could last through the morning, two nice big bouquets. They dipped a couple of old newspapers in the creek to wrap around them so they wouldn't fade before they could get them into big jam jars.

They found two of them, up at the graveyard left over from Decoration Day, and even two of those white wicker flower baskets with big round handles that looked so nice on graves. They were careful about which ones they took. One of the Escew boys contributed from the Escew plot and Jethro Catlett took his brother Ephraim's. He whispered that Ephraim would do the same thing if he were there.

They filled the jam jars in the little wide pool in the branch up above Seven Stars that they had all used as a swimming hole when they were too little for the big creek.

Then they started off around the mountain behind Seven Stars so they would come down to Godley drift mouth from the ridge. They walked single file, in and out of moonlight, surefooted.

The tents looked to Mr. Roundtree as if they had been there for years, dark, still, sunk into the black pasture. The lit window at Jake Catlett's house was a low star. Mr. Roundtree felt his way in a circuit around the snake fence. When he found the path and was nearly to the house, the light defused and took the shape of a window. Against it he saw dark figures on Jake Catlett's porch. He couldn't hear voices, only the loud ticking of a clock. Even when he walked up the steps, no one moved. Then he saw why. Side by side in the rockers three women were asleep. He could see Mrs. Catlett, Mrs. Pagano, and an old woman he didn't know. After the walk across the still valley, the alarm clock he saw on the porch rail seemed loud enough to wake the dead. Somebody was snoring.

Mrs. Catlett woke first. She said, trying not to wake the others, "Jake? Is that you?" and then sat upright, remembering that Jake had already come in and passed by them without a word. She had heard his bed creak and his shoes hit the floor upstairs. "Who is it?" she whispered.

"Roundtree."

"What are *you* doing up here?" The old woman had waked up.

"I need help. I have to find Eddie Pagano."

"What do you want with him?" The old woman was making herself speaker. He knew then who it was.

"Mrs. Jones, Eddie's in trouble . . ."

"What's that to you?"

He wanted to say, Why, you're Irish. I can hear it in your voice. Mr. Roundtree didn't, as usual, say what he wanted to.

Mrs. Pagano had heard his voice. She raged up out of her rocker. "You get out from here," she yelled. "What you done . . ."

He had to grab her arms to keep her from hitting him. "Quiet!" he said. "We've got to find your Eddie. We've got to get him away from here."

"Hush." Mother Jones took her shoulder and pulled her away

from Mr. Roundtree. They stumbled a little over Essie's feet. She didn't move. "Listen to the man, anyhow . . ."

"Thank you," he stopped to tell her.

"Don't thank me. Now speak your piece."

"The men up at the Club House are out of hand, Mrs. Jones." They spoke together as if they were alone on the porch. "One of them came to me and told me they were after Eddie."

"Why?" He knew she didn't believe him.

"They want to make an example . . ."

She didn't answer him. He could see her, taking it in, understanding. She let go of Mrs. Pagano's shoulder. "Go down there to your tent and tell your boys to come up here. We'll take care of our own." Mrs. Pagano watched them both. "And don't wake up everybody on God's green acre. I want some sleep."

Essie's voice interrupted them. "Better go ahead and do what he says. Eddie can't hide long enough if them fellers are after him. If they can't find him they'll git theirselves another one." She was in the shadows behind them. Her rocker was going slowly back and forth.

"Look here. You must bring Eddie up here with you. I am going to take him over the back road to my house." Mr. Roundtree still didn't like to admit that Lily would help. "I'll get him on the upriver train." Mrs. Pagano threw her apron over her face and started to sway and sob.

"Oh, quit that," the old woman told her. "You ain't got time." She seemed to know what would move her, even if it was cruel. "Now you listen to me, that bunch of gun thugs up there don't know one Dago from another except for your boys. Do what the man says." She settled back into her rocker. "I learned a long time ago to git sleep when I could." She didn't say another word. Her rocker creaked back and forth, slower and slower, then stopped.

Mr. Roundtree watched Mrs. Pagano go down the path. Her dark shadow stumbled under the pallor of the late moon. She seemed to sway to one side, and he saw her sink down. She was so still he thought she had fainted, and started to get up and run down to her. Then he saw that she was sitting, her back to him, like a monolith.

Neither of the women on the porch said another word to him. He hoped they were asleep again. He sat down on the steps and listened to the clock tick and thought about Lily and Eduardo, and saw himself as Friar Lawrence, and didn't like it at all.

Annunziata had seen the stump that Lily had sat on under the trees. She went to it and eased herself down like an old woman. She had to stop. She could hear her heart, a drum in her body. It seemed, in the night, loud enough to alarm the sleepers awake if she ran by the tents like that. She had to let the hackles she could feel risen along her neck when she saw Roundtree subside, let the sweat that had spurted under her heavy hair, the sweat between her legs cool, so that when she did move again she would move like a fighter, not like Stephano, that pig, that heavyweight of blind dumb temper, but light and ready. She made herself wait inside for the crouch and ease of a cat, ready to spring, but not yet. Not yet. There was too much in her that she had to face and get rid of before it would come, the power that she knew would surge when she was ready.

She had begun to sway a little on the stump. Everybody had told her how she felt, but nobody had asked her. She had to find out; she had to listen to herself before she woke the gabble of their voices, the pushing and pulling. She was still doing what they expected, the panic on the porch, the wailing, even the throwing of the shawl over her face like a common Calabrian. It was right that she should. She knew that. If she acted as they expected, they would act as she expected, but only if she were in control of herself, as she always had been.

She felt the stump. Pine. Sour earth. They should have taken it out, root and all, and put lime on the ground. It was all a waste, the sparse grass, the heavy soil.

She did not pray. She knew her De profundis, but she had called enough from enough darkness in her time. It was too late and too early for that. She smoothed the cloth of the skirt that wasn't hers. It was silk. She felt kindness in it. She didn't remember who had lent it to her. Her mind was blank about spaces of the evening, fogged with fury. That's what she meant to do, clear her mind, polish it. She knew she couldn't see through fury and sorrow and shame. She had to see—libera la mia mente, she told herself, make it trasparante, luminoso. It was the first time since the explosion of her house—she saw it as that in her mind—that she had had a chance to pause and be alone for a minute. It was not a new habit. Unlike most long habits, Annunziata could remember exactly the minute it had begun. She let herself think about that. It was a way she had learned to clear her mind so she could act. Act! The word made her smile in the midst of all her trouble. The stranieri said act when they meant do; to act was to play the part they expected to protect yourself. Every woman knew that. So she waited to know how to act. She knew it would come. It always had, ever since she was a girl in Italy.

Sant' Anna, Sant' Elena and Santa Chiara had run away. They were new pullets and didn't know any better. She was sitting under a tree outside the Porta St. Angelo where it was her duty every day to take the hens. She was fifteen years old, a new daughter-in-law without a minute to herself.

As for being a wife, she had only been one for seven months, long enough for Stephano to begin to move and kick her from inside. It was the most peaceful time of the afternoon, when she took the chickens out of their roof cages into the basket, hiding the basket under her apron so they wouldn't panic, hearing them cluck and churtle, feeling Stephano kick the basket, as she walked along the Corso Garibaldi and passed through the great gate to find free grass under the trees. Even then she wasn't alone. Her best friend, Angelina, who was not yet married, gabbled along beside her like the chickens, asking question after question. "Does it hurt? Do they listen?" Oh, yes, they listened for the bed to creak as Francesco, beautiful Francesco, covered her and sometimes, old as they were they caught the rhythm, and she could hear them, too, their bed creaking, and then there had been the women's question, "Are you pregnant yet?" She had only gone through two disappointing times of blood that made her feel a failure and then she proved fertile. "Does it take long?" She told Angelina no, it did not take long, every time she asked.

They turned the chickens out to scratch the ground and they

sat under a tree and talked about God and marriage and how they liked to go to mass to Father Donato because he had diarrhea and the mass was always short.

Annunziata called it all back quickly. She needed to be there, right at the first time, more than she had ever needed anything in her life. She looked up as she had looked up then from the grass, seeing not darkness and vague tent shapes under the moon, but grass and the horizon moving under the sun's heat and the tall cypresses that lined the stations of the Cross up to the monastery on the hill beyond the road that led down to the Tiber. She saw them again. Sant' Anna, Sant' Elena and Santa Chiara, tail feathers high, running across the dirt road to the valley, and was up and away, after them. The pullets stopped, heads down, pecking at the roadside.

She got nearly to them, carefully, quietly, was just reaching for Santa Chiara, hands cupped to grab her when they began to run again up the long, long steps—hopping, pausing just ahead of her.

Halfway up the hill steps, she had to stop and get her breath, right beside Santa Veronica in her niche. She sat down on the stone step. She looked around at the trees, the steps, the space, the stone city on the opposite hill. Terror came to her and knelt over her. At fifteen years old she was completely alone for the first time in her life. There was no one to call to, no voice to answer. The terror lifted. Wind touched her face. She forgot the chickens. She almost forgot where she was. She was the only one like herself in the whole world who had ever sat there in that space, in that body, just like that. She felt free and new and her own voice came and told her this mighty thing. She sat there stunned. The hope that Angelina would stay away, that nobody would disturb the silence came as an intrusion to the silence itself. The sun on her hair was only for her, the trees, the rock.

She didn't remember the rest. She supposed she caught the chickens and ran back with them into the company of Angelina, the poverty of the stone city, the duties, the perpetual noise of being with people all the time, sleeping, working, eating. She learned to find that stillness again, in corridors, on the street, on errands, draw it to herself, only in the seconds she had to do it. Her mother-in-law noticed her dawdling and said she was getting used to her pregnancy, but her father-in-law laughed and said she had him to thank that the priests didn't get Francesco.

Then she had learned another way to bring it back. She sewed, and when she did that, she felt like all the women, a long procession of women handing down a secret without saying a word to each other. She saw in their eyes when they were busy that some of them knew, too, how to be alone among so many. As she sewed, embroidered, tatted lace for the edges of the old linen sheets, a long-collected women's fortune of care, she learned to listen without hearing, to look without seeing, to go back to the secret place under Santa Veronica in the sun. When she was there the voices she heard were her own and the faces she saw were her choice.

She considered none of this. It was a place within herself. She took it for granted, as granted to her. She called it talking to the Virgin, who came as often as she had time to let her in. As the years passed outside herself, no time passed there. Sometimes the face of the Virgin was of plaster and she wore a blue robe, but sometimes she had Annunziata's own face at fifteen, new woman, sitting full of child and wonder on the monastery steps.

She saw then, sitting on the stump in a night darker and more naked than she had ever known, that she was going to have to strip down beyond hate in order to see clearly. She let herself see again the whole great history of her times of silence in thread turned into lace, flowers, leaves, on the sheets, the bedcovers, the clothes, all of it thrown, shredded, trampled by the cold stranieri on that foreign harsh ground, in the foreign creek she had tried to make hers, all fragmented, as if at last her private self had been raped and torn. She let hate take her body then, let it stiffen her, rise in her throat, in her muscles, clench in her hands. It was necessary and she was a practical woman. Hate surged and shook, poured out of her with faces, voices, shapes.

She was going to have to cross gulfs of hate in order to reach the place where she would know what to do. She did not consider it any more than she would have considered prayer, planting or lying under Francesco when he needed her. She let it come. Her own voice told her Mother's words, " 'They don't know one Dago from another.' We do not exist at all. That is the worst they have done to us."

"Men are cheaper than mules," she called without sound. "Use Dagoes for mine props." She was doing what the saints did when they whipped their furies out of their bodies to get to the blood that never lied, the Preziosissimo Sangue, like a deep dark well covered over with time and habit.

She could see the men again, the men in black, the gentlemen without names or faces, without hearts or blood. Their skin was like white paper scribbled with hair, their eyes did not bother to look at you. Their laughter was at something else. She could see the dresser Francesco had carved easing slowly out of the upper window, see it splinter on the ground below, see the stove slowly as in a dream coming apart in the air falling falling never touching always falling, and shook herself out of threatening sleep, the stupefaction that came with hate.

If there was going to be a lynching, there would be a lynching. That was what the old woman had been trying to tell her. A lynching was like lust. When men had it building up in them, nothing could stop it; the only protection was that it peaked and died down again. Lust and lynching left no residue of longing, not like love and hate and hope.

There had never been a time in her life when she needed as she did then to go back to where she was young, unafraid, and full of hope, and face the falseness, even of that. Hope, she had told herself a long time ago, was a thread that seemed as soft as silk until you drew it through your fingers to sew with it and it cut like a razor. You left it behind and felt lighter, free of it, and then it would come again, soft and cutting. It was not an illusion. It was a way of seeing softly, too softly for the world. Eduardo still had it even if she had tried to slap and shock him out of it.

Illusions? She had none. They were garments she dressed herself in. They were their illusions, not hers. They were her gift and necessity for the others, sewn as carefully of the fragments of the past as one of the stranieri's quilts. She had to keep that illusion about the past from tearing, from wearing out. She had always felt herself strong enough to see things as they were, but she doubted the others. Men were tender and they failed in the face of things, failed and fell. To keep them from falling, sons and husband, was for a woman to do. She had kept her eye always on the face of things, no matter how terrible the face was, but she demanded that they did not look.

She made them be careful with her as if she were getting old, bore their love and misunderstanding. What they did not know was that, in those pauses when they thought she was dreaming of a past that never was, she was getting young, unpanicked and decisive, where Santa Chiara pecked on the steps above her and the silence was hot and the leaves turned their backs, a place where no one could push her into indecision or pull her into guilt or fury.

Every decision had been made there, alone, and when she came back, her garments of fury or impatience or sadness were her own to use. Even the lies, oh that fine city of lies to cover the stone poverty of her real memory, kept up their spirits. So long as they had to placate her they dared not fall into their own despair. She, who had looked at the face of things more than any of them, knew when to demand all of their concern.

So she went back to where the biggest hope began, the promises. She made herself remember how she had first loved the riches of coal, all you wanted to keep you warm, trees, topsoil untouched, virgin topsoil, not trodden and turned by generations. She had loved the luxurious ugliness of things wasted, the trash, the water she could listen to, the Jenny Lind house where all the space around it had been hers.

That was the courtship of hope, when all she had dreamed of seemed to be there for the taking. Then, at the doors of her dream there were the cold faces. She saw again, the first straniera woman who had ever spoken directly to her, standing at the door in her huge hat. She remembered her thin mouth and the hair in her nose.

The light was still on in the high tower across the dark valley, where people said she watched the whole town, missing nothing, and Annunziata knew she was still watching. Maybe she was suffering, too. Annunziata hoped so. She smiled when she remembered the old woman in the barn, shutting out the strega, Miss Lily, shutting her out as she had been shut out always from the high towers when they had no right-of-way. Because she had used those words so seldom, Annunziata used them in her own way, her own right-of-way.

She sat, now part of the wooden stump, not man, not woman, but still flesh against wood, down to where she was ready to listen to the sangue del proprio sangue, her own flesh and blood, the voice of her blood that never lied.

When the decision came it was so simple, so right, that she was surprised. It came in the voice of the Mother of God, as she knew it would, but the words were her own, "They want a Dago. Your protect your own."

She answered, "*You* did it yourself." She told the Mother of God, "You took your own into Egypt and left the innocents to be slaughtered."

At last she felt the quietness and the peace that came after decision. She smoothed the silk skirt, got up as slowly as she had sat down, put the shawl over her head and prepared for the hysteria they would expect and that would make them concentrate on her and not take time to argue.

She wished by Sant' Elena, the mother of Constantine, that she would guide her through the politics and gestures she would need to make them do what she saw they had to do.

She ran down among the tents as lightly and silently as she had run to catch Sant' Anna, Sant' Elena and Santa Chiara.

Stephano was sleeping just inside the tent. She smelled his tobacco sweat on his undershirt. He liked to dress like that, senza proprietà, like the stranieri miners who sat dirty on their porches. She put her hands hard over his loud mouth, her mouth against his ear. "Vieni," she whispered. "Mother says come." She knew Mother to him meant the old woman and not her. "She says don't make a sound." She felt him nodding under her hands.

She stepped across the borrowed blankets with their still forms and knelt down beside Eduardo, touched his cleanliness like good earth, found his thin hand and shook him gently. "Go to Jake Catlett's. Now. Don't wake the children."

She waited until they had slipped out of the tent. Then she went to Francesco, and shook him, knowing he was harder to wake. "Caro mio," she whispered to him, "the boys are in trouble.

238

You go to Jake Catlett's. Maria and I will bring the children." She kept her hands on his face until she knew he was awake, his map of a face. Her fingers traveled up the deep rut of worry on his cragged jaw to his mouth and closed over it.

After the men had gone she woke Vera and Vanya. Vanya whimpered, but her command, "Basta," shut her up again. Maria stirred and sat up. She smiled in the hint of moonlight, still half asleep. Annunziata touched her soft curls, the young warm sleep dew on her forehead. "Here," she whispered to her, "take Vera." As soon as the children were in their arms they went to sleep again.

Only Carlo Michele was left asleep in the corner. When Maria started over to him, Annunziata held her back.

"No. Leave him here. Let him sleep," she whispered, "he's come a long way. He needs to sleep."

Lily brushed her hair in the light of the only lamp she dared use. She had taken off her dress, rolled it up in a little bundle and put it in the bottom drawer of the chifforobe to give to Essie to wash before her mother found it. She didn't consider that she wouldn't be there to do it. She had washed away the grime, and the dirty tear stains. She was two separate people, one on her way to the heart of things, one still the girl she was at home, doing the duties she had been taught, before she went to bed.

She stood in her camisole and petticoat, barefooted. She leaned her head to the right and brushed fifty strokes down the long fall of her hair. In the mirror she watched herself lean her head to the left, her hand flipped the bright fall over her left shoulder and she began to count the strokes again. She heard nothing. The shadows were deep in the room behind her.

The face appeared behind her shoulder, white, gaunt, hair gone wild. The brush stopped. Lily didn't dare move. It was the face face of an old witch, floating, not a dream.

"Young lady, are you aware that it is two o'clock in the morning?" The face disappeared out of the small pool of light. She heard the bed creak.

She didn't move.

Behind her in the darkness her mother said, "You're going away."

She didn't answer. She watched her figure in the mirror, frozen, the brush in her hair.

"I can read your mind," the voice went into her, ice. "I always could. You're going away."

She said "Yes," to the figure in the mirror. She saw her body relax.

"Are you aware that this will break your father's heart?"

There was nowhere to go, nowhere to move.

"Something happened. You don't have to tell me." Lily watched Lily in the mirror. "You're free to tell me. I won't admonish you." Nothing, no movement in the mirror.

The bed creaked again, a shift of weight, a sigh. "Your father is a dying man. You wouldn't notice that. You're the selfish one. You're always thinking about your own wishes, never anybody else's." The voice was more comfortable. "We have made great sacrifices for you. Took it all for granted. Took everything for granted," a chant, turning inward. "Nobody thinks about me. This will kill your father, leave everything for me to decide. He doesn't care. He doesn't think. I know. I know. I know everything. I'll just have to deal with everything on my own."

Lily's face in the mirror was still and blank.

"Don't go. Don't leave me to deal with everything," her mother said, but not to her. "I won't have a soul to talk to. Oh I always knew the others would marry the first man that asked them, but Lily would be above that. She would find other outlets." She sobbed on, "Lily wouldn't stoop to that. She would be my companion. I've got a mind too. Fat lot anybody around here cares about that. We were going to read things together." She began to plan: "We wouldn't need all this space. We would find a nice place in Canona, smaller." She seemed to realize that the girl was there. "You were the one. I never wanted a boy. Boys are a nuisance. We would have such a nice time. There wouldn't be a bunch of men sitting around on their backsides demanding things. I'm intelligent, too, don't you forget it. I just never had the advantages. You got your brains from me. Oh, turn around!"

Lily did as she was told. The witch had left her mother's face. In the faint light from the lamp, she looked softened, a girl again, a sister. She sensed this. "We would be like sisters. I never had your advantages. That's why I insisted on you being educated."

Lily looked so small and thin, standing there barefooted in her camisole and her petticoat with her hair hanging down, just like a little girl, that she held out her arms and said, "Honey, come here."

Lily didn't dare fall into the well of her mother's arms. She did come and sit down on the bed.

"Red and white," her mother said. She passed her hand over the quilt. "I made this for you with my own hands. I know what you like. I always did. Red flower baskets on white. All for you." The hand had freckles on it.

They were both so still that the night sounds came into the room.

"You haven't answered my question. What do you intend to do?"

Lily didn't answer. She was waiting. She didn't know anymore what she was waiting for.

"All I ask, and it's little enough, is that you finish Vassar."

"I don't want to use your money." Now Lily found some voice, even if it was still and small. "It's such a burden on you."

"Never mind about that. It's what we want to do for you. We're doing it for you." She studied Lily's face as if she were reading it for the first time. In it she saw herself and she spoke to the self she saw. "Well, if you've made up your mind." She even smiled. "God knows I don't blame you. But you listen to me. You prepare yourself." Then, knowing at last, she thought, whom she was persuading, "I want you to tender me a solemn promise. You're too hardheaded for me to persuade you to stay here. But a woman has to have weapons and you're naked as a jaybird you poor little fool. You've got to go back to Vassar. I'll help you any way I can. You know that. You've always known it."

"I can't . . ."

"Don't be a damned fool." Her mother sat straight. "Now you listen to me. I wouldn't stay in this one-horse town for a minute if I had my way. Go on. You go on. Live in Washington. Go to New York City for the summer. That's what I'd do." Now she was a conspirator. Lily had not felt in such danger in her life. The woman beside her was taking her decision, weak as it was, and using its energy for some secret self of her own. She was as nearly a stranger as Lily had ever seen her, drawing on her for a new excitement. "I used to think of it. To be young and live in Greenwich Village . . . for a while. Oh!" She rocked, clasping her knees. "Now let's see. You'll need money. How much have you got?"

"Two hundred dollars."

"You'll need more." She turned away, planning, clearing things out of the way. "You haven't promised. Promise."

"Yes ma'am," Lily said.

The woman got up, sighed a little. "Well, that's done." She had taken over the management of the affair. She went to the door, turned around once more in the shadow. Lily saw her mother again. "Oh, honey. I knew you were bored here. I'd bought you the prettiest evening gown for your birthday. I was going to take you to White Sulphur at least—not for long. We can't afford it for long." She waited for Lily to answer. Then she went out and closed the door.

It was done. Whatever it was, it was done. Lily saw herself as if she were standing in front of the mirror forever, the brush frozen halfway down her hair. Her mother hadn't asked her where she had been. She was taking over where she was going.

Lily got her suitcase and her typewriter out of the bottom of her closet, and set them on the bed. She wound her bedside clock, set it by her watch, and set the alarm for four-thirty. She opened the top drawer of the chifforobe and got out two camisoles, two knickers from the second drawer, two pairs of stockings from the third drawer, two petticoats from the big drawer below the mirror, counting as she had counted the strokes of the brush. She got her locked diary from under the petticoats, found the key in her jewel box, and put them into her suitcase first, then covered them with underclothes. She moved in a simplicity of packing, empty girl, mind not made up at all, but simply moving from one small chore to another.

She wanted to slip down to the kitchen and make herself a sandwich.

She wanted somebody to ask her to stay.

242

"I don't know what *you're* moping around for," her mother said, dumping an armful of clothes on the bed. Lily hadn't heard her come back. She turned away. She hadn't realized she was moping.

"Now. We've got a lot to do," her mother took her thought. "I suppose you'll be going sometime tomorrow."

"Six-thirty," Lily told the clothes in the closet. She reached up.

"No." Her mother watched. "Don't take those. Speak softly. We don't want the girls prowling around. You want to look like a schoolgirl? People notice things like that. Wear your new white suit on the train and your brown hat. No, not black. Ladies don't wear black with white. You can't tell who'll be on the train. All the ladies from Canona go to Richmond to shop. They know who you are." She was inspecting the underwear in the suitcase. "That isn't enough. You've never had to wash out your own things. I brought you the traveling iron. Good grief, undergarments take three days to dry. You'll need three of everything. Always wear clean underwear. You never know what will happen. I mean a wreck or anything." She was whisking around the room behind Lily. "I'll send your school waists and skirts to Vassar. Oh take one. No, that one." Her hand reached up and grabbed a dark green skirt from its hanger. "Three waists at least. Oh, a hot-water bottle."

She was behind her at the bed. "What's this? Oh, your diary." A giggle. "You needn't to hide that. I've read it all. You always did leave it around hoping I'd read how unhappy you were. *I* knew you wanted me to read it, leaving the key in plain sight. I always did." Lily could hear the flicking of tissue paper. "That Christmas when we'd done all we could for you you wrote that nobody loved and understood you around here. That made me laugh. Here. Come help me."

It was the giggle that freed Lily's body, made it new. She had no secrets; her mother, in the words she always used, "had seen to that." It was only the reading of a diary, not important, but it freed her of the woman who was folding tissue paper into her petticoats. She didn't even look up when Lily picked up one of the waists she had chosen. She only saw the girl's hands, trembling. "No." She grabbed the waist. "Not like that. You can't do an earthly thing for your own self. Roll. Roll it in tissue, like this. That way you just shake it out and hang it up. Look at your new dress. Crepe de chine, with gold fringe. It's all the rage. *Vogue* says so. I sent off for it from Miller and Rhoades. Oh yes. You'll take it and like it, my girl. You might have need of it. Besides, you have to look rich. It's a great protection in this world."

She did look up then to see if Lily liked the dress, read it in her face. What she read was no longer a frightened girl. Something had freed her of that. She smiled, and spoke to Lily for the first time in her life as a separate person. "I'm no fool, you know," she said to the new face she saw, as if that explained it all.

"Now. Don't argue. Here's another two hundred dollars. I had saved it for a purpose. Your typewriter. Mmm. If you think that's the answer you've got another think coming. There, all packed." She sat down beside the suitcase. "Oh yes, look rich by all means. Put on the armor of God!"

It was the recognition of her that finally broke Lily into tears, that separate withdrawn woman, taking her understanding for granted. She wanted her mother.

When the woman held out her arms, Lily came into them and sobbed on her mother's shoulder. "Oh Ma. I'm so ambitious," she made her confession.

"I know, honey, I know." Her mother patted her back. "I was, too."

She moved the suitcase and the typewriter off the bed. "Now, honey, don't take a bath. It will wake up everybody in the house, you just wash good, you hear me? The money's in your handbag, and a few things." She was vague for the first time. Lily heard her open the door. "You get some sleep," she said.

Not sleep. Lily was too excited for that. She was going on the train. She was going to live in Greenwich Village in New York City for a whole summer! She had enough money to volunteer. She didn't see the shadow from the lamp on the ceiling. She saw herself marching right down Fifth Avenue with Mrs. Belmont and Mrs. Peabody and Carrie Chapman Catt, carrying the banner. VOTES FOR WOMEN. LILY LACEY, huge red letters. She was happy about the new white crepe de chine dress. They might even invite her to dinner. After all, she was a Vassar girl.

She got up to go and wash herself again like her mother told her to.

She sat at the window in the dark in her kimono and watched the moonlight begin to fade into first dawn. She had long since given up any idea of sleep. She had to face it. She was what Mary Rose would call scared to death. It was one thing to be the brightest one in the little valley, besides Mr. Roundtree, of course, but she'd seen things they hadn't seen and knew things they didn't know. She watched the lilacs begin to be defined, turning gray. She looked out at the only center she knew. The hurt, the vitality, the questions she had to ask were someplace else, where another center had a secret name, and there was no direction to it.

"I have to know," she said to the lilacs, but what she had to know only whirled in her dawn mind. Essie would have said she was waiting for a sign. She saw the bright women, walking close together, seniors and virgins, their shrill sure voices floating behind them, a closed circle she could only watch, as one of the girls who trailed along after them with not quite their money and not quite their brains. She saw them marching up perpetual library steps, new women without a doubt in the world. "I'm no fool," she said to the lilacs in her mother's voice. She knew she didn't have the hard crystal mind and will that would be needed to take her place in a man's world and not mind. It was the not minding she couldn't manage. She hated being so tender, but she knew she was.

She must have slept a little without knowing it, because she started up at the scream of birds. The sky was alive with birdcall. The dawn was pale gray, not white yet. She looked back at her little clock. There was enough light in the room to see that it was four o'clock. She was cold. The dawn was damp on her kimono sleeves.

She could see movement across at the tents; women in their dawn-gray aprons. They moved like animals. The bird shrieks could have come from them. Bacchante, she thought and was pleased at that. She liked classic references. For a second she yearned again as she had in the night to be them, their circle around her, but she wasn't wanted and she told herself she didn't care, not really. It was education they needed. She knew that and

245

forgave them. They were moving up toward the barn, away from her, always away.

Mr. McLeod's fury took a pure form. It came straight from John Knox. When he was drunk he would tell Mr. Roundtree that every Scot had a twin soul. "You live like Bobby Burns; you dream like John Knox. Or, you live like John Knox and you dream like Bobby Burns." He had been dreaming in Gaelic again after fifteen years, and that was a Bobby Burns dream. He had been a lover in his dream. "Ach, I'm a terrible lover of women," he had told Mr. Roundtree, also many times.

Now, not walking, but processing, a company of one Scot, sternly down the hill from Mr. Roundtree's house in the white dawn of four o'clock, he knew what Mr. Roundtree was up to, and at such a time. Well, the English were weak in a crisis. He'd knocked on the locked door, he'd knocked at the curtained front window. He'd gone all the way around the locked and curtained house. Even Mr. Roundtree's dog was inside, in the kitchen. Blue had barked at him.

Finally Mr. Roundtree had answered his pounding, like a stranger.

"What do you want?" he'd called from upstairs.

"It's four o'clock," Mr. McLeod had stood back in the yard and called through his cupped hands.

"Go ahead. I'll come when I can," Mr. Roundtree had called out.

Mr. McLeod had listened. There were voices up in Mr. Roundtree's bedroom. He heard them whispering.

He had turned in disgust. Mr. Roundtree had a woman in there. He knew it. He carried it down the hill with him. A woman, at a time like that. What he thought about the matter was not anything from Keir Hardie. It was straight Wee Free Kirk of Scotland. Down ahead of him, he could hear the men at the Club House, still playing setback.

Somebody hollered out, "High! Low! Jick! Jack! and Game!"

He walked between whoring and drunken gambling to do his job, and thought of Scotland. It was a comfort to him. Nothing in the whitened mist-laden valley was real to him. He'd walked that way through half the world but his soul had not left home. Every month he sent his brother money for his own burial fund so that if he died out in one of the places of the ungodly his body would be sent back to rest in Scotland. The thought of that calmed him. He had known since he was a bairn at his mother's knee that he would have to go among strangers to earn his living. It was more than the law. It was the certainty of his life. The eldest son worked the croft, the others went away. It was nothing even to question.

When he looked in the mirror to shave, watching his face get older, more gnarled, more like his father's, he told himself that that was the way of things. When the homesickness got too bad, he went back, back from Australia, back from Africa, dependable as a wild goose on a flyway. He said to himself, "It's near time again." It was. He had saved almost enough to buy a croft and have a wife. It was unthinkable to do anything else. If they only knew what is behind this wee face, he told himself. Behind it was home, where the whole cycle would begin again. He would have sons, and the first would have the croft, and the others would go away, to the sea, to the mines.

He was almost to the Boarding House before he realized where he was.

Inside it smelled of sleep, of men, chamber pots, damp wood. He felt a kind of dead sadness. It made him stand in the bare-board hall for a minute, sensing their fear as part of his own. Ach, that feeling for them made him shake, the other soul coming to take over in him at the wrong time in the wrong place.

By four-thirty the men were up and fed. There were three Italians missing already, the filthy foreigners. He did just as he had done in the past, pushing feeling aside. He had the mine to think about, and he had to do it all himself, of course, do Mr. Roundtree's job for him while he stewed in sin. He assigned an experienced strikebreaker to each of the foreigners. He told them that he would not dock them for tools unless there was trouble. He'd long since learned to do it that way.

They moved in silence with heavy sleep still on them, out into the morning. The guards were leaning against the porch of the Club House, their black hats pulled low, their rifles sloped. Some of them yawned, catching it from each other. A few had just left the setback game. They stretched their backs, stiff from playing all night. Inside the clubroom they could hear the murmur of that fool Dan Neill's voice, instructing his "company." They didn't pay much attention. They were Goujot's men. They did what he said and nobody else.

The transportation men saw them when they shuffled out of the Boarding House. They huddled on the porch, afraid to move.

"You men. Move along. They're here to protect you." Mr. McLeod forced his way through and began to herd them out into the road. He had commandeered one of the trained strikebreakers to help him. He pushed a dog wagon full of tools.

Mr. McLeod stood in front of the men, still bunched together.

"Now form ranks!" he said, not yelling. The dawn quietened his voice, muted the early breeze, faintly moved the creek mist. The men who understood pushed the rest into some parody of ranks. Goujot called from the Club House porch.

"Aye! McLeod! Are ye ready?"

Of course he was ready. He always was.

Goujot strolled along the road. Mr. McLeod had never seen him walk briskly in all the weeks he'd been there. He had to admit, though, that even if he didn't have a soldierly bearing—well, not what a Scot would call a soldierly bearing—he had to be a courageous man. The Congressional Medal of Honor was like the Victoria Cross. Mr. McLeod admired a courageous man, even if he did stroll.

Goujot stopped and looked down at Mr. McLeod.

"Sergeant, I've only to hand out the tools." Mr. McLeod stood to attention. It was a natural thing for a man to do in the circumstances.

"Jesus," Goujot murmured. He looked along the line of men.

"I quite agree with you." Mr. McLeod looked with him. "The company expects me to get coal out with that. White niggers. I've worked African niggers looked better," he complained.

"White niggers," Goujot agreed.

Thirty men stood in a snaggled line. Their ages ranged from fourteen to sixty. They had washed because they had been told to, but they still carried train dirt and boat dirt in their clothes. Not a face had any life in it, except for the French boy, who had

248

begun to cry again. Nobody looked at the dawn. Nobody's head turned up toward the trees. They waited, numb, for something to be over. One of the men caught Goujot's eyes as they passed him and tried to smile. He looked apologetic. It was the huge Pole. When Goujot's eyes passed, his face went numb again.

"I've only to hand out tools," Mr. McLeod complained. "Tools! Ach! There are only ten men who have ever been in a mine before. I don't know what they're thinking of, sending this material after what we ordered. Mr. Roundtree will lodge a complaint."

"Whurs he at?" Goujot was grinning.

"Mr. Roundtree is engaged on important company business," Mr. McLeod told him with all the dignity he could muster when he had to look so far up and lie right to the man's face.

Essie had made a big pot of coffee in the pot she used at the Baptist church. She had twenty tin cups and she said they'd just have to make do with that. By the time she and Mrs. Pagano's girl, Maria, had hauled it all across the creek, the barn was half full of women. Babies were crying. Women were trying to pin up their hair after they'd dressed, half asleep still. She said to Ant Annie that it looked like they was getting ready for a Baptist picnic. Ant Annie said it wasn't nothing of the kind, not with them foreigners. Essie told her she was too old to go running around. "If she ain't too old, I ain't too old." Ant Annie settled that argument.

Mother Jones looked as neat as a new pin. She stood up on the box again and looked over what she had to work with. Half of the women looked scared to death. There weren't enough women. She knew there had been a barnful at the night meeting.

"Keep them youngins quiet. You want to wake up Jerusalem the Golden?" she called out, letting her voice draw them toward her. "Give them some titty but not too much. We're going to need that noise later."

Some of the women were pushing one of the younger wives forward to the front, and she wasn't liking it.

"Well, what is it?" Mother asked her.

"Ma'am. They's things we want to know," the girl found her

voice, not much, scared as she was. She was a pretty girl. She looked sixteen, and about seven months gone.

"Well, spit it out," Mother ordered her.

"Air they agoin' to shoot at us?" Her question released other voices, a jumble of questions. "Air we gonna git hawled off to jail?" That question was asked in a low voice by a woman with a slat body and a carved mouth. Her eyes looked from under a porch of eyebrows. She was completely calm. She wore a brand-new apron, and she carried a Civil War rifle. Mother had seen plenty of them. She singled the woman out and motioned her up to her. The woman was so tall she towered over her, even standing on the box.

"What's your name?" Mother ignored the other women.

"Miz Escew." The woman's voice was low in her throat.

"Can you carry a tune?"

Nothing surprised the woman.

"Yes," she said slowly. "I sing in church."

"Loud?"

The woman grinned a very slow grin. "To wake the dead," she told Mother.

"All right. Put down that rifle. We ain't goin' to need nuthin' like that."

"Ladies," Mother called out, "shut up and listen." While she talked to Mrs. Escew she had used the time to figure out a way to calm the women's fear.

"Hell's far, we ain't goin' to break the law. And we ain't goin' to picket. Why, can you see me breakin' the law in this fine state of West Virginia?"

Several of the women laughed. Another slow grin spread Mrs. Escew's mouth straight out. "Now you listen to me. Goujot's a Moose and Neill's an Elk and they give the orders." She didn't know what in the hell Goujot and Neill were, but that didn't matter. She sensed the beginning of the kind of calm excitement she needed, and she rode it. "What good American Elk or Moose would shoot a woman at a prayer meetin'?"

It worked. The women milled, and whispered. Some were laughing. Prayer meeting. The words had put solemnity as a meeting expression on some of the faces.

250

"Be quiet. Now you ain't goin' to do nuthin' layin' in the bed. Some of you gwan down and git them other women. Tell 'em we're havin' a prayer meetin' and they ain't nuthin' to worry about."

"Mrs. Pagano, you get the Italians out. Miz Escew—" She pushed the woman, or she pushed the air behind her. Mrs. Escew had already started to walk to the barn door, still carrying her rifle.

Essie disapproved of the whole thing. She tried to tell Ant Annie so but Ant Annie was grinning like a Chessy cat and didn't even answer her.

Annunziata thought about it as she ran down the hill. She'd thought about it ever since Mother had told her when they ate breakfast in Miz Catlett's kitchen while it was still dark. She wondered about praying in public like that in front of people who weren't Catholics. She saw in a rush all the public prayers, the swish of skirts as they knelt on the street stones as the Saint was carried past in his glass box, a real body but it looked like leather, and the new shoes on its skeletal feet, always tiny new shoes made by the nuns, red shoes with jewels. She could hear the prayer rising from the kneeling bodies, in front of tourists and strangers. It would be like that. It would be all right.

At four-thirty it was still clammy cold in the morning mist when they lined up on the road to Godley. They carried babies, and pans and wooden spoons. Some had rolling pins. Their aprons were bright white in the flat light. Some of the youngsters were fooling around, trying their dishpans with little bangs, tuning up. One started to sing and the others joined her.

> *"Just like a mule*
> *A goddamn fool*
> *Will scab until he dies."*

Mother Jones stomped along the ranks. The young girls stopped singing and shoving. Some of the older women smoothed their already smooth clean white aprons, shuffled their feet into straighter ranks, and made themselves taller.

"You ladies quiet down. We ain't singin' none of that kind of thing. This here's prayin'. God's work, not fightin'."

She marched back to the head of the procession. All she carried in her hand was her little black beaded reticule.

"What about 'Onward Christian Soldiers'?" Miz Escew said. She didn't look at Mother. She was staring straight ahead.

"I don't like it," Mother said, and raised her voice to a yell.

"Now. Forward march. Miz Escew, start singin'. Something everybody knows. Not one of them moanin' hymns. Sing a marching hymn to the glory"—she raised her voice to the dawn—"of God Almighty."

"This here is a pick." Mr. McLeod raised his voice so the foreigners would understand. "And this here's a shovel. This is a mine hat with a lamp. Your buddy will show you how to use it. Now ten of you men are going in with experienced miners. That leaves ten of you to do dead work. You're good for nothing else. You will go in with me. The rooms are blowed down. I did it myself." He had to brag a little in front of Sergeant Goujot. "I've inspected the entries. No gas where you're going. I've put down warnings where you're not to go. If you see a plank across an entry with the word 'Gas' written on it, stay out of the entry. No smoking. I'll tell you when you can eat. Any questions?"

Il Professore Antonio Morelli, who understood what he was saying, but had sense enough not to admit it, whispered to the other Italians.

"Silence in the ranks!" Mr. McLeod called, to show the sergeant he could keep order.

"Vafanculo," Morelli muttered, and one of the Italians laughed. The French boy was still sobbing. Professore Morelli, who was a syndicalist anarchist and who had been a waiter during his last exile from Italy in Lugano, leaned forward and tried, in French, to tease him into being a man, speaking so low that McLeod couldn't hear him. The boy sighed deeply, trying to stop.

"All right, men," Goujot said to the guards who had followed him away from the Club House. "If they was goin' to picket, they'd be here. Only need a few of you to keep these fellows moving." Several of them lounged over, rifles sloped, and stood, some in front, some behind the straggled column.

It was just as they got to the tipple that Mr. McLeod heard the goddamnedest noise he'd ever heard in his life.

252

They appeared out of the white mist of the creek. They came through the trees like ghosts. They marched up the road. They kept time to their hymn with their dishpan drums, and their spoons. They shouted out in the white air. The whole hollow filled with their noise. After the muttering of the men their voices pierced the sky, and seemed to shake the trees.

" 'O Beulah land, Sweet Beulah land, as on the highest mount I stand!' "

Mr. Roundtree's dog howled far away.

Mother Jones came ahead of them, singing good and loud, Miz Escew kept step with her. " 'I look away across the sea.' "

"Halt." Goujot ran to stand in front of them. He raised his rifle.

" 'Where mansions are prepared for me.' " They poured around him. The babies wailed, scared by the noise. The spoons beat on the dishpans in rhythm with the hymn. " 'And view the shining glory shore.' "

"You can't come up here. This is company property." Goujot put his hand to his rifle's safety catch.

Mother Jones covered the front of the barrel with her hand and held it up so the women could see what she had done. "Son," she said under the noise, "this here's God's creek. We're havin' a prayer meetin'. We're law-abidin' citizens and you know it you son of a bitch."

" 'My heaven my home for evermore!' " The sound engulfed the transportation, the rhythm shuffled them.

"Listen to me!" Goujot called. "You'll get somebody shot."

"You touch one of them women you'll get cold cocked. They ain't listening to no thug. They're listening to God Almighty!"

The transportation was hemmed in by women. The mothers with babies gave them the tit as Mother had told them to. There was a pure silence as the sunrise gilded the tops of the mountains and sent the first faint glow of color to the leaves, the creek water, the women's hair, their clean faces raised to God in the mist. Mr. McLeod started to say something, but never got to say it.

Mother Jones lowered herself to her knees on one side of the staring men. The women around her sank down to the ground. She lifted her eyes to some point above the tipple and began to pray. On the other side of the men, Annunziata knelt in the shadow of the coal cars and crossed herself. She motioned the other Italian women down behind her.

"Oh Lord our heavenly father who looks down on poor misguided sinners," Mother Jones called.

The women called after her, ". . . poor misguided sinners!" Some of them began to sway back and forth in time with their singsong voices.

Doggo Cutright from over on Cain Creek took off his black slouch hat and laid it on his chest. So did Pat Hand. He glanced to both sides, embarrassed that he hadn't shaved. Some of the other Baldwin men started to take off their hats.

"Put your goddamn hats back on," Goujot growled.

Mother Jones grinned. The voices of the Italian women, led by Annunziata, fell into the rise and fall of their prayer.

"Pater noster, qui es in caelis . . ."

Mother let them finish. ". . . Ah . . . men."

The men were dead quiet. A bird sang.

Annunziata called, "Exsurge, Christe, adjuva nos."

"Et libera nos propter nomen tuum." Some of the transportation muttered, along with the women.

"Oh God Almighty in your mercy, don't let these poor misguided men . . ." Mother Jones paused.

"Misguided men," the women called.

"Uomini delusi . . ." Annunziata led. "Uomini delusi," the women around her answered.

"Git blowed up!" Mother yelled. "Git blowed up," the women followed.

"Scoppiarsi," Annunziata intoned, and the women after her, "Scoppiarsi."

"Don't let no rocks fall," Mother begged the sky; her women cried it out behind her. They swayed against each other.

"Non fare cadere la massa di roccia su di loro." Her women answered Annunziata, pure Gregorian chant.

"Crushed and bleeding," Mother caught the chant.

"Schiacciato e sanguinante."

Mother could feel the movement of the transportation, like dogs on her leash.

254

"Mashed in the mine," she called, trying not to chant.

"Macerato in miniera." Annunziata felt a chill. She had chanted the word for mashed and left to rot.

"Macerato in miniera," the women chanted. One of them sobbed.

"Legs severed," from one side of the transportation.

"Gambe stroncate!" from the other.

"Runaway mine cars."

"Vagonetti sfuggiti."

The singsong of the English prayer, the chant of the Italian was too lulling to suit Mother. She broke the rhythm.

"Oh Lord, if you can see your way clear to change the minds of these poor benighted slaves who have been bamboozled and lied to and locked up and half starved . . ." It was too long to chant back. The women called "Yes, yes," and "Amen, Sister Mary," and "Oh Jesus, oh Jesus."

Doggo Cutright said "Amen" too. He didn't give a shit what Goujot said. This was praying and he knew what was right.

Annunziata, following Mother's lead, had taken off on her own with the most familiar prayer she could think of. The Italian women took it up by the third word.

"Sancta Maria, Mater Dei, ora pro nobis peccatoribus, nunc et in hora mortis nostrae."

They were words that the French boy recognized. He shook away from the strikebreaker who was holding his arm and ran up the road like a panicked animal.

Mr. Goujot turned, took a bead, and shot him in the leg.

After the shot there was dead silence around them all, but in their ears the crack of the rifle.

Some of the women started to cry.

"All right, men, go git him. I just winged him. Now ladies—" Goujot turned and bowed, in a courtly imitation of Dan Neill. That amused him. "Your prayer meetin' is over." He raised his voice. "All right, men, hit's time to git to work. First man breaks ranks gits a bullet in his laig."

Behind him the men watched two of the detectives pick up the boy and haul him into the Club House. His screams grew fainter and fainter as they began the slow climb uphill to the drift mouth from the tipple.

Mr. McLeod looked at his watch. He was pleased. It was only five minutes past five. He hadn't wasted any time even with Mr. Roundtree neglecting his bounden duty, and those damned women taking the Lord's name in vain.

The women watched and cried and let their babies cry. Pans and spoons and rolling pins lay in the road. Mother didn't bother to shut them up. She was hardly listening. She was intent on standing still so she wouldn't wobble and walk old after all that kneeling on her stiff knees. The morning had satisfied her. She decided she was eighty-two and not eighty, and she had learned that you didn't win all at once, you used what you had to hand and you went on to the next thing. She gazed at the sodden skirts, the red faces, the furious tearful eyes. What, to her, was one transportation going into one mine, one boy winged, not even hurt much, compared to the fact that these women wouldn't forget, and they wouldn't let their children forget, not even the babies on their hips that were still setting up a racket and beginning to get on her nerves? Butcher Goujot was a fine shot, even if he was a son of a bitch.

"Git them youngins on home," she hollered. "They're about to drive me crazy. Mrs. Pagano, you git your women back down-creek; you got things to do. Now git!"

By the time the Italian women reached their tents, the others were strung out all along the mile from Godley to Seven Stars, some still so furious that they walked blindly, some already forgetting enough to help enjoy the pretty new colors of morning.

Miz Escew walked slow at Ant Annie's pace.

"If I'd of had my rifle I'd of shot the hell out of that man," she stated as a plain fact.

Essie, on the other side of Ant Annie, said, "That's why you didn't have it." She was just sick and tired of the whole thing.

Way behind them because she needed a little rest from all of them, Mother Jones walked very slowly, admiring the clean morning. She heard shots behind her but she wasn't worried. She could tell it was just those damned fool detectives, letting off steam, firing in the air.

*   *   *

256

Up at the drift mouth after the transportation had been herded inside, Goujot and the men were firing at the bunches of daisies in their baskets, set on top of poles outside the entry. They didn't quit until the daisies were shredded and the fragments of both funeral baskets bounced in the dirt and shale, shot full of holes.

Way inside the mine as the men walked in the darkness toward the dead silence ahead of them, they could still hear the faint echo of the shooting, rumbling against the entry walls half a mile behind them.

The faraway singing and the throb of drums woke Lily from a little nap she didn't admit she'd had—well, only a few minutes anyway. Her head jerked up from its cradle in her arms. She was still huddled in the window seat, cold and stiff. The lilacs had turned purple and their morning scent, she made words of it, assailed her nostrils. She stretched herself awake. A prayer meeting. She smiled. In any crisis people like that turned to prayer. Somehow it made her feel homesick for their simplicity, the simple faith of simple people. She realized with some guilt that all through the thinking and planning night, she hadn't once thought of poor Eduardo or even of Mr. Roundtree.

The little clock said nearly five o'clock. She ran to turn off the alarm before it woke anybody and she had to say goodbye.

She dressed carefully, first in a new camisole and knickers edged with lace, then she fastened her suspenders to her knickers and pulled on the new white stockings she had saved for some event that waited to happen. She laced up her best brown shoes. Then, no matter what her mother thought about it, she put on her white man-tailored waist and tied her brown ascot. She did wear the ivory wool suit, even if it was going to be hot on the train. It was too heavy to pack, and it would be absolutely perfect to parade in. She put on her brown silk hat. Except for a guimpe, she looked just like Mrs. O. H. P. Belmont at the head of her Political Equality Association, marching down Fifth Avenue. For a minute she marched beside her, right alongside of Mrs. Belmont and Mrs. Belmont smiled at her.

She stood in front of the mirror, in front of the cheering, some jeering crowds. "Where's your husband?" "Go home to your babies." "Can't you get a man?" She could almost hear the shouts. Her head went up, a jingle in her mind: color of my eyes, periwinkle blue, color of my hair, honey blond, color of the clothes I'm going to wear, white for purity, white for emancipation, to tell you who I am and what I stand for.

She was pleased. She looked older than eighteen. She knew she did. She thought she ought to check her suitcase for the last time. She lifted the new dress, liking the sound of it in its tissue paper, checked her waists, her skirts, her underwear, her evening shoes, her dress stockings, her sponge bag, Hines Honey and Almond Cream, toothbrush, tooth powder, Castile soap, Pond's cold cream, hot-water bottle and a package of Golden Glint she had been saving, and had decided she would try as soon as she got to Greenwich Village. She got out her etui and checked the needles, thread, scissors. Her hand touched the diary.

She drew it out carefully so she wouldn't disturb the packing and sat in front of the wastebasket and tore out page after page and ripped them into tiny pieces so meddlesome-matty Mary Rose couldn't fit them back together and read her secret longings. When she had finished the wastebasket was full. Seven years of her life. She thought she ought to feel more about it than she did. She laid the wasted leather volume right on top for her mother to find. She took a last look at her room, wanting some sentiment about it, but she was too excited. She thought her heart would wake the house.

The sun had come up over the eastern mountain, and her last vision of her own safe room was gilded, even the air; the chifforobe showed flashes of gold on its white surface, the mirror gleamed. The cloisonné music box her grandmother had given her flashed. She had packed her silver brush, comb, mirror, and nail buffer. The places where they had always sat showed faint shapes, nothing more. She picked up the music box, and put it in her suitcase, then, dutifully, her copy of Montaigne to read on the train. When she snapped the suitcase shut, the music box began to play the Merry Widow Waltz so faintly under her clothes that it seemed to be whispering in her head, a memory of a waltz.

She had to look in the mirror one more time and straighten her skirt so the buttons were in a correct line below the buttons of her jacket. She was absolutely sure she'd forgotten something.

She crept down the stairs, keeping close to the railing so they wouldn't squeak, still hearing the music. She carried her suitcase in one gloved hand, and her handbag and typewriter in the other. The conservatory ahead of her was washed with the newest sun she had ever seen, the greenest leaves. The African violets were so bright she wanted to cry and didn't know or care why she was suddenly caught like that.

She was caught. Her mother stood in the kitchen door, fully dressed. Lily stopped dead. She was coming with her. No. She wasn't, not in an apron.

"You're not to leave this house without a substantial breakfast." Her mother motioned her into the kitchen.

"Whatever else," her mother said, following her.

She stood over Lily while she ate eggs, bacon, toast. She made her drink two cups of good strong coffee. In the corner Lily could still hear the waltz, but her mother didn't mention it. She was too busy.

"God knows when you'll get a decent meal," she said, and picked up Lily's handbag. "Let's see. Four hundred dollars! The keys to the kingdom." She laughed. "Here. Here's something that I was planning to give you. You might as well have it now." She took her garnet necklace from her apron pocket and poured it slowly into the bag. "It belonged to Beverley's mother. It never was right for me anyway, not with my coloring."

Lily couldn't thank her, her mouth was full of toast. She didn't have a word left anyway.

"You'll be late. It's a two-mile walk to the Depot. Lord's love, if it wouldn't get everybody riled up I'd wake up Beverley to help you." For the first time she said Beverley instead of Mr. Lacey, or "your father." The waltz had stopped. Lily picked up the silent suitcase.

They hugged each other, awkward among the conservatory plants.

"I know there's no use asking you to reconsider," her mother sighed and turned away. "You know where I am if you need me."

She didn't say goodbye.

Lily stood on the side porch looking over the lawn. She felt she owed herself that. She heard the creak of one of the rockers on the back porch.

Her father's voice called "Lily," carefully, almost a whisper, but not quite.

She had to go around and see him. She couldn't just run away, weighed down as she was.

He sat in his favorite wicker rocker, just letting it move a little. He was dressed, too, in his best white linen suit that was too big for him. His face shone with new shaving. His mustache was still wet. The sun caught it and brought out the faint auburn tinge. The rambler roses were so red they seemed alight. Lily closed her eyes against the power of all the color. She had never seen things so bright.

"Poor little onion," her father said, not to her but to the rambler roses.

She stood in an empty space on the porch, forgetting to put down her suitcase and the typewriter. She felt as if she were being punished, and not punished. Her father hadn't called her his little onion since she was ten. He called calves that, and pups, and foals, and once, a long time ago, so long she couldn't remember, she'd heard him call her mother that, too.

"Honey," he was saying what he had to, with a sigh, "we haven't seen eye to eye about things. Sometimes you might have thought I didn't love you."

She wanted him to stop. She wanted to run.

He seemed to sense it. Whatever else he had planned to say was lost in silence and the sunrise.

"We have a charge account at Altman's," he said instead. "You're free to use it when you need anything." Then he added, ". . . within reason."

He took more time than she had ever seen him do, getting up from his chair, and she saw for the first time that he was going to be old.

"I'll walk with you to the Depot." He took her suitcase from her. He seemed to wilt to one side.

She had to speak. "Papa—" She had to tell him in order to get

260

away. "Mr. Roundtree is waiting for me. He's got Eddie Pagano with him. I'm going to . . ."—she tried to find the word—"accompany him out of the state."

"I don't believe one word of this." She could see fury and protection of women flare in his face.

"No, Papa, it isn't what you think. Mr. Roundtree knows all about it. Some of the guards are after Eddie." She had to plead. "We have to get him away."

"Why didn't Roundtree consult me?" Her father had put down the suitcase. There wasn't time to persuade him. She had to take over.

"There isn't any time to argue," she said and he heard the strident hint of her mother's voice. "I'll be perfectly safe. Mr. Roundtree will put us on the train. Eddie will see to me . . ."

He was defeated by the voice. There was only one thing left to do. He sought for it.

"How much money do you have?" He found his way to her father again.

"Four hundred dollars. That will last me until I go back to Vassar."

"It's not enough. Here—" He opened his jacket and took out an envelope. He unbuttoned her jacket pocket and stuffed it in. "You shouldn't carry all your money in one place when you're traveling. It isn't safe. Go into the dressing room and put some of it in your corset." He picked up the suitcase again.

Anne Eldridge watched them cross the lawn together, or watched their shimmering shapes. She was crying too hard to see any more clearly. She was grieving like a child, noisy and not caring who heard her.

"They have taken away my . . ." she sobbed and couldn't remember the rest, and then burst out "God damn you," and beat her fist against the glass and made herself stop before she broke it. "I won't have a soul to talk to," she said again and leaned her head against the sweat mark her fist had made, feeling the sickness coming on. But she stopped to water her violets before she began the long trudge up the fifty-five steps to her tower room and her sick headache. She only paused once in the upstairs hall and tried to remember if she'd watered the violets, and went on climbing.

Mr. Roundtree decided that there was nothing more embarrassing than two men standing together on a dirt road in nowhere who had found out they didn't know each other and had long since run out of anything to say. He consulted his watch again. It was already five-thirty. There didn't seem to be a movement up at the Big House. Eduardo watched the trees with his hands in Mr. Roundtree's pockets. The worst thing Mr. Roundtree had to recognize was that Eddie Pagano looked better in his old Norfolk jacket and his plus fours than he ever had. Insouciant was the word for him. Mr. Roundtree resented that deeply. He was in the wrong place when he ought to be at the mine, and insouciant was the farthest thing from the way he felt. He felt, and he was ashamed of it, full of resentment.

He had fought resentment all night long and he was exhausted. Eddie had been able to sleep, actually roll over on the sofa in his, Mr. Roundtree's, underwear, best Jaeger's, and Mr. Roundtree's Argyle knee socks, as if there were nothing to worry about at all. He hadn't even asked the right questions. He seemed to take for granted that he was in danger, take it in stride. He had even laughed. "We live with that," he had said, and put Mr. Roundtree in his place, didn't even say "sir" after all that was being done for him. He had pocketed the hundred dollars as if it already belonged to him and said, "Thank you. I'll pay you back when I get work."

That was all. Mr. Roundtree had to admit that if he'd groveled and slobbered his gratefulness, he would have resented that even more.

What was behind all the little pricks of annoyance was the big one. He was running off with Mr. Roundtree's chosen girl and he hadn't even mentioned her name all night. He'd planned, demanding a confidence that Mr. Roundtree wasn't prepared to give. He had forgotten anything he had thought he owed Eddie Pagano, but so had Eddie. Eddie's mind was on the future; he was going to be an engineer, and his eyes were as glowing as if the future were shining on them.

There was finally something to say. "There they are," he muttered to Eddie. It was unnecessary. He was already watching, too.

She came across the lawn, her skirt damp with dew, frail Lily, frail as a lily on her father's arm as if Mr. Lacey were handing over a precious burden to him, Mr. Roundtree, to have and to hold. They came through an aisle made by the lilacs.

Mr. Lacey shook hands with Mr. Roundtree, ignoring the children.

"I think you should have come to me," he said.

Lily interrupted. "I told him there wasn't time."

"I think we ought to hitch up the trap."

"There isn't time." There was an unseemly edge to Lily's voice that Mr. Roundtree found he didn't like.

All three of the men stood with their hands in their pockets, watching each other.

Mr. Lacey moved first. He took Lily's gloved hand and placed it on Mr. Roundtree's arm. "You look after her," he told him.

He turned to Eduardo. "Boy," he said, "now you see that Miss Lily has a seat on the parlor car." He handed him the suitcase and the typewriter. "Hand her over to the parlor car conductor. His name is Rufus. He's a good boy. He knows the family." He started to hug Lily and then said over his shoulder, "If you require a reference I'll give you one. You're a good boy. I know that."

His face had dried from the shave and his skin felt flaky and dead on Lily's cheek. "Goodbye, honey. I'm always here if you need me." Then, knowing there was nothing else to say, but having to speak, he told Mr. Roundtree to look after his little girl and Mr. Roundtree promised.

They stood in a row and watched him go slowly back across the lawn.

Beverley was relieved that he hadn't had to take her to the Depot. He didn't know if he could walk that far.

"There's plenty of time," Mr. Roundtree said, and consulted his watch again.

Nobody answered him.

They turned and walked down the back road under the green roof of trees that met over their heads.

Lily walked between them. If somebody didn't say something soon she was afraid she was going to giggle. They looked just like Tweedledum and Tweedledee dressed up like Bernard Shaw in Mr. Roundtree's identical suits.

Fortunately Mr. Roundtree couldn't stand the silence. "This damned third-growth timber," he said bitterly. "There's not a virgin tree left in this forest."

Eduardo Pagano didn't say a word all the way to the Depot.

McLeod could see them in the light of the entry, cavorting around like a bunch of wild Indians. They had stopped shooting at last. He ran the last hundred yards out of the dark tunnel as fast as his bandy-legs could carry him. His day crew for dead work were huddled inside the entry watching the men in black pick up fragments of wicker and show them to each other.

"All right. That's enough of that," McLeod yelled, too furious to remember that Goujot was a sergeant.

"My boys was just lettin' off a little steam." Goujot was leaning against a wood prop of the entry. His cheek was fat with a cud of tobacco. "Go on down, boys, we got work to do. Now"—he didn't bother to look at McLeod—"we got to come to an understanding." He spat a long brown stream at one of the daisies. "You tell Roundtree they's things we ain't astandin' fer."

"If you have a grievance, tell it to him. I've got my work to do." Mr. McLeod was tired of all the interference. "All right, you men, come out here." The ten men inside the entry didn't move. "They don't understand nothing." He reached in and caught the first man he could grab by the arm. Slowly he brought them out into the sun.

"What they done to a woman," Goujot said behind him.

McLeod was too busy to listen.

Goujot moved away from the post, as slow as ever. There was some damned thing about search and seizure. He remembered the words from somewhere but he didn't remember any more and he didn't care. It sounded legal, and what he was looking for was something that sounded legal.

"We got the right of search and seizure. We're deputies. In the case of a felony," he added.

Mr. McLeod turned and looked at him at last. "I ken not a damn thing about that. My business is to put these men to work. Men!" he said, disgusted, and looked at Professore Morelli. The man looked like an apple, pink and smooth. He looked as dumb as an apple. His hands were white and useless-looking.

"Pick up that shovel," he ordered.

"Non capisco," Morelli said politely.

Mr. McLeod put the shovel in his hand with great patience and pointed to a pile of gob, then to an empty tram car.

Professore Morelli smiled. He began to shovel gob.

When Mr. McLeod remembered Goujot again he was already halfway down to the tipple. Then he saw the engine, stoked up and smoking. There were Baldwin men hanging all over it, on the roof, on the cowcatcher. One man was leaning out of the fireman's window, gesturing with a gun. They looked like black flies, swarming over the engine, black flies with rifles.

"Goddamned fools," Mr. McLeod said, caught trying to do his job between damned fools and white niggers.

He didn't bother to look again, but he could hear the engine puff and the whistle blowing and the chuff chuff going faster and faster as the Bull Moose gathered speed.

Just before she went up to Jake's, Mother gave her boys their instructions.

"They're comin'." She stood them in a big circle under the big oak tree by the railroad track. She liked the tree. She figured it to be on C&O property, and it pleased her to use C&O property. "I don't know when but they're comin'," she told them. "Now you boys resist not evil, let it pass through ye like a dose of salts."

She could hear the whistle blowing up-creek as she stationed the last of her boys around the tent colony. By the time they were all in place she could hear the engine starting. She didn't look back. She didn't look at Jake, who was sitting on the porch. She went on into the kitchen to help Essie wash the tin cups.

The guards stopped the train at Seven Stars tipple and poured off it at a run. They ran into a stone wall of morning calm. Boys fishing in the creek didn't even look up. There were men lounging under the trees; some seemed to be just basking in the sun, some

265

were whittling. There were two circles shooting craps. "How do," one of the crapshooters called politely. They let the thugs flow around them. Nobody ruffled a feather. Mother had said there was more than one way to kill a dog. The Baldwin men were slowed down by the familiarity of the morning. Up ahead of them the women were hanging out washing on the restored clotheslines. When they got closer, the women seemed so friendly that it made Pat Hand feel like a damned fool.

Matt Daingerfield had been drunk for four days. The sun hurt his eyes. He stopped beside one of the crap games.

"You rednecks count high enough to read them dice?" he said, and looked around to see if one of his own men was laughing, but the other guards had already walked on ahead of him. Matt felt so alone it ran a chill up his back.

The men hunkered around the crap game didn't look up.

"Don't pay no 'tention," one of them said, low in his throat.

Mother had said not to.

Dan Neill knew he had to say something before the fury he had been building in them all night died down. The damned riffraff looked like they were about ready to turn around and go home.

"Men," he called, "we are on official business. Now stay here with Mr. Goujot while I go talk to Catlett. Fall out!"

His men sank against the tree near Jake's barn, some sank all the way to the ground and lay out and closed their eyes, dog-tired and drunk to morning sober sadness. Goujot spat out his quid and started to shave himself off another one from his block with a pocketknife. He hunkered down with Pat Hand, grinned at him, and handed him the block and the knife.

Jake didn't stop rocking. He just watched Dan Neill come up the hill path, nice-looking boy. Everybody was safe. Everything had been taken care of. He knew he could defuse Dan Neill, boy who he known ever since he'd peed in his lap. Lord, he'd crawl right up on his lap looking for the jawbreaker he never did forget to bring him when he went across the river to Beulah. Of course, since he was a man and they moved on down to River Street and Middle Dan had passed on, he never had claimed kin. He'd waited for the boy to do that himself, but he never did. Times was just different than when him and Middle Dan was boys. You didn't

266

claim kin then, you was or you wasn't. Of course the boy was too much of a gentleman to act embarrassed about it like them women of Middle Dan's, but, well, if he never laid claim Jake wasn't about to.

"Mornin', son," he said, looking forward to a little talk. "I'ze lookin' fer ye last night."

Dan Neill didn't say a word. He didn't even look up at him.

"C'mon up here and take a pew. You look wore out," Jake told the top of his hat. He'd say one thing for Dan Neill. He always looked like he stepped out of a bandbox.

Dan finally looked up. "Jake," he had to call him that. He'd never called him anything else in his life. "Goddammit you fellows have started something and we're going to finish it."

"Don't use bad language, son. Essie's right inside. She'll hear ye." Jake didn't stop creaking the damned rocker.

"I didn't come up here to pass the time of day. My men are ready—"

"Hell, son, look down there. They ain't nobody doin' nuthin'."

Dan Neill didn't stop looking at him, like some stranger got in his way.

"They ain't goin' to find nuthin'," Jake told him.

Dan Neill's face was as white as a sheet. The boy looked sick.

"You gwan back to Godley and git some sleep." He couldn't make the boy answer him. One of his cows started to bawl, way up the branch. The clock still ticked loud on the porch rail. A butterfly flew right across the boy's face and he didn't move a muscle. Jake felt he had to melt him. What Essie called melting in church. He was worried.

"Hell, son. I've knowed ye so long ye've peed in my lap," he tried to reason.

Dan Neill's face didn't move. Jake knew that pride. He'd seen it in his own father, in his cousin Middle Dan. God damn, that Catlett blood made them hardheaded as mules.

"I got to do my milkin'. A cow don't wait." Jake got up and came down the steps. He put his hand on Dan's shoulder. Because he'd been so fond of the boy's daddy he thought he'd tell him. "I sure did set store by your pappy, son," and added, "don't you worry about a thing." It wasn't enough. He looked for more words.

"May the good Lord take a likin' to you," he said, and went on out over the branch to get his milk pails.

Essie usually did the milking. He wouldn't let her in time of trouble. "You can't tell what kind of white trash is hangin' around them woods," he told her. Essie said she could look after herself, she always had. But she seemed pleased that he thought enough of her to take over the milking.

Dan Neill had stopped questioning anything. He moved as if he were carved out of wood. He knew what he had to do. That was the only thing on his mind, to keep moving toward what he had to do. He'd left the whys of it behind on the night road. He put one foot in front of the other, thinking, if he thought at all, one step at a time.

When he got back to the tree where his men lounged, his voice was sharp enough for once to get them to their feet. Even Goujot looked up, surprised.

"Fan out and search those tents. We're looking for a felon."

The men got up, unwound, spat quids out. They sloped on down the hill and out among the tents. They didn't stop at the tents where the American women were washing. They had to step around them, though. Doggo Cutright had to walk all the way around Miz Escew. She still had her rifle set right behind her up against the daub chimney of her tent. He said, "Excuse me, ma'am," and she said, "You go to hell." She didn't even raise her voice.

They might as well not have been there. Nobody looked at them, nobody stepped aside. You'd have thought the women had been there all morning instead of raising hell up at Godley tipple.

Four of the guards found themselves walking abreast, even though Dan Neill had told them to fan out. It was treating them like they didn't exist that made them do it. In front of them a bunch of youngins were playing mumbledepeg with a jackknife. Not even they looked up when the guards walked around them. The knife landed right beside Pat Hand's boot and quivered in the ground. He just saw the boy's hand reach over and get it and throw it again.

When they got to the Dago tents they fanned out again. The

women were washing, just like the Americans. There wasn't a Dago man in sight.

Goujot turned one of the women around from her washtub, and held her by the shoulder.

"Whur's yore man?" he asked her.

"Non capisco," she said, and she shook herself away and went on washing.

Across the clothesline Pat Hand stopped another one of them.

"Gone to Ohio. He look for job," she told him. She bobbed a little curtsy and smiled. She seemed real friendly.

"Non capisco." "Gone to Ohio." "Non capisco." "Gone to Ohio." They got so damn sick of the repetition that even before they got to the last tent they were ready to turn around and go on back to Godley. There wasn't a soul around the last tent downcreek. If Goujot hadn't thrown back the canvas flap and pushed his way into the tent none of the rest of them would have bothered.

"Hell, let's git on back," Pat Hand was saying. "We done what he said. Let's go."

Carlo Michele was still asleep when Goujot kicked him. "Get up," he ordered him. The men outside heard his voice. They stiffened, felt alive again, like they did after a long hunt when the dog finds a bird.

Carlo Michele pulled the blanket over himself. He was still half asleep, but he didn't want the man to see he'd slept in his clothes.

Goujot kicked him again. "You Pagano?"

The straniero figure was huge and black against the light from outside the tent. Carlo Michele rolled away from the foot. "Pagano. Sì," he recognized enough of what the man was saying, at least the name. He knew if he answered politely the man would stop kicking him. He wished he could find his shirt. He reached around for it.

Goujot's Army training came in handy. He saw the boy reach out for something in the pile of blankets—reach meant gun. He shoved his rifle against the boy's stomach. The boy stumbled to his feet, and raised his hands over his head.

"You're under arrest." Goujot smiled. He had to. The boy's

pants were loose. His galluses were hanging down. He ought to know better than to go to sleep without his galluses on. Goujot could have told him that.

"Non capisco," the boy said.

"Non capisco hell. You Dagoes been in this hollow too long for that talk. You know damn well what I'm saying." He whirled him around, put the rifle to his back, and marched him out of the tent.

"One of you men put them galluses up. Don't want him to lose his pants in front of ladies."

That released some laughter. It made the women look up, and keep on looking, dumb.

Dan Neill only saw Eddie Pagano's back. Goujot had goaded him over to the snake fence. Dan Neill didn't go any nearer. He told himself somebody had to watch the women in case they caused trouble.

Nobody moved.

"Git him over onto company property." Goujot forced the boy to climb the fence. "A gun don't need no language. You men remember that."

They were going to let him go. Carlo Michele couldn't believe it. He saw the clear meadow ahead of him. The men behind him weren't stopping him. They weren't saying a word.

He started to run up toward the woods as well as he could, barefooted. He knew the woods were safe. The old woman had taught him that. He wasn't even conscious of being afraid. He seemed to be running in place with the woods coming nearer and nearer.

He was too far away to hear anything.

"O.K., men, let's go," Goujot ordered. "He's trespassing on company property." They walked out of gunshot of each other, four men widening out across the meadow, slow, bird hunting.

John Lacey was trying to find his cow. He'd let her out into the woods above Nigger Hollow. She usually came back by morning. When she didn't he had to go looking for her. He wasn't worried. He was enjoying his walk. The woods smelled good in the morning; some of those little tiny plants you couldn't find but they gave off a smell like flowers when you stepped on them. The sun was filtering through the trees in long, thin rays. There was still enough mist to make them faint like breaths of sun. The Church of Christ looked that way in the morning, when the sun came through the stained-glass window.

It was his favorite time of the day. The trees were bigger on the mountain, big enough to leave corridors of mast under them where the old abandoned log road ran along the ridge. Mr. Lacey let them shoot squirrels up there where the road was wide enough for a good clear shot. It was where Samantha always went when she ran off. He knew he wouldn't have any trouble finding her. He never did. There was no underbrush, just a few weeds and flowers where the sun touched the ground.

He saw her up ahead, peaceful, just feeding on some weeds. He wasn't in any hurry to get to her; he was enjoying his walk. He could see she was full of milk; all his people to feed, he was glad of that. He felt rich.

Samantha raised her head. He stopped. She didn't run away. She ambled toward him like she always did, kind of shamefaced, if a cow could look like that. He caught her rope tether.

Beyond her he saw a white man running along the road through the corridor of trees. He was in a white undershirt and dark pants. John Lacey watched. He prayed that Samantha wouldn't low and get them caught on company property when the white folks were having a strike. He was trying to urge her, gently, gently, around so he could head her home when he saw the others, the white men in their black suits. They came up through the woods like hunters, Baldwin men. White men chasing a white man. He knew better than to see what he saw but he went on looking.

Away ahead of him he saw one of the men in black take aim and fire. The figure, too far away to look like a man, just a moving target, like a deer, crumpled, only a white spot in the leaves. He watched the Baldwin men walk up and surround the white spot of undershirt in the leaves. They were standing in a long shaft of sunlight. He saw them point their rifles down. He heard a volley of shots. He could smell gunpowder as far away as he was.

He drove Samantha back into the woods, out of the corridor before anyone had seen him. He drove her slowly, deeper into the woods. Behind him, he heard another volley. The sound skipped against the trees.

John Lacey knew better than to say a word, not to anybody. He'd known all his life that there were things a black man did not see. He went on driving Samantha slowly so she wouldn't drag her full bag on the underbrush, carefully so her thick udders wouldn't get torn.

The mine guards walked slowly, close together, at the ready, guns up. They came out of the woods into the sun, across the north pasture and climbed the fence. They marched in close formation through the tent colony. There wasn't a soul in sight, no women, not even kids. The tent flaps were closed. Miz Escew's rifle was gone. The fishermen had left the creek. There was only a circle of bare ground where the crap game had been. They had all disappeared like snakes. There wasn't a sound, no wind in the trees. The thin columns of smoke from the abandoned chimneys rose straight up. They could hear the creek rippling. That was all. The whole place was as still as the dawn of Creation.

When the engine started to roll back up-creek to Godley, the men were slumped over it. Nobody sloped a gun. Nobody said a word. Nobody climbed into the fireman's box with Dan Neill. They left him in there alone.

Matt Daingerfield couldn't stand it any longer. He yelled out over the slow chuff on the engine.

"Boy we sure taught them Dagoes and rednecks who was boss. We sure . . ." He didn't get the next brag out.

Goujot said, "For Chris' sake shut up."

Miz Escew took her hand away from her least one's mouth. She gave him a slap. "I tole you to quit that sniveling," she said and pushed all six of her youngins out of her tent.

Three women watched out of Essie's kitchen window. Twice Essie told the kids to shut up and eat. That was all. She had no idea who the boy was, running across the north pasture. The Italian men had all gone downriver on the six o'clock train. Mrs. Pagano knew that, but she stood like she was half dead. Her body started once to move but Mother Jones held her arm. "They ain't nuthin' you can do now." She saw the old woman look at Mrs. Pagano like they knew something together. There wasn't another word said for half an hour. They stood there in a row and watched the empty pasture; the old woman's hand clutched Mrs. Pagano's arm. It wasn't until they heard the engine start back up-creek that any of them moved. The only sound was Mrs. Pagano, sobbing and muttering some foreign thing.

Essie took over. She knew what to do in such a case. She said so. "The things I've seen don't bear tellin'," she told the porch when she marched out of her door.

"We got to go up thar and git him. I know where he's at." Of course she knew. She could read the direction of the shots. It was up there where her boys hunted squirrels. She didn't explain this to the others. She just gave orders. She stuck her head back in the opened door. "You stay right here with the youngins," she told Maria. "This ain't nuthin' for a young girl to see. You," she told Mrs. Pagano, "you got time for that later. Come on." She didn't speak to Mother Jones. She didn't care whether she came or not.

By the time she had made Mrs. Pagano help her lift a shutter off the side window, the woman had quit her carrying-on. When Mother Jones tried to take a side to help carry, she said, "We don't need you. Her and me got the strength."

It was six-thirty by the time they got to the logging road. He was easy to find, that flick of white undershirt in the filtered sun. There wasn't much white left when they got to it, though. There was blood all over it. They'd shot the boy full of holes. He lay in the red mast. Essie said a little prayer to herself. "Thank God he's layin' on his face."

Mrs. Pagano fell over the body. She was howling like she'd shot him herself, beating her chest like a crazy woman. There wasn't any shutting her up. She started wailing some foreign words and Essie heard the old woman join in behind her. Mrs. Pagano raised up and beat her chest again, right in the middle of it. Her face and her whole apron bib were blood-soaked. There wasn't anything to do but let them finish. She stood up finally but she couldn't stop that muttering and crying blood and tears down her face.

"Honey, it ain't Eddie. It ain't nobody we know," Essie finally said to calm her, and put her arm around Mrs. Pagano's shoulder.

She was trembling like an animal. Essie was afraid she was going to light out in a blind run through the woods. She tightened her grip. "It ain't Eddie, honey, look!" It didn't do any good, though. The woman began to scream, and she couldn't have that. She slapped her hard. "Now help me roll him onto this here shutter," she ordered. They hadn't touched the boy's face. It was Essie who reached down and stopped him gazing at the sky.

They carried him down out of the woods and across the north pasture. Essie led the way around the outside of the Catletts' fence. She didn't know why she did that. By the time they got the shutter down across the creek and laid it on the ground, there was such a crowd of foreign women pushing at her to get to the body, she had to step back and lean against a tree. She had enough to think about.

They had killed a man, and nothing was ever going to be the same. She could hear the change like a creek swell, flooding nearer and nearer, and all the former things were passed away. It wouldn't never be the same, not in her lifetime, never the same, never the same, she kept saying over and over like a prayer, not knowing she was saying it out loud.

She had to admit the Italian women did things right. They undressed that poor little skinny thing and washed his body in the creek until the water had run clean of blood. A little way downstream, minnows swarmed around the last threads of red.

Then they laid his naked body on a sheet and rolled him into it and sewed it together. She didn't hold with burying him stark naked like that, but she decided it was some custom they had. Mrs. Pagano had stopped wailing and falling around. She was folding the clothes into a little bundle. Essie understood that. They wasn't a bit of use to waste them when they'd lost ever last thing they owned. There was just a body-shaped sheet on the ground by the time the men had dug a grave on the C&O right-of-way between the track and the big oak tree. Essie hadn't realized Jake was there until he came up and stood beside her. "I didn't think hit was fittin' to put him on Beverley's land," he murmured. He never mentioned that they hadn't put him on Catlett land, but she understood that. They used the graveyard on the hill. The foreigners had their own on Godley land where their priest came up twice a year and said their funerals, but there wasn't any way to take him up there.

They laid him in the ground. The foreigners all said some prayer. Essie knew it was a prayer in their language when they crossed themselves.

By seven-thirty they had led Mrs. Pagano away still in that blood-soaked apron. It had already turned brown. She had to be hauled off the grave like a sack of meal; it wasn't even one of her own boys, somebody none of them knew. All that carrying-on. Essie was disappointed that they didn't sing a hymn.

Only Jake and Essie were left by the tree. There was an unspoken fitness in staying back until the foreigners had finished their funeral and gone away. Mother Jones seemed to feel that too. She just stood there looking at the mound of earth and shale and track-side gob. She had been crying. Her old face was swollen up, but she'd dabbed it dry.

Jake went up and stood beside her. They looked down at the mound for a long time.

"Mother, what air we agoin' to do?" he finally asked her.

"Use it," she told him.

No. 6 was late. Time crawled and the river crawled out beyond the stationmaster's office window. Lily stood with her back to the sun and watched the water. The sun touched it and the water threw back flashes of gold. Dragonflies flirted with the surface. A johnboat moved slowly in the middle of the water. Somebody was raising a trotline, far too late in the morning. She couldn't think anymore. She was too excited, but her room kept coming back and she turned around in it forgetting something. She tried to plan, but she was too dog-tired. Behind her she could hear Mr. Osborn's telegraph going dit dot dit dot, and from time to time a man's voice. They didn't say much, "Montgomery, Thurmond, Prince, Covington." Once in a while Mr. Osborn said, "Good mornin' to you," to people he knew. The train was never going to come. She watched the red light at the downriver curve and willed it to turn green.

Behind her Mr. Roundtree watched the sun touch her lovely hair as she turned to look downriver. "Goddammit, I'm only thirty years old," he told himself.

Edward Pagano, who had changed his name on the long walk to the station, watched them all to see how they acted. That was important. Any sense of danger had long since left him. The train was taking him right along the map of his plans and nothing was going to stop him. Mr. Roundtree's plus fours itched against his knees. Mr. Roundtree had told him what to do, and it was the last time anybody was going to treat him like he didn't have good sense. Mr. Roundtree crossed one leg over his knee. Edward Pagano put one leg over his knee. He liked that, it looked as if you didn't give a damn.

He hadn't needed to ask why they were sitting in the station-master's office instead of the waiting room, or out on the platform, where a bunch of Baldwin men were patrolling. Lily's family had had the privilege of waiting in Mr. Osborn's office ever since he'd seen the girls for the first time, marching behind their mother as if they owned the C&O railroad. He felt his mustache itch and touched where it had been, forgetting that Mr. Roundtree had made him shave it off and cut his hair so that it didn't show under Mr. Roundtree's cap. "Now I don't look like no Dago," he'd said to the bathroom mirror in the middle of the night. He liked what he saw, nice-looking young boy. Behind him Mr. Roundtree said, "I don't look like an Italian," correcting him like he always had, but he could tell Mr. Roundtree's mind was somewhere else.

Miss Lily came over and sat down beside him, but she didn't look at him. She didn't say a word. Miss Lily. He could still hear her father's voice.

Mr. Roundtree got up then, and looked out of the ticket window over Mr. Osborn's shoulder. He came back and stood in front of them. "There are detectives out there—" He waited until Mr. Osborn was busy selling a ticket to speak. "Now, Eddie, I told you. You've got a seat in the parlor car. They don't expect to find anybody in there. Here—" He reached in his breast pocket and handed him a dollar. "Get yourself some breakfast in the dining car. You haven't eaten. That's even safer until you get beyond Thurmond. Go in just before Montgomery." He'd already told him that once, and he wasn't even looking at him. He was looking at Miss Lily like a dying calf. Edward Pagano felt a little sorry, an older man feeling like that.

The downriver signal light turned green. Mr. Osborn went out to see to the mailbags. The train whistled for them from the downriver curve.

They stood in the doorway until it came to a stop by the Depot, and the brakes sighed.

Down at the day coach some Baldwin men were piling onto the train.

Nobody else was getting on the parlor car. Nobody else was having a step with a rubber top put down for them. A black parlor-car porter took Lily's hand to help her up. Edward Pagano gave him her suitcase and her typewriter. She sailed up on that train in her big brown hat and her fancy suit like she was the queen of Sheba. He heard her say, "Good morning, Rufus."

"Good mornin', fine mornin'. You goin' to Richmond?" The old man was walking ahead of him into heaven. He did remember to look back and wave to Mr. Roundtree.

"Sir?" He didn't know the porter was talking to him for a minute. "Sir, hyears a seat for you right by the window." He had put Miss Lily across the aisle. Edward felt Mr. Roundtree's shoes sink into the carpet.

The train pulled out, and found its rhythm. The wheels said Going Eddie Going Eddie Going and the river rolled by outside the window. The johnboat disappeared, the trees moved faster and faster. Across the aisle Lily opened her inevitable book. She smiled at him, though, that same smile that made him remember all their secrets instead of her father's voice saying "Miss Lily" to him as if he was a nigger.

Lily looked back at Montaigne, trying to see the words, but her eyes bleared with tears. She couldn't understand why she always boohooed like that when she left home after all her hoping and dreaming. She blinked the tears away so she could see the page. "A brilliant and sharp clarity is needed to kill people; our life is too real and substantial for supernatural fantastical incidents." It was like Essie dipping into the Bible. It was telling her to stop sitting there sunk in hopes and tears when she still had a job to do.

She got up and held on to Eduardo's seat back and touched his shoulder. He jumped a little. She knew he would be scared to death until they got to Covington, poor boy.

"I'll go into the dining car with you. We're almost to Montgomery."

They went along the aisle, trying not to lurch against the ladies with their hats like ships.

There were many things he had not seen, and many mountains he had to climb. What he hadn't known was that the first step was a half of a yellow fruit that he'd never seen before, sitting in a silver bowl. He didn't know that it would be strewn with knives and forks and three spoons on a white tablecloth. He sat still and waited for somebody else to show him what to do.

He watched a fine, big man with a diamond stickpin across the aisle until he picked up a spoon with a sharp edge and dug into the fruit. Very carefully, Edward did the same thing. His first taste of grapefruit was bitter. At home he would have spat it out.

Lily leaned over and whispered, "Put sugar on it."

"I know that," he told her. It was better with the sugar but he told himself he never was going to eat grapefruit again, except when he was in a dining car and everybody expected him to. His hand trembling the spoon was the center of his being and he knew everybody on the dining car was watching him.

Lily did watch him. He looked all right, even handsome in Mr. Roundtree's suit. At first glance, without his mustache, he could have passed for any young man going to college. His eyes were still rimmed with coal dust, though, and his fingernails were torn and thick.

That will go, she thought, and thought about baths, lots of them, and then Mr. Dick, "I should—I should wash him!" That made her giggle. He looked up and she knew he thought she was laughing at him. He sulked all the way to Thurmond.

She couldn't worry about him. She was dropping away the miles behind her. She didn't know where he was going when he got off at Covington, but she knew at last where she was going. She leaned back and dreamed and didn't care what Montaigne said. There was clarity in dreams, too. She dreamed, lulled by the train, of getting off at heaven or New York City, whichever she got to first.

About the Author

MARY LEE SETTLE is the author of eleven books, including *Blood Tie*, for which she received a National Book Award in 1978. With the publication of *The Scapegoat* she completes a series of five novels which trace the inter-related histories of several families in the Appalachian coal country.

A native of West Virginia, Mary Lee Settle now lives in the Tidewater city of Norfolk, and divides her time between writing and teaching at the University of Virginia.